HUGO DUCHAMP INVESTIGATES:

Chemin de

Compostelle

BY

GN HETHERINGTON

First Published in 2023 by GNH Publishing.

The right of Gary Hetherington to be identified as the author of this work has been asserted by him in accordance with the Copyright, Designs and Patents Act 1988.

www.gnhbooks.com

Merci

As time goes on, I'm still amazed there is always a new "merci" page to write. How did I get past one book and then on to another and another? Well, the simple answer is I have amazing people in my life who have always pushed me, even when I didn't want pushing.

It began with my husband Dan and a lady I'd just met, Joy Edwards, who demanded the first chapter of what turned out to be 'Un Homme Qui Attend' and then they demanded more. Reluctantly I agreed (honestly I did!) and now here we are, seven years and almost twenty books later. I'm indebted to each one of you who helped me along the way, the vocal ones and the quiet ones. I hope you still enjoy these books.

Special thanks to Chris & Bill Bailey, June Russell, Jackie Waite, Jennifer Trieb, Suse Telford, Sandra Scott, Kathleen Pope, Margaret Cox, Pam Pletts & Dylan. Merci Bastien Greve for all his help and Sheena Easton and Julien Doré for the inspiration.

For my boys. I love you.

Notes:

The story, the places and the characters are a work of fiction. Chemin de Compostelle (the way to Camino) is a story I've wanted to write for a long time, but the truth was the idea and concept just weren't easy to work out. I couldn't quite figure out how to make a murder mystery out of such a poignant and well-known journey. My concerns always inform my ideas about how to do justice to something that is real and important to people and yet still turn it into a book without disrespecting anyone. So, this story is part travelogue and part murder mystery, I hope I've done both justice.

For the purposes of this book, I have incorporated several real factors, but for the most part, the places mentioned are fictional.

For further information, exclusive content and to join the mailing list, head over to:

www.gnhbooks.com

We are also on Facebook, Twitter and Instagram. Join us there! The artwork on the cover, the website and social media accounts were created in conjunction with the incredibly talented Maria Almeida. I'm so grateful she continues to work with me and understand my crazy ideas (often on a scrap of paper!)

For Charlie, Seth and Dawn. Tu me manques.

Previously in the "Hugo Duchamp Investigates" series of books:

Hugo Duchamp, a Frenchman by birth, has spent much of his adult life living and working in London and has risen to the rank of Detective Superintendent in London's Metropolitan Police. He lives a solitary but content life. In 2015 in **Un Homme Qui Attend** (A man who waits) Hugo finds himself ripped out of his organised life and supplanted back in the country of his birth when he is seconded to a small town called Montgenoux, a town reeling from the brutal murder of a young girl and a corrupt police force. Warned against getting involved, Hugo is soon embroiled in the investigation when a second girl is murdered and he finds himself in a race against time to catch a murderer that culminates in a fiery and deadly confrontation.

Months later, Hugo is thrown into another investigation, **Les Fantômes du Château** (The Ghosts of the Chateau) while still reeling from the aftermath of his previous investigation and trying to balance a new life in France and a blossoming romance. Following the murder of a maid working in a grand Château on the outskirts of Montgenoux, he finds himself pitted against two new adversaries and a family at war in an investigation that forces him to face his own mortality.

Battered and bruised, Hugo faces the prospect of a serial killer in Montgenoux in **Les Noms sur Les Tombs** (The names on the graves). A spate of apparent suicides share an unusual link, a mound of soil at the feet of the deceased and before long Hugo realises that there is someone in Montgenoux who is following a dangerous and baffling plan that threatens the lives and safety of those he has come to love.

The fourth instalment in the series **L'hombre de L'isle** (The Shadow from the Island) picks up after the shocking conclusion of Hugo's last investigation and the action switches to Ireland where Hugo races against time to solve the brutal murder of a priest in his most personal investigation yet which will leave him questioning everything he thought he knew and believed in.

In **L'assassiner de Sebastian Dubois** (The murder of Sebastian Dubois) Hugo's two worlds collide. His new life in Montgenoux is affected by an investigation from his past and he finds himself having to deal with a past he thought he had left behind and a pair of criminals who are determined to wreak their revenge on him. As he attends a crime scene at the newly opened Montgenoux prison, Hugo and Dr. Chapeau find themselves taken hostage and face a deadly race against time to escape their grasp of violent criminals with only one thing on their minds, Hugo's death.

The discovery of a thirty year old skeleton buried under the Beaupain vineyard in Montgenoux (**L'impondérable**) triggers a horrific series of events in the modern day resulting in the murder of a prominent citizen and a murder/suicide. It all seems like an open and shut case. Hugo faces a complex web of lies and crimes dating back to the eighties which have devastating effects upon Hugo and those he has come to love.

Fulfilling a promise, Hugo and his family journey to Moscow, Russia (**Le Cri de Coeur**) but soon find themselves in mortal danger when Hugo is called upon to assist the local police following the discovery of a mysterious box and its grisly contents. After a body is discovered on the grounds of the Chinese Embassy Hugo finds himself trapped inside with his family in danger on the outside. The clock is ticking and the killer has only just begun their deadly game.

After a fire tears through Montgenoux, Hugo and his team must deal with the shocking aftermath of the death of an entire family (**La Famille Lacroix**) (The Lacroix Family) and the fallout as racial tension erupts through the town. When the prime suspect is murdered, Hugo must put aside his own grief to unravel one of his most complicated and heartbreaking investigations.

After decades away, Hugo returns to Paris (**Les Mauvais Garçons**) (The Bad Boys) after a request from the Minister of Justice, Jean Lenoir, following the death of a young man who apparently threw himself from the Eiffel Tower. Hugo soon finds himself face to face with his past as he tries to save the lives of a group of young people whose lives are in grave danger.

A horrific accident in 2010 triggers a chain of events in present day Montgenoux (**Prisonnier Dix**) (Prisoner Ten). When the body of a young medical intern is discovered on the grounds of a scientific research institute, Hugo discovers she had a very difficult past, and the investigation leads to a family torn apart by a deadly secret and an evil murder. Hugo and his team must race against time to protect the innocent before a deadly killer strikes again.

After tragedy strikes at Baptiste Beaupain's school, Hugo agrees to go with him to the seaside town of Beaufort-Sur-Mer (**Le Bateau au fond de l'océan**) (The boat at the bottom of the ocean), where he is immediately thrown into a murder investigation. He is also reunited with faces from his past and together they must work together to fight a murderer who will do anything they can to keep their identity hidden.

SEMAINE UN / WEEK ONE

SAINT-JEAN-PIED-DE-PORT / CHEMIN DES PÈLERINS / MONTGENOUX

Dorothy & Irene

Dorothy Chapeau lifted her head upwards and closed her eyes. The sun felt pleasant on her skin and, for a moment, she felt warm. She had not felt warm for what seemed to be a long time, when in fact it had only been three short months. Three months since her world had been irrevocably altered.

She extended her hand, her finger moving slowly around the handle of the cup. She was sure the café was fine, but it tasted bitter to her, just as the salad which remained half-eaten in front of her was most likely delicious, but each mouthful she took tasted worse than the last. Dorothy did not need to open her eyes to know her daughter would be staring at her, green eyes fixed squarely, sparking with deep concern. Dorothy reached for a strand of copper hair, which had fallen from the pile on top of her head and secured it back in place.

'Can I order you something else, mama? You really…'

'… have to eat,' Dorothy finished the sentence for her daughter. Her voice was baritone, but there was no harshness to it when she spoke. She opened dark eyes flecked with red and smiled. 'I know you're just concerned for me, darling Irene, but I am fine. I WILL be fine,' she added with as much reassurance as she could muster. She did not want to sound fake because she knew she could not fool Irene in the slightest.

Irene Chapeau's rosebud lips pulled into a smile. Her hair was redder than her mother's and cut into a smooth bob, but they were similar in every other way. Small and svelte and both with keen, alert faces. There were just twenty-five years between them, and the passing of time had been kind to both of them.

'Just because I'm only a nurse, not a doctor, doesn't mean I don't know the importance of looking after myself,' Dorothy added. Again there was no maliciousness to her tone, only a gentle teasing.

Irene smiled and reached across the table and touched her mother's hand. Their eyes met, and it took just a moment for them to mist, forcing them to look away rather than face the emotion they were both running from. Irene turned her body, rearranging the blanket around Bruno, her five-year-old son who had fallen asleep in the afternoon sun.

'I'll just have a little nap, and then we can go back to the hotel,' Dorothy stated, closing her eyes once again.

Irene turned back, a cloud sweeping over her face. 'Mama, you really shouldn't be...'

Dorothy lifted a hand from her lap and wafted it towards her daughter. 'I am doing exactly what I should be doing, and I'm doing it because I need to.' She lowered her head and narrowed her eyes towards Irene. She wanted to be sure that her daughter understood and accepted what she was about to say. 'I asked you to come with me because I thought it would be an enjoyable experience for us to share, but if it's going to be problematic for you, we can always rethink our agreement.'

Irene smiled. 'People have always asked me where I get my stubbornness and determination from. I don't think it would take a genius to work out where I got it from.'

She reached across the table and touched Dorothy's hand again. 'I am a doctor, but more importantly, in this time and space I am nothing but your daughter, and all I am here to do is to be with you, to share this with you, but please understand one thing, dear mother, I will not, I CANNOT keep my mouth shut if I think you are endangering yourself. That was and remains my one condition. My line in the sand, if you like. I can be your daughter until I have to be a doctor, and that most certainly trumps you feeling mollycoddled.'

Dorothy stuck out her tongue.

Irene snorted. 'And while we're at it, I feel as if I should remind you of something someone very wise once said to me; you can be as stubborn and as obnoxious as you like, but the sooner you accept I have nothing but your best interests at heart, the better.' She smiled at her mother. 'And I am following that advice, so I won't let you chase me off or shout me down just because I'm concerned you might drop dead on this folly of yours...'

'It is no folly,' Dorothy berated.

'Désolé, I didn't mean to be dismissive, mama,' Irene breathed. 'My point is. I am here because I love you and support you. But as I said, I am a daughter who is also a doctor. I can't ignore anything obvious.' She held her hands up. 'That is my only point. Other than that, knock yourself out and have a hell of a time, but when I am concerned, you will listen to me, or else there will be trouble. Am I making myself completely clear to you, mama?'

Dorothy turned her head to hide the smile on her face. 'Honestly, I don't know where you get your pig-headedness from.'

Irene snorted again and picked up the fork on her mother's plate and handed it to her. 'Oui, you do. Now eat your damn salad, or I'll send you to bed early.'

Dorothy snatched the fork. 'I should never have taught you to speak,' she said, moving the salad into her mouth and playfully winking at her daughter.

Hugo Duchamp fell backwards onto the sofa headrest and placed a cigarette in his mouth, seconds later blowing smoke rings above him. He emitted a contented sigh.

On the other side of the cramped, overflowing living room, Ben Beaupain laughed. As usual, his hand rose to push away the mound of curls which bounced onto his forehead. It did no good. The curls returned a moment later. 'One of these days, we're going to have to talk about your smoking,' he announced.

Hugo did not answer, instead taking another drag and releasing the smoke with clear joie de vivre.

'You're enjoying your day off, I take it?' Ben asked.

Hugo smiled. 'Do you know until I came to Montgenoux, I don't actually remember ever taking a day off? I suppose I must have, but I don't remember it. I mean, what would I have done with it?'

Ben's face clouded, biting down on his lip.

Hugo noticed it, and his face creased. 'Désolé, I meant nothing by that, and I certainly didn't want you to feel sad about my past, something you had absolutely no control over.'

Ben moved quickly across the living room and threw himself onto the sofa next to Hugo. He threw his arm over him and snuggled into him. 'Je t'aime,' he breathed.

Hugo reached over and kissed the top of Ben's head. 'I'm not sad. Not anymore. You know that.'

Ben nodded. 'I guess I just don't like to talk about the dark years before we met each other,' he said, snuggling into his husband.

Hugo kissed Ben's head again. It had been almost seven years since his return to his native France, after a decade or so of self-imposed exile in England where he had worked as a police officer for the Metropolitan Police. He had never imagined he would return to the place of his birth, but the decision had been taken out of his hands when he had been seconded to investigate a town rife with corruption and the vicious murder of a young girl. He had hoped the investigation would be brief and he would be able to return to his staid life in London before much time had passed.

However, in the end, it was not to be the case because he had discovered something he never thought would be possible for him. That he wanted to be with people, and more importantly, he was able to love someone again. His heart had been cold and locked for more years than he cared to remember, and despite the occasional love affair, Hugo had never been able, or perhaps willing, to allow himself to become close to anyone again.

Everything had changed upon his arrival in Montgenoux, a small town on the southern coast of France, a little over ten kilometres from the Atlantic coast. The town had, mostly, welcomed him, and it had shown him love and compassion. And some years later he found himself still in charge of Montgenoux Police Nationale and married to a man he loved with all of his heart and could not imagine a life without.

Together they shared a ramshackle Swiss-style cottage, along with the young man they had adopted. Baptiste Beaupain, like Hugo, had barely survived a troubled upbringing, thanks in part to a problematic and fragmented family, however, under the care and guidance of his new adoptive parents was blossoming into a strong and happy man. It was not lost on Hugo; it was a life he had never imagined nor envisioned for himself. But somehow, just somehow, it had fallen into place and continued to work. He could not imagine leaving Montgenoux and as time passed, he found he recognised his former self less and less. It was as if he had two shadows emerging from one body, always following him, but both slowly diminishing by the light around him.

'Are you happy?' Ben asked.

Hugo smiled, ruminating. 'I suppose I am. I never really understood the concept of being happy. My parents left me when I was so young and I'm not sure either of them cared for me, not really. And then when I was fifteen I fell in love, or at least I think I did because honestly, I had very little understanding of what love was. Bien sûr it fell apart, and it left me devastated, mais,' he gave a sad smile, 'the sun came up, and then soon after I had a chance to love again, but again, that really was more to do with my insecurities. In all that time, I think there was only one person who had ever truly loved me, and then when she died I suppose you could say it set me on a path I didn't want to get off because I realised it suited me to be alone.' He grimaced, bowing his head melodramatically, a mop of blond hair cascading across his face. 'Tragedy did seem to follow me, I thought.'

He laughed. It was short and filled with sadness. 'I imagined that was going to be the pattern of my life, and it actually was, until I was dragged out of my misery and implanted in this crazy town.' He sucked in his breath. 'And it was only then I realised you were the reward for my misery.'

Ben wiped his eyes. 'Shut up you,' he quipped, playfully punching his arm. 'You have too much game, and it annoys me as much as it turns me on.' He moved away and grabbed his iPad. He nodded his head towards a closed door. 'And as our son is home, I'd better make better use of my time and try to finally get through to Irene.'

Hugo nodded. Irene Chapeau was one of the first people he had met when he arrived in Montgenoux, an eminent world-class pathologist. She was also Ben's best friend and had been instrumental in bringing them together. Hugo and Irene had worked together on several tough investigations, and their professional relationship had grown into a deep, personal one of mutual respect and affection.

Following a series of professional and personal setbacks,

Irene had decided to take a leave of absence from her job and undertake a period of travel with her son before he was due to begin full-time schooling. She had been gone for over six months and Hugo knew how much she was missed, particularly by Ben. Their friendship was long-lasting and they were as close as family to one another.

Ben flipped open the computer on the table and clicked some buttons. Moments later, the screen filled with Irene's beaming face, a smile as radiant as the sun.

'Oh Dieu, I miss seeing the two of you snuggling on that sofa!' Irene gulped, peering into the camera.

Ben reached across and touched her face on the screen. 'You promised me you were coming home,' he whined petulantly. 'It's been six months now, and you promised me.'

Irene nodded sadly. 'Je sais, je sais. Believe me, I was intending on coming home, mais...' She trailed off and lowered her head.

'How is your mother?' Hugo asked.

Irene moved her shoulders slowly. 'She says she's fine,' she replied as if she did not believe it, 'but then I catch her staring into space and I see the sadness written all over her face.'

Hugo nodded. Before she had a chance to travel, Irene had decided to spend some time with her parents who lived in Northern France. She had only been with them for a few weeks when her father suddenly passed away.

'I think the fundamental problem is she never got to say goodbye to him,' Irene explained. 'He was sitting there at the dining table, telling me about how well his vegetable garden was going, and then he just stopped and he was gone. It was as simple and as quick and undramatic as that. He was in the middle of a sentence and it was like the words were just hanging in mid-air, waiting for him to finish the thought he'd started.' She choked, her hand pressing against her mouth. 'But he didn't. He couldn't.'

She visibly shuddered before continuing. 'I've seen death up close before. We all have. And more times than I care to remember. But this was different, and not just because it was my father. I've seen so much death, but by the time it gets to me, well...' she trailed off as if searching for the words. 'I think it was just a shock to see someone disappear in front of my eyes. I was only on the opposite side of the room, but by the time I got to him, I knew it was over. He was gone, and I knew it. That is the only way I can think to explain it. His body was still there, but whoever he'd been before was gone.'

Hugo turned his head, a long blond fringe covering his eyes. Irene's words had catapulted him back into his past. The day of his eighteenth birthday and looking into the eyes of someone he loved very much, the only person who had ever truly been there for him, his Grand-Mère, Madeline Duchamp. He had sensed her strength and her light diminishing, even if he had been unable to articulate it at the time. He understood exactly what Irene meant because when he had first seen Madeline laid out, he knew instantly that whoever she had been had dissipated and all that remained was a decaying, once-inhabited shell.

'I wish I'd been there for you,' Ben grumbled, pressing his fingers against the computer screen. 'I SHOULD have been there for you.'

Irene reached forward and touched the screen so their fingers aligned. 'You were in every way that counts,' she said reassuringly. 'And besides, there wasn't time. Mama wanted a grand Catholic service, and she wanted it quickly. And since then, well, she won't talk about him any more. All she mumbles is, "thirty-nine years, eleven months and twelve days."'

Hugo and Ben exchanged a look.

'That's when they first met,' she added sadly. 'She keeps saying it, over and over.' Irene looked around her. 'And that's why we are where we are now.'

'And where are you exactly?' Ben asked, straining to see behind her. It appeared to be nothing special, a standard nondescript hotel room.

'We arrived in a place called Saint-Jean-Pied-de-Port late last night,' Irene explained. 'It's where the Camino de Santiago begins, or rather, the point where it began when my parents met all those years ago.'

'I remember this story,' Ben smiled wistfully. 'They met on a pilgrimage to Santiago, didn't they?' He smiled contentedly and wrapped his arm around Hugo. 'So romantic. When you know, you know.'

The nostalgia caused a cloud to pass across Irene's face. 'It was love at first sight. My mother travelled from Scotland where she was born to make the pilgrimage. She'd saved up for years to be able to afford it, and she ended up joining a tour group of strangers and papa was part of the group. After a few hundred kilometres, they had very sore feet,' she added with a sad laugh, 'but more importantly, they'd fallen in love. They were married the year after and not long after, along came me.'

She exhaled. 'I've probably told you this before, but my parents were both very religious, and while I didn't necessarily share their beliefs growing up, it actually didn't matter. They didn't force it onto me, and because of that, I could enjoy it for them when I needed to. I went to mass and the usual annual services. I did it for them because it meant a lot to them. They understood that, and they appreciated it, but they always allowed me to follow my own path.'

She paused. 'When I was pregnant and not married, I imagined they would have hated it and been terribly embarrassed by me, especially in front of their friends, but it was never like that. They never pressured me to do anything other than make sure I allowed them to be a part of Bruno's life.' She sucked in a breath. 'My father was a good man taken far too soon, and my mother is a

19

woman who left behind her entire life for a man and a country she didn't know. I honestly don't know what she's going to do with herself now.'

Ben took a deep breath. 'I always wanted to meet your parents,' he exhaled, 'because I could tell by the way you talked about them how exceptional they were,' he added with a clear intonation of sadness.

Irene nodded. 'They were, and I think without papa she's just a little bit lost. And it seems as if she's drifting aimlessly without him. The sad thing is, I understand losing my father and what that's done to me, but if I'm honest, I don't understand what losing the love of your life does to you. I've never been so lucky, and because of that, I just feel useless. I can't advise her, and I can't help her because I've loved no one enough to understand what it might be like to lose them.'

Hugo and Ben exchanged a look and entwined their hands.

'I've had love affairs,' she continued, 'but I've never had *love* affairs, if you know what I mean.'

Ben raised his fingers to his lips and kissed them, and then pressed them against the screen.

Hugo moved closer to the screen, pulling the glasses from his hair. 'What is your plan, Irene?'

Irene's face contorted. 'Well, according to my mother, she plans on walking the entire way.' She shook her head. 'It's difficult. It seems the original group from forty years ago has been trying to arrange this as a kind of pilgrimage reunion for years. The same group of people from the first Camino walk. They've all kept in touch, you see. But it seems as if for one reason or another, it never really worked out before now.'

'Forty years is a hell of a long time to wait to revisit the past,' Ben stated.

Irene murmured her agreement. 'And that's what makes it even more awful. They'd finally got everything into place after so many attempts. Something always derailed their plans. And then finally everything fell into place. My parents decided to do the pilgrimage again for their anniversary and to meet up with some old friends who had been there at the beginning of their relationship. It would have been perfect, and they were both so looking forward to it…' she trailed off, lowering her eyes.

'Désolé, Ree,' Ben mouthed.

Irene appeared to blink away tears, and when she spoke, her tone was forceful. 'Obviously, after papa died, I didn't think for a second the walk would take place,' she continued. 'And then when she mentioned it, I assumed she wouldn't go ahead with it, alors… my mother, being my mother, is very stubborn. It's very annoying…'

Ben snorted, immediately covering his mouth, his eyes flashing with embarrassment.

Irene tutted. 'I heard that Beaupain, and I'll deal with you later,' she chastised. 'Anyway, mama is insistent she's still going to go ahead with it. The fact is, I'm not even sure she's capable of doing it. It's hundreds of kilometres if she does the whole thing, which she seems insistent on,' she grumbled bitterly.

Hugo nodded. He did not fully understand the pilgrimage that so many people took every year, walking towards the tomb of Saint Jacques de Compostelle in Galicia. Although religion was somewhat lost on him, over the years he had spoken to several people who had undertaken the journey, often for contrasting reasons, but all of them had remarked they had emerged very different people.

The people he had spoken with had claimed the pallet of landscapes, experiences and emotions that had been triggered had changed them forever, essentially bringing them closer to God. Hugo had concluded whatever they had found, whether it be God, or themselves, it had been enough for them and given them what they needed. His approach to religion had always been simple.

Don't judge me and I won't judge you.

'Is it such a bad thing?' Ben asked. He turned his head to Hugo. 'Loss is something I think about every day, but honestly, I try not to think about it at all, not really, because if I did, I'm not sure I'd get out of bed or allow Hugo to get out of bed either.'

Irene frowned. 'What do you mean?'

He shrugged. 'Only that your mother has lost something I can't bear the thought of losing, and she's doing the only thing she can think of. The fact is, she's just trying to survive. She's taking a step forward without her husband because it's probably the only thing she can think of doing. Moving forward is all she can do because the only other choice is to hide under her duvet.'

Irene stuck out her tongue at him. 'I hate the fact you two boys are so wise.' She shrugged. 'I agree with everything you say. The truth is, Mama is in her sixties and she has health limitations…' she trailed off. 'And because of all of that, I can't let her do it alone, and that's why I'm going to do it with her.'

Ben's eyes widened. 'Are you sure?'

She laughed. 'Bien sûr, non, I'm not sure. The whole thing is difficult. And I don't think Bruno can cope with it, and I'm not certain I can, either,' she added with a sad laugh. 'All I know is this - I have to be here for her. I'm hoping she'll see sense, but I have to stay just in case she needs me. It's the least I can do.'

Hugo nodded. 'What about your job at Montgenoux hospital?'

Irene extended her hands in front of her. 'I don't know. When I took my leave of absence last year, I assured them I would be back by now, but the fact is I just can't, not yet at least. Not until I've seen this through. They may have to hire a permanent replacement, but I can't think about that right now. I have to do what I have to do and then worry about the consequences later.'

'Then you're really going to do the whole pilgrimage?' Ben laughed. 'It's so far and I've never seen you walk in anything but heels. You're not imagining you can do it all, are you?'

Irene snorted. 'Obviously not.' She took a deep breath. 'The fact is, I never got the chance to say goodbye to my father, to say what I should have said. So because of that, I want to make sure that I spend as much time as I can with my mother, while I still can. It's really important to me that I do this.'

Ben exhaled. His own father had died a few years earlier, but their relationship had always been strained and his death had come before either of them had attempted any kind of reconciliation. 'When my father died, I was sad only because we had never got over our impasse,' he said. 'And because of that I cherish every moment I get to spend with my mother, so I do understand your reasons.'

Ben and Irene stole a sly look at Hugo. He had finished his cigarette and immediately lit another. Both of Hugo's parents were alive, one in Paris, the other possibly in America, but their relationship was so strained it was unlikely there would ever be any kind of reconciliation. At one time it had troubled him, but no longer. He had closed that door and did not care to open it again.

Hugo noticed both of them looking at him. He shook his head. 'I understand what you're saying, but you also have to understand, I won't have any regrets concerning my parents, and that is the truth. They haven't been part of my life since I was a child, and that's honestly fine with me.'

Irene stared at him. 'Don't you think you'll regret the decision not to reach out to them?'

Hugo shook his head. His hair fell over his eyes and he pushed it away. 'I understand why you might think that, but you've never met my parents. It took seeing them face to face as an adult to understand that we are just three people who have nothing to share with one another.' He stubbed out his cigarette. 'But it doesn't mean I don't understand why you need to do what is the right thing to do, and that is to spend some time with your mother.'

23

Irene nodded. 'It just feels as if I have to seize this opportunity and spend this time with her while I still can.'

'I completely agree with that,' Hugo said.

She sighed. 'As for the logistics of it all, well, we'll just have to see how it goes. The complete walk is a guided trip using the same guide they used forty years ago, believe it or not. And as worried as I am about mama, from what I understand, the plan is to only walk a maximum of ten kilometres a day.' She shrugged. 'Mama assures me there are lots of stops along the way and apparently there's also a handy bus trailing just behind us should we need shelter from the elements. I can't imagine how we're going to manage it, especially with a five-year-old, but all I know for certain is I have to be here with her.'

Ben smiled and touched the screen again. 'Bien sûr, you do. And I wish I could be there with you, as well.'

She laughed. 'Non, you don't, not really, but I appreciate the sentiment.' She glanced at her watch. 'Listen, I have to go. There's a big get-together for everyone who's doing the pilgrimage tonight and I want to try and get Bruno to sleep for a while before that, so he's not rambunctious.'

'You will keep in touch, won't you?' Ben asked, concern creeping into his voice.

'I'll try my best,' she replied, 'but they've already warned us that cell service isn't always great in these areas.'

'Well, try to check in every couple of days, at least,' Ben responded, 'just so we at least know you're okay. We miss you and we can't help but worry about you and Bruno.'

Irene smiled. 'That's sweet. I'll call when I can, but listen, don't worry too much. What could possibly go wrong apart from an abundance of blisters and a little bit of sunstroke?' She touched the screen again. 'Au revoir, darling boys. I love you both, and I'll see you very soon, I promise. And don't worry, I'm sure everything will be fine.'

Maurice & Alain

Maurice Rousseau turned the cigarette lighter over, slowly moving it back and forth between his fingers, all the time his attention focused on the people ambling around the square in front of *Café Compostelle*. The café itself was small, perched on the side of a tall building, with a large outdoor space lined with ramshackle tables and chairs. Above it was a basic, but serviceable hotel.

Rousseau was seventy-years-old, a tall and foreboding man, who carried himself with the gait of a much younger man. A slice of grey running across the middle of thick untamed shoulder-length dark hair was the only real hint of his true age. His eyes were dark and watchful and appeared to be always on alert. He was a man who was always prepared for the unexpected.

Maurice had passed most of his days in *Café Compostelle*. He always took the same table, the one perched to the left of the entrance, the one affording a panoramic view of all around him. To an outsider, it would appear as if he was waiting for someone. The assumption would be correct, but Maurice was waiting for someone he knew would never return.

The Café was situated at the bottom of a steep, long stairway which led to a row of ramshackle houses, and several larger buildings, the stairs and path conveying on a narrow bridge which was the only way in or out of the village he had been born in, and the one he knew he would die in. Maurice knew every step, every corner, every ancient brick of the houses he had helped build.

Chemin des Pèlerins, or the "way of the pilgrims" as it was known by the hoards of visitors who descended upon it every year, was a tiny village, a hundred kilometres from Saint-Jean-Pied-de-Port and had been built long before Maurice's birth by his father and a handful of men and women who had sought to create a refuge for those who sought to walk the Camino and needed a respite from the gruelling pilgrimage they had undertaken. Maurice had taken over from his father, architecting and restoring the crumbling homes and buildings.

The village, while not large with barely a dozen full-time inhabitants, was busy most of the year with pilgrims returning or passing by the quaint village at the bottom of a valley, often remarking once they crossed the bridge it was like stepping into another century.

Maurice, like his father before him, had spent his life as a guide for passing pilgrims. In his youth, Maurice would often walk with the pilgrims, but as time passed and his advancing age brought health problems, Maurice would follow them in the rickety old bus he had been using for decades, offering them support and help should they need it.

A man coming out of the storeroom behind him jolted Maurice back into reality. Alain Bonnet, the proprietor of *Café Compostelle,* wiped his hands on the apron which barely covered his ample stomach and walked out of the dimly lit Café, a large pitcher of beer in his hand. He set it down on Maurice's table and refilled his glass and poured one for himself. He took a seat next to Maurice and slapped his hand on his shoulder.

Bonnet was as physically different to Maurice as possible. Whilst Maurice Rousseau was tall and thin, with a long, narrow nose, Alain Bonnet was small, with an expansive stomach straining under an apron, and wide short legs, thick dark hair shoved carelessly under a chef's hat. They had known each other all of their lives and it was evident they shared the comfort and ease of two men who could say anything or nothing to one another without it mattering at all. Their proximity was all they needed. They both had dark eyes, tired but at the same time alert as if they were designed for a simple, tranquil life, but were always watching in case something changed.

'It's almost 14h00,' Alain stated, pointing at the enormous

clock in the centre of the town square. His voice was light and as he spoke, and his jowls moved in tandem.

Maurice nodded. 'I'm seventy, old friend, and senility hasn't yet prevented me from being able to read the time,' he retorted, slurping the froth from the top of his beer. His voice was deep and masculine, though there was a sadness to it, almost as if it was exhausting for him to have to speak at all.

Alain snorted. 'Well, far be it from me to remind you, old man, but aren't you supposed to be meeting your new batch of pilgrims in Saint-Jean-Pied-de-Port in two hours?'

Maurice took another sip. 'There's no hurry. I've made the journey hundreds of times and I could probably do it with my eyes closed.' He set the cup down. 'This time I find myself...' he stopped as if he was searching for the right word. 'Hesitant? Oui. Hesitant. It's almost as if I have been waiting for this for so long that I can barely believe it is finally happening.'

Alain looked at his old friend over the top of his glass. 'Maurice,' he began softly, 'I don't know what you hope to achieve from all of this, mais... the past is the past, n'est pas? What good can come from stirring it all up again? Don't you think it's consumed you for too long as it is?'

Maurice slammed his fist on the table, causing a passing woman to jump. He raised his hand in an apology, mouthing a platitude in her direction. He turned back to face his friend. 'She has been dead for over forty years and yet I have nothing. I don't even have her grave to visit. Do you know how much that has eaten away at me? I feel it like a cancer gnawing at me, even after all these years.'

'I know, I know,' Alain sighed. 'Olive was your wife, but she was my girlfriend first, non?' he asked with a tired smile.

Maurice gave his friend a sad snort. 'When you were five years old, peut être! Once she saw sense, she saw me. And then she was happy.'

27

Alain stared at Maurice. A vein under his eye throbbed, a shadow passing across his face as if he was remembering something unpleasant. He said nothing, instead taking another drink. He drained the contents and refilled both their glasses from the pitcher. Finally, he cleared his throat. 'You should have left here a long time ago. Olive would have wanted that for you. She wouldn't have wanted you festering here, consumed by anger.' He rubbed Maurice's shoulder again. 'Olive would have wanted you to start again with someone else. You know that to be the truth.'

Maurice shook his head. 'I could never leave this village,' he said forcefully, 'and there could be nobody else for me.' He stabbed his finger in the staircase's direction. 'Not until I finally know where she lays. If I could, don't you think I would have left and sought justice in the outside world? I would have followed them all, dragging the truth out of them if I had to.' He shook his head, long hair falling over his shoulders. 'Non. I have waited a long time for these people to return to the village and they're not leaving until they finally give me the answers I've been waiting for.'

Alain touched his friend's shoulder again. 'You don't know what happened to Olive, let alone who was responsible for it. You've spent decades pining and imagining scenarios, you can't begin to know if there is any truth to them.'

Maurice touched a folder on the table in front of him. 'It was one of them. I've always known it. I've always felt it here.' He jabbed a thin finger against his heart. 'I just could never do a thing about it. But now they're back. Maybe they think no one cares, or that no one remembers. Mais I do, et,' he touched Alain's arm, 'you do too. We are the only ones who truly knew Olive and remember her for the young vibrant, beautiful woman she was. And that means we are the only ones who can avenge her.'

'Avenge?' Alain interrupted, his voice rising to a shrill panic.

Maurice's lips twisted into a cruel smirk. 'Do you imagine I haven't waited long enough to finally learn the truth?'

Alain cocked his head and bit his lip as if he was preventing himself from saying something he should not.

Maurice noticed his reaction. 'You have something to say, cher ami? Then say it. You've never held back before. Why would you think to do so now? If you cared for Olive as much as you claimed to, why are you not interested in finally putting her to rest?'

Alain took a deep breath. 'Because I am worried at what cost it will come.'

Maurice shrugged bony shoulders. 'What does it matter so long as we settle a debt? An eye for an eye, isn't that what the bible says?'

Alain took another sip. 'I've lived in this pilgrim village all of my life, but it doesn't mean I buy into all the religious pontifications. It just means I was too damn lazy to stretch my legs and walk further afield.' He sucked in a breath. 'Mais, you're probably right about one thing. I suppose I always hung around because I expected Olive to walk into this bar one day and order a glass of wine as if it was the most natural thing in the world and as if she had been gone but for a second. I think of that often every time I look at the top of those stairs and see a new bunch of foreigners coming into our village.'

He reached across and touched Maurice's hand again. 'We're old, Maurice, but we're not infirm yet. We both know that will not happen.'

Maurice nodded. 'I know.' He clambered to his feet and pointed at the clock. 'Which is exactly why I'm going to greet the only group of people who know the truth. They will tell me what happened to her, or there will be hell to pay.'

Alain watched as Maurice walked away, kicking dust into the air with his dirty boots. 'And what do you imagine will come of this? As far as anyone is concerned, Olive's death was nothing but a tragic accident.'

Maurice did not look back. 'I never believed it then, and I

believe it less now. Non, these people will tell me what happened to my Olive, or if they don't, they'll end up in a watery grave of their own. And my face will be the last they see and I'll make sure they understand why.' He stopped and turned back to face Alain. 'You've never been against me before. So, are you with me, or are you against me? Are your words of love for our childhood sweetheart just lip service, or do they actually mean something?'

'Bien sûr, they mean something,' Alain cried desperately.

Maurice nodded. 'Bon. Then I can count on you when the time comes?'

'When the time comes for what?' Alain asked cautiously, fear flashing in his eyes.

Maurice smiled. 'For retribution. Do I, or do I not, have your support?'

'Maurice, I don't know what you think this is going to achieve, but I beg you not to be hasty, for all our sakes,' Alain begged. 'Apart from anything else, we're too old to end up in jail.'

'I don't care about that. I've been waiting too long for this,' Maurice waved his hand dismissively. 'And therefore, I could hardly be accused of being hasty. But I'm no fool and I realise this is probably my last chance of ever discovering what really happened. So, I'll ask you again. Are you with me or against me?'

Alain's eyes dropped toward the beer. He grunted a response. 'You know I'm with you. I've *always* been with you.'

Maurice strode away, a smile appearing on his face. He scratched his jaw as if it was the first time in a very long time since he had smiled. 'Then let the games begin,' he cackled, throwing back his head and laughing.

Elke Huber pulled Dorothy Chapeau into an embrace, smothering her with a sweet, floral perfume. She pulled back and the two women appraised one another with the keen eyes of people who had not seen each other for a long time as if scanning the face for signs of the person they had once been.

Elke was small, with a narrow face and long grey hair wound into a bun at the back of her head. 'I'm sorry about Willum,' she said in broken English with a thick German accent.

Dorothy's hands dropped to her side. 'I received your bouquet. The flowers were beautiful.'

Elke looked awkwardly at her feet, kicking her shoes into the ground.

Dorothy cleared her throat. 'Over forty years since we last saw each other,' she said, with seemingly enforced bonheur. 'It feels as if it passed in the blink of an eye.'

Elke nodded. She gestured to the bar. A plump bald man with wide shoulders was engaged in what appeared to be a heated debate with the bar owner. 'We met both of our husbands on this magical journey,' she stated, pointing at the plump man. 'And as you can see, my Wolfgang has lost none of his ability to argue the point over a few pennies.'

Her husband trudged out of the bar, a tray of drinks in his hand. He dropped it onto the table. 'They think just because I'm old they can shortchange me!' he snorted, 'I tell them, I wasn't a police officer for thirty-two years because I let people get one over on me!' He extended his hands, pulling a reluctant Dorothy into another embrace. 'You look as wonderful as you did last time, Dotty,' he pronounced.

She laughed. 'Nobody has called me Dotty in a long time, Wolfgang. It is good to see you both.' She turned around and pointed at Irene and Bruno, who were seated at a table outside the bar. The night was still warm and bright and Bruno was excitedly watching a gang of pigeons playing in the square. 'May I present my daughter, Irene, and my grandson, Bruno.'

Elke moved quickly across the bar, Wolfgang following her with the tray. He set it in front of them. 'You're as beautiful as your mother, young lady.'

Irene smiled. 'Merci. That's very kind of you to say.'

'Can I get you a drink?' he asked.

'We already ordered while we waiting,' Dorothy interjected. 'We arrived early. It seems we're the first here.'

Irene sipped her wine. 'I still find it amazing you have all kept in touch all of these years.'

Dorothy slid into the chair next to her. 'Well, not kept in touch exactly,' she responded. 'Cards at Easter, birthdays, Christmas.' She gestured for Elke to sit next to her. 'These were the days before the infernal internet when a person actually went to the trouble of handwriting a note or a card.'

Elke shrugged, her eyes misting wistfully. 'Yet it was enough, wasn't it? We managed to follow each other's lives just as well.' She turned to Irene. 'Your mother told me you're a doctor of some kind?'

'Oui,' Irene replied. 'I'm a pathologist.'

Elke's face crinkled with distaste. 'Yes, that's what I understood. It must be, I'm sure, a very interesting job.' she said as if she was sure of no such thing.

Wolfgang chortled. 'You must forgive my wife, pretty lady. She spent her life as a stenographer, so unless it involves replacing typewriter ribbons, she's rather lost trying to understand the real world.'

Irene looked to Elke. There was something about Wolfgang's tone that irritated her, because it sounded like he was mocking his wife, but not in a kind way, rather a cruel one, and she could see the pain on the German woman's face. It was resigned, almost as if she was used to being belittled in such a way.

Irene turned sharply towards Wolfgang but noticed the expression on her mother's face. *Don't pick a fight,* was the clear warning. Instead, Irene cleared her throat. 'Well, actually, I've always been rather jealous of talents such as your wife's. I never really learnt to type properly, and it's rather hampered me, I find.' She smiled at Elke. Elke lowered her head, smiling gratefully at Irene.

Irene ignored the disapproving look from her mother. 'So, who else is making the pilgrimage?'

'There were ten of us on the first pilgrimage,' Dorothy answered. 'Your father and I, and Wolfgang and Elke, of course. All young and carefree, ready to experience the joy of walking towards... towards something?' She shrugged. 'I don't know exactly what my intentions were, but in the end, I left this journey with God deeper in my heart, and your father's hand in mine.'

Irene touched her mother's hand, her eyes wide as she fought back tears.

'It was a wonderful pilgrimage,' Elke agreed, 'and one which has sustained me for these past years.'

'There were six other people?' Irene asked. 'And they're all coming again? That's incredible, really.'

Dorothy shook her head. 'Sadly, not all of them. Firstly, there was the Mitchell family.' she answered. 'An American couple with their teenage son. Anne and Frank and their son Sam. Sadly, both Anne and Frank died a number of years ago, that's why the last planned reunion never took place.'

'They both died at the same time?' Irene questioned.

'In a car crash,' Wolfgang replied. 'As I recall, it was a hit and run. Some bastard ran them off the road.'

'That's right,' Elke agreed. 'It was awful, especially for poor Sam.'

'Sam? Irene asked.

'Their son,' Dorothy replied. 'He was with them on the walk to Camino.' She smiled. 'He was only fifteen or so at the time, and of course, he obviously didn't want to be here with them, and all of us, for that matter, but as I recall, he was a pleasant, well-mannered boy.'

Elke smiled. 'And it's wonderful he's joining us on this adventure.' She stole a look at her husband. 'I emailed him.' She winked at Irene. 'I can do that now, you know. Anyway, he replied to me, he doesn't normally bother. Apparently, he is a travel writer now.'

'Didn't he used to be a football player or something like that?' Dorothy enquired.

Wolfgang nodded. 'He was, and a very good one, as I recall. He was injured some time ago on the field and that ended his sporting career.'

'And that's when he took up travel writing,' Elke continued. 'He told me he imagined it would make a marvellous book about retracing the journey he started with his parents forty years ago and completing it with his son, their grandson.'

Wolfgang laughed. 'A writer, a writer who writes about travelling.' He shrugged. 'I could do that. Anyone could.' He cleared his throat. 'I walked, it was hot, and it was dusty and I was tired and then I went to sleep… Sounds like a bestseller to me!'

'Wolfgang,' Elke stopped him. Her voice was meek, but her gaze sent an obvious message. *Stop embarrassing me.*

'Who else is coming?' Irene continued, ignoring the frisson between the German couple.

'There was a British couple, Tony and Jane Wilkinson,' Dorothy replied. 'Sadly, Jane died a few years ago. She was a lovely woman, I liked her very much, although I always got the sense she was a sad soul. As for Tony, well, I never really got to know him in the same way.'

'Because he thought he was better than all of us,' Wolfgang quipped. 'Just because he was some high-flying banker.'

'At least he's coming back,' Elke interjected. 'He replied to my email. He also rarely bothers. It was always Jane who kept in touch. He said he was looking forward to seeing us all again, and that he was bringing along his daughter, Sarah.'

'And then finally there was Edith,' Dorothy said with a chuckle. 'Edith Lancaster. I still find it incredible she's coming. She already seemed old forty years ago.'

'She's eighty-two now,' Elke answered. 'And yes, she says she's not only coming, she's also determined to walk the entire way to Camino.'

'Probably by using her broomstick,' Wolfgang added, a wry smile on his face.

Dorothy laughed. 'Don't be cruel, Wolfgang. Edith is harmless enough. Or at least, her bark is certainly worse than her bite.'

'Easy for you to say. She terrified me!' Elke cried. 'The way she always looks at you, it's as if she's working out the best way to kill you with one of those knitting needles she always has in her hands!'

'Actually, you're right,' Dorothy replied. 'She may be tiny and frail, but I imagine she's stronger than most men and certainly more determined.'

'She'll terrify God himself when they finally meet,' Wolfgang added.

'She sounds like a fun lady,' Irene concluded.

'Don't listen to them,' Dorothy stated. 'The simple fact is, Edith can be a little... foreboding, but she's not as scary as she can... *sometimes* come across.'

'Well, I'm certainly looking forward to meeting her, and all the others,' Irene stated.

Dorothy clasped her hands together. 'Oh, I can't believe

we're about to do this again after all of this time!'

Irene reached across and touched her mother's arm. 'You sound happy, Mama,' she exhaled before pulling her lips together as if she was attempting to stop herself from crying.

Dorothy shrugged Irene's hand away, a guilty expression spreading across her face. 'I'm just looking forward to seeing everyone again and spending time with them.'

Wolfgang rose to his feet and pointed into the street. 'Well, you're about to get your wish, dear lady. Here's the airport shuttle, they'll be on that. Shall we go and greet them?'

Dorothy beamed. 'I'd love to. We've…' She stopped, her face clouding. '*I've* been waiting a long time to come back to this place and see all of you again.' She moved past Irene, heading swiftly in the direction of the bus, a loud sniff emerging as she did.

Edith Lancaster lowered herself into a chair in the corner of the outside bar area and immediately pulled knitting from a carpetbag she placed on her lap. Seconds later, two knitting needles were moving in rapid succession, whilst Edith's eyes remained focused entirely on the scene unfolding in front of her. The elderly English woman was rake thin, with dark grey hair cut into a short, severe bob. Her eyes were catlike, alert and bright, and vibrated as they moved from one point of vision to another.

'I was sorry to hear about Willum,' she spoke into the air. 'He was a good man, a God-fearing man. So, we can take comfort he is safe in the embrace of the Lord now,' she added dramatically.

Dorothy Chapeau positioned herself in a chair between Irene and Bruno. Bruno, still a child and filled with burning curiosity, stared at the elderly English woman as if he was not sure what to make of her. 'I'd rather he was in my embrace, not the Lord's,' Dorothy muttered under her breath with such bitterness it caused Irene to take a sharp breath.

Edith narrowed her eyes at Dorothy. 'And the Lord hears everything, as you should well know, Dorothy,' she stated, although she was ten feet away from Dorothy.

Sam Mitchell threw back his head and laughed. 'You haven't changed at all, Edith, not even after forty years, you're still a great old broad.'

She fixed the American travel writer with an intensely withering look. 'And nor have you, boy. Even then, you didn't know how to address an elder with respect.'

He extended his hands and laughed again. 'I was a fifteen-year-old football jock back then,' he replied. 'I didn't know any better, and if it hadn't of been for a busted knee, I would still probably know no better.' He was an athletic-looking man and despite being in his fifties, he had retained the blond buzz-cut hair and square jaw of his youth.

Edith sniffed. 'I've read one of your… "books" and I admire you immensely…'

Sam cocked his head. 'Really? Wow, that's amazing,' he interrupted, clearly taken aback.

Her lips pulled into a sly smile. 'I hadn't finished my thought. What I was going to say, had you allowed me,' she sniped, 'was that I admire you immensely for actually getting anyone to agree to pay you to write a book about travelling across America where the major part of your diatribe centres solely upon the difference between hamburgers from state-to-state. I was a librarian for over sixty years, and one of my major problems was always people borrowing books and enjoying them so much they just simply refused to return them.' She smiled again at him. The smile was sweet, but it did not appear genuine. 'I had no such trouble with any of your books.'

The young man to the right of Sam guffawed. 'She got you there, dad,' he giggled.

Sam threw his arm over the young man's shoulder. 'She sure did, kid. Hey everyone, this is Casey, my son.'

Casey lowered his head, his cheeks flushing and floppy black hair falling over his face. He lifted his head slowly, pushing dark-rimmed glasses back up his nose. 'Hi,' he said with evident self-consciousness.

'And while we're making introductions,' a deep British voice announced, 'or rather, re-introductions, my name is Tony Wilkinson, and this is my daughter, Sarah.'

The group all waved acknowledgement at the newcomers. Tony was a tall, thin man with a pinched face and a mop of dark hair on top of his head, which clearly was a toupee. His daughter, Sarah, nodded, raising her hand to her mouth and nibbling anxiously on her fingernails, a curtain of black hair hanging over her face. Dark, shy eyes seemed to plead with everyone not to look in her direction.

'I don't believe it,' Dorothy gasped, rising to her feet. She stepped into the street. A canary-yellow bus was pulling into the car park. It was old, with rusted panels and dirty windows, and it backfired as the driver tried to reverse it into a parking space. 'It's the same bus.'

Elke appeared next to her. 'It can't be,' she responded. 'It was old and decrepit forty years ago.' She shook her head. She pointed to the side of the bus. 'But I think you are right. Look, aren't those the stickers we added to it after each stop on the pilgrimage?' Her hand flew to her mouth. 'I clear forgot about that. Willum used to place each one in such a way so that anyone from the outside wouldn't be able to see us necking.' She blushed. 'His words, not mine, and I can assure you, we kept the necking to a minimum.'

Edith Lancaster dropped her knitting. 'That's not what I recall. It was quite indecent what was going on in the back seat.'

Dorothy covered her mouth, eyes widening. 'Edith…' she pleaded.

'Mama, and when I think of every time you chastised me for being caught kissing my first boyfriend!'

Edith raised an eyebrow. 'Well, the apple didn't fall too far from the tree, it seems,' she sniffed.

Before anyone else had a chance to comment, Maurice Rousseau jumped from the driver's seat with a resilience belying his age. He hurried toward the bar, a large open windbreaker flapping behind him. He stopped, his head turning quickly between the group. 'Then we're all here.' His voice was soft and welcoming, but his eyes were wide with interest as he looked at each individual in the group in turn.

Dorothy pulled him into an embrace. His body was stiff, and it did not relax. She moved backwards. 'I can't believe it's really you, Maurice. I imagined… I imagined…'

He cocked his head, appraising her with interest. 'You imagined what, Madame Chapeau? That I'd be dead as well?'

Dorothy stumbled backwards, bumping into Irene. Irene stood up, wrapping her arm around her mother again.

'This is my daughter, Irene,' Dorothy stuttered, her eyes wide with confusion.

Maurice nodded coolly towards Irene, but said nothing, leaving Irene with a confused look on her face. Maurice looked around again, his eyes crinkling as if he were assessing the mood. When he spoke again, his tone changed. It was light and cheery. 'I can't tell you how happy it makes me. We are all, mostly, at least, reunited after such a long time. We made so many memories together last time. And I don't know, but I just have a feeling we are going to do it again this time.'

Irene watched her mother's face as the guide spoke. Her mouth had twisted, and she appeared troubled by something. Dorothy noticed Irene watching her, and the expression changed as quickly as it had appeared.

Maurice smiled. 'As always, the Chemin de Compostelle will be illuminating for us all.' He clapped his hands together. 'So, tonight get reacquainted, but then rest well. We'll begin at first light.' He moved away. 'I will wait for you by the bus at 06h00. Bon soiree.'

Irene watched as he made his way across the courtyard. He glanced back over his shoulder, dark eyes narrowing coldly. She shuddered.

'I would like to welcome each and every one of you to what I am sure will be a momentous and life-changing journey for us all,' Maurice Rousseau began.

'I welcome you, my dear pèlerins,' he stopped, casting his eyes around the group, 'or pilgrims, for those of you not yet fully acquainted with the beautiful French language. I would like to explain what to expect in the days and weeks ahead. I know some of you have undergone the pilgrimage before, or at least part of it, but for some, it is an unfamiliar experience which has no doubt filled you with concern and doubts. Let me also begin by assuring you those feelings are perfectly normal and understandable.'

Irene sank into a chair, pulling a still-sleeping Bruno close to her chest, his head instinctively falling into the crook between her shoulder blade and her neck. The morning was fresh; the dawn throwing a dim light over the car park. She looked around. Most of the younger people who had gathered appeared tired and grumpy, whereas the older generation, dressed in their best hiking finery, seemed alert and keen, ready to engage in the daunting journey which lay ahead of them.

Maurice cleared his throat. 'Even before I was born, my family made it their mission to help people make the pilgrimage from here, in Saint-Jean-Pied-de-Port, to the final destination, Santiago de Compostela. Forty years ago, I met most of you for the first time. I was freshly married, and my heart was filled with joy and happiness, although my mother and father had died within a year or two of each other. But our remit was clear, and that was to carry on the mission created by my parents.'

Edith Lancaster bowed her head. 'And a very admirable job you made of it, Maurice,' she said.

Maurice noticed her walking stick and he smiled. 'However,

we realised not everyone, despite their best intentions, could make the entire journey using their own two feet.'

Edith raised an eyebrow, the warning clear on her face.

He stopped, giving a modest smile. 'I myself have only managed the entire seven hundred and seventy kilometres twice on foot. My darling wife and I believed it was important that if someone wanted the experience, they need not be put off by the enormity of something their human bodies were incapable of allowing. That is why we decided we would create a guided tour that was quite unique. It was a tour to be taken for as little, or as much as the human spirit could endure.'

He stepped slowly around the bus. 'My father, a staunch and pious man, thought it blasphemy. He insisted the Chemin de Compostelle was not supposed to be a straightforward journey. Each step, each blister, was part of the journey towards the Lord, is how he described it. We disagreed because the intent to walk towards the Lord should not be just for those who are more physically able. The Lord wants us all to walk towards his light in our best way, not in a way which hastens our journey to Him.'

'Amen,' Edith Lancaster interrupted, genuflecting.

Maurice smiled at her. 'However, we went against my father because we believed it was more important to include those who needed to make the journey but were afraid because of limitations. It was my wife's idea that this bus she found rusting in a yard became a part of the pilgrimage. A place of salvation when needed. A place to compose oneself in readiness for the next step.'

'Because of this,' he continued, 'we are able to offer the full Camino Frances experience, all 770 kilometres, or as much or as little of the seven stages. The first stage, the stage we are about to begin today, will take us from here, Saint-Jean-Pied-de-Port, on a journey of almost one hundred kilometres to Pamplona through the French Pyrenees. We will make this first leg of our journey by walking approximately ten miles per day,' he continued.

'The bus will accompany us, offering a respite from the elements on our carefully chosen path, which allows us to stop and rest when needed and take refreshment and shelter if we should,' he added. 'After our daily walk, we will stop for the night at various sanctuaries along the way.'

Sam Mitchell laughed. 'I remember those "sanctuaries" well! Rock hard bunk beds and tiny shared bathrooms.'

'Some of the hostels are rudimentary, it's true,' Maurice conceded.

Edith Lancaster glared at the American travel writer. 'The journey to the Lord is not meant to be a five-star luxury vacation.'

Maurice laughed at the elderly British woman's harsh tone. He addressed the pilgrims. 'As I said, the sanctuaries might be basic, but they are warm and clean and safe, and believe me, at the end of a long day walking, you will welcome them very much, for they will offer all you need.'

Irene raised her hand. Maurice smiled. 'You don't need to raise your hand, jeune femme. What can I do for you?'

Irene pulled Bruno close to her. He looked up at her and grinned. 'As you can see, I have an almost five-year-old. He's delightful most of the time, but I worry he could be precocious if he gets bored or tired.'

Maurice laughed. 'As can we all.' He waved at Bruno. 'Mais, as I stated, this tour is designed in such a way we can stop when needed and you can rest for a few days in one of the pilgrim's rests we pass by. In fact, before we reach the end of the first stage, we will pass by *Chemin des Pèlerins,* the village where I live. I would recommend we stay there for a few days before proceeding. We should reach the village in a few short days.'

He reached down and ruffled Bruno's hair. 'If the young garçon needs a break, you can stay longer and we have people in *Chemin des Pèlerins* who will transport you to however far ahead the rest of the group has advanced. You see, we have thought this all through. We have been doing it for a very long time, after all,' he added proudly.

Irene nodded, stealing a quick look at her mother. 'That's an excellent idea should... should any of us need to recharge our batteries.'

Dorothy smiled. 'My daughter imagines I'm going to drop de...' she gulped and shook her head before correcting herself and continuing, 'She thinks I'm too old and frail to undergo such a journey.'

'Nonsense,' Edith Lancaster interrupted. 'The Lord will lift you, or else the rest of us jolly well will!' she added with a guffaw.

Dorothy laughed. 'I do not doubt that, Edith.'

'Actually,' Irene replied tartly, 'I was talking about myself. Have you seen how unfit I am? I barely manage to do more than three laps in my friend's pool back in Montgenoux.'

'I'm sure that's not true at all, chérie,' Maurice continued to Irene. 'But in any event, as I have just explained, there is no need for concern. We are here together and we will complete as much or as little of this journey together and with each other's support.'

Irene nodded. 'I'm sorry to be negative. I suppose it's my job. It's not just that I am a concerned daughter, I am also a medical doctor. The journey you describe is intense, even for a young, very fit person. And as I said, I count myself as being neither young, nor particularly fit. My concern,' she smiled at her mother, 'whilst irritating to some, is also based purely upon my own limitations.'

Maurice fixed her with a stern look that caused her to pull her head back. 'Then perhaps you should pray. Dieu will give you the strength you need if you do.' He turned away from her abruptly. 'Now, shall we begin?'

Dorothy clapped her hands together excitedly. 'I can't wait.'

Les Pèlerins - Deuxième nuit

Irene walked slowly, tightly gripping Bruno's hand and swinging arms with him. She stared ahead. Dorothy was striding in front of them, happily stabbing two hiking sticks into the ground as she chatted with her friends. To Irene's shame, she also noticed eighty-plus, Edith Lancaster was far in front of her making it appear easy. *This is going to be a long trip,* Irene thought glumly, her breath already laboured. Then she saw her mother smiling, *properly* smiling, probably for the first time since losing her husband, and it warmed Irene's heart and made her realise that at the very least, she could do this for her.

From her vantage point at the back of the crowd, Irene took the opportunity to evaluate the other people in the group. In the short time since she had first met Elke Huber, Irene had noticed the German woman had begun to open up as if a weight had been lifted from her shoulders. Irene watched as Elke hugged Dorothy and the joy passing between both women was clear and touching.

As Irene remembered it, her mother had very few girlfriends back home. Dorothy and Willum had always seemed more comfortable and content in each other's company, with no actual need for outsiders. It had bothered Irene when she was a child because sometimes it felt as if she was invading the great romance between her parents. But now she was older, she saw it for the wonderful thing it had been, and she regretted the negativity she had felt at the time. And more importantly, it broke her heart because she could not quite imagine the loss her mother must now be feeling without the love of her life by her side.

Further ahead, Elke's husband Wolfgang was far ahead of the group, his head lifted high as he watched the road ahead. He was the designated leader, it appeared, and he was seemingly very proud of it. Irene had not warmed to him and had decided to try harder,

45

especially if they were all going to be spending a long time together.

Casey Mitchell sidled up to Irene from behind and ruffled Bruno's head. Bruno grinned at him and for the first time, Irene thought she saw the young American relaxing. In many ways, he reminded Irene of Hugo Duchamp, shy and a little awkward and prone to hide behind floppy hair and glasses. Irene imagined it was difficult growing up as the child of an all-American ex-football star when you did not fit into the same mould. He passed them, walking quickly ahead on a path of his own. Irene followed him, hoping he would get something positive from the experience.

'You're a people watcher I see,' an English voice called out from behind her.

Irene turned her head, smiling at Tony Wilkinson, the Englishman with the oddest toupee she thought she had ever seen, and made her wonder why no one in his life had mentioned it to him. Her mother had said he was a banker of some kind, which surprised her because if he was rich, she was sure he could have gotten something better to wear on his head. 'Désolé,' she responded. 'I find in my occupation, it has become rather an annoying habit.'

He nodded. 'Ah, yes that's right. You're a pathologist, aren't you?'

'I am,' she replied. 'Or rather, I was,' she added. The truth was, she was not entirely what she was at that precise moment. After a difficult few years, Irene had decided to take a break and spend some precious time with Bruno before school life took him away from her. 'I don't know what lies ahead of me,' she said sullenly.

Tony pointed in front of them. 'The road to Santiago. The answers you seek may just lie in front of you.'

Irene gave him a doubtful look. 'That's putting a rather lot of pressure on a road,' she replied. 'So, tell me, what's your story?'

The Englishman's eyes widened, and he coughed.

'I didn't mean to pry,' Irene apologised, sensing she had said something she should not have.

He shook his head. 'No, it's okay. This journey is bittersweet for me. I first came here with my wife. We were newly married at the time and the Camino was very important to her.' He laughed. 'Can you believe it was technically supposed to be our honeymoon?'

'There are worse places to go, I suppose,' Irene conceded.

'I didn't mind, not really,' Tony continued, before adding with a splash of bitterness. 'Not that I had a lot of say in the matter. She and her entire family were devoted Catholics and when they suggested it for our honeymoon, well, I suppose I considered it odd, but it was the price I had to pay.'

Irene frowned because she was not sure what he was trying to say. He said nothing else, and she did not feel it right to question him further.

'Jane had been poorly for a long time before she passed,' Tony said. 'But she talked about this journey a lot. We did this walk together and I suppose after she died, I was always ashamed that I didn't enjoy it as much as she had. It was really important to her, and I had always dismissed it as boring and taking me away from my life back in London.'

'She was happy when she got back to London, though, and that's when we had our daughter,' he continued. 'But it didn't last. Mental health is no joke.'

Irene nodded. 'I am very sorry for your loss.'

Tony smiled at her. 'For the longest time I feared she would leave us by her own hand, but in the end, it was not the malady that had consumed her, rather some idiot behind the wheel of a car. I'm afraid I was furious for a long time, first because of her illness and then by her death. I suppose I didn't really deal with it well and our daughter has always suffered from the loss of two parents.'

Irene watched Sarah Wilkinson. She was walking solitarily to the left of them, her head down, black greasy hair falling over her face as she kicked the ground with Dr. Martin boots. Like Casey Mitchell, Irene recognised the awkwardness of someone who had too much to live up to, which had resulted in them not even attempting to try.

Whatever problems she had, Irene would always be grateful for the caring and loving upbringing she had received from her parents. It was something she aspired to give to her own child. She could imagine nothing worse than seeing a grown Bruno walking ahead as if he wished the ground would open up and swallow him and she knew she would do whatever she could to prevent it.

'We can all only hope to do the best for our children,' Irene offered Tony, 'but it isn't always easy.' She looked at Bruno, still skipping contentedly in front of them. 'My son doesn't know his father and I think about that every day because I know he should, but his father isn't interested, so I have to be enough. And believe me, I know I'm not enough all the time, but I just keep trying. I'm sure Sarah understands what happened.'

Tony lifted his head. 'I'm not sure she does. She hates me and she's right to because I most certainly deserve it. That's why I finally accepted the invitation to revisit this walk. She saw the invitation and asked if we could do it.' He shrugged. 'It wasn't just the first time she'd asked me for anything in a long time. I realised it was also the first time she had actually spoken to me in a long time. I found I could not refuse her this one request.'

Irene smiled. 'And I'm sure she appreciates it.'

Tony looked ahead at his daughter. 'We'll see,' he grimaced. 'I hope if anything, it might make us both less angry.'

'Angry?'

'Yes, angry,' he replied. 'I think both Sarah and I have always blamed my wife's religion for her illness. I know that must sound strange, but it's true. Jane put more faith in God than she did in medicine and was convinced He would save her, not her doctors.

She spent most of her life hiding, her hands always wrapped around a dog-eared bible. It always felt as if she was more attached to that than us.'

Irene nodded. 'But you're here now. Perhaps it will make things better for you both.'

He nodded. 'I hope so. When the email popped up from Elke, a woman I barely remembered, an email talking about this pilgrimage and her attempt to bring together the original group, well, it just seemed to be a sign.' He looked at his daughter. 'I thought I could spend some time with my daughter, and hopefully reach her, and...' he trailed off.

'And?' Irene questioned.

Tony reached his head to the sky. 'I thought if there were such things as miracles, what better place was there to look for one? I want my daughter to be well, and as I am sadly all she has left in this world, I figured I could use all the help I could get.'

Irene smiled. Behind them, Maurice Rousseau's van draw to a halt and he tooted the horn and leaned out of the window. 'Dejeuner, pilgrims?'

Bruno Chapeau spun around and clapped his hands excitedly.

Dorothy & Irene

Irene watched with concern as her mother dropped heavily onto a wooden bench and pulled off one of her walking boots, wincing as she massaged her foot. It was all Irene could do to stop herself from rushing over to Dorothy, but she did not because she knew it would not be appreciated.

They had walked in silence for several hours following a particularly terse head-to-head between mother and daughter the previous evening. After a long day on the trail, Irene had been dismayed by the hostel they were to stay in, informing her mother she was sure they had used the hostel as the basis for a horror movie she had once seen.

Dorothy had made clear her feelings on the subject and when Irene had suggested she did not think it a good idea to continue, Dorothy had informed her in no uncertain terms that Irene and Bruno were welcome to leave anytime, but they would do so without her. She had then terminated the discussion by insisting she would no longer tolerate any interference with her plans.

Irene sat next to her mother, offering a conciliatory smile. Bruno was playing again with Casey Mitchell. 'Bruno really likes Casey,' Irene broke the silence.

Dorothy lifted her head slowly. 'He does, and I think Casey likes him too,' she replied, her tone frosty.

Irene sighed. 'I don't know if you're aware of this, mama,' she began, 'but I tend to overreact and overthink things when it concerns people I love.'

Dorothy snorted loudly. 'You're just like your father,' she added, her tone softening. 'He was also insufferable at times,' she added.

Irene touched her hand. She had always loved that when her mother was angry or happy, her Scottish accent returned, even though she was speaking French. 'I am like him, aren't I?' she asked sadly. 'Dieu, I miss him, and I think… well, I think him dying so suddenly has knocked me off my feet and all I can think about is…'

'The fact I'm old and setting off on a fool's errand which might actually kill me?' Dorothy suggested, her left eyebrow arched challengingly.

'Well, I may not have phrased it that way, mais…'

Dorothy squeezed Irene's hand. 'And you're probably right. I may well be an old fool, but this is what I need to do. I miss your father every day in every way, but he was MY husband, not just your father. He was the man I lay with each night and woke to each morning for a long, long, LONG time.' She shook her head so vigorously, copper-coloured hair fell out of the loose knot she had tied to the top of her head. 'And I'm sorry to put it in these terms, but the fact is, you got to leave us and move halfway across the country to live your own life…'

'Mama…' Irene cried.

Dorothy shook her head. 'This isn't about scoring points. But it is the truth. You have a whole life ahead of you, love affairs not yet imagined. I'm not sure what I have to look forward to, death, perhaps?'

Irene gasped. 'Mama!'

Dorothy laughed. 'Oh, don't pout, Irene. I'm merely being melodramatic, a trait I suspect you inherited from me, sadly. You really picked up the worst of your parents' traits, didn't you?'

Irene slapped the side of her head. 'I do not know what you're talking about! I happen to think my parents were pretty perfect.' She looked sadly at Bruno. 'I'm just hopeful I can do half as good a job with my angel.'

Dorothy pushed her hand through Irene's smooth hair. 'You already have.'

'Even though I'm not married, and the father isn't around?' Irene asked.

'Your father and I were Catholic, Irene,' Dorothy replied. 'But we would never judge you. I know some people might, but they don't speak for me or your father. If anything, we were both more proud of you for making the decision you did. Despite our beliefs, I would hate the thought you saddled yourself into a marriage just because you were pregnant with a man who was not worthy of being your husband or a father to Bruno.'

Irene's eyes widened as if she was fighting back tears. 'I know we never really talked about it, but I always imagined…'

'We were saying a lot of Hail Marys on your behalf?' Dorothy interrupted. She threw back her head and laughed. Her laugh was deep and haughty. 'I can't deny there was a little bit of that going on, but no, all we were concerned about was you being happy. You are happy, aren't you?'

Irene took in a sharp breath. It took her a while to answer. 'I've spent most of my life planning my future. My career, my life, everything neat and organised. And then came along the spanner.'

Dorothy laughed. 'But what a spanner!'

'Indeed, what a spanner,' Irene agreed. 'The problems I've had in the last few years, with work especially, have changed how I look at things. I suppose my priorities have changed and I'm just not willing to settle like I was before.'

Her mother nodded, shifting her head to the side. 'Then just maybe you're in exactly the place you need to be.' She extended her hands around her. 'And you might just find answers to questions you didn't know to ask.' She took Irene's hand. 'None of this has to be anything other than what it is in the moment. I don't need you to worry about me, but I need you to understand something important.' She gestured to the road ahead of them. 'And this is just as much about me as it is about your father. I'm doing it for both of us.'

She pointed at her feet. 'And as painful as it is, something strange is happening. I feel as if your father is here with me, more than when I'm rattling around the big, empty house we shared for most of our lives. And for the first time since I lost him, I feel him in a way which doesn't just seem like I'm trying to force him back into my memory so that I don't lose him. This feels real to me.' She paused. 'And I meant what I said last night, although I wish I had said it in a nicer way. The fact remains, I don't need your protection, darling Irene, and you don't need to be here. But I do. I need to be here, and I will remain here as long as I can.'

'Then you want me to go?' Irene whispered.

'No, of course I don't,' Dorothy snapped. 'I'd love you to stay, but this is my journey, not yours and not Bruno's. Stay if you want, or as long as Bruno will allow, but only do so if you can enjoy it and not because you have a ridiculous need to mollycoddle me.'

Dorothy fixed her daughter with a steely gaze. 'Those are my rules. The question is - can you follow them? Because if you can't, there is little point in ruining this entire experience for us both. I want to share this experience with your father and his spirit, but you can only be here if you understand I'm not a child and am more than able to understand my limitations.'

Irene stared desperately at her mother. 'I can, and I will, but you have to meet me halfway. Know your limitations and if you ever, EVER feel as if it's too much for you, or you're struggling, then you come to me.' She narrowed her eyes. 'And that's non-negotiable, mama. Don't be stubborn and don't be proud, just be truthful, okay?'

Dorothy raised an eyebrow. 'Again, bossy, just like your father.' She wrapped her arm around Irene's shoulder. 'It's a deal, darling. Now help your old mother get her boot back on and we'll hit the road again.'

Irene kissed her mother's head. 'Je t'aime, mama.'

Irene lowered herself onto the narrow wooden bench. The ancient seat groaned underneath her. She stared at her feet and though she knew it was her imagination, they actually seemed to have swollen to four times their usual size.

Bruno lifted his head, giving her a heartwarming grin displaying his latest missing tooth. Whatever the reason, he was still enjoying the experience and had barely complained. She pulled him to her and kissed the top of his head. Bruno's father, Jean Lenoir, the French Minster of Justice, was a cold and selfish man, and fortunately it appeared Bruno had inherited none of his traits. Jean Lenoir had shown no interest in his son, and though she knew it should trouble her, Irene only felt relief that Bruno was not exposed to such a man.

Elke Huber entered the dining hall and waved at Irene. 'May I join you?' she asked.

Irene smiled and gestured for her to sit down. 'Of course, Elke. I thought you were having a nap?'

'I'm too excited to sleep,' she responded. 'And besides, Wolfgang is snoring and it sounds like a pneumatic drill. I'm amazed anyone else can sleep through it.'

Irene smiled. 'Everyone's exhausted, so that probably has something to do with it.'

Elke touched Irene's arm. 'And how are you doing? I know you're worried about your mother, but Dorothy is a powerhouse. If anyone can make it to Camino on sheer force of will, it's her.'

Irene laughed. 'You're probably right and I am trying my best not to worry.' She stared sadly at Bruno. 'It's just hard not to when we've lost so much already.'

'My parents both died when I was young,' Elke replied. 'And as much as I loved them, I never really felt their loss so intensely as

54

I might have if I'd known them longer.'

Irene nodded. 'I understand. Do you have children of your own?' she asked.

'No,' Elke answered with clear sadness. 'Wolfgang doesn't like children,' she stopped, noticing the expression on Irene's face that she had not managed to hide. 'I know what you must think of him, but Wolfgang isn't a bad man. He's stubborn, set in his ways and there are days when I could gladly stab him in the back,' she laughed, 'but he is my husband and we made our vows before God.' She shrugged. 'And he might change. There's always hope,' she added with a deep laugh. 'As long as there's still life, there's still hope!'

Irene watched as Maurice Rousseau entered the dining room and poured himself a drink from the urn. As he left, he nodded curtly at Irene and Elke.

'How well do you know the guide?' Irene asked Elke in a lowered voice.

'Maurice?' Elke responded. 'Not very well, really. It's been over forty years since I saw him. Before email, we had the occasional card from him, but it was sporadic at best. Why do you ask?'

'I'm not sure,' Irene pondered. 'At first I wondered whether it was because he just didn't like me. I am a single mother, after all, and I know some people don't approve of that sort of thing. There's just something about the way he looks at me which seems a little off.'

Elke smiled. 'Oh, I wouldn't take it personally. I think it's just his way, and if I recall correctly, he's not particularly religious either. I'm not saying he doesn't enjoy what he does, but it's also his job and he gets paid for it. I don't think he's the sort of person who would judge unnecessarily.' She paused as if she was assessing whether to continue. Finally, she turned back to Irene and spoke in hushed, conspiratorial tones. 'The last time we were here, his wife,

Olive, died, and I didn't think it's something he ever got over. As I recall, he was extremely devoted to Olive.'

Irene narrowed her eyes. 'His wife died on the pilgrimage forty years ago? I don't recall my mother mentioning it. What happened?' she asked with interest, realising for the first time just how much she was missing being away from Montgenoux and investigating complicated crimes.

Elke bit her lip, her face contorting. 'I suppose it's something none of us liked to talk about. There was an accident. It was tragic, and it was awful,' she gave by way of an answer. She turned her head away, and moments later, Irene could tell she was crying.

'I'm sorry, I didn't mean to upset you,' Irene gushed.

'Don't apologise,' Elke replied. 'It was a long time ago, and I think I'd just put it out of my mind. Olive was a lovely woman, full of life and vitality, and then one day she just wasn't there anymore. It's hard when that happens. Even though I didn't know her well at all, it didn't matter. Of course, it was worse for Maurice. He was just devastated, especially under the circumstances.' She stopped speaking abruptly.

Irene frowned. There was something about the way Elke spoke which troubled her, but she was not sure whether to press further.

'I don't want to talk about Olive,' Elke said, her voice no longer soft. 'And I can't imagine Maurice would either, so it's best not to bring it up, I think,' she added with bite.

'Again, I apologise. Curiosity comes as standard in my line of work,' Irene reasoned. 'And that's not always a good thing.'

Elke opened a bottle of water and sipped it slowly. 'I understand. All I can tell you is this, Maurice went through a loss that can't be explained, and one I'm sure he never recovered from.'

Irene nodded, making a mental note to speak to her mother about it later. She looked to the kitchen. 'Well, I wonder what's for supper tonight,' she said cheerfully.

Elke sighed. 'Stew. It's always stew.'

Dorothy and Irene caught up with Edith Lancaster. It was a new day and after a light breakfast, the pilgrims had left the hostel and begun the next stage of their journey. Dark clouds rolled above them and there was a dampness to the air. The elderly spinster was walking with determination, her eyes fixed firmly on the road ahead.

'I can't talk,' Edith snapped. 'I have to concentrate and I find chit-chat, exercise and the need to convey with the Lord do not always go well together at my advanced age.'

Dorothy and Irene laughed and stepped back. Irene glanced over her shoulder. Bruno was a few steps behind them, again swinging on the arm of Sam Mitchell's son, Casey. Irene was pleased to see the normally timid young man come out of his shell when around Bruno, and she was happy to leave them together, not least because it seemed to work, keeping Bruno active and interested in the journey. The added bonus was it gave Irene more of a chance to spend time with her mother.

'I can't believe how fit Edith is for her age,' Irene whispered to Dorothy. 'She's putting me to shame.'

'I've walked at least five miles a day for most of my life,' Edith boomed over her shoulder. 'And my hearing is just as good as everything else, thank you,' she snipped, glancing around. 'So, you might all want to bear that in mind!' she warned into the air.

Irene chuckled, her mouth contorting, realising her faux pas.

Dorothy squeezed her hand. 'How are you doing, darling?' she asked.

Irene scoffed. 'Oh, so you're allowed to ask that question, and I'm not?' she reasoned.

'Don't be petulant,' Dorothy gently chastised. 'Are you enjoying yourself?'

Irene nodded. The truth was, it was not at all like she imagined it would be and she was enjoying the experience, but at only five days in, she was not sure how far that pleasant emotion would be extended. If she was honest, the thought of her own bed back in Montgenoux was becoming more and more appealing.

'I am,' she responded. 'It's wonderful to spend time with you, of course, and the rest of the group seems nice.' She pulled out her cell phone. 'I am concerned about one thing, though. The weather reports suggest we are in for an almighty storm in a day or so. It seems to suggest we might be in for torrential rain for days. And I'd be lying to say the thought isn't exactly appealing to me.'

Dorothy scoffed. 'Forty years ago, we walked for two days in non-stop rain and it never did us any harm. Waterproof coats and boots are all we need.'

'Forty years ago, peut être...'

'How many times do I have to keep telling you I'm not decrepit?' Dorothy snapped. She spoke in French, and Irene was well aware that the only time her Scottish-born mother spoke in French was when she was angry and wanted to make a point. Since arriving in France and marrying Irene's father, Dorothy had always insisted on speaking English when they were all together. She reasoned it was her way of keeping her past alive without her birth family around her.

'I know,' Irene responded apologetically. 'I just worry about us all, especially Bruno. He's being particularly good at the moment, but I can't imagine for a second he'll cope well with walking for hours in heavy rain.'

Dorothy nodded. 'Then it's good we'll be in *Chemin des Pèlerins* in a day or so,' she reasoned. 'As Maurice explained, we can rest up and ride out the storm, and if need be, you can stay with our darling boy and catch us up later. There are people in the village who can transport anyone who is left behind so they can catch up with the others.' She narrowed her eyes and spoke again in

French. 'And we are not having this discussion again,' she stated definitively.

Irene coughed, remembering how it was to be a child and be chastised by the bossy nurse she had for a mother. There had been moments in her youth when she had been fearful of her and her fiery temper. It was ignited quickly but often dampened as fast. In the end, after her adolescent hormones had subsided, Irene had come to understand what a wonderful woman her mother was. Stubborn and often obstinate, but wonderful nonetheless. Irene's father, Willum, had been the polar opposite. A quiet and stoic man whose voice was barely ever raised past a whisper. Irene had never understood how their marriage had worked, but it had, and she had witnessed nothing but complete and devoted love between her parents.

'I wouldn't dare suggest you're anything but Wonder Woman,' Irene informed Dorothy. 'Actually, speaking of Maurice Rousseau. Last night, Elke mentioned that forty years ago, on the last pilgrimage, something happened with his wife.'

Dorothy stopped dead in her tracks, causing Irene to bump into her. 'Mama?' Irene asked in concern. Dorothy began moving again, her steps quick. 'Dear, dear Olive,' she exhaled. 'What a lovely, lovely woman. It's odd. I thought of her often over the years, even when I did not want to.'

'What happened to her?' Irene asked. 'Elke was a little vague.'

'Nosiness isn't nice, Irene,' Dorothy informed her haughtily.

Irene laughed. 'Like I told Elke, it's a bit of an occupational hazard, I'm afraid. You were a nurse, so you know that as well as I do,' she added.

Dorothy fixed her daughter with a tired smile. 'Maurice and Olive ran the tour together. They both came from religious families, though I am not sure religion was something which interested either of them very much. I'm not saying tour guiding was necessarily just a business for them. Rather, it seemed it was just the way things had always been done and it was expected of them to continue the tradition,' she explained. 'I imagined Olive had dreams of a life outside of the village, but for Maurice, I think what he had was enough for him.' She closed her eyes for a moment. 'The nearest to religion Maurice ever got was his devotion to Olive. And that's why it was all so tragic.'

'Tragic?'

'There was a terrible storm the night she disappeared,' Dorothy explained, staring off into the distance. 'We were in *Chemin des Pèlerins* at the time. As well as running the tour, Olive's family also ran the local supermarket, and they kept lots of animals. Sheep, chickens, pigs, cows, goats, that sort of thing. Anyway, as the storm got worse and worse, Maurice was looking after us pilgrims and Olive made her excuses, and said she had to see to her flock.'

Dorothy gave a sad laugh, a shadow passing across her face. 'She didn't say flock though, she said children. That's what she called them, *her children*. Maurice even made a joke about it, saying she thought more of them than she did him. That night we were all in the tavern. A wonderful man called Alain Bonnet ran it, and at some point, I can't even be sure when we all suddenly remembered Olive had been gone for an awfully long time. We all looked out of the windows, but the weather really was terrible, so we couldn't see a thing. Anyway, after a while, Maurice got impatient and he and Alain, along with a few of the other men, your father included, braved the storm and went looking for Olive.'

'And did they find her?' Irene demanded, eager to hear the rest of the story.

Dorothy shook her head. 'They went to the market. The animals were all loose still, as if Olive hadn't even gotten to them. Your father said they tried desperately for ten, fifteen minutes, to get them all safely into their cages and coops, but all the time there was no sign of Olive.'

She shuddered. 'They searched for most of the night, and once it got to daybreak, the rest of us joined them. At about 05h00 the storm finally broke, for a while at least, and we were better able to see, but still, there was no sign of Olive.'

'What happened next?'

'Well, with it being light, we could see a little better. Because it's at the bottom of a valley, there's only one way in or out of *Chemin des Pèlerins,* you see and that's via a bridge over the river. Olive's market bordered the town, and it overlooked the river. With all the rain, it looked as if the embankment had turned into a mud bank and when we got there, it was clear by the tracks in the mudslide that someone had fallen from the bank into the river. There was no one else missing, so it had to have been Olive.'

Irene gasped. 'Are you sure?'

Dorothy shrugged. 'There was no other explanation. We searched for days for her, but it was obvious what had happened. She was gone. The police confirmed it wasn't the first time such a thing had happened in the area during a storm. They reasoned she'd fallen and was carried by the river downstream.'

'But they never found her body?'

She shook her head. 'I don't believe so. I heard nothing about it. Years later, Elke told me they had declared Olive officially dead. The whole thing was just awful.'

Irene's mouth tightened. 'And you continued with the pilgrimage afterwards?'

'What else were we to do?' Dorothy reasoned. 'Edith said we should use our journey to pray for Olive's safe return. But really, we were all there, a group of strangers with nothing to do other than what we had come to do in the first place.'

'And Maurice?'

'He came with us,' she replied. 'We told him not to, but he said we'd paid for a guided pilgrimage and that was what we would get. It was awful and terribly, terribly sad,' Dorothy continued.

'I don't think any of us spoke about it again on the entire pilgrimage. It was like this giant elephant in the room. I remember thinking, praying we would hear something and news of Olive would reach us and that she had been found and was recuperating in a hospital somewhere. But it never happened. There was no word, and we had to accept Olive was dead.'

'I thank you to keep my wife's name out of your mouth.'

Dorothy started, her hand flying to her mouth. She halted and turned around. Maurice Rousseau had appeared seemingly out of nowhere. 'I'm sorry, Maurice,' she blurted.

'We meant nothing by it,' Irene added. 'I was just wondering, that's all.'

'Then don't,' he snapped. 'My wife is dead, and I don't want to hear you speak of her again. Not until I tell you to speak her name. Do I make myself clear?'

Irene and Dorothy exchanged an anxious look. They both nodded quickly, watching as he pushed past them.

'What was that about?' Irene asked.

Dorothy watched his retreating figure, her face crinkling. 'I honestly don't know, but I don't think I've ever heard him speak like that.' She grimaced. 'He's obviously still not over what happened to Olive. I hope he didn't think we were gossiping. I should go after him.'

Irene grabbed her arm and shook her head. 'Non, Mama. I think you'd better just leave it, for now at least. Let him cool off.'

Dorothy nodded, watching after him. 'Perhaps you're right.'

'*Not until I tell you to speak her name*,' Irene repeated with a curious frown. 'What on earth did he mean by that?'

Irene lifted the cell phone above her head in an attempt to get a signal. The bars finally moved and after a few moments, Hugo and Ben's faces filled the screen.

'Ah-ha!' Irene cried triumphantly. 'I can see your wonderful faces.'

Ben clapped his hands together excitedly. 'How's it going? I miss your beautiful face, too.'

'Ben has been following your progress online, tracking your journey,' Hugo added.

'Tracking my journey?' Irene laughed. 'That sounds positively stalker-ish.'

Hugo reached over and kissed Ben's cheek. 'That's exactly what I said…'

'Psssh,' Ben bristled. 'The fact is, I've been checking the weather reports, and it looks like there's a doozie of a storm heading your way,' he stated. 'In fact, according to the statistics, you foolishly have chosen the exact wrong time of year to embark upon your pilgrimage because BONJOUR it's rainy season.'

Hugo pulled Ben to him and ruffled his hair before turning back to Irene. 'I'm afraid Ben is suffering from terrible separation anxiety.'

Irene blew them both a kiss. 'As am I. But don't worry, we're all fine. And oui, we've heard about the rainstorm. Luckily, we're due to arrive in a local village, *Chemin des Pèlerins* later. It's the home of our guide and we're spending a few days there before carrying on. Merci Dieu!' she exclaimed. 'And thankfully, it also means it should shelter us from most of the storm.'

Ben gave her a doubtful look, pushing his hand anxiously through the abundance of curls on his forehead. 'I want regular check-ins,' he demanded. 'And by regular, I mean at least one call a day, or if you don't have enough signal, one text. I demand it. Am I making myself clear?'

She chuckled. 'Oui, *Maman*.'

He nodded happily. 'Bon. Make sure you do, or else you'll be in trouble, comprendez?'

'I wouldn't dare argue,' she responded.

Hugo smiled at the screen. 'What are the rest of your travellers like?'

'They're fine,' she drawled.

'Fine?' Hugo questioned, his voice rising.

Irene shook her head. 'I can't get anything past you, can I?' she laughed.

'What is it?' Ben demanded. 'What's wrong?'

She raised her hands. 'Rien, rien!'

'Tell me,' he snapped.

Irene sighed. 'Honestly, it's nothing. I just thought there was something off about our tour guide, Maurice Rousseau, but I spoke to my mother about it and I think he's just had a lot of problems.'

'A lot of problems?' Ben shrieked so loudly, Hugo had to pull him into a hug. 'What kind of people are you travelling with?' he demanded, panicked.

'Don't worry, there's nothing to be concerned about, I'm sure,' Irene said passively. 'Anyway, I'd better go before I lose the signal again. Luckily, Bruno has been occupied with a nice American kid, but I don't want to push my luck. And besides, believe it or not, all the older pilgrims are striding ahead. I tell you, I have trouble keeping up with them!'

Ben pushed his face against the screen. 'D'accord, but like I said. I want at least one phone call or text per day, or else…'

'Or else?' she interrupted, clearly amused.

'Or else I'll come out there and drag your damn ass home, that's what,' he responded.

Hugo chuckled in the background. 'And you know he means

it, Irene.'

Irene reached for the disconnect button. 'I love you, crazy boys. À Bientôt.'

Irene lifted her head upwards, her face contorting at the ominous black, swirling clouds overhead. Bruno buried his head in her chest, his griping and wriggling informing her he too could sense the impending storm. She looked to her fellow travellers, all now trudging in more or less a single file straight line. It was as if the sudden change in weather had already dampened everyone's mood, or rather the novelty of walking over ten kilometres a day with no proper rest, decent food, or a comfortable bed and workable shower, was taking a toll on them.

As if sensing her thoughts, Dorothy slipped her hand through Irene's and pulled her daughter close to her. 'Don't worry, darling. We'll be in *Chemin des Pèlerins* soon and safe from the storm, and then we'll decide what to do next.'

Irene nodded. She was pleased they were due to rest for a few days. She only hoped it was in better surroundings than some of the hostels they had already been staying in. 'What's *Chemin des Pèlerins* like?' she asked.

'Oh, it's beautiful,' Dorothy answered cheerfully. 'Such a quaint little village, completely cut off from the real world. When you cross the bridge and walk down the stairs into the town square, it's like waking into another century.'

'It's been forty years since you've been there, mama,' Irene reasoned. 'I expect it's changed quite a bit in that time.'

Dorothy laughed. 'I wouldn't count on it,' she retorted. 'For one thing, the villagers who live there wouldn't allow it! Every now and then, your father and I would get a letter from Alain Bonnet. He owns and runs *Café Compostelle*. It's the only restaurant and hotel in the village. The letter would often include a photograph, and as far as I could tell, it looked the same as it ever did!'

A weary look passed across Irene's face. Dorothy playfully

pinched her. 'Don't be a worrywart, darling. *Café Compostelle* has beautiful rooms, with proper beds and everything, and as I recall in one of his letters, Alain even bragged about finally getting indoor bathrooms and toilets!'

'Well, aren't we in for a treat!' Irene exclaimed.

'Irene...' Dorothy chastised wearily.

'I mean it,' Irene added as cheerfully as she could. 'But I won't lie to you. Sitting out a storm in a nice Café with my feet up and a very large glass of wine in my hand is rather appealing to me right now.'

Dorothy looked down at her feet. 'If I'm honest, it does to me too!' She flashed her daughter a warning look. 'Just don't go reading too much into that.' She slapped her thighs. 'There's plenty of life left in these old things still!'

Irene reached over and kissed her mother on the cheek. 'I don't doubt it.'

Without warning, the pilgrims stopped abruptly, and Wolfgang Huber clapped his hands. 'We're here!' he exclaimed excitedly.

Irene placed Bruno on the ground, and they moved forward. 'Wow!' she gasped, half impressed.

The road had taken a sharp turn, guiding them into a steep incline and a winding road leading towards a long, thin bridge which seemed unlikely to be able to sustain a dozen people at the same time, and certainly not a vehicle of any kind. Past the bridge, Irene could make out a row of houses lining the embankment, almost as if they were standing sentry to keep out intruders. The houses were ramshackle and clearly in need of repair, but she could see what her mother had meant. It was like stepping back in time and they had a charm that was missing in most modern towns.

Dorothy stopped suddenly, covering her mouth. 'What is it, mama?' Irene demanded.

'I'd quite forgotten until this very moment,' Dorothy

whispered. 'That bridge. It was where your father kissed me for the first time.' She twisted her head at her daughter. 'Isn't it awful I completely forgot the first time your father kissed me?'

Irene rubbed her mother's shoulder. 'You had a lifetime of kisses, mama,' she breathed. The moment was not lost on Irene because she realised what it meant for her and her own current predicament. *I don't remember my first kiss and I don't remember my last.* She had enjoyed romances in her life, but there had always been something holding her back. She had imagined it was because she had always focused on her career, but in the last few months of spending time with her parents, she had come to just one conclusion. *I want what they have and I don't think I'm ever going to get it.*

'That will never be enough,' Dorothy mumbled before turning to her daughter. 'It will happen to you, and when it does, you will know.' She stared at the bridge in front of them. 'Just like I did.'

Irene nodded, her mouth twisting. She had seen it in her parents, and she had also seen it in the love between Hugo and Ben. It was unconditional, and it was total. When she had left Montgenoux, Irene had been involved in a love affair with Etienne Martine, the forensic expert who worked with the police. He was the sort of man any woman should be so lucky to love. He was kind and romantic. But no matter how hard she tried, Irene had come to only one conclusion. Something was missing and Irene was not sure whether it was missing from him or from her, but she suspected the latter, and it was something she did not know how to fix.

In one of the last conversations she had with her father, Irene had told him of her concerns and he told her in no uncertain terms the only person she had to care about was herself. *Love will find you if you allow it.* His words still echoed in her head, now more so because he was gone, and particularly because she did not know what they meant, and she did not have the chance to ask him to explain.

'What I do remember,' Dorothy continued, 'is that it was pouring with rain and all I was worried about was my lovely curls clinging to the side of my face,' she laughed. 'Although, as it happens, a few seconds into the kiss, I don't think I cared very much.'

'I miss him,' Irene breathed.

'As do I,' Dorothy replied. She extended her arms towards the sky. 'But he is here with us. Not the way we want, but he is here.' She stabbed her finger against her heart. 'I feel it here, and,' she tapped her head, 'here. Willum will never leave us so long as we remember him. That is God's gift to us.'

Irene took a breath and held it for a long time. She looked at the road towards *Chemin des Pèlerins* and smiled, wrapping her arm around her mother. 'So, tell me - how good a kisser was he?'

Dorothy pushed her away. 'A mother should never have those types of discussions with her daughter, but,' she winked, 'it was the best kiss I think I'd ever had. And the first was as good as the last. Although one was happy and one was devastating.'

Irene wiped her eyes irritably, determined not to cry in front of her mother. 'Let's get to shelter before the rain starts.'

Maurice Rousseau jumped from the bus, like a man belying his age. 'Ah, we have arrived at my home. And this will be your home for the next part of our journey.'

Dorothy smiled at him. 'I am very much looking forward to it.'

Maurice walked past her. 'As am I. I have been waiting for this moment for a very long time.' He looked over his shoulder. 'Now follow me before the storm begins.'

Les Pèlerins - Sixième jour

Irene stepped outside *Café Compostelle*, contentedly sipping an espresso. She filled her lungs with fresh, damp air. It was barely 07h00, but she had awoken early as was usual when she was in a strange environment. An environment filled with strange sounds and light which moved in different ways through a room, casting shadows on places she did not recognise. A cabinet, a chair. In that instant, she felt panicked because she did not know where she was or what might be lurking in the darkness.

In reality, *Café Compostelle* was much better a respite than she had imagined it would be. While still rudimentary and basic, the rooms were at least private and filled with antique furniture, giving them a bijou feel. She had also been relieved to discover she was sharing a double room with her mother and Bruno and there were only two other rooms on the first floor, occupied by the elderly British woman, Edith Lancaster, and the German couple Wolfgang and Elke Huber. But more importantly, she had been more delighted by the fact each floor had its own bathroom. Not quite the type of hotel she was used to, but Irene was more than pleased with it after some of the other places they had stayed at in the preceding days, where neither bathrooms nor cleanliness were in abundance.

She drained the remnants of her café, her lips slapping happily. It was strong, just as she liked it.

'You appear to be enjoying that.'

Irene turned around. Alain Bonnet, the proprietor of *Café Compostelle,* had appeared from the kitchen. She smiled warmly at the man she had met only the previous evening but had warmed instantly to. The small, rotund man with a kind face and thick, dark hair had pushed past all the adults and grabbed Bruno into a tight embrace, dashing him through the air, making airplane noises as he

71

moved him back and forth. Bruno had been initially confused but had soon collapsed into contented giggles.

'I'll deal with the rest of you later,' Bonnet called out, 'once I get my priorities sorted and deal with the little boss here.' Bruno had instantly bonded with Alain and it had broken the ice between them all.

Irene drained the remains of her drink. 'I love your village,' she said. 'It's not only beautiful, it's also very tranquil.'

He tipped his head. 'You're probably right, but it's not a place for a woman such as you,' he responded.

Irene raised an eyebrow. 'A woman such as me?' she repeated sharply. She was used to men judging her for her choices and the older she got, the less interest she had in tolerating it.

He touched her arm, smiling as he pointed towards the staircase which led to the edge of the village. 'Don't imagine just because I am old, I am judgmental. People such as you have always paid my bills, and,' he paused with a cheery laugh, 'I find those who aren't so moral tend to tip better.'

Irene tipped her head, grinning. 'That's probably true. Keep the chardonnay coming, and so will the tips, as far as I'm concerned,' she added.

'That is something I can mostly certainty do,' he replied, gesturing behind him to the bar, 'so long as we don't run out.' He pointed again to the bridge above them. 'All I meant was, young woman like you, your place is on the opposite side of that bridge. Where there is a world full of adventures. Sadly, there are no adventures to be found here,' he added. 'And frankly, I imagine it would bore you to death. Nothing happens here, not really, certainly nothing you might consider important.'

She shrugged. 'Still, just lately it seems as if I have been wishing I could just step away from the crazy world outside of here and enjoy a more sedate life.'

Alain laughed. 'It would bore you rigid, I'm sure. But it's

been enough for me, and others.'

There was something about the way he said it, which caused Irene to turn to him. 'How many people live in this village?'

'Twenty,' he replied. 'Although at this time of year, most of the younger ones go to the next town because that's where the work is. The older ones help out with the tourists. As boring as it might sound to you, for us, it is enough.'

Irene smiled. 'I understand enough. I thought I was happy with my life and had everything I needed, and then suddenly I imagined everything was wrong, but now, here in this moment, I'm just not sure.'

'Ah,' Alain said, sounding impressed. 'So, that's why you're walking the Camino. You're looking for answers.'

Irene shrugged. 'I'm not sure about that. I'm here because... well, because we lost my father and...'

'*And?*' Alain pushed.

She met his gaze, her eyes widening as if she was conceding something. 'Maybe I'm a little lost, too. And by little, I mean *minutely* lost,' she laughed. 'I'm not religious...'

He reached over and touched her hand. 'The Chemin de Compostelle isn't always about religion. I've seen hundreds of people passing by here and without fail, they all say the same thing. It's about the journey. That is the only important thing about it. It's always just about opening up to Dieu and allowing Him, or whoever it is you need, to help you and to give you the answers you need.'

Irene sighed. 'I left my parents' home mainly because I didn't want to stay in the same town I was born in. For no particular reason, you understand. I'm not proud to say my only thought was to get away from the people I knew and the people who knew me.' She stopped speaking. 'Désolé, I don't know why I'm telling you any of this.'

Alain smiled. He pointed to the Café behind them. 'I do

understand. I was born in this village, in the room upstairs, as it happens. It wasn't as fancy as it is now, of course. My parents were devout Catholics,' he continued, 'and their biggest disappointment was I never gave them grandchildren to carry on the family line, mais, it just wasn't meant to be, in the end.'

'I'm sorry to hear that,' Irene said.

He shrugged. 'I fell in love once, but it didn't work out the way I wanted it to, and I suppose I gave up on love after that.'

Irene nodded. 'I hear you. None of our lives really works out the way we imagine, but I don't believe we should ever give up on searching for what we want.'

'Even at my age?' Alain snorted.

'Absolutely!' she said forcefully. 'Life may be short, but I've always believed age is just a number, and as far as I can see, you've got plenty of numbers still to go.'

He tipped his head. 'I appreciate that.' He looked behind him, noticing the others were entering the Café. 'Ah,' he said, 'I see you're not the only early riser. I'd better get cooking. The pilgrimage seems to give people very healthy appetites.'

Tony Wilkinson pushed the plate away, smacking his lips contentedly. 'Forty years ago you made an amazing breakfast, Alain, and it appears you still haven't lost your touch.'

'I learnt from my father,' Alain replied. 'Because believe it or not, my mother was a terrible cook. What she was good at was building,' he added, gesturing around the Café. While rudimentary and paling in comparison to more modern establishments, the Café had a charm of its own. The walls were lined with pictures of people who had passed through its doors. 'And she built most of this entirely by herself. She was really ahead of her time,' he added proudly.

'Way to go,' Tony's daughter, Sarah, replied. She immediately blushed as if she was embarrassed to speak and suddenly having everyone pay attention to her, and she began gnawing at already too-short fingernails.

'Fine people, both of them,' Edith Lancaster, the elderly British woman, stated.

'Merci,' Alain replied. 'Is this your third or fourth pilgrimage?'

Edith placed her knitting in front of her. 'This will be my third time,' she answered proudly. 'Fifty years ago was my first. I travelled alone and only came across this village by accident, but your parents took me in and made me feel very welcome. They were good, God-fearing people, and I was very sorry when there were taken so young.'

Alain exhaled. 'They died within a week of each other. Maman first, she went as she lived, banging a nail in a wall!' He laughed with melancholy. 'And I don't think papa knew what to do without her, so he just willed himself into death to be with her still.'

Edith muttered a prayer under her breath, but no one else said anything.

Irene finished her wine, her eyes moving across the photographs on the wall. She gasped at seeing a picture of her parents, forty years earlier, barely acquainted, but it was clear even in the faded photograph that the two were in the first flush of love. Instinctively, she jumped to her feet and moved to the counter, extracting her cell phone as she moved. She lifted the phone and snapped a picture of the photograph.

Alain watched her quizzically before the realisation passed across his face. 'Ah, I see. The fledgling love story.' He tapped the photograph with his index finger. 'Would you like it?'

Irene shook her head. 'Non, merci.' She lifted her phone. 'I have a copy here. No, I think…' she paused, 'well, I think the original belongs here,' she added swallowing hard.

Behind her, Dorothy nodded. 'I think so as well. After all, this is where it all started, and I take comfort in a little piece of us always being here together in this place.'

Irene exhaled, trying not to let the emotions rising consume her. She and Dorothy had spent the day exploring the village. It was so small it did not take them long. It was just as Irene had imagined it would be. Quaint and deafeningly quiet, but it was a place Irene was more than happy to spend a few days. She stared again at the photograph and looked around the Café, searching for the exact spot where the photograph had been taken. She found it, and although at that moment the space was occupied, she knew she would spend as much of the rest of her stay in the hotel there, hoping against hope to feel closer to a man who was no longer around, just because he had once inhabited the same space.

Irene and Dorothy had walked around the village for as long as they could, but because of the storms rolling in, they could not go further. By early afternoon, it was already as dark as night and the air was thick with the heaviness of what was approaching. Irene was sure that whatever was coming, it was going to be quite a storm, another reason she was pleased the hotel was to be their home for the foreseeable future.

Dorothy cleared her throat as if she was attempting to steer herself away from an emotion she could not face. She turned to Sam Mitchell, who was sitting at the end of the table with his son, Casey. 'I find it fascinating you became a travel writer, Sam, especially after having such a different career to begin with.'

Despite being in his fifties, the athletic blond American had the appearance of a much younger man. He chuckled. 'You're not the only one, Dorothy. I think a lot of people, my ex-wife included, thought I was just made up of brawn, not brain.' He stopped, noticing the pained expression on his son Casey's face at the mention of his mother. The young man turned his head as if he was forcing himself not to cry.

'I downloaded your book about your travels in Tibet last night,' Irene interjected, hoping to ease whatever tension had just passed between the Americans. 'And I found it thrilling. Your prose was so good it made me feel as if I was on the trail with you.'

Sam tipped his head. 'Why that's a very kind thing for you to say,' he responded in a way which showed he was used to being complimented.

'Downloaded,' Dorothy cried despairingly. 'Whatever happened to the days of enjoying the pleasure of a book between your hands?'

'Many people still feel that way,' Sam replied. 'In fact, I think I have a few copies in my luggage. I could let you have one if you'd like.'

She smiled warmly at him. 'I would like that very much...' Before she could continue, they were interrupted by a deafening roar of thunder and a sudden flash of lightning that illuminated the night air. 'Oh my goodness!' Dorothy cried.

Alain pushed the door to the Café open. 'I think we'd better take shelter inside. Unless I'm very much mistaken, I think it's going to get messy out there.'

Irene picked up Bruno and helped her mother to her feet, and they hurried inside. Moments later, the heavens opened, throwing torrential rain onto the ground with such force one of the tables which had just been occupied collapsed to the ground, smashing plates and glasses against the cobbles.

Irene's eyes widened. 'Wow, we made it just in time.'

Les Pèlerins - Septième jour

Irene awoke with a start, and it took her a few moments to get her bearings. Then she heard the rain crashing against the windowpane. It sounded violent and angry as if it was tapping out a powerful message. She shook her head, realising she was feeling spooked by the strange surroundings. She reached to the bedside table, her cell phone telling her it was only 05h55.

She was not sure how much sleep she'd had. A lot of the night had been spent attempting to calm Bruno, who had never experienced such a storm and had been terrified by the unfolding tempest. Even Irene had been shaken by it because the storm had been relentless and at one point she was convinced it was going to destroy the Café.

Finally, the night had passed, and the building had miraculously survived, and it appeared so had they. She looked at Bruno, who was snoring heavily next to her. Dorothy was in her bed and Irene could hear her soft breaths as she slept. It almost sounded as if she was speaking to someone. *At least we're safe and not on the trail,* Irene reasoned.

She closed her eyes, hoping that the storm would at least allow her to sleep for a while longer, but something caught her attention and she tried to understand what it was. Finally, she got her bearings and, as far as she could make out, there appeared to be a commotion coming from the ground floor beneath her. Male voices talking in forceful but hushed tones, preventing her from understanding what was being said. However, it was clear to her something appeared to be wrong. She raised herself slowly from the bed, pulling a jumper over her head and sliding into her jeans. She moved slowly so as not to wake Bruno or her mother before slipping out of the room.

The ancient, winding staircase creaked as she moved deftly

downwards, spurred on by the increasingly loud and agitated voices. She pushed open the door to the bar area to be greeted by the Café owner, Alain Bonnet engaged in a heated exchange with the tour guide Maurice Rousseau and the German pilgrim Wolfgang Huber. They all looked at her, their faces a mixture of irritation and concern.

'What's going on?' Irene demanded.

'Désolé, Mademoiselle Chapeau,' Alain replied. 'I'm sorry if we woke you.'

Wolfgang waved his hand dismissively. 'Yeah, go back to bed, girlie.'

Irene's eyes widened with anger. She was sure the former police officer was used to talking to the people in his life exactly as he saw fit, but she was determined to disabuse him of the fact it was acceptable to her, but before she could respond, she noticed the worried look on Alain's face. 'What's happened?' she pushed.

Maurice let go a long, weary breath. 'I'm afraid the storm's causing a lot of damage,' he said reluctantly.

'It's taken out the bridge,' Alain blurted. He shook his head angrily. 'I've been saying for years we need to do something about it. It was only a matter of time before something like this happened.'

Irene recalled the wide wooden bridge they had crossed to gain access to the village. She had not thought it particularly unsteady, but it was old. 'Was anyone hurt?' she asked.

Maurice shook his head. 'Non, most of the people are either here or holed up in their cottages.'

'The problem is, it's our only way in and out of the village,' Alain explained. 'We're at the bottom of a valley here. The only way is up,' he added glumly, 'so it appears we're stuck.'

Irene frowned. When she and her mother had previously explored their new surroundings, they had come to the edge of the village and discovered a tall, imposing cliff, one Irene imagined would be almost impossible to navigate. She looked at the telephone on the counter. 'Well, we can call for help, can't we? Someone will come and I'm sure they can figure out a way to make it possible to get us over to the other side.'

Alain said nothing, instead crossing the Café and picking up the telephone, holding the receiver in the air. There was no noise. 'It seems the storm has also knocked out the phone lines. It often does.'

'Oh, damn,' Irene tutted, pulling out her cell phone and lifting it in front of her. Her eyes narrowed. 'Merde, I don't have a signal either.'

Wolfgang Huber tutted. 'As he said, girlie, we're at the bottom of a valley. Your cell phone won't work down here.'

'Will you stop calling me girlie? I have a name, and it's Irene,' Irene snapped, harder than she intended, no doubt fuelled by the impending panic she was trying to fight off.

Wolfgang gave her an amused nod. 'Sorry, *Irene*,' he said in a tone which suggested he was not sorry at all.

Irene turned her entire body away from him, facing Alain and Maurice instead. 'Well, I imagine it's only a matter of time before someone notices we're cut off, non?'

The two men exchanged a look, which worried Irene even further. 'People must come and go to the village all the time?' she pushed.

'Bien sûr,' Alain reasoned. 'Although the Café and hotel are fully booked, as you know, therefore we wouldn't be expecting more pilgrims to arrive, because the checkpoints wouldn't point them in our direction.'

Irene shook her head. 'But you must have deliveries coming in?'

He nodded. 'Oui. We have a weekly delivery, mais…'

'Mais, what?'

'The last delivery was yesterday,' he replied.

Irene sank onto a wooden stool. 'Then it could be six days before anyone notices the bridge is out?'

Alain extended his hands. 'C'est possible.'

'Once the storm breaks,' Maurice continued, 'and it will break, if not today, certainly tomorrow. Then it's only a matter of time before the phone companies realise the phone lines are down again and will send out a repairman, and he'll see what happened. It's probably not more than a day or two at the most.'

Irene nodded, suddenly feeling relieved.

'And we have plenty of food and wine,' Alain reasoned. 'So, we'll be perfectly comfortable in the meantime.'

Wolfgang laughed. 'It doesn't sound too bad to me,' he said. 'And as far as I'm concerned, I'd rather be comfortable here than adding more blisters to my already sore feet.'

Despite herself, Irene smiled at him. 'I can't say I disagree either.'

'You see?' Maurice said cheerfully. 'Everything is going to be fine.'

Les Pèlerins - Septième nuit

Irene stared out into the town square, dismayed it had not yet stopped raining, and as far as she could tell, it actually appeared to be getting worse. The cobbled pavements were already underwater, but because of the direction of the slope, it was draining away from the Café rather than toward it. However, she was sure if the rain continued as it was, and with nowhere else for it to drain, it would end up coming back to them and most probably flood the Café. The thought terrified her.

The rest of the pilgrims had taken the news of the broken bridge in their stride, reasoning they had already planned on spending a few days in the village and even with the worst-case scenario, it would only extend further their stay by a few more days. And as most of them were on no particular schedule, none of them seemed concerned by a delay.

Irene stared at her phone again for what felt like the thousandth time. The "no signal" icon seemed to taunt her. She knew she was overreacting, but she would feel better if at least one person in the outside world knew about their predicament.

She turned her attention to her fellow travellers surprised none of them appeared to share her concerns. She reasoned it was probably because in her line of work she had come across many dangerous situations, some of which had ended very badly, therefore she was programmed to always expect the worst. It was not a good way to live, but it had made her acutely aware of everything going on around her and how events could change in a split second. And there was something not right about her current situation. She felt it in a way that just seemed instinctive.

Dorothy appeared from the dimness of the hallway, dropping into the seat next to her daughter. 'Bruno's finally asleep,' she said wearily. 'I swear he's just like you were at his age. Curious about everything. Now that he's gotten over the shock of the storm, he just wants to know all about it. Every question I answer there's the same response. *Pourquoi?* It's you, all over again. Another doctor in the family, I don't doubt.'

'Oh, I don't know about that,' Irene replied.

Dorothy raised an eyebrow. 'Rather that than following his father into his profession... what is that again, exactly?' she asked coolly.

Irene rolled her eyes. She had spoken at length with her parents about Bruno's heritage and the decision that had been reached. They did not understand it, but she thought she had convinced them it was for the best. Bruno did not need a father in his life who did not want to be in it, and that was the end of it as far as she was concerned. Irene had decided a long time ago it was the only decision which made sense.

Dorothy raised her hand. 'Sorry, I forgot I'm not supposed to have an opinion on the matter.'

Irene turned her head, not willing to repeat a dialogue which could have no end. Instead, she stood, pressing her nose against the doors. 'I don't think I've ever seen so much rain, especially for so long.'

Dorothy shrugged. 'At least we're safe, and we're warm and looked after. Help will be along soon enough, I'm sure.'

Wolfgang pushed himself back, his chair scraping against the ground. 'Speaking of which, where is old Alain? I have a hankering for one of his special omelettes.' He moved across the Café, peering behind the counter. 'Hey Alain, are you there? What about giving us one of your special truffle omelettes?'

He continued walking, stepping behind the counter, peering towards an open door behind the bar. 'Where are you hiding?' he asked, peering around the corner. 'Ah, there you are. Don't think you can hide out down there. You have famished pilgrims to feed...'

There was something about the way he stopped abruptly that caught Irene's attention. She dashed after him, moving his now rigid body out of the doorway. Narrowing her eyes, she peered into the dark shadows of the storeroom. It took her a few moments to acclimatise, finally focusing on the Café proprietor, seemingly bent in the corner, his small round body covering a row of boxed canned goods.

She stumbled backwards, unable to stop herself from crying out loud.

'What is it?' Dorothy demanded from behind her.

Irene spun around, grabbing her mother firmly by the shoulders and spinning her around. 'Don't look,' she said forcefully.

'What on earth are you talking about?' Dorothy demanded, attempting to peer over her daughter's shoulder. Irene continued to move her back into the Café.

Maurice Rousseau appeared, pushing open the doorway and filling the Café with rain and howling wind. He struggled to close it again, finally kicking the door into place with his boot. He shook the rain from his coat and dropped it to the floor. 'Oh, it's still crazy out there,' he said. 'I don't know…' He stopped abruptly as if alarmed by the expressions on the faces of Wolfgang and Irene. 'Que s'est-il passé?'

Wolfgang continued staring into the storeroom. 'He's dead… He's dead…' he repeated, shaking his head in disbelief.

'What are you talking about?' Maurice grumbled irritably, pushing him out of the way. 'Who is dead?'

Irene moved next to him, barring him from entering the room.

Maurice glared at her. 'What are you doing?'

'Alain Bonnet is dead, I'm afraid,' she replied, staring at the Café proprietor's body in the corner of the storeroom, a large knife sticking out of his back. 'And it appears he was murdered.' Her eyes moved quickly from side to side as she began to assess the situation. 'Which means we need to preserve evidence,' she stated as calmly as she could.

'What gives you the right…'

'I am a doctor, and I am a pathologist,' she continued. 'And in those capacities, it is my responsibility to declare this a crime scene.' She looked around the room, considering. 'Now, stay here and allow me to examine Alain. There's just a chance he could still be alive, so I have to move quickly.'

Maurice glared at her. 'Save him, or I swear, there will be hell to pay!' he bellowed.

SEMAINE DEUX / WEEK TWO

SAINT-JEAN-PIED-DE-PORT / CHEMIN DES PÈLERINS / MONTGENOUX

Ben stared at his cell phone on the dining room table as he had been for most of the morning, hoping that by the sheer force of his will, it might finally ring. He looked to the doorway. Hugo was busy filling his backpack and readying himself for his day. Ben knew he had most likely kept him awake too, and as sorry as he was about it, it did not erase the fact he was worried.

'Now, where are my damn cigarettes?' Hugo grumbled aloud, staring around the cramped living room. The Swiss-style cottage they shared with their son, Baptiste, was never tidy and between the three of them, they were always searching for something. 'Ah!' Hugo cried, clearly relieved to discover his cigarettes were in his pocket. As if reassuring himself, he pulled one from the pack and deftly lit it, quickly releasing a contented sigh.

'You were beginning to panic, weren't you?' Ben asked, in an amused and slightly scolding way.

Hugo happily blew smoke rings in his direction. 'Don't you have to get to the hospital?' he retorted.

'Not for an hour,' Ben replied. 'I was supposed to be heading over to the hotel, mais...' As well as working as a nurse in Montgenoux Hospital, Ben was also overseeing the building of a hotel in the heart of their town. It was a special project for him, a way to help those who needed help in a way which allowed Ben to use the fortune he had inherited since his father's death.

'I can drop you off if you like...' Hugo offered.

Ben did not respond, instead continuing to stare at the cell phone.

Hugo sighed. 'She'll call, or she'll send a message when she's able. You know that, she promised,' he said reassuringly.

'It's been three days since we spoke to her and there's been nothing since then, not even a text message,' Ben stated, the desperation clear in his voice. 'And she's not responding to a single one of my messages either,' he added. 'You were there. We had a deal. A text or a call a day, without fail. End of discussion.'

Hugo smiled warmly at him, touched by the concern and love his husband felt for those in his life. He also understood there were times when he was prone to overreact, a trait they both shared, most likely because they had come close to losing one another on more than one occasion. Irene's situation was not usual. She was not in a hotel somewhere, surrounded by technology. She was in the middle of rural France, travelling between small villages, with very little around them but the open air. Hugo also suspected at any moment a backlog of texts would suddenly appear on Ben's cell phone after having been floating around the cosmos waiting to be delivered.

'You've been following the weather reports,' Hugo continued, hoping to allay any fears. 'There are awful storms over that part of the country at the moment. Irene and her fellow travellers are likely just holed up somewhere in a pleasant hotel, resting and waiting for the storm to pass, like she said they would be. And the fact she has no signal isn't surprising either, especially considering the weather and their remote location.'

He stopped and kissed Ben on top of his head. 'Now, stop worrying and we'll go to work, d'accord? And then I'm sure by the time you get there, you'll have heard from her.'

Ben rose reluctantly to his feet. 'Fine, but I swear if I haven't heard from Irene before tonight, then I'll... I'll...'

'Then you'll what?' Hugo asked.

Ben grabbed his bag. 'Well, let's just say I'd better hear from her,' Ben mumbled, stomping petulantly towards the door.

Irene & Maurice

Irene moved quickly but carefully across the storeroom, her eyes ensuring she did not compromise any evidence. The room was dimly lit, adding to the difficulty. A single bulb on a long wire swayed gently above them throwing eerie shadows across the room. She stopped, taking a moment to fully assess her surroundings. One wall was lined with large tins of beans, peas, and meat, and another filled with enormous bags of potatoes and other vegetables. Barrels of beer and boxes of wine covered the third.

At the far end was a small door with a sign indicating it was a walk-in freezer. Alain Bonnet was slumped over several boxes, his back to Irene, a large knife protruding from it. She inched forward and immediately noticed something which told her there was something very wrong. She pushed her hand through her hair, tucking fine red hair behind her ear. It took her a moment to completely understand what she was seeing.

The knife in Alain Bonnet's back was large, but it was not its size which concerned her. It was the minimal amount of blood around it, and there was only one plausible reason she could think of for that. She moved slowly around his body. Alain's head was pressed against the concrete wall. Irene was conscious she had no forensic gloves, so she pulled down her jumper sleeve and gently lifted his head.

She did not need to study it for very long. Alain Bonnet had clearly suffered a very serious and most likely catastrophic head injury. There was a large amount of blood splattered down the wall and there was clear evidence of the force of the blow to his temple. Irene frowned. Even without properly examining him, her instinct and years of experience informed her with almost certainty the cause of death.

As she lifted Alain slowly by the shoulder, Irene noticed the pained expression on his face. One eye was swollen shut with blood, the other staring straight at her. *Je suis désolé, Monsieur Bonnet,* she whispered, before continuing with a cursory examination of his body. There were no other obvious signs of trauma or assault.

When she was finished, she gently lowered his body back to where it had been found. She was conscious of Maurice Rousseau standing in the doorway. Irene did not need to see him to know his eyes were locked on her, boring into her back expectantly, desperately hoping for good news. She stood up, slowly turning to face him.

'Why aren't you saving him?' Maurice snapped. There was little conviction in his voice, as if he had resigned himself to the truth, but did not want to face it.

'I'm sorry, but I'm afraid he's gone,' she breathed.

Maurice stepped forward. 'Can I?' he asked.

Irene gestured to the path she had taken, along the side of the boxes lining the lefthand side wall. It had occurred to her it had likely been some time since the storeroom had even seen a sweep, so it was very unlikely a forensic examination would prove fruitful, but all the same she had to ensure they preserved as much potential evidence as possible.

'Walk down the side as much as you can, and try not to touch anything,' Irene instructed.

Maurice inched forward, his head facing directly at his friend. 'Who on earth would want to stab Alain?'

'I don't think it's as simple as that,' Irene replied, immediately biting her lip. She had not meant to speak aloud her suspicions, least of all to someone who was not a police officer and who could also very possibly be a suspect.

'What do you mean?' Maurice snapped. 'There's a goddamn knife sticking out of his back.'

'All I mean,' Irene responded evenly, 'is that until a professional examine him properly under better circumstances, we can't assume anything.'

'Aren't you a fancy doctor?' he demanded. 'Why can't you examine him?'

Irene shook her head. 'I can't. This isn't my jurisdiction... it isn't proper.'

'*Proper?*' Maurice screamed. 'Is it proper that my best friend is lying there with a knife sticking out of his back?'

Irene took a deep breath. 'Non, it isn't. All I meant is that we have to think about what happens next,' she explained.

'Next?' he asked with a frown.

'It's clear your friend was murdered,' she continued. 'And whoever is responsible needs to be punished for it, and the truth is, I can't tell you how many times in my experience someone has gotten off on a technicality, often because of a forensic error. That's all I'm saying. We have to preserve evidence and not give any defence avocat an excuse to argue about procedural errors.'

Maurice nodded slowly. 'I understand what you're saying, but what are we supposed to do in the meantime? It could be several days before anyone gets to us, or the phone lines start working.' He stole a sly look at Alain. 'I mean, won't he... won't he go off or something?'

Irene looked at the freezer doors. She nodded. 'Oui, you're right. I'm afraid we don't have a couple of days before decomposition begins,' she said softly. 'As reluctant as I am to move Alain, under the circumstances, I don't think we have much choice.'

Maurice followed her gaze, his eyes widening in horror. 'You want to freeze him like he's a fucking dead pig?' he spat.

'I realise it's not ideal,' Irene responded. 'But in a morgue, we do store bodies for extended periods of time under controlled conditions. At least this will allow us to preserve as much evidence as we possibly can. Alain has only been dead for a few hours at most. Rigor mortis isn't present, and that makes it even more important we try to preserve him as best we can until he can be properly examined.'

Maurice wrapped his arms around his chest. 'We don't have a choice, do we?'

'Unfortunately, I don't think we do,' she replied. 'But I can't do it alone. Would you help me carry him into the freezer?'

'Bien sûr,' Maurice answered as if it was the last thing he wanted to do.

They crept back to Alain's body. Irene pushed open the door to the freezer, the cold gust of air making her stumble backwards.

'The light's on the left,' Alain pointed.

Irene flicked on the light, illuminating the walk-in freezer. She looked around it. There was a wide table in the corner of the freezer which was clear and she imagined would hold Alain's weight. 'The table in the corner,' she directed. 'Take his legs and I'll guide him by the shoulders.'

Maurice nodded. 'Why is there so much blood on his head and the wall?' he asked, his brow crumpled.

Irene did not answer, instead shuffling on her feet to lift Alain by the shoulders. 'Let's get him in the freezer,' she said.

They moved slowly as they shuffled him into the freezer and placed him on the table. Maurice retreated quickly, Irene a step behind, panting because of the cold and exertion.

She closed the door, securing the lock in place. 'We should talk to the others,' she said.

'What are we going to tell them?' Maurice asked.

Irene stared at him but did not respond because she knew she was faced with a dilemma. And it was to whether or not she should assume control of the situation. Despite the fact she had no jurisdiction, her professional training meant she was better placed than most to secure the crime scene until the proper authorities could take charge.

'I don't know,' she responded finally. 'I honestly don't know.'

Les Pèlerins - Huitième jour

Irene stared at the wall clock in the centre of the Café. Its tick seemed almost deafening to her, and with each tick, it got closer to the time when Bruno would wake and demand her attention. She wished more than anything she could just leave with him because she did not want him to notice what had happened. And more importantly, she wanted to protect her family because there was a murderer on the loose.

She took a moment to observe her fellow travellers. Everyone was seated, their heads lowered, nursing cold drinks as if searching for something, anything, to do to occupy their time. Edith Lancaster, the elderly British librarian, had been stirring the same cup of thé for a long time, her lips moving in silent prayer. The rest, Irene's mother, the German couple, the American and his son, and the Englishman and his daughter were all placed around the Café, not really looking at anyone, or each other for that matter. Against the doorway, Maurice Rousseau, their tour guide, was staring out of the window, his hands pressed against either side of the door, almost as if he was willing the rain to stop.

Irene had been mulling over what to do next, especially if it might be a few days before help arrived. She reasoned all she could do was her best effort to preserve evidence and keep a watchful eye.

'I can't be the only one thinking this,' Sam Mitchell broke the silence, slamming his fists on the table. 'Someone in this room killed Alain.' He turned his head, narrowing his eyes to the other people in the Café.

Maurice spun around. 'We don't know that at all, you fool,' he hissed. 'Anyone could have come to the village before the bridge was destroyed.'

Elke Huber raised a shaking hand to the door. 'But the door

was locked, wasn't it?'

He shrugged. 'How the hell am I supposed to know that? Alain could have let his murderer in, for all we know.'

'Maurice has a point,' Tony Wilkinson interrupted. 'And other people are living in the village.'

Dorothy Chapeau shook her head. 'Alain told me there are only elderly people still living here. Most of the younger ones leave the village looking for work,' she added.

Maurice's nostrils flared. 'It doesn't matter. What does matter is who on earth would want to stab Alain in the back? There was no better man in this world, and that's the truth. He would have done anything for anyone without uttering a complaint.'

Edith Lancaster nodded. 'That is indeed the truth.'

Maurice turned back to Irene. 'There's one thing I keep coming back to in my head - why was there so much blood on Alain's head but not on his back?' he demanded.

'Oh, my God!' Elke Huber cried, her hand flying to her mouth.

Irene coughed. She was still struggling with the thought of becoming further involved, but with no other suitable authority, she believed it was the only choice. Her primary concern was the preservation of the crime scene and making sure no one attempted to tamper with the evidence.

'I believe it's likely that Alain didn't die as a result of being stabbed,' she blurted out before she changed her mind.

Wolfgang Huber clenched his fists. 'What are you talking about, you foolish woman?' he snapped. 'There was a goddamn knife in his back!'

Dorothy raised her hands. 'I remind you, Wolfgang Huber, that my daughter is considered to be one of the foremost pathologists in the whole of France. If Irene says Alain wasn't stabbed, then you'd better believe her, or else you'll have me to deal with.'

Maurice looked to Irene expectedly. 'What are you saying, Dr. Chapeau?'

Irene glanced anxiously over her shoulder. The storeroom door was open, and there was no lock on it which troubled her. 'While I only performed a cursory examination on Alain,' she began carefully, 'it is quite clear there is very little blood around the knife wound.'

Sarah Wilkinson, the British teenager, lifted her head, dank hair falling over her face. 'What does that mean?'

Dorothy stared at Irene. 'It means he was already dead when he was stabbed,' she stated.

Irene held her mother's gaze. For most of her adult life, Dorothy Chapeau had been a nurse, primarily working with elderly patients suffering from awful diseases such as dementia, but she had also worked in intensive care for a time, only leaving when it had become too much for her. Irene nodded.

'Then how did he die?' Dorothy questioned.

Irene shrugged. 'I'm afraid I can't answer that, not now, not here at least,' she answered. She lowered her voice. 'I don't have any equipment,' she added, suddenly feeling very helpless.

Maurice shook his head angrily. 'If you're really a doctor, you must have some idea what the hell happened.'

'As I said, I performed a preliminary examination, that's all,' Irene continued reluctantly. 'And there is some evidence of a haematoma on his head, suggesting they struck him with something, something very hard. There is blood on the wall of the storeroom, so it's certainly possible he hit his head on the wall, but a forensic technician will need to confirm it.'

She paused as she spoke of a forensic technician, instantly seeing Etienne Martine in her mind's eye, the forensic expert in Montgenoux and the man she had left behind. Walking away from him had been easier than it should have been, and she was not sure if she was going to go back to him. It made her angry at herself because he was a good man, but every time she saw Hugo and Ben together, the same thought always popped into her head. *I want what they have,* and each time the realisation hit her, she did not believe she had it with Etienne.

Elke scratched her head. 'I don't understand what you're saying. It makes no sense. Either poor Alain was stabbed, or he wasn't.'

Her husband emitted a long, weary sigh. 'It's abundantly clear what Dr. Chapeau is saying,' the rotund German admonished his wife.

'It might be to you, Wolfgang, but it isn't to me,' she snapped back.

'And nor me, I have to say,' Dorothy agreed.

'I can't begin to say with any degree of certainty,' Irene responded. 'Monsieur Bonnet needs to be properly examined. Only then might we able to piece together the events that led up to his death.'

Wolfgang stood and began pacing in front of the bar. 'I was a cop in Germany for over thirty years, and in all that time, I saw more than my fair sure of terrible things. Crimes which made no sense, or so we thought. In the end, every crime has an explanation. It is just knowing where to look. Whatever happened to our friend, we will discover the truth, one way or another.'

Irene nodded. 'I hope so,' she replied. 'I've already spoken with Maurice about this, and the fact is until the local police get here, all we can do is try to preserve the crime scene as best we can.'

'It doesn't change the fact someone murdered him and that it's one of us,' Sam Mitchell stated again.

'That's not helping, Sam,' Dorothy interrupted.

'But it's the truth,' Sam snapped.

Edith Lancaster pushed back her seat and rose. 'I'm going to my room, and,' she produced a knitting needle from her oversized carpet bag, 'if anyone follows me, I'll stab them in the eye with this.'

'We need to remain calm,' Dorothy raised her hands, 'and we most certainly can't start turning on one other.'

Sarah Wilkinson turned her head towards the storeroom. 'It's a little late for that, don't you think?' the young, normally shy young English woman said, with a hint of amused malevolence in her voice.

Hugo drew his beaten-up old Citroën to a halt and clambered out of it. It groaned underneath him as if it was relieved to have finally stopped. He knew he had no business driving the car, particularly as it was likely not as roadworthy as it should be. However, over the years he had attached some kind of sentimentality to it, primarily because it had saved his life on more than one occasion.

He stopped and lit a cigarette, taking a moment to appreciate the place he now called home. In his wildest dreams he had never imagined living in such a place, but from the second he had first seen it he had known it was special and that so long as he was there, he would always be surrounded by love.

Stepping across the path, Hugo pushed open the large double entrance doors which led into the ramshackle living room, and he was immediately greeted by a scene of pandemonium. Ben was rushing around the room, throwing various items into a bag. It took Hugo a moment to realise what was happening.

'Ben, what's going on?' he asked with evident concern.

Ben stopped in his tracks, fixing Hugo with a stern look. 'I don't want to hear what you're about to say,' he said forcefully.

'What's going on?' Hugo repeated.

Ben took a deep breath. 'I have to go, Hugo. I don't have a choice. Irene and Bruno are my responsibility.'

Hugo grimaced. 'I'm not sure that's true…'

'What would you know about it?' Ben snapped. 'Irene was my family when I barely had one. She means more to me than…'

'Than what?' Hugo interrupted, realising they were heading into dangerous territory.

'I can't do this now,' Ben said, folding a t-shirt and putting it in his bag. 'My flight leaves in two hours, and…'

'You can't be serious!'

'I don't have a choice, Hugo. I can't just sit around waiting. It's been three days since we last heard from them.' Ben raised his hands. 'And before you say it, I don't care about the storm, because I know Irene would have found a way to get a message to me if she could,' he reasoned.

'But the weather is bad,' Hugo sighed, realising he was fighting a losing battle. The bond between Ben and Irene had been formed long before he had arrived on the scene. He had never felt jealous of it, particularly because Irene had welcomed Hugo with open arms. Although he was sure Ben was overreacting, Hugo understood why he would be concerned.

'Give me a day or two,' Hugo sighed. 'I'm in the middle of giving evidence in a court case, but once that's done, I can get away and we can go together.'

Ben grinned at him, pushing the curls away from his forehead. He rushed over to Hugo and kissed him on the cheek, pushing his hand through Hugo's long blond fringe. 'I love you for that,' he said. 'Besides, we both know I'm overreacting, and I just don't want to drag you into my madness.'

Hugo sighed, knowing he had lost the battle. 'What about the hospital? And the hotel renovations?'

'I've cleared my schedule,' Ben reasoned. 'I was due some leave from the hospital anyway, so I just took it a little earlier. And as for the hotel, well, the renovators are taking forever and if I don't have a break from them, then I'm going to go apeshit at the amount of extra money they're costing me. Money I don't have. So, I gave them an ultimatum this afternoon. Be finished by the time I get back, or else.'

Hugo raised an eyebrow. 'And how did that go?'

Ben laughed. 'I don't think they believed me, and then I reminded them that my mother is Mayor and she can cause them a lot of problems.' He shrugged. 'Hey, I'm not proud, so long as it gets the job done, that's all I care about.' He narrowed his eyes. 'Do I have your permission to go?'

Hugo gave him a quizzical look. 'You don't need my permission, you know that. We're married, but that doesn't mean I own you.' He fixed Ben with his emerald-green eyes, his face softening. He felt nothing but love for the man he had married. 'But it also means I'm allowed to be concerned about you. I understand why you feel you need to go, but I'm not sure Irene needs rescuing or would appreciate the sentiment.'

'Probably not, but I keep replaying the last conversation we had with her. Irene suggested there was something off about the tour guide. What if...'

Hugo reached over and touched Ben's arm. 'Irene didn't sound worried to me. You know what we're like. It's an occupational hazard to always imagine the worst in people,' he added as lightly as he could.

Ben sighed. 'I know I'm...' he coughed, *probably*, overreacting. We've created our own little family here, and neither of us had much of a family growing up, did we? But since I met Irene and then you came along, and Bruno and Baptiste, we've just formed this crazy little nuclear family and I love it so much, so yeah, I panic when it feels like we're in danger. I mean, we have had our own fair share of danger, haven't we?'

Hugo nodded, again reminded of the occasions when they had nearly lost one another and there were some nights when it still kept him awake, haunted by what they might have lost.

'And not to mention Bruno doesn't even have a proper father to watch out for him,' Ben snipped. 'So, it falls to us to at least make him feel like he has people who care about him.' He glanced at his watch. 'I really have to go, but don't worry, I'll call you and text you all the time.'

Hugo exhaled, defeated. 'Do you even know where you're going?'

Ben gave him a sheepish look. 'I know where to start and where they were headed. But don't worry, I'm not a complete plebeian. I checked online and I've arranged for a guide to meet me at the airport and they've agreed to go with me.'

Hugo tried to hide the relieved look on his face. 'Probably a good idea with your sense of direction.'

Ben playfully punched his arm. 'Hey!' He pulled Hugo into an embrace and kissed him hard on the lips. 'Je t'aime, and don't worry, everything's going to be fine and we'll all be back before you know it.'

Hugo watched helplessly as Ben grabbed his bag and headed for the door. He took a long drag on the cigarette as he watched his husband disappear around the corner. He wished the feeling of foreboding that was an occupational hazard would, in this instant, desert him.

Irene, Maurice & Wolfgang

Irene looked across the table. Wolfgang Huber and Maurice Rousseau were staring at her expectantly as if they were waiting for her to provide answers she did not have. They were seated in the Café, the rain still pounding against the windows. The other members of the group had all retreated to their rooms, unsure what else they should do. It was almost as if the safety of a closed door was providing a safe sanctuary for them.

Irene held her head high, shifting her gaze between the two men. One, the leader of the pilgrimage, the other a retired German police officer, both decades older than her. She was not sure she liked or trusted either of them, a fact that was not lost on her saying as how they were supposed to be a pilgrimage towards spiritual enlightenment.

'Maurice and I have been talking,' Wolfgang began. 'And as you are,' he paused, flexing his hands in front of him, '*technically* the nearest we have to a serving officer, we accept you should take charge, however,' he paused, thick lips pulling into a snide smile, 'as I spent decades on the force, we also believe I should use that experience to guide you. What are your thoughts on the matter?'

Irene faced the German. 'I didn't ask to be in charge of anything. As I keep saying, my only concern is that we try to preserve as much evidence as we can until the proper authorities arrive,' she replied coolly.

Wolfgang gave her an amused look. 'You don't like me very much, young lady, do you?' His eyes flecked with anger. 'You don't know me, but you don't like me.'

Irene held his gaze defiantly. 'I could say the same about you.'

He shrugged. 'I mean no harm. I suppose to you, men like me, and my friend Maurice here, must seem like dinosaurs, with opinions right out of the dark ages.' He raised his hands as if fending off Irene's impending denial. 'I saw the way you looked at me when I was talking to my wife. And while it might be true that I sometimes take my lovely Elke for granted, and speak to her in a less than gentlemanly way, believe me when I say this; she is the single best thing I have done with my life, and I love her more than she could ever know.'

'You could try telling her that, rather than just expecting her to know,' Irene retorted tartly, before immediately regretting it and biting her lip. 'Sorry, it really is none of my business.' She leaned forward. 'Listen, I'm sorry we got off on the wrong foot. It wasn't my intention. I suppose I'm not myself these days.'

'You lost your father and you're worried about your mother,' Wolfgang said softly. 'It's not so hard to understand, really.'

Maurice Rousseau sighed. 'Now that you've made up, can we get back to the issue at hand?'

Wolfgang nodded. 'Of course,' he turned back to Irene. 'How would you proceed, Irene?'

Irene wondered if he was being sincere and realised whatever his motives or their opinion of each other, the two of them were the only qualified people to hold the scene until the local police arrived. 'Well, first things first. We need to make sure we're protected. The door to the Café was locked, but that doesn't mean it was always that way. Our murderer may not be amongst us, but we can't say that definitively, so we have to be careful.'

Maurice shook his head. 'I still can't imagine someone from the village murdered Alain. I mean, why would they? And more to the point, why now all of a sudden?' He narrowed his eyes. 'Non, the only explanation is someone staying in this hotel murdered Alain.'

'It's certainly possible,' Irene conceded reluctantly, 'but by the same theory, it could be someone hiding in the village who may not have escaped because of the bridge being destroyed.'

'I agree,' Wolfgang added. 'At the very least, we need to perform an extensive search of the village. You and I should do that, Maurice. Dr. Chapeau, I'd like you to stay here and make sure no one enters or leaves the Café.'

Irene nodded. 'I will, but at some point we're all going to need to go outside, even if just for some fresh air.'

Wolfgang considered. 'It's probably a good idea, but let's wait until we've had a chance to search the entire village first. I don't want people wandering around if there's a madman out there.'

'You're right, of course,' Irene agreed. 'And we should stick together. No one should be alone, because...' she trailed off.

'Because?' Maurice questioned.

'Because you have a point,' Wolfgang answered for Irene. 'If our murderer didn't come from the outside, he...' he lifted his head towards the ceiling, 'came from the inside and is most likely one of us.' He stood. 'Okay. Let's begin our search.'

'And then?' Irene asked.

'We interview our witnesses and see where it takes us,' Wolfgang replied.

Irene nodded. The only thing she knew for certain was that neither she nor her mother had murdered Alain Bonnet, but she could not say the same about Wolfgang Huber and Maurice Rousseau, but at that point, she knew she had no choice but to go along with the plan and hope the local police arrived sooner rather than later.

Ben & Viviane

Ben stepped out of the airport arrivals gates, suppressing a yawn. The flight had felt longer than two hours, especially since he had not slept, moving in and out of a troubled sleep, plagued by dark thoughts formed by an overactive imagination. There was no reason to assume Irene and Bruno had come to any home, but it did not translate into logic in his consciousness.

Putting use to the time, Ben had tried to formulate a plan of action, and he had reluctantly come to one conclusion and that was he had not thought it through. Hugo had been correct, and in hindsight, Ben realised he had acted hastily and it saddened him that he had not allowed Hugo to accompany him, primarily because he knew if they were together, they would have at least come up with some sort of plan. Ben had known from the first moment when had met Hugo that his life would be forever changed for the better by his presence.

As it stood, his plan had involved little more than arriving in Saint-Jean-Pied-de-Port and then hoping for the best. He looked at the line of people in the arrival lounge, his eyes falling on a young woman holding up a sign bearing his name. He lifted his hand and waved awkwardly at her.

Viviane Auclair sipped her drink and smiled warmly at Ben. In her early twenties, she was a tall, thin young woman with smooth black hair pushed under a wide hat. She was dressed in a long floral oversized floral print dress over dark leggings, not what he had expected for a tour guide.

Ben sipped his beer. 'I'm really grateful you agreed to be my guide at such short notice,' he said.

Viviane smiled. 'It came at the perfect time because my last customer dropped out yesterday and I was resigned to cooling my heels around here for the next few weeks with nothing to do because of the weather.'

'You do this sort of thing all the time?' Ben asked.

'Just this year,' she replied. 'I'm taking a gap year from university and one of my teachers suggested this would be a good way to make a little money and get some experience for my dissertation.'

Ben nodded. 'And what are you studying?'

'And I have to admit, I was intrigued by your message,' Viviane continued, without answering his question. 'I rarely get clients who want to walk the Compostelle just because they're looking for someone, someone other than Dieu, of course,' she added with a smile. Her voice was soft and her dark eyes were expressive and appeared to radiate only kindness.

'Yeah, I'm suddenly feeling very foolish about that,' Ben stated honestly. 'My husband tried to talk me out of it, but I wasn't having any of it. I'm not proud of the fact I can be rather stubborn when it suits me.'

Viviane shrugged. 'You're worried about someone. That's understandable enough. Though I'm not sure what we can do if we have little to go on.'

'Je sais, je sais,' Ben said with a weary sigh.

Viviane sipped her drink. 'Well, all is not lost. I mean, we know the general direction your friend and her party were travelling in, and because the weather has been so terrible, the chances are they're still holed up somewhere trying to wait it out.'

Ben nodded. He had been replaying the last exchange with Irene over and over his head, but he could not recall the exact details. 'My friend Irene said something about that,' he said. 'She told me they were going to stop in a village somewhere for the storm to pass, but for the life of me, I can't remember the name. I'm fairly sure her guide is called Maurice, but I don't remember his surname.'

Viviane flipped open a laptop lid. 'I may be able to help with that. When you mentioned the name Maurice, it rang a bell. There aren't too many guides around, especially ones who have been around for forty-plus years like you suggested. So, I did a little digging, and I found only one Maurice on the official guide list. That's not to say there aren't others, but it's a start, non? Anyway,' she pointed at a picture on the screen. 'This is Maurice Rousseau, a real veteran of the scene and a bit of a character,' she added with a laugh.

'You know him?'

Viviane nodded. 'Not well, but I've met him a few times. He knows his stuff, he should because he's been doing the walk for most of his life. Anyway, if your friend mentioned they were going to his home village, then I think that's a place called *Chemin des Pèlerins*, or the way of the pilgrims, as it's also known. It's actually a really cool place, a tiny village at the bottom of a ravine. I've been there a couple of times because I have a friend who lives there. Once you cross the bridge into it, it's like you're walking into another century. The tourists really dig it,' she added cheerfully.

'*Chemin des Pèlerins*,' Ben repeated, tapping the side of his head. 'That sounds like the place Irene mentioned.'

'And if they were walking there, it would fit the timeline,' Viviane continued. 'It would take about a week to get there by foot.'

'Good. Then how do we get there?'

She smiled. 'I take it you don't want to do the walk yourself?'

'Dieu, non,' Ben added with a shudder. 'That's okay, isn't it?'

Viviane shrugged. 'Yeah, so long as I get paid, I don't mind how we get there.'

'Bien sûr,' Ben replied. 'Can we get a taxi, or hire a car maybe?'

Her mouth twisted. 'It's about one hundred kilometres away,

and,' she glanced at her watch, 'it's going to get dark soon. I think it would be better to wait until tomorrow morning, rather than trying to search in the dark.'

'I really don't want to wait any longer,' Ben complained.

'One night won't make much difference, will it?' Viviane reasoned. 'Besides, there's a bus that leaves right across the road from here at 07h00 in the morning and it passes right by *Chemin des Pèlerins*. We would be there by lunchtime.'

Ben gave her an unconvinced and desperate look. 'I wanted to get started today.'

'I honestly think this is the best option,' Viviane said. 'There are a lot of rural roads, and many of them aren't lit. It would be dangerous, especially since the weather is still pretty dire.'

'Fine,' Ben replied grumpily.

She gave him a warm smile. 'Bon! D'accord, I'll show you where the local hotel is and then I'll come back for you in the morning in time for the bus. Sound like a plan?'

Ben nodded. 'Oui.' He looked outside the airport, the rain beating against the revolving doors. *I'm coming, Irene, keep safe,* he breathed.

Maurice & Wolfgang

Maurice Rousseau and Wolfgang Huber trudged in silence through the rain, carefully sidestepping the mudslides which had gathered along the sloping edges of the square. The rain had been relentless for days, only stopping for short periods of time and was showing no sign of easing up.

Maurice lifted his head towards the storm clouds. 'The storm's breaking,' he declared.

Wolfgang gave him a doubtful look, shaking the rain from the hood of his rain jacket.

'I've lived here my entire life,' Maurice began, 'and you might say I feel it in my bones. The storm will pass in a few hours, I'm sure of it, mais it won't mean it's over forever, rather we'll have a respite for a few days.' His head turned towards the steep staircase that led to the top of the village. 'A break from the rain should speed up help getting to us.'

Wolfgang turned his head to the tour guide. 'Has this sort of thing happened before, Maurice? The bridge falling down, I mean.'

Maurice stared straight ahead before responding, 'The bridge was old. I mean, you saw it. The matter of replacing it comes up now and then at town meetings, but we always find a reason to put it off. The fact is, it comes down to money and who is going to pay for it?'

Wolfgang snorted. 'Well, saying as it's now at the bottom of a ravine, I guess someone is going to have to find the cash.'

Maurice grimaced. 'Oui. I'm looking forward to our tax increase next year.'

The two men trudged in silence for a few minutes, turning their heads back and forth. Despite the storm's severity, the village appeared to have only suffered minor damage. The small, rickety houses were all still standing, seemingly with minimum damage, no doubt protected in part by the shutters covering their doors and windows.

'Most of the people still in town are spending their days together in the Mairie,' Maurice said. 'We imagined it would be the best idea under the circumstances, safety in numbers and all that. Most of them are even older than me, if you can imagine such a thing!' he added with a sad laugh. 'Being seventy years old is actually damn depressing.'

'You don't need to tell me,' Wolfgang replied. 'When I turned seventy, it felt like a sledgehammer to my skull. Suddenly it was like I was on a rail track peering into a dark tunnel knowing that any second it would be...' he slapped his forehead. 'Bam!'

Maurice laughed again. Wolfgang stopped him and pressed his hand onto Maurice's arm. 'What do you think happened here, Maurice?'

Maurice gave him a quizzical look. 'I don't know what you mean.'

Wolfgang stopped. 'The hell you do. Someone stabbed Alain Bonnet in the back or smashed his head against the damn wall. Who the hell knows for certain at this point? And as far as I know, Alain was a decent man, and certainly not the sort who would attract enemies.'

Maurice sucked in a breath. 'I would agree with that. I've known him all of my life, and I can't think of a single reason why someone would want him dead.'

Wolfgang's lips twisted. 'Nor I. He was a good man, and being stabbed in the back is just... it's just cruel and unusual, don't you think? I mean, in my line of work, such a modus operandi is, well, unusual. Two apparent manners of death, one more obvious than the other.'

'What are you suggesting, Wolfgang?'

The German police officer shrugged. 'Only that we are dealing with a very unusual situation. As far as we can be sure, the

Café was locked when Alain was murdered, which means we have to think of the alternative. The killer came from within.' He noticed the distressed look on Maurice's face. 'It's not a thought I want to entertain either, my friend, but it is one we cannot ignore.'

'We'll talk about this later,' Maurice said. He pointed to a metal pair of doors. 'Let's check in on the villagers.' He pushed open the door and led Wolfgang into a large, open-spaced area. They were greeted by a dozen or so expectant faces, mainly elderly men and women, their faces etched with concern.

Maurice moved quickly into the room, walking along the gangway and stopping in front of a large platform. He raised his hands. 'Ches amis,' he began. 'I hope you are well and keeping safe and calm in such trying circumstances.'

'Alain is dead,' Maurice announced gravely. 'And his murderer is amongst us,' he added, casting his eyes around the room.

'It has to be one of the pilgrims,' an old man in the crowd added angrily.

Maurice raised his hands. 'We can't be certain of anything at this moment,' he stated passively. 'And the only thing we have to concentrate on is getting through this storm and waiting for help from the outside. Once help arrives and the bridge is repaired, the authorities will make sense of what happened to our friend.'

'And if they don't?' the old man demanded.

Maurice narrowed his eyes. 'This village is ours,' he stated with a smile. 'And we look after our own. We always have, and we always will. And if a stranger invaded *Chemin des Pèlerins* and murdered Alain, then we don't need any police authority to solve the problem for us. We are more than capable of looking after and protecting ourselves.' He turned his head slowly in front of the crowd. 'Whatever happened here, now and in the past, it is all about to become clear and make sense.'

Wolfgang stepped forward. 'What do you mean?'

Maurice's mouth twisted. 'Alain may be dead, and for that, I am very sorry, but his death has confirmed one thing I have suspected for a very long time.'

'And what is that?'

Maurice clenched his fists. 'Forty years ago, a murderer walked into *Chemin des Pèlerins*, and then left without giving a second thought to the devastation they left behind.'

Wolfgang scratched his head. 'I don't know what you mean.'

Maurice stabbed his finger towards the exit. 'Only that forty years ago, one of your friends came into this town and murdered my beautiful wife, and now they've returned and murdered again. That much is obvious to me.'

Wolfgang shook his head. 'Maurice, you're not making any sense. What does any of this have to do with your wife's death? Olive was a wonderful woman, and I'm very sorry for what happened to her, and to you, but you have to know what happened then has nothing to do with what happened now.'

Maurice shrugged. 'We'll see. The only thing I know for certain in here,' he stabbed his finger at his heart, 'is that no one is leaving until I get the answers I've been waiting for.' He pointed above him. 'If you think the storm above us is bad, wait until you see the one raging inside of me. I've kept it chained for a long time, but no more. It is time for it to be freed.'

Wolfgang stared at him and shook his head, uncertain how to respond. 'We should get back to the others,' he said solemnly, struggling to hide his concern.

Maurice nodded. 'That, my friend, is a splendid idea because no one is leaving here until I finally know what happened to Olive and that is what is going to happen. You have my word on it. I will discover the truth, and there will be hell to pay.'

Ben watched the roads pass by as the bus ambled along. He knew the slow progress the driver was making should not irritate him, nor the fact he kept stopping periodically, cheerfully hanging out of the window and chatting with and encouraging pilgrims trudging through the rain, but it did.

Ben had spent a restless night checking and rechecking his cell phone. His own signal was weak, and he had to use the hotel landline to call Hugo in Montgenoux, feeling even more foolish for having to do so. Hugo had been kind, not needing to remind him that at any moment there was likely going to be a multitude of delayed messages and voicemails appearing on his phone.

'You look worried,' Viviane Auclair said softly.

Startled, Ben turned to Viviane. He liked the young tour guide. There was something quirky about her which appealed to him, her oversized clothes and hair pushed under her hat made her stand out from other people her age. He had also noticed she was wearing dark sunglasses, which seemed odd considering the weather and the dark skies above them.

Viviane noticed him looking. She tapped the glasses. 'I like to wear sunglasses because it allows me to look at people when they talk to me. I always feel a little awkward if I don't.'

Ben nodded. 'I understand. My husband is the same, though he has no reason to be.'

'So, listen,' Viviane began. 'Remember, I told you I had a friend who lived in *Chemin des Pèlerins?* Well, I called him last night. He's not actually in the village at the moment. He's like me, does a lot of pilgrim guiding at this time of year, so he hasn't been back to the village for a few weeks. Anyway, he rang his parents who still live in the village, or at least he tried to ring them. It looks like the phone lines are down.'

'The phone lines are down?' Ben repeated, his voice rising sharply.

She touched his arm. 'Don't read too much into that. Apparently, it happens a lot, especially when there's a bad storm. And that makes sense, non? That's why you haven't heard from your friend. Not only can't she get any cell signal, but there's also no landline either. As we said all along, they're probably just in the village waiting out the storm.'

Ben took a deep breath. 'I know I'm a drama queen,' he stated finally, pushing the light curls away from his forehead. As usual, they bounced right back. 'But I love my friends. They're family to me, more than family, really. I didn't have the best when I was growing up.'

Viviane smiled. 'I understand all about family, or lack thereof,' she responded, her tone suddenly becoming harder. 'And I've always believed families are what we make for ourselves, not what we're given by birth.' She shrugged. 'I haven't got there yet, but I will one day.'

Ben nodded his understanding. 'I'm sure you will. It took me a long time, but when you get there eventually, it'll be worth the wait, trust me.'

The bus suddenly ground to a halt again and the driver leaned over his shoulder. 'We're just going to take a quick break, folks,' he said cheerfully.

Ben groaned. 'Is this normal?' he asked Viviane.

She laughed. 'Buses tend to run to their own schedule in this part of the world. Don't worry, we'll be at *Chemin des Pèlerins* soon enough. Just be patient.'

Ben sighed. All he needed was to see Irene and Bruno were safe and then he would be able to relax. 'I'm afraid patience isn't my strongest virtue.'

Irene watched as her fellow travellers made their way slowly into the Café, each glancing slyly over their shoulder toward the storeroom which housed the remains of Alain Bonnet. It had not been a peaceful night for Irene, troubled by what had happened, but more concerned about what lay ahead.

The only conclusion she had arrived at was that it was imperative they left the village as soon as possible and got as far away as possible. Irene knew her mother would not be agreeable, but at that point, she did not much care. There was only one fact certain at that point and it was that there was a genuine possibility at least one member of the pilgrims was a cold-blooded murderer. And as far as Irene was concerned, the only thing she cared about was getting her family to safety and she would force her mother to leave if she had to.

'Have we received word from the outside?' Edith Lancaster demanded. As usual, the elderly British woman began knitting as soon as she sat.

Maurice shook his head. 'No, but it won't be long now, a day or two at the most.'

Edith clicked what sounded like dentures before lowering her head, concentrating again on her knitting.

Wolfgang stood up. 'We thought that under the circumstances of the tragic passing of Alain...'

'His murder, you mean,' Casey Mitchell interrupted, instantly recoiling from the angry look shot in his direction by his father, Sam.

'Yes, yes, of course,' Wolfgang flustered. 'Anyway, as I was saying, under the circumstances and until the local authorities arrive to take charge, we think it prudent that I, in my professional capacity as an ex-police officer, and Dr. Chapeau, a current pathologist working for the French Republic, take control as we try to understand what happened here.'

'What does that mean, Wolfgang?' Elke asked her husband.

Edith gave a haughty laugh. 'It means they think one of us here stabbed poor Alain.'

All eyes turned to Irene and Wolfgang as if waiting for confirmation.

Wolfgang took a deep breath. 'We don't know anything for certain, and that's a fact. The point is, we want to make sure everyone is safe, and that involves trying to understand what happened to Alain, and under the circumstances, I, for one, don't believe we can afford to wait for the police to arrive. I'm not accusing anyone of committing this horrendous crime, but until we know otherwise, we have to assume the killer is still in the village.'

'What do you want us to do?' Dorothy inquired.

'I propose we speak to you all individually,' Wolfgang replied.

'Then you DO suspect one of us,' Tony Wilkinson griped.

Wolfgang narrowed his eyes. 'It's a perfectly normal way to proceed. Rather than talking to you all in a group, we are far more likely to be able to piece together a timeline if we have individual recollections rather than a collective one.'

Sarah Wilkinson nervously bit into a fingernail. 'And what will you do if you discover one of us is the killer?' the young English woman asked anxiously.

Wolfgang shared a look with Maurice. 'We'll cross that bridge when we come to it,' he replied, a wry smile appearing on his face, 'if you pardon the expression. But to answer your question - should we come across evidence implicating someone in the crime, I will use my authority as a former police officer and place the said person in protective custody until the local police arrive.'

Irene raised a hand. 'I would also like to ask your permission to record our talks on my phone.'

'I'm not sure that's entirely legal,' Tony Wilkinson

interrupted.

'I'm not suggesting it is,' Irene reasoned. 'Rather, we're only doing this to make sure the authorities have all the information they need to perform a proper investigation when the time comes. Recording our memories when they are still fresh is crucial for an investigation. I know this to be a fact,' she added. She had worked with several police officers, Hugo Duchamp most lately, and she wanted to make sure she put into practice everything she had learned from them.

Dorothy Chapeau nodded. 'It's the least we can do, and the fact is, what else do we have to pass the time? I think it's a fine idea, and I have no problem with it.'

Some of the group nodded their understanding, but no one spoke.

Wolfgang clapped his hands together. 'Good, I'm glad you all agree.' He looked at his watch. 'How about the ladies rustle us up some breakfast and we'll get started right after?'

'Sexist,' Sarah muttered under her breath.

He laughed. 'I may be, young lady, but ask my lovely wife as to the extent and edibility of my feeble attempts at culinary endeavours and I'm sure she'd agree it's best I keep as far away from the kitchen as possible.'

Elke nodded. 'It's true. Nobody should have to experience Wolfgang's attempts at cooking, especially now. I think we've all been through enough already,' she added with a dry laugh.

Wolfgang smiled warmly at her. 'Then it's a deal. Don't look so worried everyone. Everything is going to be alright. You have my word.'

Irene, Wolfgang & Elke

Elke Huber slowly sipped from the glass of water, her hand gently shaking. She was staring anxiously at her husband. It confused Irene because she could not think of a reason why Elke would be afraid of Wolfgang under these conditions.

'We're going to ask everyone the same questions,' Wolfgang began. 'We simply need to try and understand the events which led to the demise of our dear Alain.'

Elke made the sign of the cross. 'I've been thinking about it and praying, but none of it makes sense because I can't think of a single reason why someone would want to hurt such a wonderful person.'

Irene leaned forward. 'You kept in touch with him over the years?'

Elke's eyes misted. 'Not as much as I should have. I tried, but, well, life just passes by without you realising, doesn't it?'

Irene noticed Elke was not looking at her husband when she spoke. It was almost as if she was afraid to.

'I tried, anyway,' Elke continued. 'Men aren't always the best at reaching out, but over the years, we talked a little and my opinion of him never changed. He was a fine man.'

'He was indeed,' Wolfgang agreed.

'When was the last time you saw Alain alive?' Irene asked.

Elke turned her head towards the storeroom. 'Just after lunch. It was about 13h00, I suppose.'

Irene nodded. 'And did you notice anything unusual?'

Elke considered before finally shaking her head. 'I don't think so,' she said distantly, her head moving back and forth as if she was trying to retrace steps. 'No, everything just seemed normal. After we'd eaten, Alain collected all the plates and went to the kitchen.'

'And what did everyone else do?' Irene pushed.

Elke frowned. 'Well, I can't be sure. I know I remained in the Café for a while, finishing my drink and reading my book.'

'And you were alone?'

She nodded. 'Mostly. People came in and out, I suppose, but I can't say I noticed who they were. Despite the storm, people were foolish enough to leave the Café.'

Irene nodded her agreement. 'I was one of those fools because I went for a walk too,' Irene stated. 'I was trying to find a cell signal, but I couldn't.'

'As did I,' Wolfgang added. 'I went to the bridge to see if there was anything that could be done to get us out of here, or to get help in.' He shrugged. 'Sadly, I found nothing.'

'After an hour or so, I went up to our room,' Elke continued. 'I mean, what else is there to do? We're rather stuck here, aren't we? There aren't many ways to pass the time. I suppose I went up just to have something different to do to break up the day.'

Irene nodded her agreement. 'I know that only too well with a five-year-old.' She paused. 'Tell me, did you see Alain again?'

'No,' Elke replied with assurance. 'Although I'm positive I heard him banging about in the kitchen, or the storeroom, doing the dishes or something.'

'I didn't see him either when I came back,' Irene added.

Wolfgang nodded. 'Nor did I.'

'I'm sorry I can't be more help. I wish I could,' Elke said, helplessness clear on her face.

Irene reached across and touched her hand. 'Don't apologise, Elke. We're just trying to make sense of this whole tragedy.'

'What if we can't?' she retorted.

'Oh, we will,' Wolfgang snapped. 'One way or another, we'll find out exactly what happened here before we leave this damn village. I wasn't a cop for thirty-two years to let a murderer walk away from his crime, and I'm not about to start now. Whoever is responsible will pay. You can count on it.'

Ben shook the rain from his head and looked irritably at the sky. He did not want to tempt fate, but the clouds suddenly seemed less imposing and the rain appeared to be lessening.

'The road down to the village should just be around the next bend,' Viviane Auclair called out above the deafening roar of the ancient bus as it pulled away from them.

'Oh, great!' Ben exclaimed cheerfully, breaking into a trot.

They rounded the corner and stopped dead in their tracks. 'What the hell?' Ben lapsed.

Viviane moved quickly past him, peering down the steps towards what remained of the broken bridge. 'Damn, the storm must have wiped out the bridge,' she said.

Ben frowned. 'There must be another way in, surely?'

She shook her head. 'Non, there isn't. Like I said, it's at the bottom of a valley. There's nothing but a mountain on the other side. You can only get in or out through the bridge.' She peered over the side, looking down into the river below them. 'Most of which appears to be at the bottom of the ravine.'

Ben stepped forward and turned his head slowly, shaking it in disbelief. The gap between the two sides he guessed to be at least sixty feet, and about the same to the river below. He grimaced, realising not only was it impossible to get across, even jumping down into the water would be dangerous, and even then the sides of the bank were wet with no obvious way of climbing up.

'It's a disaster,' he cried.

Viviane touched his arm. 'Not really, and it probably explains a lot. The storm knocked out the bridge and the phones. Help is most likely on the way to sort it out.'

Ben rounded on her. 'But what if it isn't? What if no one actually knows what happened here?'

Viviane bit her lip, twisting it as if she was contemplating something. 'There's another village, Millieure, about ten kilometres away from here. It's probably the nearest place we could go to for help.'

Ben turned back to face the village and began screaming at the top of his lungs. 'Bonjour! Bonjour!' Shouting so hard, his voice finally cracked. He looked around anxiously, waiting to see if his shouts had attracted any attention.

'They probably can't hear you because of the weather,' Viviane reasoned. 'And they're probably all down in the village, anyway.'

'Then what do we do?' he asked desperately.

'We can go to the other village and get help,' she suggested.

Ben stepped away with determination. 'Then let's go. Do you know what time the next bus is due?'

Viviane shrugged. 'I don't think there is one. We're probably going to have to walk there.'

Ben strapped on his backpack. 'Then we'd better get started.'

Viviane watched helplessly as he strode ahead. She looked over her shoulder back towards the village, a dark look flashing across her face. 'Wait for me, Ben!' she called after him.

Irene, Wolfgang & Sam

Sam Mitchell dropped heavily onto a chair opposite Irene and Wolfgang. The chair groaned under the athletic man's weight. He grinned at them, running his hand across his buzzcut.

'Is this where we come for our interrogations?' he asked cheerfully.

Irene smiled, wondering quite what the American had to be so cheerful about. 'It's not an interrogation,' she replied evenly. 'As we said, we're just trying to make sense of this whole situation until the local police can take over.'

'Where were you the afternoon before Alain died?' Wolfgang interrupted in a tone which suggested he was not fond of the other man.

'I went for a walk with Tony around the village,' Sam replied. 'As well you know because we ran into you once or twice on the circuit. *Chemin des Pèlerins* isn't exactly a bustling metropolis,' he added with a wry smile.

'And when was the last time you saw Monsieur Bonnet alive?' Irene asked.

Sam considered his answer. 'I guess I saw him when Tony and I came back from the walk. It must have been around 15h00, maybe later. I can't say I paid it a lot of attention.'

Irene nodded. 'And what was he doing?'

'When I saw…' he shook his head, 'not so much saw him. What I mean, I suppose, is that I heard him,' Sam continued. 'He was in the storeroom talking with someone.'

'Who was he talking to?' Wolfgang demanded, cocking his head keenly.

Sam frowned. 'That's the thing, I don't know. I could only make out Alain's voice, and I didn't want to stick around, to be honest.'

Irene leaned forward, tucking her hair behind her ear. 'What do you mean by that?'

He shrugged. 'Listen, after everything that's happened, I don't know whether it's just my imagination playing tricks on me, but when I think about it, it seems as if he was having some kind of argument with someone. Not the knock 'em out sort, but a heated exchange, if that makes sense?'

Wolfgang raised an eyebrow. 'About what?'

'I don't know, and that's the truth,' Sam replied. 'My mother always told me not to eavesdrop, so I just made my way to my bedroom and spent the rest of the afternoon on my laptop, working on my book.'

'And you don't want to say what he was fighting about, or with whom?' Wolfgang asked angrily.

Sam gave him a surprised look. 'Why would I lie about something like that?'

Wolfgang snorted. 'Why indeed,' he mused. 'Why indeed?' he repeated sarcastically.

Before the situation escalated, Irene spoke, 'How well did you know Alain?'

'Not well,' Sam answered. 'Before this trip, I only met him once, and that was on the original pilgrimage forty years ago. I guess my parents kept in touch with him and the others, but I can't say I paid much attention. I mean, when I first came here I was a popular jock back home, my girlfriend was the head cheerleader and then out of the blue my parents said I couldn't spend my summer at the beach with my girl and instead I was going to spend it with them and a bunch of oldies trudging through the elements across France and Spain to search for God, or whatever. Yeah, I was *delighted*,' he concluded with a bitter laugh.

Irene laughed, immediately covering her mouth and muttering an apology.

'A bunch of oldies,' Wolfgang sniffed huffily.

'Sorry,' Sam blurted. 'I didn't mean to offend. Dad always said I was a loudmouth jock, and I guess he was right. At the time, I thought busting my knee and ending my football career was the end of my life, but in the end, it was actually just the beginning. Travelling and writing and seeing the world as my parents did has changed me.'

He looked to the staircase which led to the bedrooms, a sadness passing across his face. 'Not always for the better, but I'm still better than the snotty-nosed kid who came here the first time. I hated every second of it, and I hated my parents for dragging me away from my happy life. My girl, by the way, lasted a whole week without me before she shacked up with my so-called best friend, the quarterback.'

Sam sighed. 'I gave my parents such a hard time about that,' he added with a sad smile. 'I'd pretty much forgotten all about this place, until one day I received an email from Elke inviting me to do the pilgrimage again.' He laughed. 'Obviously, the first thing I did was delete it.'

Wolfgang tutted loudly.

'I know! I know!' Sam exclaimed. 'I told you I'm still an asshole, but only half a one these days. Anyway, I spent the rest of the day thinking about it and it was like someone or something was niggling at me the whole time. My folks died together, run off the road by some idiot who didn't even care enough to stop and check if they were okay. They'd talked about going back to Camino SO much over the years, but each time they couldn't do it, usually because of me. Either I was in hospital, or rehab, or whatever. And I guess that email got to me, and made me feel sad and I guess I thought maybe I could finally do something good for my folks.'

'And write a book about it,' Wolfgang muttered under his breath.

'You're right,' Sam conceded. 'My publishers have been nagging me for a while about getting on with and writing something and there were vague mumblings about them asking for the advance back, so...' he extended his hands, 'here we are.'

'Actually,' he continued, 'I thought it might be a chance to reconnect with my own kid. He doesn't exactly worship the ground I walk on, and the thought of spending a summer with him filled with uncomfortable silences and dragging his reluctant ass from one stupid activity to another, wasn't exactly something I was looking forward to, so I had to ask. When I mentioned doing the walk to Camino, he actually didn't seem turned off by the idea, so before either of us had a chance to change our minds, I booked our tickets.' He snorted. 'But it hasn't exactly worked out as I'd hoped. And he still hates me.'

Wolfgang raised an eyebrow. 'However, suddenly your book has taken a rather interesting turn.'

Sam's eyes widened, and he shrugged but said nothing.

Irene took a deep breath. 'For what it's worth, this wasn't exactly how I planned on spending my summer either, and the current circumstances notwithstanding, I'm cherishing the time with my mother. Bruno's only five, so I don't have a lot of experience with teenagers, but I've seen enough to know that when they get through the fog of adolescence, they do often emerge as reasonably decent human beings.' she laughed. 'And I'm sure Casey will come around and appreciate the time with you, too.'

Wolfgang emitted a bored sigh. 'Dead man in freezer,' he mumbled, gesturing for them to get on with the matter at hand.

Irene flashed him a dirty look before turning back to Sam. 'Is there anything else you can think of that might help us?'

Sam shook his head. 'I've been racking my brains and I'm not even sure if it's my imagination, but I think whoever Alain was talking to, he sounded afraid of them. As I said, I couldn't make out much of what was being said, but when I think about it, as I was heading up the stairs, it sounded as if Alain was saying something like - *it wasn't my fault*, and saying it over and over.'

'Are you sure?' Wolfgang asked.

Sam shrugged. 'I'm not sure of anything. I wish I was because I want the monster responsible for this to be caught. Are we done? Can I go?'

Wolfgang nodded. 'Of course. Could you ask your son to come and see us next?'

Sam gave him an anxious look. 'I'll send him down, but just be careful with him, he's really anxious. He's a good enough kid, who's just had a crappy set of parents. He deserved better.'

Irene watched as the American moved slowly across the Café towards the stairs.

'What do you think?' Wolfgang demanded of her.

Irene did not know what she thought. 'All I know is that I wish Hugo Duchamp was here.'

Irene, Wolfgang & Casey

Casey Mitchell moved hesitantly into the Café, peering at Irene and Wolfgang through a mop of fine black hair. He sat in front of them, pushing the glasses back up his nose. They immediately slid down again, and he irritably pushed them back up, his eye twitching rapidly.

Irene studied the young man, and it was all she could do to stop herself from reaching out and embracing him in the same way she did with Bruno when she sensed he was uncomfortable or in distress. The young American, the polar opposite of his athletic father, scratched irritably at an angry circle of acne on his left cheek.

'I saw nothing,' Casey stated, his voice cracking as if it had just broken, although he was most likely in his later teenage years.

'We'll be the judge of that,' Wolfgang snapped. 'Where were you, Tuesday lunchtime?'

'Well, I wasn't sticking a knife in the cook's back, if that's what you're asking,' Casey quipped, flicking his hair from his face.

Wolfgang slammed his palms on the table. 'Now, listen here boy, don't get smart with me or I'll… I'll…'

Casey gave the German detective an amused look. 'Or you'll what? Beat it out of me? I know we're stuck in some backwater shithole, but it's not quite Nazi Germany, as far as I can tell.'

Irene coughed, noticing Wolfgang's reddening face next to her. 'Casey, we're just trying to understand what might have happened to Alain Bonnet, and asking for everyone's help.'

Casey glanced at her, before turning away as if he was too embarrassed to continue. 'I told you I saw nothing.'

Irene nodded. 'Just tell us what you remember. You had lunch here with everyone, then what did you do?'

He shrugged. 'Went to my room, lay on my bed and listened

to music.'

'And you didn't hear or see anything?' she continued.

Casey shook his head.

'Nothing at all?' Wolfgang interrupted, his voice suggesting he did not believe the young man. 'You expect us to believe you spent the entire afternoon on your bed listening to music?'

'What else is there to do?' Casey countered haughtily. 'It's not like there's any internet here or anywhere civilised to go. I had my headphones on and the only time I got up was to go to the bathroom.'

'And when was that?' Irene asked.

Casey considered. 'Two, three o'clock, something like that. At least it was the first time I went out.'

'The first time?'

He nodded. 'Yeah. Someone was in the bathroom when I first tried. I knocked, but they didn't answer, so I went back to my room and listened to some more music. I think I may have fallen asleep for a while, and then I woke up and I REALLY needed to go pee, so I went out again, but they were still in there. They still didn't answer when I knocked again.'

Wolfgang sighed as if he was clearly bored. 'So what did you do? Piss in the sink?'

Casey gave him a dirty look. 'No, I'm not a pig. I went to the bathroom on the first floor.'

Irene tapped her chin. 'Who do you think was in your bathroom on the second floor?'

He shrugged again. 'I guessed it was the stuck-up British chick,' he answered.

'Sarah Wilkinson?'

'Yeah,' he replied. 'My dad was out walking with her dad, and the third bedroom on the second floor was empty, so I figured it had to be her. You know what chicks are like once they get in the bathroom,' he added with a sarcastic laugh. 'Anyway, I went to the bathroom, and then back to my room and that's where I stayed until my father came back and we went down for dinner. And, well, you know what happened next.'

Wolfgang exhaled. 'If only we knew what happened next, young man. *If only.*'

Ben edged forward, each step feeling slower and more forced. It was almost as if he was stabbing his feet into quicksand, slowly sinking more and more with each step. He was not even sure where the sense of foreboding came from, other than it was something he had become accustomed to in recent years.

Montgenoux, the town of his birth, had been swathed in darkness for a long time, beginning decades before his birth. The culmination of evil, much of it stemming from his father and the men he called brothers. Together they had created a devastating series of events which had put Ben and the three people he loved most in mortal danger on more than one occasion. His father was now dead, but the fallout of his legacy was something everyone who knew him was still having to deal with.

It was also the reason why, he supposed, he had jumped on a plane on what he was sure everyone was calling a fool's errand. Apart from Hugo, Ben thought unable to hide the smile that danced across his face every time he thought of him, his spirits already lifting just by the thought of the gentle giant who held him in his arms each and every night. Hugo had taught Ben everything there was about love, even though Hugo knew little of it himself. It was simply because he was naturally filled with love.

'Whatever you're smiling about, I'm jealous you have something that makes you so happy,' Viviane Auclair said with a warm giggle.

Ben looked at the cobbled path ahead of them. It was uneven, several of the stones broken and upturned and it was necessary to pay careful attention to each step or it was likely a person would take a tumble. 'I was just reminded of my own rocky path and how easy it becomes when you have someone to walk with,' he replied with a sad lilt to his voice.

'You're lucky,' Viviane said glumly.

'You're damn right I am,' Ben agreed. 'And I know it, well, most of the time, at least. But listen, your turn will come.' He noticed the doubtful look on her face. 'Je sais, je sais! When someone says that to you, it's annoying. I used to feel the same. I never thought my turn would come. I truly didn't. But it did, and yours will too. Isn't there anyone on the horizon?'

She shrugged, a flush appearing on her cheeks. 'There is someone,' she breathed. 'Trouble is, he doesn't know I'm alive.'

'Then he's blind,' Ben told her. 'But either way, move on to someone who isn't. That's my advice.'

Viviane snorted. 'I wish it was that easy.'

'Oh, I never said it was easy,' Ben reasoned, 'and I never said I was any good at it myself, mais…' he laughed again, 'I am older and wiser and I've made it through to the other side… eventually!'

She sighed sadly. 'Anyway, we should be at the next village in a few minutes.'

They continued the rest of the way in silence. Although there was still a chill in the air and it was still dark as night, the rain had subsided, but the remnants of the storm were everywhere. Ben sidestepped a mudslide in the middle of the road, slipping and having to steady himself against a tree. He was relieved to see the road was ending and opening up into a small village.

'Is there a police station here?' he asked.

Viviane shrugged. 'I doubt it. There's probably a radio office, but they're not always manned. The best bet is to head to the bar. That's where everyone will be, I imagine, and the owner will know who to call.'

Ben nodded. 'Good idea. Lead the way.'

Viviane stepped in front of him, guiding them through what appeared to be a deserted village, but as they rounded a corner, he was relieved to see there was a large bar in the corner and it was crowded with people, many of them young. Viviane called out, waving her hand excitedly.

'Hey, Viv!' a young man called out, jumping over the veranda and striding towards them.

'Hi, Xav,' Viviane replied awkwardly as if she was both embarrassed and pleased to see him at the same time.

The way her face lit up told Ben everything he needed to know. This was the young man she had been talking about. Ben guessed he was, like Viviane, in his very early twenties.

'Ben, this is Xavier Cadieux,' she said breathlessly, her cheeks flushed. 'He also works as a guide. Xav, this is Ben Beaupain, he hired me.'

Xavier held out his hand and shook Ben's. 'Nice to meet you, man,' he said in a deep, breathy voice.

'You too,' Ben smiled. In a former lifetime, when he was a young man desperately looking for love, Ben had come across what seemed like hundreds of men exactly like Xavier Cadieux. Excessively and almost ridiculously handsome young men. Wide eyes and unblemished skin with dark, thick curly hair and a tall and lithe body poured into too tight a t-shirt and jeans. Fleshy lips always pulled into a suggestion, head turned in a confident and somewhat predatory stance. Ben had had his heart broken on more than one occasion by someone like him.

Xavier continued, staring at him. 'Do I know you?' he asked.

Ben shook his head. 'I don't think so, not unless you've been to Montgenoux.'

'Doubt it,' Xavier replied. There was no judgement in his voice, but Ben thought there was something curious about him.

'We need your help, Xav,' Viviane said quickly. 'It looks like the bridge to *Chemin des Pèlerins* was blown down during the storm.'

'Dammit!' he hissed. 'I kept saying this was going to happen and no one would listen. Too tight to spend money to fix it and instead praying to Dieu to save it! Ridiculous,' he added angrily. 'The phone lines being down is one thing. That happens pretty much every time there's a storm.'

'Xav is the friend I was telling you about,' Viviane explained. 'He lives with his parents in *Chemin des Pèlerins*, most of the time,' she explained to Ben.

Xavier glanced over his shoulder. 'Hey, buddy,' he called out to one of his friends. 'Bring some beers. Our pilgrims here look a little road weary'

'Sure thing,' his friend replied.

'We shouldn't really,' Ben replied. 'I need to find my friends…'

'And you will,' Xavier said, slapping him on the back, 'but we have to wait for help and that's gonna take a while, so you might as well be comfortable, non? Okay, wait for your beers and I'll go and make some phone calls.'

Ben nodded reluctantly.

Ben sipped his beer and took a long drag on a cigarette and for the first time in days, he began to feel relaxed as if there was a light at the end of the tunnel. He hoped there was. He just wanted the whole sorry business to be over and back to his nice, safe cottage in Montgenoux.

Xavier appeared from the bar. 'I talked to the flics,' he called out. 'They'll do what they can, but everything is backed up because of the storm,' he added.

'Damn,' Ben complained.

'What about the phone line and the bridge?' Viviane asked.

'They're working on it,' he replied. 'But it's going to be a couple of days at least before anyone can get out to fix the bridge.' He shrugged. 'I've ordered some more beers. It looks like you're going nowhere for a while, at least.'

'I really need to get there,' Ben cried desperately.

'Are you sure your friends are even in *Chemin des Pèlerins?*'

Xavier asked.

'Not exactly,' Ben replied, feeling foolish yet again. 'Mais it was where she said they were heading the last time I spoke to her and that they were going to spend some time there until the storm passed.'

Xavier nodded. 'Sounds like a sensible thing to do. So, what's the problem?'

Ben took another drag. 'Well, she said she would call or text every day, but I've heard nothing, not for days now.'

'As Viv said, the phone lines are down and the Wi-Fi signal around here is atrocious,' Xavier reasoned. 'Your friend is probably just holed up in the hotel, bored out of her skull.'

'Probably,' Ben agreed. 'And I know I'm being oversensitive, but the last time we spoke she also said something a little weird, something about her tour guide Maurice Rousseau and that something was off with him.'

Xavier laughed. 'Yeah, that sounds like Maurice.'

'You know him?'

'Only for most of my life,' Xavier replied. 'And yeah, he is a little off. Harmless enough though, I suppose.' He paused, his eyes narrowing. 'Wait, your friend isn't part of the reunion group who are here for the first time in forty years, is she?'

Ben nodded. 'Oui. She's here with her mother, who was with the rest of the people on the last pilgrimage. Why?'

Xavier and Viviane exchanged a look. 'It's nothing, really,' Xavier began. 'As I said, Maurice is a bit of an oddball, that's all. As far as I can remember, he's been going on and on about something that happened forty years ago and that one of these days he'd finally get answers.'

Ben sucked in a breath. 'What happened forty years ago?'

Xavier shrugged. 'No one talks about it. All I know is he's been desperate for revenge over something for longer than I've been alive.' He noticed the panic on Ben's face. 'Désolé, I didn't mean to worry you. You must know what it's like in small villages like these. People bear grudges for no real reason. And your friend wasn't even on the last pilgrimage, so it has nothing to do with her.'

Ben shook his head irritably, pushing the curls away from his forehead. 'Non, but her parents were, and not to mention Irene is there with her five-year-old son, so they could all be in danger.' He paused. 'This man, Maurice Rousseau - what's he like? Is he dangerous?'

Xavier and Viviane exchanged another look. 'I wouldn't say dangerous. A few bar fights, that's all.'

'Didn't you once tell me he beat someone up so badly they ended up in a coma?' Viviane interrupted.

Xavier glared at her. 'Yeah, but that was just another bar fight over a gambling debt, or a woman, who knows?'

'But it shows he has a temper, and he's dangerous and if you're right, he's been nursing a grudge for over forty fucking years,' Ben said, clenching his fists. 'Dieu knows what he's capable of.' He lowered his head. 'What am I going to do?'

'They have rooms in the tavern, so you can stay here until help arrives,' Viviane suggested.

'I can't just sit here for Dieu knows how long,' Ben cried. 'Especially if this Monsieur Rousseau is out for revenge and Irene is caught up in the middle of it.'

Xavier tapped his chin, looking at Ben pensively. 'When I was younger, there was a way we used to sneak in and out of the village,' he explained. 'They used to lock the gates on either side of the bridge, you see,' he added with a laugh, 'worried that some outsider might actually want to waste their time sneaking in!'

Ben leaned forward keenly. 'What do you mean, sneak in and out? We've been there today. Without the bridge, there's a sheer drop to the river, and it's far too far to jump.'

Xavier grinned. 'Yeah, but you probably didn't notice there are trees on the left side, just in front of the embankment and behind them, there's a narrow gap, which means you can sort of climb down the trees and once you get to the bottom, you can swim to the other side and climb up the tree on that side.'

'I never knew that,' Viviane said.

'We told no one,' Xavier replied, 'because we certainly didn't want our parents to know we were sneaking out to party because if they did, they'd have cut down the damn trees, I'm sure!'

Ben lit another cigarette, slowly tapping his chin. 'Then we'll do that. We'll get into *Chemin des Pèlerins* that way.'

Xavier shook his head forcefully. 'It's not possible. We did it when we were kids. The fact is, it's dangerous, and the gap is narrow and it would be so easy to fall down.'

'I may be older than you, but I'm NOT that old,' Ben stated tartly.

Xavier stared at Viviane. Her mouth contorted as if she could not decide. He shrugged. 'I suppose I should check on my parents too,' he said finally. 'Maman hasn't been well and I hate to think of her and Papa cut off.' He glanced at his watch. 'I can't go tonight, though. I have to meet someone in the next town.'

'Can't you cancel?' Ben asked desperately. 'I'd pay you for your time.'

Xavier shook his head. 'I can't. I promised them and I'll get into trouble with the agency if I leave a paying customer high and dry, and I really need this job. We can go tomorrow first thing, I promise.'

'I can't wait,' Ben said. 'I'll go on my own.'

Xavier sighed. 'D'accord. Listen, go with him Viv and keep an eye on him and I'll catch up with you both tomorrow?'

Viviane nodded. 'Bien sûr.'

Xavier stood. 'I'll get going then.'

Ben smiled gratefully at him. 'Merci for everything, Xavier, I mean that.'

The handsome man with dark eyes grinned a perfect, even

smile at him. 'My pleasure.'

'Will you check up on the police and the bridge repair, too?' Ben asked.

'Absolutely,' he replied before retreating off into the distance.

'Shall we go?' Ben asked Viviane.

'Can you give me half an hour?' she asked. 'I just have to let my friends know where I'm going.'

Ben exhaled, realising he should also make a call. 'Good idea. Can you show me to a phone? I should call my husband and let him know what's happening.'

'Sure, follow me. And don't look so worried. Everything's in hand now. Xavier's super. He'll make sure everything is sorted out and before you know it, you and your friends will be on your way home.'

Ben crossed his fingers, mouthing a prayer he desperately wanted to believe.

'I can't tell you how good it is to hear your voice,' Hugo exhaled as if breathing properly for the first time that day.

'Oh, I have an idea. I only wish I could see your beautiful face,' Ben replied, lowering his voice because he realised everyone in the bar could likely hear the discussion. 'Are you mad at me? I knew you would try to stop me by using common sense, and I didn't want to give you the chance because you could talk me out of anything just by looking at me. Do you hate me?'

'Non, bien sûr, non,' Hugo answered quickly. 'I told you I understood your reasons. Anyway, what's happening?'

'Well, the storm seems to have passed, for now at least. I found the village where I think Irene and the others are, but the phone lines are down and, to make matters worse, the storm has demolished the damn bridge, which is the only way in and out of the village.'

Hugo was silent as he took in the news, taking a moment to light a cigarette. He knew he had to be supportive of Ben, but he had a feeling he would not like what came next.

'The plan is I'm heading back to the village with my guide, Viviane,' Ben continued, 'so hopefully in a few hours I'll have found Irene and the others.'

Hugo took a long drag on the cigarette. 'Wait. You said the bridge was destroyed, and it was the only way to get into the village. If that's the case, how are you going to get in?' he demanded.

Ben did not answer the question. 'Viviane's friend, Xavier, is also a guide, and he's alerted the authorities, so help is on the way, but they don't think they can get anyone to fix the bridge for a few days at least and I just don't want to wait. Before you say it, I know, but then Xavier confirmed there's something off about the tour guide Maurice Rousseau. I don't really understand, but something happened forty years ago on the last pilgrimage and he's had a hankering for revenge ever since.'

'Ben, this isn't something you should be getting involved in,' Hugo said wearily. 'At least wait until the local police arrive. Let them deal with it…'

'I wish people would stop telling me to leave it,' Ben snapped angrily. 'I'm not some stupid, helpless damsel in distress.'

'And nor is Irene,' Hugo retorted. 'And we're only saying these things because we care for you.'

Ben noticed Viviane had finished her own call. 'Listen, cher, I have to go. Just don't worry, okay? I'll call you as soon as I can, but if I can't get through, you can call the hotel here. It's a village called Millieure, and it's about ten kilometres away from *Chemin des Pèlerins*. Ask for Xavier Cadieux, if he's not around, I'm sure they'll know how to get in touch with him.'

Hugo scribbled the names on a notepad.

'Oh, and he's a bit of a hunk, so don't think of flirting with him, okay?' Ben added lightly.

'I wish you weren't doing this,' Hugo said, knowing again he had already lost the argument.

'Don't worry, it'll be fine. Au revoir, mon amour.'

Irene, Wolfgang & Tony

Irene watched as Tony Wilkinson entered the Café from the narrow, winding staircase. He walked with the gait of a man who was confident in his own skin and his position in life. She recalled Dorothy telling her he was some kind of investment banker in London, so Irene imagined he was a very successful and, most likely, rich man.

Tony sat down, smoothing down the black hair on top of his head that was not his own. He glanced at Irene's cell phone on the table. 'My earlier point stands. Recording conversations is highly unorthodox.'

'And yet you know you're being recorded, so what's the problem?' Wolfgang responded, clearly bored.

'You were part of the original pilgrimage forty years ago?' Irene asked, eager to move along. She realised there was probably not a lot to learn from the pilgrims, but it felt good to be actually engaged in something constructive.

Tony nodded. 'Yes, along with my wife, Jane. We had always intended on coming again. However, life had different plans for us,' he responded, his voice hoarse. 'We tried, but it was not meant to be. She died a few years ago, even though the grim reaper took his time to claim her.'

'I'm sorry to hear that,' Wolfgang replied. 'I recall Jane to be a rather special, delicate woman. The archetypal English rose, no?'

Tony lowered his head, shaking it slowly.

Wolfgang gave Tony a moment to compose himself. 'What do you recall about the afternoon of Monsieur Bonnet's death?'

Tony lifted his head, moving his shoulders nonchalantly. 'Very little. I accompanied Sam Mitchell for a walk around this delightful village. I can't say exactly how long it lasted. Much of it was a case of dodging showers, but it was pleasant enough. Though we have as little in common now as we did forty years ago, but as I said, it was agreeable enough. We walked and then Sam went back to the Café. I stayed outside for a while, taking shelter under a canopy, making some notes concerning work back home, and then when I was done, I also returned to the Café.'

'And did you see anything or anyone when you returned?' Wolfgang asked.

Tony shook his head. 'No. The Café was deserted as far as I can remember.' He considered. 'Yes. I'm fairly sure there was no one either inside, or outside. I then went upstairs for a nap.'

Wolfgang nodded. 'And your daughter?'

Tony stared at him, his eyes fixed. 'She was resting,' he stated, before adding in a lighter tone. 'I mean, what else is there to do?'

'And there's nothing else you can think of?' Irene asked.

Tony smiled. 'Not a single thing.'

Hugo & Etienne

After a particularly long and tedious day in Montgenoux court, Hugo knew the only thing he should be thinking about was going home, dangling his feet in the swimming pool, drinking ice-cold beer and smoking copious amounts of cigarettes and wrapping his free arm around Ben. However, he knew that was not going to happen, at least not anytime soon.

Etienne Martine appeared in the doorway to Hugo's office. A civilian forensic expert working for the police judiciaire, and one of the foremost in France as far as Hugo was concerned who had helped solve a myriad of complicated and often despicable crimes. Etienne had also become one of the few friends Hugo had ever managed to accumulate in his life. He was an unorthodox man, prone to dressing in flip-flops, board shorts and bright Hawaiian shirts, despite the occasion or the season, it seemingly made no difference to him. With Etienne by his side, Hugo knew he had someone whose superior intellect and ability were a direct assault on those fighting against good.

'How's it going?' Etienne asked, his voice devoid of its usual lightness.

Hugo recognised the tone. It was the same one he had heard from Etienne in the months since Irene Chapeau had decided to take a sabbatical from her job and her life in Montgenoux. The two were in a relationship of sorts, but not one Hugo understood or felt comfortable enough to ask about.

Hugo grimaced and lit a cigarette, although he had just extinguished one.

Etienne jumped into a seat. 'Spill, H.'

Hugo sighed. 'Ben's worried about Irene, and while I understand it, I'm not entirely sure I agree, and yet...'

'And yet?'

He shrugged again. 'As reluctant as I am to admit it, something seems off about the whole situation. But that's probably more to do with the fact I'm paid to never take things at face value.'

Etienne pressed his hands against the desk, leaning in and studying Hugo's face intently. 'And what aren't you buying in this instance? If there really is a problem with Irene and Bruno, we shouldn't ignore it. We *can't* ignore it,' he added forcefully.

'Oui, oui,' Hugo conceded, he was not sure how much Etienne knew about Irene's current situation and although he was reluctant to discuss it, he was also aware that if there was anything amiss he was going to need Etienne's assistance. He took a deep breath and explained everything he had learned so far.

'A village cut off by a storm? A dodgy tour guide who may have a grudge to bear about something that happened forty years ago? No phone lines? Have I missed something?' Etienne repeated, his tone displaying his concern. His lips twisted as if he was attempting to reassure himself. 'I mean I suppose it could just be Ben's imagination causing him to worry unnecessarily...'

'I agree,' Hugo replied, relieved to speak his concerns aloud. After a moment, the concern returned. 'Ben is worried, and because Ben is worried, I have to be, too. Although at this point I'm probably more concerned about the fact Ben seems intent on finding his way into a village that has lost its only way in and out. He dodged the question about how he intended on getting in, which probably troubles me more than anything.'

Etienne laughed. He had known Ben for a long time and was well aware of how determined he could be when the situation called for it. 'What can I do?'

Hugo smiled, dragging slowly on the cigarette. 'Are you busy right now?'

Etienne smiled. 'For the people I love, I always can find time. I take it you want me to find everything I can on the mysterious tour guide and the pilgrims?'

Hugo stubbed out the cigarette. 'If anyone can put this to rest, it's you. It would be nice to convince Ben the only bad thing going on is a horrible storm.'

Etienne jumped to his feet. 'Order in some pizzas and beers from *Arienne's* and I'll be back with everything I've discovered before you know it.'

Irene, Wolfgang & Sarah

Sarah Wilkinson's entrance to the Café was distinctly different to her father's. She lingered by the stairs; her face almost completely covered by fine, dark hair. She slowly made her way towards Irene and Wolfgang, pulling a chair from under the table and positioning it carefully, all the time chewing anxiously on her fingernails. Irene gave her a warm smile, hoping to make the young woman feel less scared. Their eyes met and for a moment, Irene imagined it was not fear in the young Englishwoman's eyes, but rather anger.

'How are you feeling?' Irene asked slowly in English.

Sarah moved her shoulders slowly but said nothing.

Wolfgang rolled his eyes as if he was bored with having to deal with the other members of the group. 'As you know, we're asking everyone to recall their movements on the afternoon when our friend died. What do you recall, my dear?'

'Nothing,' she answered sharply.

'Nothing at all?' Irene questioned.

'Nothing at all,' Sarah repeated. 'Why would I? I was in my room. I went there after lunch and stayed there until we came down for supper.'

Wolfgang nodded. 'And you didn't see anyone else?'

Sarah gave him a curious look. 'In my room? No, of course, I didn't see anyone else. Not least until my father came back from his walk, but I was listening to music, so I didn't pay attention to him, or the time,' she explained matter-of-factly as if she was reading a shopping list.

Wolfgang looked to Irene, his expression relaying a clear thought to her. *She's lying.*

Irene sipped her water. 'And you never left the room until you came down in the evening?'

Sarah bit down on her fingernail. 'That's what I said.'

Irene watched the young woman carefully. She was having trouble reading her. At first, she had imagined Sarah to be a shy young woman, but there was something else hiding behind her aloofness, Irene was sure of it. 'Did you hear anyone else on your floor that afternoon?'

Sarah's left eye twitched. 'What do you mean? Who would I hear? I had my headphones on. The only person I heard was my father when he came back.' She rose abruptly to her feet, pushing the chair back irritably. 'Are we done here? I want to go back to my room. I don't like it down here,' she said, glancing fearfully towards the closed storeroom door.

Noticing that Wolfgang was about to protest, Irene raised her hand to pacify him because she realised they would likely get nowhere by attempting to force Sarah to cooperate. 'You can go back to your room, Sarah,' she said softly.

Irene and Wolfgang watched her leave. Wolfgang turned his head. 'Well well well. Tell me, Dr. Chapeau, are you about to suggest the English father and daughter weren't both lying through their teeth?'

Irene was reluctant to agree with the former German police officer, although she agreed there appeared to be something off. 'I can't answer that. I'm not an expert in these things.'

Wolfgang stood up, rubbing his chin. 'Well I am, and I am here to tell you with utmost certainty that they are both faced liars.'

Irene rose, pulling the now empty chair back under the table. While her instinct told her there was something off with the English travellers, she was not sure she would go so far as to call them liars. 'The chances are whatever it is, it may have nothing to do with the murder,' she suggested. 'Everyone reacts to situations like these in different ways.'

Wolfgang looked towards the staircase. 'Yes they do, don't they?' he responded with a considered smile.

Hugo nibbled the edge of a pizza slice and took a healthy slug of ice-cold beer, smacking his lips contentedly.

Etienne appeared, laughing. 'You look like you're enjoying that.'

Hugo took another bite. 'I seem to have survived on nothing but court cafeteria food for days, and it isn't great. Have you found anything?'

Etienne dropped a file on his desk. 'I searched for Irene's tour group. Luckily official groups are registered, just so the authorities have some way of tracking who is walking to Camino at any particular time and who they're with. We're lucky because if they weren't part of a group, we'd have nothing to track.'

Hugo gestured for Etienne to take a seat and slid the pizza box over the table. He lit a cigarette. 'Anything interesting?'

'Excluding Irene and Bruno, the group comprises eight others,' Etienne began, nibbling on the edge of a pizza slice. 'Irene's mother, Dorothy. Then we have a German couple, Wolfgang and Elke Huber. As far as I can tell, Wolfgang Huber is a decorated retired police officer. A couple of reprimands for excessive force and the odd suggestion of impropriety and bribery, but nothing proved as far as I can tell. All in all, a typical cop, non?'

Hugo snorted, gesturing for him to continue.

'His wife is a retired secretary. No kids and no obvious skeletons lurking in their closet.' Etienne continued.

'Next up, we have an altogether more interesting character - Tony Wilkinson,' he added. 'He's on the pilgrimage with his twenty-five-year-old daughter, Sarah. Mr. Wilkinson is, or was, an investment banker in London, but for the last decade he's been in and out of the High Court on one charge or another, insider trading, that sort of thing.'

Hugo pursed his lips. 'Very interesting, I'm sure, but I can't imagine it has anything to do with what's happening now.'

'Probably not,' Etienne conceded. 'I only had time to pull up a few newspaper articles, I printed them in the folder for you to have a look at, but as far as I can tell, he got very rich, often despite his clients, who didn't take it too well. However, he ended up losing millions and was about to go bankrupt when...' he trailed off dramatically.

Hugo raised an eyebrow. 'When, what?' he repeated.

'His wife died under mysterious circumstances,' Etienne replied. 'I quickly checked the police reports though and nothing came of any investigation as far as I can tell. Jane Wilkinson was involved in a hit-and-run. They never found the other driver and CCTV didn't help, so they ruled the death an accident. Some might say it was fortuitous because it turns out Jane Wilkinson was from old English aristocracy and her death meant he came into a lot of money. We're talking twenty million pounds, give or take. Just what he needed at exactly the right moment. Paid off his debts and left him enough to start again.'

Hugo nodded. 'You said you checked the police reports. Was there any suggestion of Tony Wilkinson's involvement in his wife's death?'

'They certainly investigated him,' Etienne responded. 'Why wouldn't they? But he had an alibi, of course, and the investigating team found no paper trail suggesting he'd paid anyone off, so case closed, I suppose.'

'You mentioned he had a daughter?'

'Yeah. Sarah Wilkinson has been in and out of clinics, according to the newspaper articles. Some state for substance abuse, others suggest it was anorexia.'

Hugo sighed, suddenly feeling very weary. It was an awful part of his job, picking through the private lives of people just because they were involved in something he was investigating.

'What about the other people in the group?'

'There are three more. Sam Mitchell and his son, Casey. Americans. Sam is an ex-football player with apparently a promising career cut short by injury. He now writes travel blogs and books. I checked some reviews. They sell reasonably well, but they're not universally liked by the critics, it seems. He also has quite an extensive criminal record in the States, mainly DUI's, but a few assaults and batteries as well, mainly on his ex-wife. The son seems to be a perpetual student. Starts one degree but never finishes it and moves on to another.'

'And the final traveller?'

'Edith Lancaster,' Etienne replied. 'British, in her eighties and a retired librarian,' he smiled. 'So, as you can imagine, no criminal record or sniff of trouble.'

'Which brings us to the tour guide,' Hugo concluded. 'What can you tell me about Monsieur Maurice Rousseau, the man Irene seems to have been concerned about?'

Etienne gulped, his throat visibly tightening. Hugo was not sure if it was the mention of Irene's name again, or the realisation she imagined there was some kind of danger posed by the guide. 'Absolutely nothing,' Etienne grumbled in a way which suggested he was entirely dissatisfied with himself. 'Barely any mention of anything. Certainly no criminal record. The only thing of interest was a microfiche of an old local newspaper from about forty years ago, which suggested there was some kind of tragedy in *Chemin des Pèlerins*. It's all very vague, but it mentions the wife of a local man appears to have lost her footing and was swept away in a river during a violent storm. I can't even say for certain if it's him, other than it mentions the village.'

Hugo tapped his chin. 'All the same, it's interesting. Particularly bearing in mind what Ben just told me about something happening on the previous pilgrimage forty years ago and how Rousseau has been seeking some kind of revenge ever since. As always, it amazes me you manage to dig up so much in such a short space of time.'

'Give me more time and I can tell you everything there is to know about each and every one of them.'

Hugo sighed, glumly sipping the rest of his beer. 'Oh, I don't know what to do for the best,' he complained.

Etienne stared at him. 'I don't think we can ignore the fact Irene thought there was something off, and that's why Ben was worried about her, and I don't think it's just because he's being overly cautious. He knows her. You know her. I know her. What if she's not just worrying unnecessarily? The fact is, H, we've all been through some traumatic shit in the last seven years and we have our instincts. Irene may have had little to go on, but the fact she sensed something was off means something, non?'

Hugo sighed, reached to his packet of cigarettes and lit one, blowing smoke petulantly into the air.

'The same goes for Ben. He took off to the other side of the country on the off-chance she was right,' Etienne continued, his eyebrow raised. 'Because he knows too.'

Hugo narrowed emerald green eyes towards his friend. 'What are you saying?'

Etienne grinned. 'I've booked you a flight. I'm afraid it leaves at 05h45, but that can't be helped. I also found the guide Ben mentioned to you, and he's going to meet you and take you directly to the village.'

Hugo stubbed out his cigarette. 'This is quite ridiculous. I have a job to do,' he said tartly, knowing full well he was going to go anyway.

Etienne shrugged. 'The court case is concluded. Another criminal is in jail, thanks to you. Markus, Marianne, Mare-Louise and I can hold the fort here, and we'll call Nantes for backup if we can't. Go bring back our friends,' he suggested, his mouth contorting.

Irene, Wolfgang & Edith

Edith Lancaster's knitting needles moved with such ferociousness, it scared Irene because it appeared dangerous. The elderly British librarian did not look up at any point. She had entered the Café quietly and positioned herself in front of Irene and Wolfgang without uttering a word. She smoothed the skirt of a smart grey tweed suit as she sat.

'Thank you for talking to us,' Wolfgang began.

Edith tutted, barely hiding her irritation. 'I wasn't under the impression we had a say in the matter,' she sniffed haughtily.

'What do you recall of the events on Tuesday after approximately 13h00,' Wolfgang continued.

She sighed. 'I ate a passable lunch, then retired to my room. I said my prayers and knitted for a little while. It helps me to relax, especially when in strange surroundings,' she added, staring at the knitting on her lap.

Irene smiled, unsure what the item was, other than it appeared grey and shapeless.

'And then I took a nap,' Edith continued, thin lips pulling into a tight smile. 'I find as one gets older, one rather becomes like a cat, napping at the most inopportune moments with ever-increasing regularity.'

Wolfgang nodded, clearly stifling a yawn. 'And how long did you nap for?'

Edith shrugged. Irene noticed her wincing, and she again wondered how any of these people were going to manage to walk the whole Camino. Edith spotted her looking. 'Yes, getting old is a bore,' she addressed Irene. 'But I should point out one thing to you, young lady. I hear you talking to your mother, and the way you talk to her, and whilst I believe you do it out of love and kindness, I also believe it is entirely disrespectful, and, frankly, condescending,' she sniped.

Irene's eyebrow raised. 'I can assure you, that is not my intention.'

Edith continued knitting. 'I'm sure you believe that, I don't imagine you intend to be cruel. But the way you speak to your mother, and the way you look at me, and the rest of us, you are merely informing us YOU don't believe us to be capable and that you know better than the rest of us simply because you have a medical degree.'

Irene looked at Wolfgang. He tipped his head. 'She has a point.'

Edith snorted. 'I'm sure it's the first time I've ever heard you say something like that about a woman, Wolfgang Huber.'

He chuckled. 'You're probably correct, old lady, but I wouldn't get used to it.'

She narrowed small eyes at him. 'You're not so far behind me, *old* man.'

'I'm sorry about the way I've been behaving,' Irene blurted in English suddenly overwhelmed with a rush of emotions. 'I did not know I was being so... so...'

'Annoying. Patronising. Disrespectful...'

Irene held up her hands. 'Okay, okay! I get the message. I'm a worry wort.'

Edith's mouth pulled into a reluctant smile. 'My point is, just because we're old, and maybe a little stubborn doesn't mean we aren't aware of our limitations. I have longed to make this pilgrimage again, and time has finally allowed me to do so. I wish it could have been sooner, but I can't do a lot about that now. What I am in charge of is putting one foot in front of another and asking our Lord to grant me the strength to continue for as long as possible.'

'Or the wisdom to know when to stop before we end up dead in a ditch,' Wolfgang added dryly.

Edith tutted again, before dropping her knitting needles and facing Irene. 'That is my point, though I would have phrased it better, I'm sure. Your mother is a strong woman, but she is no fool. We are all walking the Camino for our different reasons, but you have to trust us when we say we know our limitations.'

Irene nodded slowly. 'I am beginning to understand that, and honestly, it isn't my intention to offend anyone.' She exhaled. 'I'll do better.'

Wolfgang clapped his hands together. 'Now we've got that out of the way. Can we continue?' He glanced at his watch. 'It's getting late and I'm rather peckish. So, let's move on. When you were in your room, do you recall hearing anything?'

Edith considered for a few minutes before finally shaking her head. 'Hearing, like the rest of the body, needs a little extra help as we age. I heard nothing,' she added, 'though whether there was anything to be heard, I can't say.'

'How well did you know Alain Bonnet?' Irene asked.

'He was a fine, fine, God-fearing man,' Edith replied, her voice cracking. 'And he always looked after us very well. Whoever plunged a knife into his back was a coward, no doubt sent directly from Beelzebub himself. I mean, what other explanation could there be?'

Irene was not sure how to respond. 'Did you keep in touch with him?'

Edith nodded. 'He and Maurice both. We exchanged letters, cards and occasionally a telephone call, though not very often. A librarian is not exactly paid vast amounts of money, which is just as well because I live a prudent life, as God advises.'

Irene nodded. 'Did he ever suggest he was having problems?'

Edith gave her a curious look. 'I can't imagine what sort of relationship you might think I have with men, but I can disabuse you of any sordid thoughts which may be circulating your twenty-first-century brain.'

For the first time in a long time, Irene felt her cheeks reddening in the same way they used to when her old teacher, Mademoiselle Fontebleu, would scold her, often for playing too roughly with the other boys in her class. *Proper girls don't behave that way.* 'I meant no disrespect,' Irene apologised.

'Of course, she didn't,' Wolfgang bristled. 'So, stop being such an old harridan, Edith Lancaster, and answer the damn question.'

Edith glared at him but seemingly thought better than to argue. 'I recall the odd relaying of problems here and there, but if you expect me to recall details, then you will be sadly mistaken, and I return to my original point. Alain Bonnet was a good man who did not deserve to be stabbed in the back.' She rose sharply, pushing the chair back irritably. 'Now, we are done here,' she stated, not as a request but as an instruction, 'and I must say my prayers before supper. I bid you farewell.'

Irene and Wolfgang watched Edith move quickly across the room, disappearing up the staircase with a dexterity of a woman half her age.

Wolfgang turned to Irene. 'What do you think of our frail English spinster, then?' he asked.

Irene watched the empty space. 'I think she'd stab any one of us with one of those knitting needles and probably not think twice about it.'

Wolfgang laughed. 'I think you're probably right.'

Irene, Wolfgang & Maurice

Maurice Rousseau entered the room. Irene's head was lowered, absent-mindedly stirring a long-cold café, while Wolfgang tapped out a symphony with his fingers on the table.

'You've spoken with everyone?' Maurice demanded.

Wolfgang's head jerked upwards. He winced with pain and rubbed the back of his neck. 'Ya,' he replied.'

'Et?'

Irene and Wolfgang exchanged a look.

'There are some concerns,' Wolfgang stated finally, with sheer reluctance. 'Whether those concerns are relevant, I'm afraid I'm hard-pressed to say at this moment.'

'What does that even mean?' Maurice snapped. 'Are they, or are they not involved in Alain's murder?'

'I simply cannot say with any degree of certainty,' Wolfgang conceded.

Maurice slammed his fists on the table. 'Then thrash it out of them if you have to! Isn't that what you people do?'

Wolfgang clenched his fists. 'I'm not sure what you mean, but if it is what I think it is, I would counsel you to remember my age and the things I have seen in my lifetime. My entire childhood was informed by the monsters who came before me. My parents and God made sure I and people like me did not travel the same path. We have asked questions,' he pointed at Irene, 'and Dr. Chapeau has preserved the interviews on her cell phone for the local authorities. If there is more to be gleaned, they must do it and not us.'

'I don't agree,' Maurice snapped back.

Wolfgang emitted a sad sigh. 'This isn't a kangaroo court, Maurice,' he said. 'And I won't allow it to become one. I may technically be a retired police officer, but the fact is, you never really retire. I know what I am doing, and I know what is right.'

Maurice clambered to his feet. 'You're in my town, pilgrim. You would do well to remember that. I'll find out what happened one way or another, you see if I don't.'

Before Wolfgang could respond, Maurice moved to the counter. 'Now, it's getting late. I'm going to arrange supper.'

Ben & Viviane

Ben and Viviane walked along the road in silence, pushing their way through the howling wind. The rain had finally become intermittent, though as night descended, the foreboding clouds were becoming even more oppressive as the moon began rising.

'Ben...' Viviane cried out, trying to catch up to him.

Ben ignored her, knowing full well what she was going to say and how they should stop before it got any darker.

'Ben,' she repeated.

He stopped, staring at her wide-eyed. 'Listen, I know. You don't need to say it. We should have listened to Xavier and waited until morning, mais...'

She touched his arm. 'I wasn't going to say that.' She pointed over her shoulder. 'It's just you were walking so fast you missed the turning to the village. Now, come on, if we're going to do this, let's do it before it gets any darker and wetter.'

They moved quickly and silently back to the turnoff and were soon faced with the remains of the bridge into *Chemin des Pèlerins*. Ben pointed to the left, to a row of trees as tall as a building, all lining the edge of the village. He peered over the verge down into the ravine. The trees appeared rooted in the embankment at the bottom.

'Those must be the trees Xavier was talking about,' Ben pointed.

Viviane nodded, and they moved across the clearing. Viviane peered behind the trees. 'Xav was right, there isn't much of a gap.'

Ben narrowed his eyes, pressing his hand between the tree and the gap. Viviane was right. There was barely room for an adult to fit and he could see why it had never occurred to anyone it might be a possible escape route to and from the village for errant teenagers eagerly searching for adventure.

Viviane pursed her lips. 'Ben, I'm not sure we can fit down there and it looks pretty ropey. It could be dangerous.'

Ben took a deep breath. 'Viviane, I'm so sorry for dragging you into this whole mess. It really wasn't my intention and I shouldn't have done it.' He pushed the curls from his forehead. 'As usual, I got caught up in my own drama and dragged everyone into it without really giving it a second thought. It's a terrible character flaw of mine, and I've been working on it for a long time. I thought I'd got better, and I have a little, I suppose, but when my family is involved, it's like a red mist descends on me and I can't see straight. All I can focus on is moving ahead and doing whatever I can to push the mist away. But, I am sorry, truly I am for involving you in this.'

She gave him a nonchalant smile. 'Jeez, I didn't want your life story. I'm here because I want to be and this is by far the most exciting guide gig I've ever had.' She tucked her baggy shirt into her leggings and sidled up to the tree. She pushed one leg through and then manoeuvred her body around the tree. 'Ah, I see. It's not so difficult.'

'It isn't?' Ben asked doubtfully.

'Non,' she replied, pointing beneath her. 'If you look, there are branches on either side spaced apart. The left is higher than the right, so,' she adjusted her weight, 'you can use them like stepping stones and move down.'

Ben watched horrified as Viviane moved rapidly down the tree, disappearing into the darkness, the reality of the situation suddenly dawning on him.

'Come on, keep up!' she called out.

Ben said a silent prayer, suddenly feeling very foolish and old and before he had a chance to stop himself and think too much about what he was doing, he threw himself behind the tree, wincing with pain as he tried to squeeze his body between the narrow gap. *Don't think about it, just do it,* he chastised himself and began climbing down. He moved quickly to keep up with Viviane. He could hear her beneath him as they descended into the darkness. The visibility was poor, but he reasoned it was not because of the impending nightfall, rather the trees rarefied the light.

'Are you okay?' Ben called out.

It took Viviane a few moments to respond. 'Yeah, still going. How far down is it? I seem to have been going down forever,' she complained. 'And we have to climb up the other side in wet clothes.'

Ben grimaced. 'Have I said I'm sorry?'

She snorted. 'Once or twice. But hey, I'm gonna expect a big tip after all of this.'

Ben laughed. 'Oh, you have no idea.' He stopped suddenly, hearing a big splash of water beneath him.

'Damn, that was a surprise!' Viviane called out. 'Merde, it's deep AND cold. Just get ready, Ben, because it comes at you without a warning. I'm swimming to the left, so I'll be ready to grab you.'

Ben nodded and continued his descent. Moments later, he felt his feet slip from the branch and his body dropped into the ice-cold water. He flailed, his arms reaching out desperately until Viviane caught him.

'I got you,' she called out. 'Just follow me. I think if we swim straight ahead, we'll reach the bank on the other side.'

They swam slowly. Ben's eyes took a moment to adjust, but he soon made out dim shapes of the trees and debris floating across the river.

'Here it is,' Viviane said, pressing her body against the tree. She looked around it. 'There, and there,' she pointed. 'Can you see them? The branches are on either side, like the other tree.'

Ben narrowed his eyes. 'Yeah, I think I see them.'

Viviane swung her body around, wrapping her legs around the tree and using her back against the embankment, pushed herself upwards, pressing first her left leg and then the right against the branches. It took her a while to wriggle into place but managed to drag her body upright out of the water. She let out a joyful cry. 'I'm on,' she exhaled, pulling herself upward to make room for Ben. 'C'mon, you're almost there. Just follow me.'

Ben swam the last few feet, his hands tracing around the tree until he found the branches and pulled himself up. He had difficulty moving his body out of the water and he wheezed as he attempted it, reminded again of how sedentary his perfect little life had become. He rarely regretted it, but at that moment as he tried to wrangle his thirty-three-year-old body between a narrow tree and the embankment, he perhaps wished he had used the gym membership he had started at least once or twice.

'I'm on,' he called, suddenly feeling very proud of himself, but wondering how on earth he was going to lift his sodden jeans a step higher.

'It's hard, but just take it slow and move when you can,' Viviane shouted from above. 'It gets easier.'

Ben laughed. 'I don't believe you!'

Viviane also laughed. 'Good, because I'm a lying bitch. Just tell yourself what you need to, to get up. You're going to find your friends, and I'm pretty sure you want to see your husband again, so use that to propel yourself up, or else the alternative is to freeze to death, or drown down here.'

Ben lifted his left leg forcefully and slammed it against the tree, wincing in pain. He pulled his hand to the right and lifted his other leg. It hurt, but he managed it. 'Come on, Ben, you can do this,' he carolled himself and it seemed to work, and for the first time he moved swiftly upwards. 'Just don't think about it, just keep going.'

They moved together in silence for the rest of the ascent, and it seemed to take much longer than the other side. Then the darkness of the trees lifted and between the branches he saw the sky above them, the moon a glittering, welcoming illumination.

Ben pushed himself up, his eyes taking a moment to adjust again to the change in light and atmosphere. The first thing he saw was Viviane's outstretched hand. Grateful, he reached out and grabbed for her and she pulled him onto the embankment. He fell onto his back, panting and allowing relief to swarm over him.

'We made it,' he said breathlessly.

Viviane jumped excitedly. 'That was amazing! Can we do it again?'

Ben sighed. 'Sometimes I hate young people,' he spat distastefully. He sat up and looked around. In the distance, he could see a row of houses. 'We made it,' he gasped again, barely able to believe it.

Viviane smiled. 'Then get up. Let's find your friends.'

Les Pèlerins - Dixième jour

It had been a long evening, and as the clock ticked past midnight, Irene noticed no one seemed to be in any particular hurry to leave the confines of the Café. She supposed they were all fed up from being cooped up in their rooms and having only a limited amount of space to exercise and despite the fact it was possible one of them was a cold-blooded murderer, there was something about their being safety in numbers which seemed to be offering comfort to the pilgrims.

They were now on their eighth day and Irene hoped it would be the last. She lifted her head to the ceiling. Bruno was sleeping, locked in their bedroom, and for the entire evening, Irene had been replaying over and over the conversation she had with Edith Lancaster and she had come to only one conclusion. The Englishwoman was correct. It was not Irene's place to judge how others lived their lives, even if her intentions were good. There was only one thing Irene could think of doing. She needed to leave her mother to do what she wanted, and she knew she could not do that if she stayed, because she would continue to worry and it might just destroy their relationship.

Irene had decided once they left the village, she and Bruno would accompany the rest of the pilgrims on the next leg of the journey and then they would go their separate ways, and Irene would take her son and return to life in Montgenoux. It had been a difficult decision, and one Irene was still not sure about, but her instincts told her it was for the best. Whatever Dorothy Chapeau needed to do, the rest of her journey had to be her own.

Dorothy reached across the table and touched Irene's hand. 'You look a million miles away, darling. Are you alright?'

Irene smiled at her mother and nodded. 'I'm fine, mama.'

'You're going home, aren't you?'

Irene looked at her in surprise. 'How on earth do you know that?'

Dorothy laughed. 'Edith told me she'd given you a talking to. I told her there was no need and that you would have decided for yourself eventually. Anyway, it's about time you got back to your life and your job, and that rather nice fellow you're too frightened to commit to just in case he doesn't turn out to be perfect.'

'Mama...' Irene protested.

Dorothy held up her hands. 'I know, I'm an old Scottish woman who has an eye for the fancy, but it's not so bad for me to want my only child to be settled and happy.'

'I am settled and happy,' Irene responded.

'And yet you walked away from your life because you'd had a few setbacks. Whatever is wrong with Etienne, don't blame him for not being what you imagine to be the perfect match for you,' Dorothy stated.

'Do you think any of us believe it to be the case when we meet someone for the first time? None of us can predict the future, and frankly judging someone just because they don't,' she paused, 'what is it you young people say these days,' she extended her fingers into air quotes, 'they don't "rock your world" is foolish. Your father enchanted me from the moment I saw him, but that's not to say he was my type. I had rather a fancy for Rod Stewart, as it happens, and your father was nothing like good old Rod.'

Irene guffawed. 'Mama!'

Dorothy gave Irene a sheepish look. 'Your father couldn't even sing,' she added with a wink. 'My point is, just because he wasn't what I imagined when I thought of my ideal man, doesn't mean he didn't end up being my ideal man.'

'Then how did you know?' Irene countered. 'Are you saying I should just spend my life with someone, even if I'm not sure it's going to work out?'

Dorothy gave her a scolding look. 'That doesn't sound like

the girl I raised. It sounds like someone who is scared. And that's not what I'm saying at all.'

Irene gave a reluctant shrug.

'There's nothing wrong with being scared,' Dorothy continued. 'Don't you think I'm scared? My life has been destroyed irrevocably. I don't know what I'm heading towards, so until I do, I'm heading to Camino, or as far as my old pins will allow. Who knows what will happen? Maybe I'll drop dead, maybe I'll make it to the end. Hell, there's even a chance I might find a man on the way!'

Irene laughed. 'As long as it's not Rod Stewart.'

Dorothy squeezed her hand. 'Oh no, he's far too old for me now. Anyway, the point is, I don't know what I want exactly, or whether I want any of those things, a man, a romance, but all I know for certain is that being scared is as boring as heck and not something I'm prepared to accept. I won't give in to being scared at my age, so you have no excuse at yours. Do you understand what I'm saying?'

Before Irene could respond, the door to the Café burst open. The women gathered around the room all cried in shock. Irene jumped to her feet, her eyes narrowing as if she could not believe what she was seeing.

Ben stepped inside, shaking the rain from his head. He grinned at Irene. 'Well, don't stand their gawping, you old fool. Pour a poor pilgrim a beer!'

Irene ran forward and flung herself into his arms.

Irene continued to hug Ben as if her life depended on it. 'What on earth are you doing here?' she gushed, barely able to get the words out.

'You didn't send me any messages like you promised, so I came looking for you,' he replied matter-of-factly as if it was the most normal response in the world.

She pushed him back, her eyes flashing. 'What are you like, you crazy boy?' she scolded.

Maurice Rousseau clambered to his feet and approached them. 'Who are you, jeune homme, and more importantly, how on earth did you find your way into *Chemin des Pèlerins*?'

'Désolé everyone, this is my dear, *dear* friend from back home,' Irene explained before introducing Ben to the other people in the Café.

Ben gave a little anxious wave to them all. He pointed to Viviane, who was still standing in the doorway. 'And this is Viviane Auclair. She helped me get here.'

Maurice gave her a curt nod. 'I know full well who she is, but you still didn't answer my question.'

Ben noticed the fire in the corner of the room. 'Do you mind if we warm ourselves first? As you can see, we're rather wet.'

Irene looked around. 'You don't seem to have brought a lot of luggage with you,' she admonished.

He gave her a sheepish grin, pointing at his sodden backpack. 'As expected, I didn't think it through, I'm afraid. I have a change of t-shirt, pants and socks and that's about it.'

Irene tutted.

Sam Mitchell stood. 'Casey and I probably have something you can borrow until your clothes are dry. You look about the same size as my son.'

'And Sarah probably has something your guide could wear,' Tony Wilkinson added.

Upon their father's suggestion, Sarah Wilkinson and Casey Mitchell left the room with obvious reluctance.

Dorothy wrapped her arms around Ben and kissed his cheek. 'It's a pleasure to finally meet you, darling boy.'

Ben snuggled against her. 'And you.'

'We'll catch up properly later,' she added, gesturing for Viviane to move next to the fire. Maurice cleared his throat. 'Patience, Maurice Rousseau, can't you see they're soaked to the skin?'

Ben shivered, arming his hands in front of the fire. 'It's okay, I can explain. We met with another guide, Xavier Cadieux, a young man who lives in the village. He told us there was a way in and out of the village the young people used to use.'

'What nonsense!' Maurice explained. 'I would know about it if it was true.'

Ben shrugged. 'I don't know what to tell you, but we just got into the village without the bridge, didn't we?'

'Then there's a way out?' Irene asked, her voice suddenly filled with hope.

'Yeah,' Ben replied, pointing at his wet clothes. 'It's not ideal, and,' he glanced around the room, 'I'm not sure it's possible for everyone.'

Edith Lancaster dropped her knitting onto her lap, stabbing a needle in Ben's direction. 'I hope you're not suggesting our ages would hamper our progress.'

Ben held up his hands. 'I wouldn't dare!' he replied, his eyes twinkling.

Despite herself, Edith smiled as if she had been disarmed and lowered her head, quickly resuming her knitting.

'Would it be possible for us to leave the way you came?' Irene asked hopefully.

He shrugged. 'Honestly, I don't know. You have to climb down a narrow gap between a wall and a tree, then swim across the river and climb up the tree on the other side. It isn't easy, but it is doable.'

Irene gave him a doubtful look.

'In any case, I don't think it'll be necessary,' Viviane interjected. 'Xavier went off and called the police to arrange for someone to come and install a temporary bridge or something. They said it might take a day or two, but I'm sure it means help will be here soon.'

'That's right,' Ben confirmed. He glanced around the room, his face crinkling as he noticed the expressions on everyone's faces. 'Is everything okay?' he asked gingerly. 'Why do you all look so worried?'

Irene glanced over her shoulder. 'We have rather a situation here,' she said, lowering her voice. 'I'll tell you about it later.'

Dorothy stood up. 'It's late. And now we know help is definitely on the way perhaps we should turn in? I know I will probably sleep much better with this knowledge.'

Edith nodded, folding her knitting and placing it in her carpetbag. 'I agree.'

Sarah Wilkinson and Casey Mitchell appeared in the stairway, folded clothes in their hands. Irene took them with a grateful smile. 'Thank you very much,' she said before turning to Dorothy. 'You go up, mama, and I'll join you later. I'd like to spend some time with Ben first.' She watched the rest of the group leave, her face etched with concern.

Maurice yanked open the front door. 'I'll be back first thing. I'm going back to my cottage,' he mumbled, slamming the door behind him.

Once she was satisfied everyone had left, Irene turned to Ben. 'We've got a real problem. There's been a murder and I'm fairly sure the murderer is in this hotel.'

Hugo & Xavier

Hugo stepped out of the airport terminal, immediately shielding his eyes from the early morning sun. The flight had been calm enough, and he was pleased to see the clouds were not as dark as he expected, with splashes of clear blue sky behind them. He only hoped it was not a temporary respite.

'Are you Hugo Duchamp?'

Hugo spun around, to be greeted by a young man almost as tall as him, dark curls cascading down his forehead as he bounced excitedly on his heels. Hugo nodded. 'Oui, I am, et toi?'

The young man extended his hand. 'Xavier Cadieux, but call me Xav. Your assistant called and left a message for me to meet you. I was worried I wouldn't get here in time.'

Hugo shook his hand. 'I'm very grateful you did, merci.' He bit his lip, looking around anxiously. 'I'm very embarrassed, but would you mind if I smoked? They don't allow it on the plane or in the terminal, et,' he glanced at his watch, 'it's been a while.'

Xavier laughed. 'Terrible habit, but sure, it's your body.'

Hugo gratefully lit a cigarette. He always liked this moment when meeting new people because it gave him a moment to study them, unaware of his attention. In his profession, it had proved invaluable in assessing potential suspects or witnesses. 'I'm sure you must think this entire business is a terrible farce,' he suggested.

Xavier shrugged. 'Not really. And hey, as long as we're paid, each gig is as good as another, and if there's a bit of drama to spice up the days, so much the better as far as I'm concerned.'

'You saw my husband?'

He nodded. 'Oui, hier soir. He went to *Chemin des Pèlerins* with his guide, Viviane. There's a way in even without a bridge. Not many people know the way, but when I told Ben it was obvious he didn't want to wait.'

171

Hugo narrowed his eyes. 'But he was okay?'

Xavier bent over, stretching his left leg in front of him, causing it to strain against too-tight denim. 'Yeah, Ben was fine. Just keen to find his friend, I guess,' he added, his mouth twisting into a mischievous smile. 'He's *quite* the character. I can see why you like him.'

Hugo sucked on his cigarette. 'Can you take me to the village?'

Xavier stared at him, fixing Hugo with such an intense stare, it made him uncomfortable. 'I spoke to a construction company about replacing the bridge. They have a lot of work because of the storms, but I managed to convince them to move us to the top of the list, so they'll be there tomorrow with some kind of fix. Apparently, they have an extendable walkway which can stretch from one side to the other. It's only temporary, of course, but it should be enough to get everyone who's been trapped in the village since the storm took out the original bridge.'

Hugo nodded. 'I understand, mais…'

'I've found you a room in the hotel nearby. You can rest there and I'll come back for you tomorrow and we can all walk over the temporary bridge together.'

Hugo shook his head. 'A lack of patience seems to run in our family, so if it's all the same with you, I'd like to head over to *Chemin des Pèlerins* right away and satisfy myself everything is okay.'

Xavier gave him a reluctant look, one which told Hugo he was not used to people not following his direction. He shrugged and pointed at a scooter on the opposite side of the road. 'I can have you at *Chemin des Pèlerins* in less than an hour if that's what you really want,' he said, his carefree tone had changed and was now suggesting he was irritated.

Hugo nodded. 'I really would appreciate it,' he said, eager to keep the young guide on his side.

Xavier gave him the once over. He gestured to a scooter on

the opposite side of the road. 'Then be prepared to get soaked. Now jump on and hold on tight. We're about to go on quite the adventure!'

Hugo watched helplessly as Xavier skipped across the road towards his scooter, reluctantly falling into step behind him.

'What the hell do you think happened here, Ree?' Ben demanded.

Irene linked his arm and they continued walking, making their way slowly around the centre of *Chemin des Pèlerins*. They had spent most of the early hours of the morning talking before finally going to sleep. Irene had taken Viviane to the remaining vacant room on the top floor of the hotel, and Ben had shared Irene's bed. He had fallen asleep immediately, exhausted by the journey and the relief of the tension finally being released.

As the sun rose, they had awoken at the same time, silently signalling to one another to leave the room while Dorothy and Bruno still slept. They had then left the Café in silence, intent on continuing their discussion out of the potential earshot of others.

'I know you told us you were concerned about something,' he continued. 'But I had no idea it was going to end up this serious.'

She scoffed. 'I was, but I didn't think for a moment something like this was going to happen.'

Ben extended his hands. 'But it proves my point. You knew something was off, and I knew it too, by your reaction. You may not have understood what you were seeing, but you were clued up enough to know there was something wrong.'

Irene shook her head, smooth red hair falling over her face. 'I don't think it's that simple, Ben. My instincts, such as they are, don't extend to...' she stared towards *Café Compostelle*, 'whatever *this* is.'

Ben scratched his head. 'You said the dead man was stabbed in the back, but that it wasn't the cause of death?' he pondered.

'That would be my initial conclusion,' she agreed, 'and the preliminary examination suggests death by blunt force trauma to the skull, mais… at this stage, it's not really possible to understand what it signifies.'

He stared at her. 'You've had a chance to get to know these people. You must have formed some sort of opinion,' he posed.

Irene shrugged. 'If you're asking me, do I imagine one of them committed this horrible crime? Then my gut reaction is no, however, the circumstances we're dealing with suggest otherwise.'

Ben stopped walking, dropping onto a wall outside a ramshackle building. 'We've both been here before, Ree. People can be surprising, and just because we think we can trust them, it often proves to be the complete opposite. Remember, I once thought I knew a boy from my youth, a sweet boy who I cared for very deeply, and what happened to him? He came back to Montgenoux for revenge against the people he thought had harmed him and because of that, he did the most horrible things.'

Irene nodded, recalling the events which had almost cost both of them their lives several years earlier. 'Murder is often about revenge, but really, is it an imbalance of the mind which causes people to do unspeakable things.'

Ben shook his head. 'I used to think that, but the more I see, the more I experience. It's just too easy to make excuses and I'm fed up with it.'

'I can't say I disagree, but it is part of our jobs,' Irene reasoned. She took a long breath. 'I wish Hugo was here,' she added with a sigh.

'You have no idea,' Ben agreed sadly. 'Things always feel better when he's around, don't they? I mean, it's not just me, is it?'

She touched his arm lightly. 'Non, it's not just you. There's a calmness and patience to him that none of us really has. He sees everything and always seems to know what to do, no matter how dire the situation is. I am genuinely in awe of him.'

They walked in silence for a few minutes. 'What about the German cop?' Ben asked. 'Has he proved helpful?'

Irene visibly shuddered. 'A veritable dinosaur,' she replied haughtily. 'Oh, I shouldn't say that. He's probably harmless enough. The fact is, he could also be a suspect, which is what worries me the most, I suppose. I don't know who to trust. I'll feel better when the local police arrive and take charge and we can go home.' They rounded the corner. Dorothy and Bruno were standing outside the Café waving excitedly in their direction.

Irene linked arms with Ben. 'Come on, let's go and get some breakfast and hope this day gets better and ends with us leaving this godforsaken place once and for all.'

Ben found after a night of rest the group of pilgrims appeared more relaxed than they had during the early hours of the morning. He supposed his arrival, which brought with it the news that help was on its way, had been an immense relief.

He slowly sipped his café, taking the time to study the people in the room. If Irene was correct, someone amongst them was a murderer. As he watched them going about their business, eating their breakfast, he found it difficult to imagine one of them could be guilty of such a heinous crime, but without another explanation, it appeared one of them most certainly was.

He turned his attention to the outside. The rain had begun again in earnest, barely giving the ground enough time to dry from the previous days of onslaught, and the village square was once again becoming a mudslide, making *Café Compostelle* feel even more oppressive.

Ben was used to being able to get up and move freely around. Leaving the sanctity of the Swiss-style cottage, padding happily to the pool area, or to his car and the short drive to Montgenoux hospital or the building site that was becoming *Hotel Beaupain*. As a teenager, Ben had thought of nothing but escaping the legacy of his father and the small town which he had always imagined would destroy him if he did not leave it, but now, in his thirties, all Ben wanted was to be in Montgenoux and to remain there surrounded by the love he had found and the life he had created for himself.

Despite *Chemin des Pèlerins* being a village supposedly built as a respite for pilgrims seeking God, he felt little peace there, and he could not shake the feeling there was something very wrong. It wasn't just the murder; it was something else altogether. All he knew for certain was he would not be happy until they all left.

Irene appeared by his side, pointing at the half-eaten omelette on his plate. 'Something wrong with your food? I know my culinary skills leave a lot to be desired, mais…'

Ben shook his head and quickly shovelled a forkful into his mouth. 'Non, it's delicious. I was just miles away, or rather, *wishing* I was miles away.'

She squeezed his hand. 'This nightmare will be over soon, I'm sure.'

He looked towards the storeroom. 'I know we're kinda used to this sort of stuff, but it feels a little strange that everyone else here is so calm about someone lying dead in the deep freeze,' he said, his voice lowered. 'I mean, isn't it a bit strange they all seem to be taking it in their stride?'

Irene shrugged. 'People react differently to situations, you know that as well as I do. And I suspect people here are in a little bit of denial because they don't want to face the reality and the danger of the situation. I think this is about just getting through the time until help arrives,' she reasoned. 'I suspect the shock will set in once people feel safe and comfortable away from this place. Let's not forget, most of the people here are deeply religious. I suspect there's a whole lot of praying going on.'

'I hope it helps,' he replied, looking around again. 'But it doesn't change the fact one of them is guilty.'

'Or more than one,' Irene added.

'What do you mean?' he demanded.

She shrugged again. 'Oh, I don't know,' she grumbled. 'I keep coming back to the same point and the fact there are two seemingly different causes of death. And I keep asking myself - why?'

Ben did not answer immediately. 'It could be a distraction. Using one to stop us looking too closely at the other.'

'It's possible, I suppose,' she replied as if she was not sure she agreed. 'They may not have realised once a heart stops it is not going to release blood at the scene of a knife wound, but then they must have known once a pathologist examined the victim, it would become clear the blow to the head was, in fact, the cause of death.'

Ben pursed his lips. 'Peut être they were relying on us assuming the victim was stabbed and fell forward and hit his head when he fell.' He stopped. 'But then again, even that makes little sense. Without the knife wound, wouldn't you have just treated it as an accident? I mean, wouldn't your first instinct of been to assume he may have just taken a tumble and accidentally smashed his head against the wall?'

Irene considered her answer. 'You're right, it would. There would have been several factors in coming to any sort of conclusion,' she continued. 'And the fact is, with no direct evidence to the contrary, any reasonable pathologist would have trouble proving it was a deliberate act.'

Ben nodded. 'That's what I thought, which makes it even more complicated. If the knife wasn't the cause of death, then why suggest it was...'

Behind them, Edith Lancaster threw her knitting onto the table, cold, pale eyes instantly locked in their direction. 'What are you getting at?'

Ben jumped, surprised she had overheard their discussion. There was a radio playing in the Café and he was sure it would have covered their conversation.

Irene and Ben exchanged a look but said nothing. 'We're just speculating, that's all,' Irene replied. 'Until there is a proper investigation, we're never going to be sure.'

Edith turned to Wolfgang. 'Why would someone pretend to murder Alain?' she demanded.

Wolfgang shrugged. 'As the doctor said, we can't be sure one way or another at this stage. It is one theory, as yet unconfirmed.'

Dorothy pulled her cardigan tight across her chest. 'The entire business is macabre.'

'I just don't understand what it could mean,' Elke Huber

cried.

Edith Lancaster tapped her chin with a knitting needle. 'It means that this is all about to become even more interesting,' she replied mystically before picking up her knitting and beginning again, thin, dry lips pulling into a mischievous smile.

Hugo & Xavier

'The trick is,' Xavier Cadieux began, 'to not think too much about it and just move quickly.'

Hugo gave him a doubtful look. He flicked on his glasses and immediately regretted it. The rain was lashing against his raincoat, whipping it up around his waist. Even in the darkness, it was clear the gap between the trees and the wall was tight and he could see the rain had already soaked the tree and branches. He also knew he did not need to look down to know there was a sheer drop into the darkness of the water beneath them.

Xavier touched his arm. 'I told you, you don't need to do this now,' he breathed. 'Help is on the way. We can chill out in Millieure and wait for them, and when they do arrive, it'll be a damn sight easier to get into *Chemin des Pèlerins.*'

Hugo reached into his pocket and extracted a cigarette, quickly lighting it and hoping it would give him the courage he needed to move forward. 'I know that's logical,' he replied, 'but I'd just like to satisfy myself everything is okay with my friends and then hopefully we can all go back to our normal lives.'

Xavier looked around. 'This is my normal life, for better or worse, so I'm fine with it.'

Hugo imagined the young man was half his age, probably barely in his early twenties, still with his entire life ahead of him. 'Isn't there something else you want to do?' he asked. Hugo was not adept at making polite chit-chat, but at that moment, he felt at least he should make the effort, particularly after what Xavier was doing to help him and his friends.

Xavier took the cigarette from Hugo's fingers, took a drag and immediately coughed. 'Not now, not yet at least,' he spluttered. 'I've got stuff to sort out and then I can figure out what I'm going to do next.'

Hugo gave him a quizzical look. There was something about the young man's response, which seemed odd to him.

Xavier smiled at him as if reading his thoughts. 'I *will* leave soon,' he added coolly. 'And I have a feeling it will be *really* soon.'

Before Hugo had a chance to respond, Xavier swooped past him and jumped around the back of the tree, wrapping his thighs around it and using his arms, began quickly descending like a spider monkey. 'Come on, Hugo, follow me.'

Not one for prayer, nevertheless Hugo said a silent prayer before moving to the tree and stepping into the darkness. He pressed his foot against the branch and immediately slipped against the wall. He let out a sharp cry.

'I've got you, Hugo,' Xavier said in a tone so soft it made Hugo feel uncomfortable. 'I'll be just below you, so don't worry if you miss a step, or slip, because the only thing you'll crash into is me and I'll have a tight grip, so we won't both fall. You trust me, don't you?'

Hugo nodded. 'Oui, bien sûr, I'm just not sure I trust myself and I'm even less sure you want me crashing down on you.'

Xavier gave him what Hugo was fairly sure was a flirtatious look.

'Let's get this over with,' Hugo mumbled.

Xavier laughed and began his descent, Hugo slipping into place behind him. They moved the rest of the time in silence for what seemed like a long time. Hugo was relieved when he finally heard Xavier dropping into the water beneath him. He braced himself for the cold, finally letting go of the tree and falling into icy cold water. Hugo fought the urge to panic and began quickly paddling. He could make out Xavier's feet splashing in front of him and he followed as best he could, grateful to have something to guide him and push him forward.

The river was moving quickly; the rain pushing it through the gap between the trees and under the hill. It was hard to keep moving because they were swimming against the current and Hugo was again reminded of how out of shape he was. Moments later, they reached the furthest tree, and Hugo watched as Xavier easily yanked himself up. Hugo tried to do the same, his wet feet slipping against the tree. Xavier reached down, extending his hand and pulling Hugo upwards.

For Hugo, the ascent felt worse than the descent, no doubt exacerbated by his sodden clothes and backpack, but he moved as quickly as he could, trying his best to keep up with the much younger man above him.

'We're almost there,' Xavier called out over his shoulder. Hugo watched as Xavier jumped from the tree onto the embankment, falling to his knees but immediately jumping back to his feet and extending his hand to Hugo, dragging him quickly from the tree and pulling him onto the land. Hugo collapsed, gasping for breath, but infinitely relieved to be on relatively solid ground.

'Welcome to *Chemin des Pèlerins*,' Xavier announced.

Hugo clambered to his feet, shaking the rain and water from his clothes and bag. He pulled his glasses from his pocket and flicked them on, his eyes moving slowly around taking in his new surroundings. What he could see of the village so far was exactly as he imagined it would be. Old and quaint, belonging to another era. The houses appeared badly in need of repair and he could see little sign of life, primarily because of the shuttered windows. There was no sound but the rain and the howling wind.

Xavier gestured for Hugo to follow him, leading him to the top of a steep staircase. 'This is the way down to the rest of the village,' he explained.

'And that's where everyone is?' Hugo enquired, barely able to contain himself that Ben and the others were now within walking distance.

Xavier nodded. 'I expect they'll be in *Café Compostelle*. I mean, it's the only place to go in the whole damn village.'

Hugo stepped onto the staircase, his hands gripping tightly onto the handrail. The rain was pouring down the steps, making it difficult to walk, and he found he had to keep sidestepping in order not to slip. Xavier skipped ahead of him as if he had done it a hundred times before.

'Once we get to the bottom, I'll point you toward the Café,' Xavier called out, 'and I'll meet you later.'

'Where will you be?' Hugo called after him.

'I have to check on my parents. They live on the other side of the village,' Xavier replied. 'Maman isn't well, so I just need to make sure everything is alright. Is that okay?'

'Bien sûr, it is. I'm just grateful for all of your help, Xavier.'

Xavier stopped and stared at Hugo. 'Don't thank me yet, Hugo.' He jumped from the staircase and pointed to his right. 'That's the Café,' he stated.

Hugo narrowed his eyes. He could barely see in front of him, but he could make out the neon sign and what appeared to be people moving around, and it made him feel a little better.

'Merci, Xavier,' he called out.

Xavier nodded, the tone of his voice suddenly cool. 'I'll see you soon, Hugo. And good luck, d'accord?'

Hugo nodded, unsure why it was Xavier thought he might need good luck. He tucked his hands in his jeans pockets and strode with determination towards the Café.

Hugo pushed open the door to the Café, the sudden gust of wind and rain slamming the door against a table startling everyone in the room. It took Hugo but a moment to spot Ben in the far corner, his lips pulling into a relieved grin.

Ben jumped to his feet, clapping his hands together like an excited child and sprinting towards his husband. 'You crazy, crazy fool, what on earth are you doing here?'

Hugo squeezed him. 'The same reason as you,' he breathed into Ben's head, taking a moment to inhale his scent. He pushed back, suddenly aware of all eyes on him, and, as usual, under such circumstances, he felt himself blushing.

Irene stood and moved quickly to Hugo, pulling him into an embrace. 'I can't tell you how happy I am to see you,' she whispered into his ear, 'not least because we have a problem.'

Hugo turned his head to study her face, their eyes locking. He recognised the look, and it worried him immensely because he realised the problem he had been envisioning was likely altogether something very different. He nodded. 'I guess we need to talk,' he whispered.

Irene nodded. 'Hey, everyone. I'd like to introduce you to my dear, dear friend. I'm sure you've heard me talking about him. But I'd like very much to present Captain Hugo Duchamp of the French Police Nationale. He is one of the finest people and police officers I know.'

Bruno Chapeau excitedly clapped his hand. 'Oncle Hugo!'

Hugo swept over to Irene's young son and pulled him up, swinging him through the air, blowing raspberries into his hair, causing the young boy to squeal with excitement. 'Je t'aime, Bruno,' he cried into the air.

'Moi aussi, Oncle Hugo!' Bruno squealed.

Irene took Bruno and gently placed him back on the seat. 'He's just eaten, Oncle Hugo,' she said, gently chastising. 'So, unless you want to wear an omelette on your coat, it might be a good idea to leave the swings until later.' Irene gestured to Ben. 'I'd love for the three of us to catch up,' she announced.

Hugo nodded. 'I'd like that. Let me just change out of these wet clothes and then we can go.'

'I have some dry clothes you can borrow, thanks to Casey over there,' Ben stated.

'No need,' Hugo replied, pointing at his backpack. 'I have a waterproof bag full of clean, dry clothes in my backpack.'

Irene snorted, punching Ben on the arm. 'You see, that's how you do it. Sensible people come prepared!'

Ben stood on his tiptoes and kissed Hugo's cheek. 'I will never stop learning from you, oh great one!'

Hugo, Ben & Irene

Hugo shook his head in disbelief. 'Are you serious?' he asked with incredulity.

Irene nodded. 'I admit I'm at a loss, which is very odd for me, but I can't help but feel out of my depth,' she continued. 'I thought I needed to leave Montgenoux because my life had become complicated and staid, but I realised since being here it wasn't that simple. I was just spoilt and used to everyone telling me how good I was, and once that stopped, it bruised my ego, so I ran.'

Hugo stopped and lit a cigarette. 'I began running when I was eighteen years old when I buried my grandmother. She was the most insufferable, demanding, difficult, condescending...' he stopped, his voice breaking, '*perfect* person I'd ever met. It took me a long time to understand that you don't always have to hug or use words to show how much you love someone. Madeline was a lot of things, but she certainly wasn't demonstrative in any way, other than when showing her disapproval,' he added with a sad laugh, 'and losing her made me spiral for over a decade. I thought it was for the best, but it wasn't. All I was doing was hiding.'

'How did you get out of it?' Irene asked.

Hugo grabbed hers and Ben's hand, a gesture which would have been unthinkable for him seven years earlier. 'They threw me into a real, REALLY weird town in Southern France and it changed everything. I took a chance, and it worked out perfectly because,' he turned his head between them, 'the pair of you taught me that chaos can be worked through as long as you have people who love you.'

Irene pursed her lips. 'You learnt too damn quickly for my liking,' she quipped.

Ben agreed. 'And I hate the fact he got better at it than either of us.'

Hugo laughed. 'Anyway,' he drawled. 'Let's get back to the rather important matter at hand. A man with a knife in his back?'

'That's only part of it,' Irene replied. They stopped, taking shelter from the rain under a canopy in front of a closed-up building. Irene looked around as if satisfying herself they were out of earshot of anyone who may be around. 'I have reason to believe the knife wound was only superficial, and that death was most likely caused by blunt force trauma to the cranium. All of which needs to be substantiated, mais…'

Hugo nodded. 'The fact you believe it to be the case is enough for me. Which begs the question - why fake a cause of death? To confuse? To misdirect?'

'That's what we thought,' Ben concluded. 'Although unless someone's really stupid, they'd have to expect somewhere along the line, a professional would spot the discrepancy.'

Hugo lit a cigarette, slowly exhaling. 'There is another possibility, a little left field, but it might just explain two different apparent causes of death.'

'And what's that?' Ben asked.

'Two attacks,' Hugo suggested, slowly rubbing his chin. 'By two different perpetrators.'

Ben gave him a doubtful look. 'That seems a little… extreme and random.'

'And still doesn't make any sense,' Irene mused.

'Unless the murderer didn't want to risk the blow to the head not being fatal,' Hugo reasoned, 'so they stabbed them just to be sure.' He sighed. 'Well, we'll be sure to ask them once they're in custody.'

Ben smiled. 'Then you'll take charge of the investigation?'

Hugo nodded. 'Only until the local police arrive. I am an active police officer, so I feel it's my responsibility to secure the crime scene and remain vigilant.' He frowned. 'Speaking of which, I would like to take a look at the crime scene if it's possible.'

'I'll take you there,' Irene responded. 'I should also tell you that Wolfgang Huber and I, Wolfgang is a German ex-police officer of some thirty-plus years, anyway, we talked with everyone who was staying in the hotel. The logic being to ask everyone for their recollections when events were still fresh in their minds.' She tapped at her pocket. 'I realise it's not legally binding, but under the circumstances, I recorded our conversations while memories were still fresh. I got everyone's permission, of course.'

Hugo narrowed his eyes. 'Legally binding or not, I think you did the right thing, and I'd like to listen to the recordings if I may.'

'Bien sûr, although I wouldn't get your hopes up, I'm not sure how helpful it was. Either someone is a damn good liar, or there just wasn't anything to be learned from them,' Irene replied. 'Shall we go?'

'I'll head inside too,' Ben added. 'I'll hang with Bruno, and I'd like to get to know Mama Chapeau and find out all the sordid secrets of Irene Chapeau: the teenage years,' he said with a mischievous wink.

Irene playfully punched his arm. 'Don't you dare listen to a word she says, and if you do and you repeat any of it, you know I can take you out!'

Hugo moved slowly around the storeroom, pulling his glasses from his head and peering at the wall. He grimaced. 'Unless I'm very much mistaken, Alain Bonnet took a hell of a blow to his head. This wasn't subtle, nor was it an accident, I'm sure of that.'

'I would agree,' Irene confirmed after a moment.

Hugo moved his head slowly around the room. 'Forensics aren't going to find much here, are they?' he asked.

Irene took a pause. 'I did my best to preserve evidence, but I think you're right, the crime scene is problematic, and it's almost certainly compromised.'

Hugo nodded. 'Can you show me the body?'

Irene led him in silence through the storeroom, pulling open the door to the cold storage anteroom. Hugo took a step back, the cold catching the back of his throat. His eyes locked on Alain Bonnet's body and the image squeezed his heart. 'Would he have suffered?' he asked softly.

Irene stepped next to him. 'If I'm correct, the blow to his head would have been catastrophic, which often suggests death would have followed quickly. He certainly would have been dazed and confused then unconscious soon after. I don't believe he would have suffered for long.'

Hugo moved back into the storeroom again, turning his head back and forth. The room was cramped, lined with boxes, and as he tried to envisage various scenarios, only one appeared sensible to him. 'He wasn't taken by surprise,' he said finally.

Irene's eyebrows knotted. 'What do you mean?'

Hugo extended his arms, and could only touch one wall, but he could almost reach the other. 'There's not enough room to freely move through here.'

Irene shrugged. 'I agree, et?'

Hugo pivoted his body around. 'Only it suggests to me that for Monsieur Bonnet to sustain such an injury, it isn't likely to have come as a surprise. It suggests he was talking with his attacker.'

Irene pursed her lips. 'And they did what? Grab him, spun him around and smashed his head against the wall?'

'He could have turned away momentarily,' Hugo suggested. 'Either way, I believe he was in here with his attacker.' He stopped, sighing. 'Not that it really matters at this point, because it doesn't tell us anything.'

Irene pressed her body against the wall. 'I can't begin to imagine what happened here, can you?'

He shook his head. 'Non.' He paused. 'When Ben left, I recalled your concerns regarding the tour guide, so I asked Etienne to investigate.'

Irene's mouth pulled into a sad smile at the mention of his name. 'Good old Etienne,' she exhaled. 'Did he discover anything important?'

'Not really,' Hugo conceded. 'You expressed concern about Maurice Rousseau, but the only thing Etienne found was an old newspaper report about the death of his wife.'

Irene took a deep breath. 'I don't know all the details, but oui, Maurice's wife was killed in some sort of tragic accident. Do you think it could be relevant?'

Hugo's mouth twisted as he considered. 'I don't see how it could be, however,' he paused for a moment, 'we can't ignore the fact that as far as we can tell, it's the only link connecting the same group of people who were here forty years ago.'

'Then you suspect one of them is involved?' Irene asked tentatively.

Hugo shrugged. 'At this point, I don't know what to think, but I also don't believe we can't rule anything out. I wish we had the option to wait for the local police, but we don't. We have to be vigilant until they arrive.'

Irene studied his face. She frowned. 'If we suspect Maurice, then we also have to suspect everyone else who was on the original pilgrimage, and that would include my mother,' she snorted, giving Hugo a withering look. 'And I'm sorry, but I just can't believe my mother was involved in what happened to Alain, I just can't.' She gave Hugo a sweet smile. 'I realise you can't just take my word on that, I wouldn't expect you to, mais I simply can't believe the woman who raised me is a murderer.'

Hugo moved forward and faced her. 'I trust your judgment, Irene.'

She smiled gratefully. 'Merci for that. Mama may also be able to give us some information about what happened back then.'

Hugo nodded. 'Maybe I could talk to her discreetly. I mean, it wouldn't harm, would it?' He moved to the exit. 'But first I would like to speak to the German police officer. I'd like to hear his thoughts.'

Hugo & Wolfgang

Hugo and Wolfgang Huber moved slowly around the village square, both huddled under large umbrellas. They had been walking in relative silence for ten minutes, occasionally exchanging polite anecdotes about their careers. There was something about the former police officer which made Hugo uncomfortable. It was not because the older man was even taller and broader than Hugo, who often towered above everyone he met, it was something else. A brooding expression lined his face and to Hugo, Wolfgang appeared to be a man perpetually on the verge of losing his temper.

'Do you have a gun?' Wolfgang snapped, breaking the silence.

'I do, but not with me,' Hugo replied.

'Well, that's stupid,' the elder man hissed. 'What is the point of having a damn gun if you don't carry it?'

'Because I'm not on duty, and I'm out of my jurisdiction,' Hugo stated passively. 'I take carrying a firearm very seriously and therefore I don't tend to take it when I travel, especially when I am not on duty.'

'Then you're a fool,' Wolfgang bristled. 'Particularly because you walked into a situation blind. In my day, a police officer would not be so foolish,' he added haughtily.

Hugo ignored the insult. He had trained extensively to become proficient in using a firearm because it was expected of him, but he did not allow it to inform how he approached his job as a police officer. 'Tell me,' he began cautiously. 'What is your assessment of the situation?'

Wolfgang gave Hugo a curious look as if he did not know what the question suggested, although Hugo had framed it in clear English. Wolfgang shrugged.

Hugo stopped abruptly, craning the umbrella between his

neck and his collarbone as he strained to light a cigarette. Once lit, he faced Wolfgang. 'You have no opinion? You have come to no conclusions?' Hugo posed forcefully.

Wolfgang merely shrugged again. 'I am sure I have no firm opinion in any direction.'

Hugo raised an eyebrow. 'Then you see no difference between a crime based purely on circumstance, and one based on something else altogether?'

Wolfgang sighed. 'I was born in Germany at a time when the entire world hated us, but not as much as we hated ourselves. I think little of circumstance and deal only with the here and now.'

'And the here and now?' Hugo pushed. 'You believe Alain Bonnet's murder was random?'

'I never said that,' Wolfgang interrupted. 'Nor did I suggest otherwise. I imagine you have spoken with Dr. Chapeau already and your mind is already awhirl with several different, colourful scenarios. I can't comment on them, but I will say this. A murder was committed on my watch, and I will forever feel as if I could have done something to prevent it.'

'In what way?' Hugo asked with genuine curiosity.

Wolfgang did not answer. 'Alain was a good man, and he didn't deserve what happened to him.'

Hugo nodded. 'Can you think of any reason someone might have wanted to hurt him?'

Wolfgang snorted. 'I hadn't seen the man in forty years and have only spoken to him once or twice in the intervening years. I know nothing about him, or his life then, between, or now, so commenting on it would be futile and pointless, don't you think?'

Hugo blew smoke into the air. 'What can you tell me about the original pilgrimage?' he asked quickly, hoping he sounded as if he was putting little importance on it because he did not want Wolfgang to know Hugo had any knowledge of it.

Wolfgang narrowed his eyes. 'What is there to say? Several

like-minded people came together to walk the Camino. Hardly unusual,' he responded. 'My parents were deeply religious and in ill health, so I suppose I came here on their behalf. You see, my father was ashamed of his part in the Second World War, and he was always looking for atonement and I wanted that for him. Our priest told us the walk to Camino was a powerful and life-changing journey.' He paused, fleshy lips pulling into a smile. 'It certainly changed my life,' he said, staring off into the direction of the Café.

He stopped, pressing his arm against the side of a building. His breath was laboured and for a moment, Hugo was concerned for him, but Wolfgang soon pulled himself together and continued walking.

Hugo caught up to him. 'There were no problems?' he asked. He did not want to directly ask about Maurice Rousseau, but he wondered whether the implication would be enough to make Wolfgang talk.

It was not. Wolfgang shrugged. 'Other than blisters and swollen ankles? No, I don't recall anything relevant to what happened here.' He lifted his hand, staring at his watch. 'Now, if you'll excuse me, it's lunchtime. My doctor insists I eat regularly to maintain my blood sugar level.' Without looking back, he stomped heavy-footed through the rain back towards *Café Compostelle*.

Hugo & Dorothy

Hugo moved to a corner table outside *Café Compostelle*. Dorothy Chapeau was already seated, slowly sipping a glass of water. Hugo was pleased to see someone had very kindly left him a very tall, frosty glass of beer.

'How was your conversation with Wolfgang?' Dorothy asked with a wry laugh.

Hugo flopped into a seat and took a healthy slug of beer, smacking his lips happily. 'Interesting,' he replied.

She laughed again. 'I bet it was. Don't be put off by his briskness,' she said. 'Because I believe underneath it all, Wolfgang is a good man, you just have to look hard to see it.'

Hugo took another drink of beer.

'My daughter and her son both love you and your husband very much,' Dorothy continued. 'And I can't tell you how happy that makes me, especially after what has happened to me lately and as I face my own mortality. It gives me great comfort, so I just wanted to thank you personally.'

Hugo smiled. 'One of the most valuable lessons I have learnt in my personal life is that family does not always have to be what we are given, it can also be what comes to us. Irene and Bruno are a wonderful part of our family, and I hope you can be too for many years to come.'

Dorothy moved her shoulders slowly. 'I've buried a husband. When my mother did the same, she told me she had done her duty. She'd raised her children, loved her husband and then buried him and all that remained was for her to wait out her time.' She slowly sipped her water. 'I thought at the time it was terribly old-fashioned, but now, I don't know if I do. I miss my darling Willum and I'm afraid I am rather counting the days until we are reunited.'

Hugo awkwardly sipped his drink, eagerly eyeing the packet

of cigarettes he had placed on the table.

Dorothy laughed. 'Irene told me all about you. Light a cigarette, young man, and let me watch. It's a terrible habit, but my husband smoked a pipe for most of his life. For the first ten years of our marriage we fought about it until finally one day, we stopped. I expect I imagined there were more important things to fight over, but I also like to think it was because I finally accepted it was simply just something that made him happy. And really, isn't that what we should aim for with a loved one? Just to give them free rein to be happy even if it goes against the grain?'

She gestured for Hugo to light a cigarette. He did. Her nose immediately crinkled. 'It's not the same, but it's close enough.' She smiled. 'The small folds around your eyes flex in the exact same way as Willum's did when he smoked. I can only describe it as pure pleasure.' She reached across and touched Hugo's hand. 'It makes me happy to see it again.'

The two of them lapsed into silence. It was not an uncomfortable silence as it had been with Wolfgang, rather one simply shared between two people passing a pleasant moment.

Dorothy finally broke the impasse. 'Irene suggested it might be an idea to discuss with you the original pilgrimage forty years ago.'

Hugo nodded.

'You believe it might be relevant?'

Hugo studied Irene's mother. Something had changed in the tone of her voice, but he could not be sure what it was, other than there was a wariness which had not been there before.

Dorothy took a deep breath. 'I don't like speaking of this,' she whispered, before adding, 'although that's not strictly true, because I have NEVER spoken of this. Not even with Willum, not really, not in any tangible way, and certainly not since we left this place the first time.' She exhaled. 'I imagine it was because I thought it was too difficult, but really it was just most likely just because I didn't want to think about it because I'm not particularly proud of myself.'

Hugo gave her a curious look.

Dorothy slowly sipped her water. 'We came to this village as young people. Most of us single. I had never been out of Scotland before, and after the pilgrimage, I returned rarely. I occasionally visited family, attended funerals when I could, but really, the pilgrimage changed everything for me. It gave me the direction I'd been searching for. I was raised a Catholic and my parents encouraged me to walk the Camino, but once I met Willum, I knew he was the real reason I was there. Willum was my reward from God, you might say.'

Hugo nodded his understanding. 'I can't say I believe in such things, but I can't deny the fact I reluctantly made a pilgrimage of my own, which certainly changed everything for me too.'

She touched his hand. 'We don't all need burning bushes to imagine the hand of God has touched us, you know. He acts in ways we can barely imagine.'

Hugo lowered his head, not wishing to offend her. 'I've always appreciated the way people are comforted by their beliefs, but I cannot agree with it when it becomes a weapon against... against someone like me,' he said softly.

Dorothy nodded. 'And that is the burden those of us with TRUE belief must reconcile. Do you judge me because I believe in God?'

Hugo shook his head. 'Not at all. But I don't accept the whole hate the sin and love the sinner trope. I'm sorry, but I don't, and nor should anyone. I believe more often than not, people who preach religious beliefs on others aren't always so literal when it comes to their own behaviours.'

Dorothy cocked her head. 'You're a spirited young man. No wonder my daughter loves you and your husband so much. And by the way: Husband and husband and wife and wife is something that should have happened a long time ago in my opinion and I'd tell the damn Pope myself if ever I met him. My point is, young man, nothing is as simple as two people looking at each other as we are now and acknowledging love in its purest form. There will always be people who judge, but there will always be those of us who know not to judge, especially when it comes to love in whatever form it comes.'

'And forty years ago?' Hugo interjected. 'Was that about love?'

Dorothy took a long, deep breath. 'Olive Rousseau,' she whispered in a way which suggested she had not spoken her name in a long time. 'What a beautiful, lively young woman!' She gestured with her hand. 'I can still see her, spinning around this floor, serving drinks, delivering meals, chatting away. She was a delight. I liked her very much, although looking back, I imagine the life she was born into was not the one she wanted. She died before she had a chance to live the life she so desperately wanted.'

'What do you mean?' Hugo asked.

She shrugged. 'She was beautiful. I mean, *really* beautiful. What you might call a natural beauty,' Dorothy continued. 'If you can imagine a combination between Sophia Loren and Grace Kelly, then that was Olive. She was barely a child then, not even twenty, I think, and her life had been spent doing little more than cooking, cleaning and looking after the pilgrims who came through this village. Her entire life had been decided for her by her parents,' she added sadly. 'And they had chosen Maurice as her match.'

'And it wasn't a good match?' Hugo asked.

Dorothy considered her response carefully. 'Who really knows what goes on behind closed doors?' she suggested. 'All I can tell you is this - Maurice clearly adored her, and back then he was a handsome young man, older than her by a few years and a serious man who wanted nothing more in life than he already had. I think Olive was fond enough of him.' She noticed the expression on

Hugo's face. 'Times were different then. Was it love's great romance? No, I don't imagine it was.'

Hugo nodded. 'And what happened?'

Dorothy stared out of the window, lifting her head towards the sky. 'The heavens opened as they have this week. The rain was relentless. The thunder defeating. The lightning terrifying,' she said with a shudder. 'I slept on the top floor of the hotel then, because,' she laughed, 'I was younger and the steps weren't so problematic. All the women slept there,' she added, her eyes twinkling, 'as far away as possible from the men. Edith Lancaster was much younger then, but just as ferocious and determined.'

'What do you mean?'

Dorothy laughed. 'She was always knitting then too, and I'm fairly sure she'd stab a man through the heart with one of her knitting needles if he tried to do something he shouldn't be doing with one of us girls.'

'And did that happen with Olive Rousseau?' Hugo asked. 'Was there a problem with one of the men?'

Dorothy's throat constricted. 'I told you about the storm. In my nightmares, I now imagine it was much worse. I don't know if it was. It may have been, I can't be sure. And as I said, these are the sort of conversations no one ever really has after the event. I mean, why would you? Someone died. Move on. We commiserate and we condole, but really, all any of us want to do is to try to forget. To forget the pain and stop talking about it.'

Hugo took a breath, painfully aware he had spent most of his life doing his best to walk away from expressing or feeling any kind of emotion. In his imagination, he had always supposed his crippling insecurity and isolation were almost exclusive to him, but he knew it was not the case. Everyone had their own burdens to carry.

Dorothy glanced around anxiously as if satisfying herself they were out of earshot of anyone else. 'I don't like talking about the private lives of others, but Irene pressed upon me the importance of keeping nothing back.' She hesitated as if she was uncomfortable. 'Although, to be frank, I can't imagine a single scenario which might suggest something that happened over forty years ago could have caused what happened to poor Alain this week.'

Hugo nodded. 'I'm not saying it does. But as Irene suggested, in our line of business, we can't always afford to ignore our instincts. Tell me what happened.'

Dorothy closed her eyes and cupped her hands together. 'We were in *Café Compostelle*, taking shelter, much like we are now, but back then, I can't quite describe how different it was. It wasn't just that we were all so much younger, rather the excitement of the adventure we were undertaking. And, of course, love was very much in the air. Wolfgang and Elke were already together,' she added with a wry smile, 'though, as I recall, you'd have been hard-pressed to tell. Then there was the Mitchells, they were very much in love, and if I remember correctly, Tony and Jane Wilkinson came together from England but weren't married yet, or perhaps they were engaged. I can't quite remember.'

She stopped and laughed. 'Though that is why I imagine Edith Lancaster kept her beady eye on them. And finally Willum and I, we had just met here you see and I suppose Edith understood what was transpiring between us, probably better than we did at the time.'

Hugo smiled, noticing the shadow pass across Dorothy's face. He could see the grief was still raw, only months after losing her husband. The emotion was plain to see on her face and he felt helpless, knowing there was likely little he could say or do which might ease her pain.

Dorothy appeared to pull herself together. 'Anyway, we were all sitting in the Café, no doubt giddy with glee and praying for the rain to stop so that we could be on our way when we suddenly realised no one had seen Olive for a while. So the men all instantly rallied together and went about searching for her. The storm was brutal, and the conditions were difficult, but off they went with determination, worried that something might have happened to her.'

Hugo frowned. Dorothy noticed it. 'Did I say something wrong?'

Hugo shook his head forcefully. 'Not at all. I was just curious about something - you used the word "suddenly" when talking about Olive Rousseau and that everyone began searching for her instantly, despite the weather. I suppose my question is what raised the alarm and the concern?'

Dorothy stared at him, her eyes widening in a way which surprised him because it suggested to him she was about to lie about something. After a few moments, she sighed and then gave a deep laugh. 'You're worse than Irene. It was always impossible to lie to her when she was a child and it's gotten even worse since she became the force she has.'

'Why would you lie to me?' Hugo asked softly.

'Not for the reason I'm sure other people lie to you,' she responded. 'Rather my own desire not to appear foolish, or a gossip.' She took a deep breath. 'As I told you when I first met Olive it was clear she was not as happy with her life and her marriage as she could be.' She paused. 'And that she may, or may not, I can't say either way with any certainty, have been involved with another man.'

Hugo raised an eyebrow. 'Another man?'

Dorothy's lips contorted. 'I don't know. But that was the impression I got.'

'One of the pilgrims?'

She nodded.

'And what made you think that?'

Dorothy exhaled. 'That afternoon I was looking for Alain.

The rain had stopped, and I was bored with being cooped up. I had a hankering for a picnic and thought I might ask Willum if he would accompany me,' she added demurely. 'Anyway, I found Alain in the storeroom, but I foolishly didn't knock and came across him and Olive.'

'Came across them?' Hugo pushed.

She shook her head forcefully. 'Not in *that* sort of way,' she stated, before adding, 'at least I don't believe so. No, I think it was more I walked in on an argument between them. It reminded me of an argument I'd once had with a friend back in Scotland. She'd been cheating on her beau and although it wasn't because I was being a prude, I took her to task. He was a nice wee chap, and he deserved better.'

Hugo smiled. 'And that was the impression you got - that Alain Bonnet was challenging her about having an affair?'

'I believe so,' Dorothy agreed. 'We were all terribly embarrassed about my faux pas, so I made my excuses and left, and Olive came out soon after me and I think she was crying. The reason I said we suddenly noticed she was missing was because Maurice came looking for her and I suppose we all assumed she was at her house, but when he came he said he had assumed she was with us in the Café, but she wasn't. There was nothing untoward about it really, and I apologise for misspeaking,' she blurted.

'Anyway, I suppose the drama came from Maurice. He said Olive had told him she would wait in the Café for him. He'd spent most of the day attaching shutters to the windows of the houses in the village because the storm warnings suggested the weather was going to get even worse.'

She shuddered. 'It really was a horrible, horrible storm, and it had come on again suddenly, so of course once we realised no one knew where she was. I suppose we all jumped into action and went looking for her. In the end, because of the weather, the women stayed in the Café and the men began searching.'

'And what happened next?' Hugo asked keenly.

'It seemed to take an eternity,' Dorothy continued, 'despite the fact the village is tiny. Our noses were pressed against the windows over there, but of course, we couldn't see a thing. The clouds were as dark as night, and the rain was thick and icy. I remember thinking all I could see were the shapes of men slipping and sliding through the mud. They searched the houses first, but it turned out no one had seen Olive all day. Her parents said she had left as usual for the Café, back then she cooked and cleaned you see, and they said they didn't expect to see her until bedtime.'

She momentarily closed her eyes, gently massaging her fingers against her skull. 'Finally, the men made their way to the edge of the village, to the bridge and that's when they found her shoe in the mud and, according to Willum, it was clear she'd slipped down the bank into the water. When the police finally arrived, they concluded the current had carried her away.'

Hugo nodded. 'But they never found her body?'

Dorothy shook her head. 'No. Apparently, the stream goes all the way to the river. I think everyone just assumed she was lost to the sea. It was awful, just awful. Maurice was beside himself. We all were. Nobody could believe such a tragedy had happened to such a lovely young woman.'

Hugo considered his response for a minute or two. 'I get the impression Maurice Rousseau didn't and still doesn't believe it was an accident. Is that a correct assumption?'

Dorothy's mouth contorted. 'That was mostly down to Edith Lancaster,' she explained. 'As we sat in the Café trying to make sense of it all, Edith mentioned that earlier in the afternoon she'd seen Olive sneaking off with a man. I'm afraid she was rather salacious about it and the way she made the implication clear to Maurice. I thought at the time it was cruel and unnecessary, but I said nothing.'

Hugo nodded. 'Then because of what she said, Maurice came to believe his wife was murdered by her secret lover?'

Dorothy shrugged. 'I suppose it was the only thing which made sense to him. He just kept saying over and over - what was she doing by the bridge unless she was meeting someone?'

'And you had no idea who her lover might have been?' Hugo asked.

'No,' she replied quickly. 'Or even if there was one, for that matter. I always assumed it was nothing more than a tragic accident, but that it was something Maurice just couldn't accept.'

'Was the bridge damaged then also?'

Dorothy shook her head. 'No,' she replied. 'In fact, I'm fairly sure it was the same bridge, and it certainly wasn't new even forty years ago.' She narrowed her eyes at Hugo. 'Why are you asking?'

Hugo met her anxious gaze and it troubled him because he had no answers to give her. 'Only my suspicious mind working overtime. No body was ever recovered and as you said, Olive Rousseau wasn't exactly enamoured with the life she'd been given, so it's not too much of a stretch to think she may have run off to start a new life.'

'It's possible, I suppose,' Dorothy conceded reluctantly. 'Although it would be a particularly cruel thing to do. She had elderly parents who loved her, not to mention Maurice.'

'You're probably right,' Hugo replied, not at all sure if he agreed. He had seen enough in his forty years on earth to know there were dark recesses in the minds of most people, which often caused them to act entirely selfishly.

'If Olive had a lover,' he continued cautiously, 'do you have any idea who it might have been? I'm guessing it wasn't someone she already knew from the village, but rather someone new, perhaps someone on the pilgrimage?'

'I'm sure I don't know,' Dorothy responded.

Hugo sucked in a breath. He was fairly sure Dorothy

Chapeau had just lied to him.

'All I can tell you,' she continued, 'is everyone was devastated by what happened and it marred the entire pilgrimage, but in the end, Maurice insisted we continue, which we did in her honour.'

'And did he speak about it?'

Dorothy considered her response. 'No. He barely mentioned it afterwards. None of us did.' She fixed Hugo with a fiery stare, one which Hugo recognised because he had been on the receiving end of a similar stare from her daughter on more than one occasion. 'I still can't imagine why you think this may be relevant now.'

'I'm not sure it is,' Hugo agreed. 'Other than the timing seems odd.'

Dorothy shrugged and rose slowly to her feet. 'I don't know anything about that. Anyway, if you'll excuse me, it's time for my nap. Old age is a drag, Hugo,' she added sadly. 'I am glad to have met you and I hope we can get to know each other better without this shadow over us.'

Hugo smiled at her. 'I hope so too.'

Dorothy stopped abruptly. Edith Lancaster was standing in the doorway, her gaze fixed firmly on Hugo and Dorothy. 'Oh, Edith, you startled me,' Dorothy gasped.

Edith pulled her cardigan across her chest. 'I haven't lived through almost nine decades for others to discuss me behind my back. I find I prefer to be asked questions directly.'

Hugo and Dorothy exchanged a confused look. 'We weren't talking about you,' Dorothy responded quickly.

Edith waved her hand irritably. 'I shall speak privately with Captain Duchamp,' she snapped. 'You need not concern yourself with this any further.'

Hugo flashed a look of acknowledgment at Dorothy, and she moved into the hotel. 'Be kind to him, Edith,' she called over her shoulder.

Edith gestured to the chair Hugo had just moved away from. 'Take a seat, Captain Duchamp, and we can begin.'

Hugo & Edith

Hugo was not sure exactly what it was about Edith Lancaster that reminded him of his Grand Mère, Madeline Duchamp. There was certainly no physical resemblance, and while their voices shared similar intonations, Hugo only recalled Madeline's admonishments as being cutting, rather than nasty. He supposed, in the end, Edith Lancaster had no reason to like him or anyone like him. They likely shared no common interests or experiences.

'You're a homosexual, aren't you?' Edith demanded.

'Is that relevant?' Hugo retorted defensively.

'To my God it is.'

Hugo locked eyes with her. 'Not to my God.'

The elderly English woman gave Hugo an interested look. 'You have a God?'

Hugo nodded. 'I do,' he replied. 'He probably doesn't exist in any way we understand, but he or she informs me in very important ways nevertheless. My God allows me to be the best person I can be without actually judging someone just because a book, most likely fiction, tells me to do so. And the same book, I must add, that allows its readers to pick and choose what rules they do or do not follow.' He smiled at her. 'I'm sure you know such books. You are a librarian, after all, aren't you?'

She laughed. 'Very well. You passed the grumpy old lady test, we can continue. Most people have always assumed because I'm a sour old spinster who spent most of her life in a dusty old library that I too was of the homosexual persuasion.' She shrugged. 'The fact remains, I find women as tiresome as I do men. None of them ever caught my attention enough for me to care one way or the other.' She picked up her knitting. 'Instead, I knit and send scarves to Ethiopia, or wherever else they can have the least positive effect.'

She gave him a demure smile. 'The truth is, my knitting allows me to be present with no one actually paying me a blind bit of attention.'

Hugo returned the smile. 'I imagine you see and hear much more than people intend for you to.'

Edith demurely tipped her head. She pulled her knitting from the carpetbag on her lap, her fingers instantly moving with such rapidity, Hugo was not sure how she saw what she was doing. 'Am I correct in thinking you are foolishly assuming something that happened forty years ago, is somehow or other connected to the death of poor Alain Bonnet?'

Hugo felt as if he was being scolded, again reminded of most of his childhood conversations with Madeline. 'I'm not suggesting anything. The fact is, we have very little to go on, but we have a basis to start. Unless we assume that someone snuck into the village with the express intention of murdering Monsieur Bonnet and their escape was thwarted by the storm, then we are left with only two alternatives.'

'The first,' he continued, 'that he was murdered by someone in the village. For me, of course, this is a much more likely scenario, particularly bearing in mind the people who came here recently are relative strangers, or strangers at least separated by forty years of absence. I find no reason to assume someone would have returned to France simply to murder someone for something that occurred forty years ago.'

Edith snorted. 'Then you have no imagination.'

Hugo laughed. 'On the contrary, I have a lot of imagination and it has served me well since I solved my first murder when I was fifteen years old. I learnt then to always look in the shadows and never assume that a truth is always a truth.'

'Then what is it you are suggesting?' Edith asked, suddenly stopping knitting, fixing Hugo with an irritated look.

'I don't know what happened here,' Hugo replied, 'other than my gut tells me someone who lived alongside Alain Bonnet suddenly murdered him at this particular moment. To further extrapolate, I would also like to move on from the possibility of a perfectly random stranger wandering into this village.' He shrugged. 'Therefore, it's not too much of a stretch to imagine a closed-door scenario, wherein several people were reconnected after a period of time, resulting in the past resurfacing and someone taking the opportunity to avenge past sins, whatever they may be.'

He smiled at Edith. 'I spent a large part of my life in England and during that time I read a lot of Agatha Christie, as I am sure have you. My grandmother approved of very few English women, but she certainly approved of her and she told me the only thing about small villages you could be certain of was that no one, absolutely no one could be trusted.'

Edith laughed. 'Your grandmother was not only wise, she was also correct. Forty years ago, we all came to this village, but not all of us left. There was debauchery. Olive Rousseau had her head turned by a charlatan and it ended in her death.'

'In what way?' Hugo asked. He was genuinely curious because he imagined whatever scenario Edith Lancaster had created in her own mind, it was at the very least something which might help the investigating authorities to make sense of what had happened.

Edith dropped her knitting, lifting her head towards Hugo and he sensed she was evaluating whether to speak further. She picked up the knitting and quickly resumed.

'In what way?' Hugo repeated. 'Who turned her head? Was it Alain Bonnet?'

Edith scoffed. 'He wished,' she cackled. 'I'm not sure what it's like for your kind, but normal…' she paused before continuing, 'I mean, heterosexual men are often foolish, led to impulsiveness and foolishness by their,' she gestured downwards before adding in a whisper, '*members*. Alain was like a puppy dog following a cruel owner. The more Olive kicked him, the more devoted he became. If you ask me, she was cruel in her apathy towards him.'

Hugo nodded. 'Dorothy suggested there was some kind of argument between Olive and Alain on the day of her death.'

'She is correct,' Edith confirmed. 'It was interesting to hear Alain actually standing up for himself.'

'What was the fight over?'

Edith pursed her lips. 'I'm sure you wouldn't like me to speculate about something I may or may not have heard or misheard decades ago,' she sniped.

'I wouldn't,' he replied. 'But I also imagine you're not the sort of woman who would speculate about anything you weren't certain of.'

She smiled demurely. 'There's nothing wrong with my hearing, even at my advanced age, but back then I could hear a pin drop in a different room,' she added. 'Although I always find when men are engaged in a heated debate they're often useless at keeping their voice low enough, making it practically impossible for a person not to hear, whether they are predisposed to or not.'

'Alain was admonishing Olive on what he perceived as inappropriate behaviour,' Edith stated firmly. 'He was correct, of course, but really, his reasoning wasn't.'

Her lips twisted cruelly. 'He made the pretence he was concerned about the honour of his best friend, Maurice, but really all he was mad about was that was she dabbling with another man. I heard it clearly in his voice. *You'll choose anyone but me, won't you, you whore?* That was what he was saying without using the actual words.'

Edith smirked before continuing. 'Whilst I don't like to speak ill of the dead, Alain Bonnet was hardly Rudolph Valentino, but in this instance, he was right. Olive didn't choose her lover for his looks. She chose him because I imagine she saw him as an escape from her life in this village.'

'You're talking about Tony Wilkinson?' Hugo interjected.

She gave him an impressed look. 'Well done, Monsieur Poirot.'

Hugo shrugged. 'Not really. Dorothy told me that the Mitchells were madly in love and that Tony Wilkinson was not yet married. I also imagine he was rich then too, so if Olive was searching for a way out of her life here, he may just have been a suitable candidate.'

'He was a pasty-faced miscreant even then,' Edith stated. 'And he was no match for a woman of her wiles. Oh, but you are correct. Olive saw dollar signs when Tony Wilkinson walked into the village, and she no doubt imagined she was going to join him as lady of the Manor back in England.'

'Except she didn't get to leave the village after all,' Hugo said softly.

'No, she didn't,' Edith said curtly. 'I'm not saying she got what she deserved, but…'

Before Hugo could stop himself, an irritated tut escaped his mouth. 'What else do you recall about that day?'

'After she argued with Alain, Olive ran from the Café in tears, the shame clear on her face,' Edith replied. 'I suppose I assumed she'd just gone home to lick her wounds, or perhaps to commit a sin with her lover. Either way, it was only some time later that Maurice came looking for her. As far as he knew, she'd remained working in the Café and had never returned to her home.'

She continued. 'With the storm being as bad as it was, of course, all the men beat their fists against their chests and went to rescue the damsel in distress. It didn't take them long to discover what had happened, and that she had been lost to the sea.'

'What do you think happened?' Hugo asked.

'Isn't it obvious?' Edith replied. 'She was running and slipped. How karmic. Committing adultery and running to a new life with her home wrecker, but God had other plans for her,' she added bitterly.

'Then he isn't a God I can get behind,' Hugo snapped.

Edith sniffed huffily. 'You don't need to, young man. Our job is to follow Him and know He is always correct and acting in our best interests. If Olive had understood that, her life may have ended very differently. Whatever you might think of Him, I know it is not always easy to understand His decisions and His reasons, but we must accept them as what has been chosen for us, even if that is sometimes difficult.'

Hugo thought for the first time the elderly English woman sounded genuinely bothered. He frowned. 'It seems as if it was a tragic accident caused by the storm,' he began. 'Therefore, I'm confused why Maurice Rousseau thought it was something other than an accident.'

'Ah, that would be down to a particularly nosey woman who just happened to be looking out of her window,' Edith answered. 'She claims to have seen Olive in front of the bridge arguing with someone.'

'With someone?' Hugo leaned forward.

Edith nodded. 'She says she couldn't see who it was because of the darkness and the rain, but that she was sure it was a man and he was manhandling Olive.'

'And what happened next?'

She shrugged. 'The woman went about her business and left them to it.'

'And it wasn't Maurice Rousseau?'

She shrugged again. 'Not according to him, nor Alain. They effectively gave each other an alibi, but it certainly made for an interesting scenario, don't you think? Maurice claimed then, rightly or wrongly, that poor Olive was pushed to her death, but of course, there was no way of proving it one way or the other. Especially without a body or no actual witness.'

'A few days later, the storm cleared, and we left the village,' Edith continued. 'Of course, we were all shocked, but the reality was none of us knew these people at all. We'd only met that week, and even Tony was most likely relieved to be free of a complication he had not envisaged when he arrived in France. No, we went about our pilgrimage and that was the end of it.'

'And Maurice?'

'He accompanied us,' she replied. 'It was his job, after all, and I suppose it kept him busy, but he kept his distance. I recall thinking at the time he was watching us all with suspicion as if he imagined we were all somehow involved.'

Hugo nodded. 'And do you think he had reason to?'

'I couldn't say,' Edith retorted. 'I know I was not involved, and my counsel is the only one which concerns me. If you're asking, did I have any suspicions? Then the answer would be no. I don't know one way or another whether Olive fell to her death naturally or otherwise. I was here for one purpose and one purpose only. To walk towards God.'

'And what do you make of Alain Bonnet's murder forty years later?'

She lifted her head and Hugo noticed her eyes were twinkling. 'I make very little of it. Other than it's rather interesting he was stabbed in the back, don't you think?'

'What do you mean?'

Edith rose slowly to her feet. 'I must rest before supper.' She stopped by the stairs, fixing Hugo with an amused look. 'Stabbing someone in the back is practically biblical. It's like someone saying, you stabbed me in the back metaphorically, so now I'm going to do it to you for real.'

'And who do you imagine Alain Bonnet metaphorically stabbed in the back?' Hugo questioned.

Edith Lancaster disappeared into the darkness of the stairwell. 'Now therein lies a very interesting question. See you later, Hercule. I imagine there will be much more to discuss soon,' she called cheerfully from the shadows.

Hugo dropped onto the bed and wrapped his arms around Ben. He had been trying to spend some quiet time away from the noise and confusion of the situation he now found himself in. It was one he did not understand, and he hoped listening to the recordings Irene had made of her and Wolfgang Huber interviewing the group might help.

'I feel so helpless,' Ben murmured.

'Me too,' Hugo agreed. 'And the problem is, I don't know what we've walked into. I don't have a lot to base it on, but it feels as if there is something really off in this village and I can't understand whether it's to do with the present or the past, and truthfully, I'm not sure it's my place to try to piece it together.'

Ben squeezed his hand. 'Who else can do it? You're kinda the best at this, y'know?'

Hugo gave him a sad laugh. 'Someone died, and it seems like there is something really weird going on. But the truth is, we can't stay. This isn't our problem, and I don't think we can make it our problem.'

'And yet here we are,' Ben replied. 'And aren't we a captive audience? What else do we have to do with our time?' he added with a smile before reaching across and touching the wall, tapping it with his fingers. 'I'd rather be doing something else, but the walls are paper thin and I imagine the English librarian will crash through it and throw a bible on my naked ass.'

Hugo chuckled. 'Merci for that particular image, cher.' He smiled, pleased with a momentary distraction from his troubles. 'I need to listen to these recordings Irene made.'

'You think they'll help?'

Hugo considered his answer. 'I'm not sure. But I feel as if I should listen. I don't know any of these people, and the fact is, we are like sitting ducks here. Alain Bonnet was murdered and we have to assume it was someone in this hotel.'

Ben shuddered. 'I hate the thought of that.'

'As do I,' Hugo conceded. 'However, it is how it appears at this moment and it is what we have to deal with. I'm not sure how listening to these recordings will help, but I admit I am curious and I would like to listen to them.'

'Then lie back and see if you can make sense of it,' Ben said, kissing Hugo on the cheek. 'And I'll be right here with you holding your hand.'

Hugo lit a cigarette and placed the notes he had made on the bedside table. Ben had fallen asleep next to him, and Hugo found his gentle snores to be soothing. He had listened twice to the recordings Irene had made because he wanted to make sure he missed nothing. He stared at his notes because at that moment he was not sure what to make of them.

'Are you done?' Ben asked, rolling over and rubbing his tired eyes. 'I can't believe I fell asleep during the day.' He pushed himself up. 'It's the relentless darkness and the rain. Everything just feels so miserable and it's like we're in the middle of the night all the time. I just want a little bit of daylight,' he said wearily.

Hugo grabbed Ben's hand. 'We'll be home soon.'

Ben crossed his fingers. 'What about Irene's recordings?'

Hugo glanced at his notes again and took his time before responding. 'There is so little to go on. Peut être if I'd had the chance to look at their faces I may have been able to form a better opinion, but as it stands I can't be sure of anything, not least why someone may have murdered Alain Bonnet not once, but twice.'

'What do you think we should do, then?' Ben asked.

Hugo took a deep breath, staring at the rain-splattered window. 'The only thing I'm sure of is that we need to get out of this village because only then will we be able to look back and have a chance of understanding. We need to get word to the local police and get them here. I suspect Maurice Rousseau is a man who thinks he had nothing left to lose. If it's true, he's been nursing a vendetta for a very long time, it likely makes him very dangerous.'

'Should we be worried?'

Hugo reached over and kissed his cheek. 'Whatever happened has nothing to do with us. We'll be fine because we're together. I won't let anyone harm us, not again.'

Ben nodded. 'I know. I trust you. If anyone can get us out of this mess, it's you.'

Hugo lit a cigarette, not sure he shared his husband's confidence because as matters stood, he had no idea how to proceed.

Hugo stared out of the Café window. Night had descended quickly, bringing with it even more rain. He glanced at his watch again, realising he had been doing it more or less every minute for longer than he could remember.

He was concerned that help had still not arrived in one form or another. Even with the bridge down, he imagined someone would have followed them into the village, at the very least, to check that everything was okay. Ben had tried to reassure him, reasoning no one outside of the village yet knew of the murder and was most likely dealing with a myriad of other problems in the surrounding areas.

'You look worried,' Ben said, slipping his fingers between Hugo's.

Hugo nodded. 'Part of me thinks I should leave the village and make contact with the local police department because the longer we leave it, the more likely evidence is destroyed, and...' he lowered his voice, glancing ominously around the room. All the guests had come down from the rooms as the women busied themselves in the kitchen making supper. 'We can't rule out the possibility of something else happening,' he added in a low whisper.

'Je sais, je sais,' Ben agreed. 'But I can't let you go, not now, not in the dark and the rain, and especially because you are the only person experienced enough to take charge of the situation.'

'There's Wolfgang Huber,' Hugo corrected. 'He's a retired police officer. He's just as capable of taking charge as I am.'

'But he is also a suspect,' Ben mouthed, before shaking his head forcefully. 'Non. If help hasn't arrived by morning, I'll go myself and contact the police and let them know what happened, and then hopefully we can get the hell out of here once and for all.'

Hugo squeezed his hand. 'We'll talk about it later.' Before he had a chance to say anything else, the door to the Café flew open, a gust of wind and rain spraying into the room. Hugo's head jerked upwards, as Maurice Rousseau and the young guide, Xavier Cadieux, pushed the door closed behind them.

'You frightened me,' Elke Humer gasped from behind the counter before going back to chopping an onion.

Maurice ignored her, instead turning around and locking the Café door. He pulled out the key and placed it in his pocket.

Hugo watched him with interest. There was something about his face that troubled him. He placed his hands on the table in front of him. 'What's going on?' he demanded. 'Why have you locked the door?'

'You're not in charge here, flic,' Maurice snapped.

Wolfgang Huber stood. 'Maurice?' he questioned, his voice wavering.

Maurice pointed to Wolfgang's seat. 'Sit down, Wolfgang,' he commanded.

Wolfgang's eyebrows knotted in confusion and after a moment he reluctantly returned to his seat, flashing Hugo a look of concern.

'I'll ask again,' Hugo said forcefully. He was concerned by the sudden change in circumstances, though he was at a loss to understand what it might mean. 'Why have you locked the door?'

A muscle in Maurice's cheek flexed. 'Because I am in charge here, not you, not any of you,' he said wagging his finger dramatically.

Dorothy stepped from behind the counter, wiping her hands on a towel. 'Maurice, you're scaring me.'

Maurice moved across the room and physically moved a shocked Dorothy back behind the counter. Irene jumped to her feet. 'Don't you dare touch my mother like that!' she hissed, her fists clenched ready to strike.

Maurice spun around and pressed his hand against Irene's

chest and, with a hard shove, moved her away from him. 'Sit down and don't move again unless I tell you to. Do I make myself clear?' He turned his head between all the people in the Café. 'Do I make myself clear to you all?' he repeated, his voice hard and cold.

Hugo gestured for Irene to take her seat. 'Tell us what this is about, Monsieur Rousseau,' he said in as even a tone as he could muster in an attempt to defuse a potentially escalating scenario.

'This is about a pain I've held inside for over forty years,' he replied. 'I have waited for the people in this room to finally return so that I could look each one of them in the face and demand they finally tell me the truth and answer a simple question. Which of them killed my beautiful Olive and robbed this earth of such a beautiful angel?'

Edith Lancaster sighed and dropped her knitting on the table in front of her. 'Not this nonsense again,' she sighed. 'We all know it was nothing but an accident. A tragedy, but an accident nonetheless.'

She raised her hand quickly as if fending off his inevitable protests. 'And before you start with the apparent recollection of an elderly woman who may or may not have seen Olive talking to a man. The police at the time saw it for what it was. Nothing. Olive died, and as tragic as it was, it was nothing but a horrible accident. The police knew it, and,' she gestured around the room, 'we all knew it.'

'The only person who was in denial then, and apparently still is now, is you, Maurice Rousseau,' Edith continued, 'and I won't allow this to mar what is most likely my last chance to walk the Camino again with your inane conspiracy theories. Olive died and there was no great mystery to it.'

He clenched his fists. 'You know that's not the truth. You of all people know it.'

Edith cocked her head, her eyes widening. 'I can't begin to imagine what you mean by that, or why you might imagine your opinion is of any consequence to me. I knew you forty years ago, Maurice Rousseau, and time has not tempered my initial opinion of you. You blamed everyone else for your lack of virility, rather than directing it to where the blame really lay and that was with you.'

'Shut your mouth, you foul woman!' Maurice roared.

Edith moved her shoulders slowly. 'I have always found the only opinions some people are interested in are their own. The actual truth is often nothing but a burden for such people.'

'Olive was murdered.'

'That's certainly a possibility,' she conceded. 'Though quite what you hope to achieve with this charade is beyond me.'

'This charade, as you call it,' Maurice snapped back, 'is for one purpose and one purpose only. To finally discover which of you murdered my beautiful girl.'

Hugo jumped to his feet. 'Whatever you think happened, whatever you hope to achieve, as a police officer I must tell you, you have to be careful how you proceed.' He pointed at Xavier. 'Xavier has informed the authorities and help is on its way, so you must remember that, because I'm sure you don't want to get carried away and do something which will, in the end, only result in you finding yourself in trouble.'

Maurice stepped back and rubbed Xavier's shoulder. 'Xavier is my nephew, or rather, he was Olive's nephew, but more importantly, he stands side by side with me in finally ensuring darling Olive's murderer finally faces justice.'

Hugo turned to the young guide. 'Xavier. You contacted the police, didn't you?'

Xavier smiled, flashing a perfect set of teeth. 'I told them the storm had been brutal, but all was well at *Chemin des Pèlerins*, and they should concentrate on helping the surrounding towns and villages, which were far more affected by the terrible weather.' He stopped, winking at Hugo. 'You didn't think for a second that I was lying, did you?' He turned to Ben and Viviane Auclair. 'None of you did.'

Viviane slammed her hands on the table. 'What the hell's going on, Xav?'

Xavier slapped his arm around Maurice's shoulder. 'For forty years, my family has been tortured by what happened to tante Olive. One of my first memories is of my mother crying because it was the anniversary of her sister's death. Maman has been sick ever since Olive died and I swear the only thing keeping her alive is one day finding out exactly what happened.'

Hugo shook his head irritably. 'I can't pretend to know all the facts of the case, but everything I've heard so far shows Olive Rousseau's death was a terrible accident caused by a violent storm. There is no sign of a police investigation suggesting otherwise, and the only suggestion she may not have been alone came from a witness who was not entirely sure what she saw.'

'The widow Lebrawski was very clear in her recollection,' Maurice snapped, his voice cold as ice. 'She remained convinced that if she'd done something, she could have saved Olive. She died soon after. The doctor said it was as if her heart had just been so broken it just stopped working.'

'I'm sorry to hear that,' Hugo replied softly. He took a deep breath, trying desperately to think of a way to defuse the increasingly volatile situation. He looked between Maurice and Xavier and he did not like what he saw on their faces. They were alert, and they were keen. *They've been waiting a long time for this and we have no idea what they are capable of, or what is coming next.*

'I have to ask: what are you hoping to achieve?' Hugo continued.

Maurice began pacing across the floor of the Café. To Hugo, he resembled a caged lion, anxiously pacing, eyes locked on its spectators as if readying itself to attack any one of them.

Maurice dropped onto a chair in front of Hugo. 'I don't really remember the first few years after Olive died. I was so consumed with grief that it took a long time for the anger to take over. But then, as the widow Lebrawski lay on her deathbed, she said something which changed everything for me. *I saw the man who murdered our dear Olive. Don't let him get away with it.'*

Maurice poured a glass of water from the decanter on the table, angrily slurping it, water spilling down his chin. 'I've waited a long time for this moment.'

Hugo frowned. He looked around the room, anxiety clear on everyone's faces, all staring at him expectantly, waiting for him to do something. Hugo faced Wolfgang Huber. The elderly ex-police officer slouched his shoulders, flashing an obvious message to Hugo - *I have no idea what we should do.*

Hugo pushed away a sigh. 'I'm very sorry for your loss, Monsieur Rousseau, but I must point out to you that holding us here is a crime, and it is a crime which will land you in prison for a very long time,' he stated evenly and calmly. 'I am a serving police officer and am therefore reminding you of this before the situation gets any more out of hand.'

Maurice pointed to the door. 'You're free to leave, Captain Duchamp,' he responded. 'I don't have a problem with you and I would prefer to keep it that way. So, like I said, you, your,' he paused, extending his fingers into air quotes, '"husband" and your friend and her son can leave right now.'

'If you think I'm leaving my mother here with you, you're very much mistaken,' Irene snapped through gritted teeth.

Maurice shrugged. 'That is your decision, young lady.'

Hugo shook his head. 'I'm not leaving anyone behind. We will all be leaving together.'

Xavier pointed to the darkness. 'It's pitch black and pouring with rain,' he stated, 'and as you know, it's not exactly easy to get out of the village without the bridge, especially,' he turned his head around the Café, 'since most of the people here are ancient.'

Edith Lancaster spluttered. 'Try coming over here and saying

223

that, young man,' she hissed through gritted teeth, before adding, 'and you'll see exactly what *this* ancient is capable of!'

'I agree,' Elke Huber added before her eyes widened with fear. 'Although, I'm not sure leaving in the middle of the night in a storm is the best idea.'

'We won't,' Hugo said. 'Regardless of whether or not Xavier told the authorities what's going on here, the fact no telephone lines are working means someone will look, eventually. But more importantly, my team in Montgenoux knows exactly where I am and if they don't hear from me soon, I wouldn't be surprised if a helicopter lands in the village square.'

'He's right,' Ben chimed in with pride. 'And then you'll be sorry.'

'As I said, you are free to leave at any time,' Maurice stated.

Edith pushed her chair back and rose. 'And leave, we will. One way or another. Now, I am going to my room because I refuse to engage in this stupidity a moment longer.'

Maurice laughed. 'You'll go when I say you can, old lady.'

She chuckled. 'I'd like to see you try to stop me, Maurice Rousseau.'

Dorothy Chapeau also stood. 'I agree with Edith. I don't want to be here, not now, not in the middle of the night.'

'Let's go, Mama,' Irene added. 'We don't have to stay here just because he says we do.' She glared at Maurice. 'And I'll be locking our door, and if anyone tries to get in 'without my permission, they'll have me to deal with, and don't be fooled by my stature. I can assure you I can still pack a punch.'

Ben gave a wry smile. 'I can confirm that.'

Maurice and Xavier exchanged a look. 'I've waited a long time for this,' Maurice said.

'It can wait until morning, Oncle Maurice,' Xavier interrupted, pushing his hand through his hair. He lowered his voice. 'And it might help to be rid of the cop and his friends. The others may be more willing to talk without them.'

Maurice's lips twisted in irritation as if he was weighing up his options. He grimaced. 'D'accord.' He extended his hands. 'Go rest pilgrims, and if any of us have been carrying a burden for the last forty years, I hope this is the last night your conscience allows you to keep lying.'

Edith tutted, searching around the table in front of her. 'Where has my knitting gone?'

'What do you mean?' Dorothy questioned.

'Of all the audacity!' Edith exclaimed. 'Imagine stealing an old woman's knitting!'

Dorothy linked arms with her, giving a sad laugh. 'I don't think anyone would steal your knitting, Edith,' she explained gently. 'You probably just left it in your room,' she added.

'Of course, I didn't,' Edith snapped, before her face clouded. 'At least I don't think so. I'm sure I had it with me. I mean, I always do.' She rummaged through her oversized carpet bag. 'It doesn't seem to be here.'

Dorothy guided her towards the stairway. 'Let's get you upstairs. We all need some rest. Things will be okay tomorrow, you'll see.' She stopped and looked over her shoulder towards Hugo. 'It will be, won't it?' she asked with clear desperation.

Hugo nodded. It pained him to see the fear in everyone's eyes because the fact was; he did not know what he could do to make the situation right. 'We'll be leaving tomorrow, don't worry. We will be leaving. I promise you everything is going to be fine,' he stated, hoping to hide his doubts.

Maurice Rousseau laughed loudly. 'It will be as long as one of you bastards finally tells the truth.'

Hugo squared up to him. 'The time for threats is over, Monsieur Rousseau. And as much as I want you to find peace, I cannot allow it to come at the expense of anyone else.'

Maurice shrugged. 'The truth will set us all free.' He smiled at the people in the room. 'All it takes is for one of you to tell the truth.' He rubbed Xavier's shoulder. 'And should any of you decide to make a run for it during the night, think again. My nephew here will make sure no one leaves.'

Xavier Cadieux stood, dragging his chair across the floor and placing it under the door lock. He dropped back onto it, a wide grin on his face. 'Consider me your sentry. Try to pass me and you'll regret it.'

Hugo, Ben, Irene & Dorothy

Hugo awoke with a start, his notebook falling from his chest. He picked it up, noticing Ben was standing by the window, staring into the village square below. Hugo could hear the rain still pounding against the glass and it depressed him almost more than he could stand.

'I was hoping it would have stopped by now,' Ben mused. 'You saw how difficult it was to get into the village. I'm just not sure how everyone is going to make it, or even if we should try. But what can we do? I don't want just one of us to go, but if they won't let everyone go, what can we do?'

Hugo reached over to the bedside table and lit a cigarette. 'Well, technically, there are more of us than them. We could force our way out and they wouldn't have much chance of stopping us.'

Ben spun around. Hugo could see the anxiety etched on his usually smooth, cheerful face. 'I've been thinking about that - but what if Maurice and Xavier have weapons? They could have guns, or knives, or both. Do we really want to take the chance?'

Before Hugo could respond, there was a knock at the door. Ben pulled it open to reveal Irene and Dorothy.

'How did you sleep?' Irene asked.

'Terribly,' Ben sighed. 'And when I did, I had nightmares.'

She nodded. 'We did too. Listen, Bruno's hungry, but I don't want to take him downstairs with those idiots. I'd rather he stayed in the room.'

'We'll make you all something and bring it up to your room,' Ben replied.

Irene and her mother exchanged an irritated look as if they were in the middle of an argument. 'Mama is insisting on going downstairs and confronting Maurice.'

'How else are we going to end this?' Dorothy snapped.

227

'Maurice has a bee in his bonnet about something that happened before you were born. He isn't interested in the three of you. This is about us, the original pilgrims, and until he gets something resembling an answer, he's going to keep going and none of us wants that.'

'Mama, he could be dangerous,' Irene cried, the knowledge she was fighting a losing battle evident in her voice.

Dorothy ignored her daughter and instead turned to Ben. 'Ben, I would like you to stay in our room with Irene and Bruno. I'd feel better knowing you were with them.' She then turned to Hugo. 'Unfortunately, I think we need you. Maurice seems to respond to your authority.'

Ben stepped forward. 'I can't let Hugo go without me.'

Hugo stroked Ben's hair, his fingers twirling around the curls on his forehead. 'Dorothy is right. I need to be there. The fact I am a police officer might just be enough to stop this from descending into something more than it needs to be. And she's also right about how it would be better for us all if you, Irene and Bruno were safely locked in the bedroom until this is over.'

He raised his hand to fend off the impending protests. 'This really is the best way, mon amour.' He kissed the top of Ben's head. 'We'll be safe, don't worry.'

Dorothy looked at Irene. 'Lock the door behind you. I'll send some food up shortly.'

Hugo stepped into the doorway. 'This will all be over soon, you'll see. One way or another, I won't allow Maurice Rousseau to carry this vendetta any further.'

Les Pèlerins - Onzième jour

Hugo and Dorothy descended the steps into the Café dining room and all attention was drawn to them as they entered. Hugo had always felt awkward, especially walking into a room full of strangers and having them all look at him. In this instance, it felt even worse because he saw the expectation and hope on their faces that he might be the one to get them out of the troubling situation.

'I thought we might cook some breakfast,' Dorothy called out, gesturing to Elke. 'Bruno is famished, and I think it's probably a good idea for us all to try to eat something.'

Elke Huber clambered quickly to her feet. 'A splendid idea, Dorothy,' she responded as if she was glad to finally have something to do other than staring out of a misty window.

Hugo looked around the dining room. Maurice Rousseau and Xavier Cadieux were by the door, engaged in a private and seemingly heated debate, but Hugo could not make out what they were saying. Wolfgang Huber was at a table in the centre of the room with the American Sam Mitchell and his son, Casey. Edith Lancaster was in the corner, eyes narrow and fixed firmly on Maurice and Xavier. The young tour guide Viviane Auclair was on her own, anxiously chewing on a piece of hair, no doubt wondering what on earth trouble she had walked into, Hugo reasoned. The only other people missing were the English father and daughter, Tony and Sarah Wilkinson.

Hugo took a seat and, not knowing what else to do, lit a cigarette, ignoring the loud tut from Edith in the corner.

Behind them, Dorothy and Elke went about preparing food. Hugo heard eggs being cracked into a pan and for a moment took solace in the normality of it all.

'Did you find your knitting, Edith?' Dorothy called out over the sizzling.

'No, I did not,' Edith snapped, casting a disapproving look around the room. 'And if it is someone's idea of a joke, then I consider it to be in very poor taste.' She narrowed her eyes again. 'I would like it returned forthwith,' she announced to no one in particular.

Sarah Wilkinson moved into the Café, stopping in much the same way Hugo had when she realised she had attracted everyone's attention. The young English woman anxiously bit her nails, frightened eyes snapping around the dining room. 'Where's my dad?'

Hugo looked around. 'Isn't he with you?'

She shrugged. 'He wasn't there when I woke up,' she responded.

Sam Mitchell pointed to the door. 'He probably went for a walk again,' he suggested.

In the shadow of the doorway, Xavier Cadieux laughed. 'I told you. No one was going to get in or out of here last night.'

Hugo stubbed out his cigarette, turning to Sarah. 'When was the last time you saw your father?'

She shrugged. 'He was in the room, trying YET again to get his phone to work so he could get his emails. I said I was going to sleep, and he said something about going to try to get some signal. I fell asleep, and he wasn't there when I woke up.'

Hugo noticed Wolfgang Huber was staring at him and he instantly recognised the look. *We have a problem.* Hugo shook his head, hoping his fear was only being intensified by what was going on at the moment.

Wolfgang clambered to his feet. 'We should perform a search,' adding, 'right now,' in urgent tones.

Sarah gave him a confused look. 'What do you mean?' She turned to Hugo. 'Where is my dad?'

Dorothy Chapeau glanced over her shoulder towards the storeroom. She took the frying pan from the cooker. 'Hugo?'

Hugo nodded and gestured for Wolfgang to follow him. The two detectives moved quickly across the floor, passing the serving counter and entering the storeroom. Hugo's eyes flicked over the crowded room. It was small and he saw nothing which appeared to be out of the ordinary. He stopped, noticing the closed door to the walk-in freezer. His legs did not want to move forward, and he found himself having to force himself to inch forward. Using the sleeve of his jumper, he yanked open the door and flicked on his glasses. He sucked in his breath as the cold air hit his face, his eyes adjusting to the darkness. He blinked several times, at first unsure what he was seeing.

'Dorothy,' he called over his shoulder. 'We're going to need Irene down here right away.'

Irene stepped into the walk-in freezer and before she could stop herself, she cried out aloud and quickly covered her mouth. 'Désolé,' she gasped, shaking her head in disbelief.

'It's alright,' Hugo responded. 'I can't say my initial reaction was much better,' he admitted.

Irene lifted her phone, the light from it illuminating the path in front of her. 'I'm not sure I've seen anything like it in my entire life,' she mumbled.

Hugo stared ahead. He still felt the same emotions he always did when stumbling upon a crime scene, and as awful as it was, it was something he hoped would never change because becoming immune was a far worse outcome. All the same, the monstrous nature of what was in front of them was certainly one of the worst he had come across.

'It's Tony Wilkinson, isn't it?' Irene asked.

Behind her, Wolfgang Huber pressed his body against the wall as if he was attempting to push his way out of the freezer whilst unable to move his legs. 'It certainly is,' he whispered. 'And whoever did that to him is going straight to hell.'

Irene inched slowly forward. 'I can't say I disagree,' she moaned.

Wolfgang exhaled. 'Well, at least we know what happened to Edith Lancaster's knitting,' he stated with a bone-dry laugh.

Hugo looked sharply at him, but he recognised the tone. The laugh was nervous, not malicious. An attempt to break an uncomfortable silence whilst faced with unimaginable horror. Hugo inched forward. Tony Wilkinson's body was slumped against a wall in the corner of the freezer, only a foot or so away from the still-covered remains of Alain Bonnet. Wilkinson's head was turned in the direction of Alain's body, a knitting needle protruding from each eye.

Hugo gestured at them. 'Is that... is that how he died?' he asked Irene awkwardly.

Irene lowered her body, flicking smooth red hair behind her ears as she surveyed what was in front of her. 'There's a lot of blood around the eyes and down his face. So,' she paused, 'I believe there's a very real likelihood he was alive when it happened.'

Behind them, Wolfgang Huber mumbled something which sounded like a German curse.

Hugo looked around the cramped freezer. 'What was he doing in here?' he thought aloud. 'Do you think this is where he died?'

Irene moved her head slowly around the room. 'It's very difficult to say, Hugo, you know that. I need to properly examine the crime scene, and for that, I need forensic lights, my kit...' She stopped before adding sadly, *'Etienne.'*

Hugo pointed at the floor. It was lined with painted white wooden floorboards. 'I see no signs of dragging, but nor do I see any obvious footprints.'

Wolfgang held up a mop. 'Someone could have cleaned up after themselves,' he stated.

Hugo sighed, shaking his head in disbelief. 'What the hell are we dealing with here?'

'I wish I knew,' Irene responded grumpily. She stared at Hugo desperately. 'We need to get out of here today, Hugo. We simply cannot wait any longer.'

He nodded. 'Je sais. I agree, under the circumstances, we can't wait.' He stepped away. 'As reluctant as I am, I believe the only viable option we have is to ask Ben and Viviane to leave the village and alert the police.' His face clouded. 'Time is now most certainly of the essence.'

He stopped, facing Wolfgang. 'I've now had the opportunity to listen to the recordings Irene made, and along with some conversations I've had with people who were familiar with the situation, I believe it's fair to say Tony Wilkinson had some sort of relationship with Olive Rousseau forty years ago.'

'You shouldn't believe everything Edith Lancaster says,' Wolfgang replied. 'She's an awful gossip and a vindictive, judgemental old woman on top of it. Now and then,' he added.

'That's possible,' Hugo agreed. 'But regardless of gossip, was there an affair between Tony Wilkinson and Olive Rousseau?'

It took Wolfgang a moment, but finally he gave a reticent nod. 'They could barely keep their hands off one another, and I'm not even sure they cared if they might get caught. Tony was arrogant even then.' He stared at the corpse, grimacing. 'Sorry, Tony, but it's true. I don't believe in speaking ill of people, alive or dead if they didn't deserve it.'

'What was wrong with him?' Hugo asked.

'Oh, you know the type, I'm sure,' Wolfgang replied. 'Obnoxious men bathed in riches, who know life ahead of them was always going to be paved with gold.'

A thought occurred to Hugo, though he was not sure it had any significance. 'I thought the money come from his wife,' he wondered.

Wolfgang shrugged. 'I can't say. All I can tell you is I didn't like him much. Pasty-faced obnoxious Brit.' He stared at Tony Wilkinson's body. 'Sorry again Tony, but as I said, I believe in telling the truth. And the truth was, I didn't like you, and you didn't like me much either, so I see no sense in being a hypocrite about it now.' He turned to Hugo. 'I don't even know why he came on the pilgrimage. He told me he didn't even believe in God.'

'Well, I can't say I do either,' Irene interrupted. 'But I am here because it was important to my mother, and what's important to her is important to me.'

'Dorothy is very lucky to have you,' Wolfgang replied. 'But I'm not sure Jane Wilkinson was so lucky to have an opportunist like Tony hitching himself to her. My wife told me Jane's father was high up in the English Catholic Church and had raised his daughter to be devout. Tony Wilkinson was here on the first pilgrimage for one reason and one reason only and that was to impress his in-laws.'

'And yet he had an affair with the first woman he met?' Hugo asked, with a confused frown. 'And if he wasn't too worried about hiding it, then your theory about impressing his in-laws makes little sense, does it?'

'I can't answer that,' Wolfgang stated. 'All I can tell you is what my impression was, and that remains, Tony Wilkinson was running around with the gorgeous young Olive without a care in the world.'

'To what end?' Hugo asked.

Wolfgang gave him a quizzical look. 'I don't understand the question, Captain Duchamp.'

Hugo considered his response. 'I suppose I'm wondering this: why was Tony Wilkinson so unconcerned about his affair being discovered if it was his wife who had all the money?'

Wolfgang shrugged again. 'Because it was a fling, nothing more.' He looked over his shoulder as if satisfying himself the door was closed. 'Sometimes men make mistakes because an opportunity presents itself to them. It often means little, other than a man having his ego polished by a pretty young dolly bird.'

He stopped, noticing Irene wincing. 'Sorry, Dr. Chapeau, I mean no harm. All I'm trying to say is that even men who love their wives can stray. It doesn't always have to mean anything.' He turned to Hugo. 'That could have been the case here. Olive Rousseau was very beautiful, and while it's possible Tony loved Jane, I'm afraid to say she wasn't much to look at it.'

Irene tutted loudly.

Wolfgang smiled at her. 'I told you...'

'Yeah, yeah,' Irene interrupted, 'you like to tell the truth.'

'Careful, Dr. Chapeau,' he responded, 'you sound like you might actually be starting to warm to me.'

Irene gave him a doubtful look.

'Anyway, I can see why it might have happened. That's all I'm saying,' Wolfgang continued. 'Jane was what you might call dowdy. Prim and proper, with not much to say for herself.' He turned to Hugo. 'Haven't you ever had a holiday romance that you knew would not carry over into real life, but was fun while it lasted?'

Hugo gulped, unsure of how to respond without sounding foolish. Holiday romances had never been something he had experienced. He had once imagined he might, but it had slowly dawned on him that sort of thing was for other people, not him. The image of a smiling Ben appeared in his mind's eye. It was all Hugo could do to stop himself from grinning at how his fortunes had changed.

'What do we make of the witness suggesting Olive Rousseau was talking and/or arguing with someone right next to the bridge?' Irene asked.

Wolfgang shrugged. 'I never put much stock in that theory, or even if it mattered.'

Hugo tapped his chin. 'Olive Rousseau died, and that appears to be an indisputable fact. We know there was a terrible storm, but the question has to be - did she fall, or was she pushed? And as far as her husband is concerned, she was murdered by the person she was with her when she died. And that question begs another question - did Maurice kill Tony Wilkinson because he believed he was involved in his wife's death?'

'Or Xavier, Olive's nephew, as we now know him to be,' Irene added. 'He could have been involved. He's certainly helping Maurice orchestrate this monstrosity we're having to live through.'

Hugo moved across the room, stopping in front of the covered body of Alain Bonnet. The knife in his back was still obvious under the sheet covering him. 'Doesn't this strike you as odd?' he spoke into the air.

'The whole thing is cuckoo, as far as I'm concerned,' Wolfgang chortled.

Hugo pointed at the sheet. 'Only a thought occurred to me just then. I was listening to the recordings Irene made of your interviews with the people in the hotel and I realised Edith Lancaster claimed Alain Bonnet knew about the affair between Tony Wilkinson and Olive Rousseau.'

Wolfgang nodded his agreement. 'Yes, that's true. I imagine the only person who didn't know about it was Maurice. Eyes as wide as puppy dogs staring at their master. I don't imagine he had a clue what was going on right under his nose.'

'You're saying everyone knew about the affair?' Hugo interjected.

'Yes, that's what I said,' Wolfgang answered wearily.

'Well, no one mentioned it in the interview, nor when I spoke to them,' Hugo replied. 'No one except Edith Lancaster, that is.' He stole a look at Irene. Dorothy Chapeau had not mentioned it either, and Hugo wondered whether that was why he suspected she was lying to him.

'I think we all just turned a blind eye to it,' Wolfgang suggested. 'After all, most of us were relative strangers and the whole thing was a little embarrassing.' He extended his hands. 'What were we supposed to do? Confront the young lovers?' He shook his head. 'It was none of our business, and in the grand scheme of things, what was the harm?'

'Well, I would imagine Jane Wilkinson and Maurice Rousseau might disagree,' Irene stated tartly.

Hugo pursed his lips as he considered a scenario. 'If Alain Bonnet, Maurice Rousseau's best friend, knew about the affair, I imagine that would rather feel like being...'

'Stabbed in the back,' Wolfgang clapped his hands. His face

crinkled. 'Damn. I get your point.'

Hugo pointed to the knitting needles protruding from Tony Wilkinson's eyes. 'And while I hate to point to metaphors, I feel I should point out this one as well.'

Wolfgang gasped. 'An eye for an eye!'

Irene's face contorted towards Hugo. 'I can't begin to imagine what happened, can you?'

Hugo considered his answer. 'I'm not comfortable in speculating, but if I had to imagine a scenario, one does present itself. Alain Bonnet had been nursing a secret for close to forty years about his best friend's wife, and then one day Tony Wilkinson walks back into his Café and it all came back to him.' Hugo slumped against the wall. 'I imagine Maurice Rousseau has had a problem about all of this for over four decades and no doubt Alain bore witness to it all. Tony Wilkinson, finally returning, may have pricked his conscience.'

'So he confessed,' Irene breathed. 'And Maurice felt like his friend had…' She paused, shaking her head. 'Stabbed him in the back,' she repeated.

'You two are crazy,' Wolfgang interrupted grumpily. 'Back when I was a police officer, we investigated crimes based on evidence, not supposition.'

'Then how do you explain what happened here?' Irene demanded.

'I can't,' he responded honestly. 'This isn't our business. The local authorities will take charge. All we need to do is make sure we survive both of the almighty tempests that have presented themselves to us.' He manoeuvred across the room, a laborious process hampered by his girth. 'All I care about now is getting my wife to safety. This is not my business and I won't let it consume me.'

Hugo exhaled. 'I agree. Getting out of here has to be our priority. As I said, I think the only choice we have though is to send Ben and Viviane back to the next village to make sure help finally arrives soon. And with them gone and help on the way, we need to distract Maurice and Xavier the best we can, because we need to buy the time we need until the police arrive. And the only way we can do that is to keep them talking and try to give Maurice what he is looking for.'

Wolfgang scoffed. 'To what end? What do you think you're going to achieve with that course of action?'

'I don't know,' Hugo replied with honesty, because the truth was, he had no idea how to proceed. There was only one thing he was certain of, he could allow no one else to be harmed. 'Whatever game Maurice Rousseau and Xavier Cadieux are playing, we have to make sure it goes no further than it already has.'

Wolfgang raised an eyebrow. 'And how do you propose to do that, Captain Duchamp?'

Hugo gestured to the door. 'We end this. Whatever Maurice Rousseau has imagined for the last forty years has most likely been unbearable for him. All I know is that it is up to the three of us to do whatever we can to ensure it goes no further.' He gestured to the door. 'I suggested we go back inside *Café Compostelle*, where this all appears to have started and we at least try to give him the answers he's been searching for.'

'And if we do, what if he doesn't like those answers?' Irene asked.

Hugo took a deep breath. 'Then we make sure no one else suffers because of it. We're here and we are the only ones who can end this. Maurice Rousseau has to see sense and we need to make him see it.'

'No matter the cost?' Wolfgang demanded, his head cocked.

Hugo gave him a quizzical look. 'The cost has already been too high.' He moved towards the door. 'Let's put an end to this before anyone else gets hurt.'

Hugo and Wolfgang moved in silence from the storeroom behind the Café counter, Irene a few steps behind them. She carefully closed the door behind them, her hand shaking as she touched the handle.

'I'll be upstairs with Bruno,' she said, flashing a hateful look toward Maurice Rousseau and Xavier Cadieux. 'And I'll send Ben right down.' She reached across and squeezed her mother's hand, leaning in and whispering in her ear. 'This will all be over soon, mama, I'm sure. But Hugo is here and if I know anything, it's that he'll make sure no harm comes to you.'

Dorothy Chapeau pulled her hand away. 'To hell with me. What about everyone else?'

Irene leaned in and kissed her cheek. 'Hugo doesn't discriminate between loved ones and complete strangers. He will protect us all.' She scampered away, her feet slapping hurriedly against the stairway. She did not look back, but Hugo felt sure he heard her crying as she disappeared from view.

Sarah Wilkinson jumped to her feet. 'Have you found my father yet?' she demanded.

Hugo nodded and gestured for her to take her seat again. He looked at Dorothy, slouching his head. Her eyes widened as if she understood the instruction and moved quickly, deftly guiding Sarah down and wrapping her arms around her.

'There's no easy way to say this, but I'm afraid I have to inform you your father is dead,' Hugo stated softly.

'What nonsense is this?' Maurice Rousseau roared.

Hugo ignored him, instead concentrating directly on Sarah. He lowered himself into the seat next to her and took her hand. 'I'm very sorry, Miss Wilkinson,' he began, ' but it appears your father was murdered.'

Sarah's head jerked angrily towards Maurice. 'You fucking bastard!' she spat.

Maurice looked anxiously at Xavier. The young guide's face remained passive. 'It had nothing to do with me,' Maurice cried desperately.

'The hell it did,' Sarah cried, before turning back to Hugo. 'What happened to him?'

Hugo took a deep breath. 'I'm afraid that will be for the local authorities to determine, but I'm afraid there's little doubt he was murdered, and,' he paused, rising to his feet, 'we, therefore, have to accept that his murderer is someone in this hotel.'

'How did he die?' Edith Lancaster demanded.

The image of her knitting needles immediately returned to Hugo, and he found it difficult to face the elderly English woman. 'The exact cause of death will have to be determined by a pathologist,' he offered. 'I can't really say more than that, I'm afraid.'

Sarah Wilkinson's head jerked and she placed a hand over her mouth to stop the sobs from escaping. Dorothy pulled her into a tight embrace, burying her mouth in the young woman's hair, muttering calming words. Dorothy gawped at Hugo, confusion and fear palpable on her face.

Sarah pulled away. 'I'm going to my room. I need to be on my own.'

Dorothy nodded her understanding. 'Very well, darling. But try to remember we are all here for you. Whatever you need. To talk, not talk, anything. Okay?'

Sarah stared at her wide-eyed and as if she had no clue what the elderly Scottish woman was saying. 'Okay,' she responded, before running up the stairs.

Hugo moved his head slowly around the room. Everyone was staring at him expectantly, clearly waiting for him to take charge and to offer them reassurances he was not sure he could offer. Before he could respond, the sound of Ben skipping down the stairway broke the silence of the room.

'Irene told me,' Ben said breathlessly. 'It's true?'

Hugo nodded. 'And I'm sorry to ask you, but I think under the circumstances we have little choice. You and Viviane should return to the next village and try to get help here as soon as possible.'

'Bien sûr,' Ben stated forcefully. He flashed Hugo a look which told him he did not want to leave him, but he understood he had to. Ben turned to Viviane. 'Are you okay to come with me?'

Viviane jumped to her feet, grabbing her coat from the back of the chair. 'Are you kidding? I can't wait to get out of here. I don't want to sit around when some madman is killing us off one by one.' She tipped her head towards the door. 'I'd rather take my chances with the storm than stay here and be a target.' She glared at Xavier Cadieux. 'I hate you, Xav. I thought we were friends.'

Xavier shrugged nonchalantly, his smooth, boyish face impassive. 'It's nothing personal, Viv,' he stated. 'This is about family.' He turned his head slowly around the Café. 'And someone here knows what happened to my aunt and they've gotten away with it for far too long. But not anymore. We're not leaving here until we know the truth, and then we'll make sure they're sorry for destroying my family.'

Elke Huber's head moved quickly, her eyes pleading towards her husband, Wolfgang, and Hugo. 'Are we all going to die?' she screeched.

Wolfgang rolled his eyes. 'Don't get all hysterical again, Elke,' he sighed wearily. 'No one else is going to die. Certainly not on my watch.'

'Are you sure about that, Wolfgang Huber?' Edith Lancaster interrupted, her tone at the same time both cruel and condescending. 'As I recall, you've never been the sort of man known for keeping his promises.'

Wolfgang's eyes narrowed angrily in her direction, his fists clenching in a way that Hugo did not understand, other than it concerned him. As time went on, the only thing Hugo was becoming increasingly sure of was that he was far behind in actually understanding the moments which might have passed between this very different group of people. The fact bothered him, but he knew he could not allow it to confuse him when time was not on his side. *Keep focused and look ahead,* he chastised himself.

'Are you going to move away from the door?' Hugo demanded forcefully of Maurice and Xavier.

The two men stared at him but said nothing. Hugo edged forward, taking a defiant stance in front of them. 'This is non-negotiable,' he pushed. 'Ben and Viviane are leaving now, and if you try to stop us…'

Xavier snorted. 'You'll do what exactly? Slap my face?' He chuckled, seemingly proud of himself.

Ben stood next to Hugo. 'Keep it up, and you'll see exactly how hard we can slap, you fucking moron!'

Hugo touched Ben's arm to reassure him. 'This has already gone too far, Monsieur Cadieux, and you and Monsieur Rousseau are already in trouble. Don't make this any worse for yourselves. Ben and Viviane will leave now and the police will arrive later, and that is a fact. Either you let them go or we'll all force our way out of here.' He looked around. 'And as you can see, there are more of us than there are of you.'

He noticed the sneer appearing on Xavier's face. 'And I can assure you, you won't find us the pushovers you seem to think we are.'

'You can be sure of that!' Sam Mitchell added, the former football star pointing to his muscular arms.

Wolfgang Huber moved next to Hugo. 'Don't be even more foolish than you already have been, Maurice. I may be an old man, but even old men can be lions when they're protecting their loved ones.'

Maurice tutted, pushing Xavier away from the door. He gesticulated to Ben and Viviane. 'Get out of here,' he said, unlocking the door and opening it. He then pointed to Hugo. 'But I warn you, I don't care who comes back. I'll burn this place to the ground with all of us in it rather than spend one more day with no answers.'

Hugo waved his fingers, indicating for Ben and Viviane to leave. He watched them go, filled with an overwhelming sadness. Xavier barricaded the door after them.

Hugo gestured to a table. 'Why don't you both take a seat and we'll see if we can talk calmly and logically before anything else happens.'

Maurice Rousseau moved reluctantly to the table. 'Then let's get started. But I warn you now, unless I get what I want, I make no promises about what will happen next.'

Hugo nodded, sure he meant it.

Ben & Viviane

Ben glanced over his shoulder as he and Viviane Auclair hurried away from *Café Compostelle*. He had not wanted to leave, but in the end, he knew it was the only logical course of action. They needed to get outside help, and they needed it fast.

He shuddered as the door to the Café slammed shut behind them. Xavier Cadieux's handsome face pulled into a cruel smirk. Ben felt foolish the young tour guide had taken him in, and as he stole a look at Viviane he had to wonder whether she could be trusted either. All he knew for certain was he needed her help, but it did not mean he would trust her or let down his guard. He would not be a fool again, not least when he was walking away from most of the few people in the world he loved and leaving them in danger.

Viviane pulled the hood of her raincoat tight against her face, but it was no use, the rain was relentless and the wind blew it back from her head. 'The storm is getting worse again,' she shouted into the air. 'It was meant to be getting better. But it just seems to be more and more relentless. If only the sun was shining, wouldn't it feel less... less dramatic?' she cried desperately.

Ben gestured for her to follow him into the doorway of a house. There was minimal shelter, but it allowed them a respite from the howl of the air. He stopped and went about securing her hood firmly around her head.

Viviane stared at him, dark, wide eyes apprising him. 'I didn't know about any of this.'

Ben nodded but said nothing.

'You don't believe me, do you?' Viviane pleaded. 'This had nothing to do with me. I swear to... well, I'll swear to Dieu if that's your thing, it's not mine, but if it helps, I swear to Billie Eilish, she's as close to Dieu as I'm willing to go, and it's all I have to say that I'm not lying. I SWEAR didn't know about any of this. If I didn't

245

have such a crush on him, then maybe…'

Ben smiled. 'I'm old, but I appreciate the sentiment. We all have our rocks we tie ourselves to. When I was growing up, I had my crushes. I locked the door of my bedroom and because of them, I could forget all the shit going on the other side of the door. The fact remains,' he added, pointing towards *Café Compostelle.* 'Those people are in very real danger and we have to get the flics here and get them the hell out of the crazy situation none of us should be part of.'

Viviane looked into the street. The rain pounded against the cobbles of the village square. 'It's going to be difficult to get out of here. The trees are going to be wet and it's going to be hard…'

Ben grabbed her hand. 'You whistle Billie Eilish and I'll whistle Julien Doré and let's just hope that gives us all the strength we need to get out of this damn village and finally put an end to this craziness.'

Viviane dragged him into the rain. 'Let's go. You're right, we don't have a moment to lose.'

Maurice Rousseau closed the blinds, throwing a blanket of darkness into the Café. Behind the counter, Dorothy Chapeau reached over and flipped the light switch. The tubes flickered, finally throwing a dull, shadowy glow across the room which seemed to only succeed in making the Café appear even darker and more oppressive than it had before.

'Even if the police arrive, they aren't going to be able to stop what has already started,' Maurice warned.

Hugo frowned. 'I'm not sure what that means, Monsieur Rousseau,' he responded, 'other than I have to tell you, whatever you imagine happened decades ago has long since been ruled an accident,' his eyes softened because he had no desire to hurt Rousseau anymore than necessary, despite what he was currently putting them all through.

'And I am sorry for your loss, mais, you have to understand we are now dealing with an altogether more serious and pressing situation,' he continued. 'Whatever happened in the past, we have no evidence of a crime, however, in 2023, we have clear evidence of two crimes. Two people have been murdered here and now, and that has to be our focus.'

Maurice stared at him challengingly. 'And what if the focus needs to stay centred on the past? What happened to my wife cannot be ignored. I won't allow it. I most certainly won't allow it. Don't you understand how long I have waited for answers?' he cried, his voice cracking.

Hugo's jaw tightened. 'I do understand, and I promise you that while we wait for the local police to arrive, we can try to make sense of it, but we can only do so if you agree whatever we discuss, whatever we might find, you will not act until the authorities arrive.'

'That's not a bargain you can make, Captain Duchamp,'

Maurice countered.

Hugo held his gaze. 'It most certainly is. And it is the only one I am willing to entertain. So, you want to talk? You have gone to great lengths to orchestrate this grand scheme of yours, and I have to question why. Why now? Why so long? I mean, I understand it has taken a tremendous amount of time to gather all the same people who, more or less, were present when your wife disappeared,' he continued, 'but as far as I can see, it didn't need to be this way. If you were so convinced one of these people murdered your wife, why did you wait so long, and more importantly, why did you have to wait for them to return here?'

'I'd like to know the answer to that question as well,' Wolfgang added. 'After all, you've known all of our addresses this whole time, haven't you?' he demanded of Maurice. 'You could have come to us at any time if you were so convinced of our guilt.'

Maurice reached into his coat pocket and extracted a pipe. He lit it slowly, inhaling the smoke deep into his lungs, fixing Hugo and Wolfgang with a look through squinted eyes.

'I have not left this village for more than a few days in these past forty years,' he began, his voice slow and drawling. 'It has been like a prison for me, even though there are no bars or locked doors. I could not leave Olive.'

'Oh, Maurice, Olive wouldn't have wanted you to live that way,' Dorothy gushed. 'She was a lovely, caring woman, and I'm sure she would be horrified if she knew what she had done to you.'

'And I don't wish to be indelicate,' Edith Lancaster interrupted, 'but you were a young man back then. Most young men would have moved on, probably starting a new family.' She narrowed her eyes. 'This should not have consumed you in the way it has Maurice Rousseau. God would not have wished it for you.'

Maurice pivoted his head, a low groan rising in his throat as if he was pushing away emotions he did not want to share. 'Don't speak to me of Dieu. If such a person existed, they would not have allowed me to suffer this way.' He smiled at Dorothy. 'You're right, my Olive was a saint, a beautiful woman not just on the outside, she was even more beautiful on the inside. She would never have harmed a soul.'

Hugo listened to the other man intently. If Maurice Rousseau was aware of his wife's alleged infidelity, he was certainly doing a good job of hiding it.

'Because of that, I could not stand to be away from her, not until I knew where she was and what happened to her.' He turned his head slowly around the room. 'Believe me, if I had been able to, I would have tracked you all down, each one of you, and beat the truth from you.'

'I'd like to see you try, old man,' Sam Mitchell sneered. 'Just see what happens if you and your thug try to pull anything else.' He flexed his arm. 'You'll soon discover we're not all the pushovers you seem to think we are.' He blew a sneery kiss at Xavier.

Hugo raised his hand to pacify the American. The last thing any of them needed was the situation escalating any further.

Maurice sucked on his pipe. 'I've spent so long waiting for a resolution, I don't think I noticed the time passing by. When I look back, each year just seems the same as the one before. What I remember is the times these people were supposed to be coming back. I remember it because the excitement built in me. It was the only time I had experienced anything resembling happiness. The thought of finally discovering the truth was enough to sustain me and get me through my pain.'

He tapped the pipe on the side of the table before relighting it. 'But then, each time there was a setback.' He stabbed the pipe towards the people seated opposite him. 'Ill health, death... the list went on and on,' he spat. 'One excuse after another. I always felt robbed, like I was getting closer and closer to an answer that never came. I put it aside, hoping for next year, but as I said, each year seemed to just melt into another until finally I woke up one day and looked in the mirror and saw how much time had passed and that I had become an old man. An old man wizened and twisted with anger and grief and thirst for revenge.'

'We're all very sorry for you, Maurice,' Elke Huber sobbed, pressing a handkerchief against her mouth. 'But this isn't to do with us. It can't be. Don't you think one of us would have spoken up if we'd known something?'

He threw back his head and laughed. 'Are you serious? The only reason everyone kept their mouths shut is that they know the truth.'

'I don't know anything!' Elke wailed.

He moved his shoulders distantly. 'We'll see. We'll see just how much of a liar you all are before this day is done. Because I can assure you all of one thing. My body may have gotten older, but this,' he tapped this side of his head. 'My mind remains as young and sharp as it was back then.'

Hugo cleared his throat. 'Then let's cut to the chase, shall we?'

'What do you recall about the events leading up to your wife's death?' Hugo asked Maurice Rousseau.

Rousseau pushed his hand through his wild mane of hair. It fell across his face and he pushed it back irritably. 'It was a normal day,' he answered finally in a way which sounded as if he was speaking it aloud for the first time. 'Just like any other. Everyone was excited to get going once the storm cleared and Alain was looking after everyone with his usual charm and wit,' he added with sadness, his attention drawn to the closed storeroom door.

'He was a fine man,' Elke Huber agreed.

Dorothy rubbed her friend's hand. 'He most certainly was.'

Hugo coughed, eager to move the discussion along. 'When was the last time you saw your wife?'

Maurice pointed to a bar stool near the window. 'She was sitting there talking with Anne Mitchell, Sam's mother. They were laughing over something, I don't know what.' His face clouded over. 'I remember I was mad at her for carrying on when we had so much work still to do. What a prince, huh?' he concluded with a sad laugh.

'As I recall, you were rather more than mad at her,' Wolfgang interrupted. 'The fights often ended up being physical.'

'What are you talking about?' Maurice hissed. 'I loved Olive. I would never have laid a hand on her,' he barked.

Dorothy shook her head forcefully. 'You can't just rewrite history, Maurice. We all saw it. And by bringing this all up, you're forcing us to confront something we were discrete about. As far as I'm concerned, you can't have it both ways.'

'Dorothy is right. And no matter how you dress it up, it is true. You weren't the husband you should have been,' Wolfgang replied. 'We'd only been here a week, not even that, but we must

251

have witnessed five or six fights between the two of you. And as I remember them, they weren't little spats, they were often full-on battles.'

Maurice slammed his fists onto the table with such ferocity, a small vase fell to the ground and smashed. He angrily kicked the pieces of glass away with his foot. 'You don't know what you're talking about, fool.'

'He's telling the truth,' Sam Mitchell interjected. 'I was only fifteen, but I remember it well. At one point, I came across you next to the bridge and you had your hands around her throat. I grabbed a hold of you and you threw me off, telling me if I laid a finger on you again you'd... you'd...' he trailed off, a worried shadow passing over his face.

'He'd do what?' Hugo demanded.

Sam lowered his head. 'He said he'd throw me in the damn river.'

Elke Huber gasped.

Maurice shook his head vigorously. 'You're lying. I loved Olive. I would never hurt her.'

Edith Lancaster tutted loudly. She reached into her carpetbag and extracted knitting needles and wool. 'I'd still like to know where my knitting went to. I was halfway through that scarf,' she grumbled as she quickly began knitting again.

Hugo and Wolfgang exchanged an ominous look.

'No one is lying, Maurice Rousseau. And we all know the real reason for your arguments.' Edith announced curtly.

'What are you talking about?'

Edith moved the knitting needles quickly. 'The affair! The affair!' she called out, her voice shrill and cold. 'Don't pretend you didn't know, because you did. We all did. She and Tony were hardly discrete.'

'Tony?' Maurice interrupted, eyebrows knotting in confusion. 'Tony Wilkinson?'

Hugo leaned forward, keenly eyeing Maurice. If he did not know better, he believed the news of the affair had come as a complete surprise to him.

'You knew damn well what the heathens were up to,' Edith muttered under her breath.

Maurice clenched his fists together as if he desperately wanted to punch something or someone. 'Non, it's not true.' he hissed, his voice heady with emotion. After a few moments, he took a deep breath and then sighed as if releasing something he had been holding in for a long time. 'I suspected something was going on, but I didn't know for certain. Things hadn't been right for a long time. I suppose I'd been in denial about it, hoping it would all die down, but looking back, I suppose I got the sense Olive was bored with her life here.' He closed his eyes. 'And like a fool, I thought I would be enough for her, that this village, this life would be enough for her, and that if I just ignored it, her unhappiness would just go away.' He shrugged. 'I guess we'll never know now.'

'And you maintain you didn't know about the affair?' Hugo asked.

'I told you, I didn't know about it. Why would I lie?' Maurice snapped. 'As I said, I knew something was off, but that week I suppose it just became too obvious to ignore. She started dressing differently and she would do just about anything to get away from me.' He tapped his pipe on the desk. 'I suspected, but I didn't know for sure and I certainly didn't know it was Tony. As far as I knew, he was with his English rose.'

'All rather convenient, if you ask me,' Edith snipped without looking up from her knitting. 'I mean, it all seems rather odd to me this sudden bout of amnesia while Tony Wilkinson's lying dead in the other room.' She placed her needles on the table. 'You waited a long time, but you finally got your revenge, didn't you?'

'I didn't murder Tony,' Maurice snapped, 'but if I'd known...' he trailed off, his words hanging heavy in the air.

Xavier stood next to Maurice. 'Do you think we've waited all this time just to kill someone?' he demanded. 'My family has suffered for long enough. We deserve more. We deserve answers and as tempting as that kind of revenge is, seeing whoever murdered tante Olive standing in a court and spending the rest of their lives in prison is far more important.'

Hugo said nothing. He understood the young tour guide's logic, but he also understood that in the heat of the moment and coming face to face with the person potentially responsible for the death of a loved one, emotions were often difficult to contain.

He looked towards the storeroom. The door to the walk-in freezer was visible. It was not too much of a stretch of the imagination to believe Maurice Rousseau had finally discovered what happened to his wife and at whose hands, and it had been more than he could cope with.

'So Tony Wilkinson was the man arguing with Olive next to the bridge?' Maurice asked, staring out of the window.

'Why would he kill her?' Xavier posed.

'It could have been an accident,' Hugo suggested. 'A quarrel that got out of hand. As I understand it, it's quite likely, particularly with the dire weather you were experiencing. The question is - did she slip or was she pushed? And I don't know if you're ever going to get the answer. Especially now if we are to believe Tony Wilkinson was involved because he is now dead also.'

Maurice glared at Hugo. 'I'll say this one more time. I did not murder Tony Wilkinson. If I knew he was involved with my wife and that he was involved in what happened to her, the chances are I would have murdered him, but I would not be ashamed of it, nor would I hide the fact. I'd be the first to hold my hands up and tell you all I exacted revenge for my Olive. I'd be proud. I would feel righteous. And I would go to jail a man with some semblance of peace of mind.'

Hugo scratched his head. 'I still don't understand what Olive was doing by the bridge,' he mused aloud. 'I mean, it could have been a lover's rendezvous, mais as we already know, somebody saw them. Why choose that time in the middle of a horrendous storm, knowing they could be seen? Is it possible they were attempting to leave the village?'

'Run away together, you mean?' Sam Mitchell asked.

Hugo shrugged. 'Why not? If it wasn't the place or time for them to be alone, and they were seen at the only way in or out of the village, we can't ignore the fact they may have just simply been leaving.'

Wolfgang blew a raspberry. 'Either way, what the hell does it matter? She's dead, they're both dead.' He stared at Maurice Rousseau. The elderly tour guide was still standing in front of the exit, but his demeanour had changed. It was almost as if defeat was beginning to overwhelm him.

'Maurice,' Wolfgang continued. 'I understand you've been waiting a long time for this, but I have to ask why? What answers do you think you're going to get? And what makes you think it will make you feel better?'

'He's right,' Dorothy added. 'We're all sorry about what happened to you, dear Maurice. But I'm more sorry you've dedicated your life to this. Forty years is too long to put your life on hold because of unanswered questions. Questions I imagine you know you'll never really get answers to, not least ones which will give you the peace you've been seeking.'

'I will not leave this Café until I know the truth,' Maurice said, rising to his feet. 'And nor will any of you, so I suggest you all unzip your lying mouths and tell us exactly what you recall.'

'And then you'll let us go?' Dorothy asked.

Maurice smiled. 'The innocent amongst you have nothing to fear from me. If you're not innocent, then you've gotten away with this for far too long, and it will end now.' He stared at Hugo as if he was ensuring his intention was perfectly clear.

'Let's talk about the events leading up to Olive's disappearance,' Hugo began cautiously.

'What is there to talk about?' Edith Lancaster snapped. 'Olive snuck off to be with her lover, despite the awful weather. I suppose that's what foolish young people do when they are incapable of controlling their primal urges,' she added with bitterness. 'And as a result, she fell, or she was pushed. It really doesn't matter now, because the only other person who might have known is...' She stopped, stabbing her knitting needle into the air towards the storeroom. 'Spending time in the deep freeze.'

Hugo shuddered at the way she thrust the knitting needles, reminded of where he had last seen the missing pair.

'Even if you didn't kill him, Maurice,' Edith continued, her voice laced with cruelty, 'someone rather stole your thunder, it appears.' The skies rumbled above them and she laughed. 'It seems somebody is listening,' she added with a flourish, before fixing Maurice with a withering stare, 'even if you aren't, Maurice Rousseau.'

Hugo stood, lighting a cigarette before moving slowly across the Café floor towards Maurice and Xavier. 'Although I may have phrased it differently,' he stated, 'I have to agree with Miss Lancaster. And while I understand your need for closure, I have to believe there is a part of you which has to know, especially now, and after all of this time, that you will never find the answers you seek. However,' he paused, staring at Maurice, 'I can't ignore what has taken place here in these last few days, because it suggests you have finally found what you were looking for and found a way to attain some kind of peace of mind.'

'And how do you imagine I might have done that?' Maurice demanded sceptically.

'Two men have died, and we must assume it is connected to what happened to your wife,' Hugo replied.

'Alain had nothing to do with it!' Maurice shouted.

Hugo locked eyes with him and shook his head. 'I'm afraid it appears Alain was aware of the affair between your wife and Tony Wilkinson. The question is - did you know about it then, or did you only find out about it now?'

Maurice shook his head angrily. 'Alain was my best friend. Hell, he's the only person who's kept me sane for the last forty years. And now you're expecting me to believe he's been doing what - keeping a secret from me he must have known would have hurt me, but would also have made me get over what had happened? He saw first-hand every day what I was going through, what Olive's family was going through. And though he would never have admitted it, the fact was he was probably as much in love with Olive as I was. To accuse him of something so heinous when he can't defend himself is abhorrent and you should be ashamed of yourself.'

'He knew, Maurice,' Dorothy said with a long sigh. 'We all knew. I can't speak for Alain, but I'm sure he didn't tell you because with Olive gone, there was no point in tarnishing your memory of her. It's what we all did. We buried the truth so as not to hurt you any further.'

'And you maintain you didn't know of the affair?' Hugo continued.

'I didn't know,' Maurice replied forcefully, his voice cracking, his face lined with confusion.

Hugo frowned. He wondered whether he should discuss the manner of Alain Bonnet's murder. While it was not his place, he was curious to gauge everyone's reaction. In the end, he reasoned, there was one way to proceed without damaging the forthcoming actual police investigation. As Irene suspected, the actual cause of death was blunt force trauma, and as Hugo supposed, there was the possibility of two murderers. If he informed them the cause of death was a knife would, would the actual killer betray themselves with their surprise?

He decided to try and cleared his throat. 'The manner of Monsieur Bonnet's death might betray his murderer's motives.'

Maurice's eyes widened. 'What do you mean?' he demanded.

'Monsieur Bonnet was stabbed,' Hugo replied. 'And he was stabbed in the back.'

Maurice lowered his head, thick hair falling over his face. 'I was there with Dr. Chapeau. I saw it.'

Hugo nodded. 'But there's a very real possibility it wasn't his *actual* cause of death. And I find that incredibly curious. Why was he stabbed in the back if he was actually already dead?'

There were several gasps and Hugo took as much time as he could to assess the reactions of all those in the room, but he was not sure he saw anything which might be helpful, just worried, anxious people all afraid to look at one another too closely.

'With all due respect to Captain Duchamp,' Wolfgang Huber spoke loudly. 'We can't keep beating around the bush. The facts are simple. Alain Bonnet was,' he stole a sly look at Hugo, '*murdered*. Shortly afterwards, Tony Wilkinson was also murdered.'

'How did Tony die?' Edith Lancaster asked.

Wolfgang looked at Hugo again. He shrugged. 'That is for the authorities to decide, not us. My point is, two men are dead, most likely by someone staying in this very hotel. Even if the door was not locked, we're stranded in a village in the middle of nowhere.'

'The arrival of Captain Duchamp and the others suggests people still can get in and out of the village,' Sam Mitchell reasoned. 'We can't rule out someone else invading the village, can we?'

Wolfgang extended his hands. 'For what purpose?' He shook his head. 'Non, as reluctant as I was to come to the conclusion, the facts are relatively simple. Alain Bonnet and Tony Wilkinson were killed for one reason and one reason only, their involvement with the death of Olive Rousseau.'

'I tell you, I knew nothing about it!' Maurice screamed.

Hugo stepped forward. 'That doesn't mean you didn't discover the truth in the last few days. And it's not too difficult to imagine what effect it might have had on you. Your oldest friend keeping a secret, and the return of the lover I imagine you'd always suspected existed but were never sure of. It's understandable if in such circumstances, finding answers was more than you could cope with and you reacted accordingly.'

'I didn't murder either of them, I'm telling you!' Maurice said, his head buried in his hands. 'I wouldn't. I *couldn't*. Not like that. It would be… it would be,' he trailed off, searching for the right words, 'a pointless end to it all.'

'And yet they're both dead,' Edith Lancaster stated calmly. 'And as far as I can tell, the only person who could possibly have anything against them is you and your half-wit nephew.'

'Hey! Careful, old lady,' Xavier Cadieux spat.

'Edith has a point,' Wolfgang interrupted. 'And we have gone as far as we can with this. One of you killed these two poor men, or both of you, and right now we are at an impasse.' He reached into his pocket and extracted a long, sharp knife. 'I took this from the kitchen because I want you to know that until the local police arrive to arrest you, I will sit here on this very seat and if either of you moves, I will not hesitate to plough this blade into your heart.'

'Wolfgang!' Elke Huber cried.

He looked at his wife. 'This isn't the time for sentimentally, my dear. These two men are murderers, and they have extracted a cruel and vindictive revenge. A revenge which I will not allow to go any further.'

'I'd like to see you stop us, old man,' Xavier laughed.

Wolfgang rose to his feet. 'You just try, childish idiot, and you'll see entirely what this old man is capable of. You won't hurt anyone else. I won't allow it.'

Hugo looked to the rain-splattered window, desperately hoping help would arrive soon and the nightmare would be over.

Ben & Viviane

Ben threw himself from the tree, flopping onto the sodden embankment with a thud. He rolled onto all fours, shaking the water from his air. 'That was even harder the second time,' he spluttered, adding with a bite, 'and I certainly hope it's the last.'

Viviane Auclair appeared behind him, athletically leaping onto the ground. 'You have a point, but the desire to get out of that damn village was all the motivation I needed.'

She moved quickly, striding forwards. Ben clambered to his feet, struggling to keep up with her. The rain had lessened, but it was still cold and the icy air slapped against his face. His hair was matted against his forehead, but for once he did not have the energy or feel the need to push it away. 'What did you make of all that back there?' he called after her.

Viviane did not look back but kept striding ahead. 'That's some fucked up shit, that's all I know.'

'How well do you know Xavier Cadieux?' Ben asked.

She stopped abruptly, causing him to crash into her. She carried on walking before answering. 'He's a good kid,' she said distantly. 'You met him. He's all about making money and doing it any way he can.'

'What does that mean?'

Viviane laughed. 'What do you think? Give the pilgrims what they want. *Whatever* they want. Some of the guides do. It's a good way to make extra money. I'm not saying he's into shady shit necessarily.'

'Then what are you saying?' Ben demanded.

'Hey listen,' she snapped. 'Just because this is a religious experience for some people doesn't change the fact people are just basically the same the entire world over. Some of them hold a bible in one hand, a packet of cocaine in another and somehow in their

261

brains they manage to ignore the hypocrisy.'

Ben nodded. He was well aware of the lies people told. His father had spent his lifetime wildly disapproving of Ben's homosexuality, while all the time he had embarked on a lifetime of debauchery, including illegitimate children with prostitutes and covering up murders committed by his friends. And all the time he had judged Ben about something he had no control over.

Ben had learnt all he needed to know from his father because of it, and it had served him well. Because of Louis Beaupain, Ben had finally understood what it meant to look a liar in the face. He had imagined he would never be able to trust anyone in his life, but then he met Hugo Duchamp and everything had changed. Hugo finally made Ben understand that not everyone was lying all the time.

'He's not a bad kid,' Viviane called over her shoulder defensively. 'And for the record, I had no idea about the whole dead aunt thing.'

'I think they've all been very good at hiding their secrets,' Ben conceded. 'And that's what worries me.'

'What do you mean?'

Ben shoved his hands in his pockets. His fingers were icy and wet and ever since an incident years earlier when he had been burnt in a fire, the cold exacerbated the pain in his damaged skin. 'Two people died in that village because of something that happened a long time ago. At first, I thought this was just about discovering the truth, but now, I'm not that's true.'

'Then what is it about?' Viviane asked.

Ben pressed his hands against his thighs in an attempt to warm them. 'It's just about revenge. Maurice Rousseau and Xavier Cadieux have been waiting a long time for it, and the fact they've murdered two people without even really bothering to hide it scares me.'

'Scares you?' Viviane stopped suddenly, cocking her head

towards him.

Ben nodded. 'Oui. Because they are dangerous and they don't seem to care about the consequences of their actions, which makes them even more dangerous.' He looked back toward the village of *Chemin des Pèlerins*, and he grimaced. 'I have most of my loved ones in there. The love of my life came to help me and if anything happens to him because of that, I don't think I'd ever recover. I can't let my friends, or Hugo,' he stopped, his voice cracking as he spoke his name, 'fall victim to this stupidity.'

Viviane took his hand. 'Then let's get to the next village and get some damn help so it doesn't come to that.'

Ben smiled. 'That's an excellent idea.'

She placed her hands on her hips and laughed. 'Then stop walking so damn slow. I mean, I know you're old, but we gotta move.'

Ben watched her forging ahead, shaking his head sadly. '*Old?*'

Sarah Lancaster appeared on the stairway, her eyes swollen with tears. She looked anxiously around the Café. 'Can I stay here?'

Dorothy rushed to her. 'Of course, you can darling, as I said, you shouldn't be on your own at a time like this.'

Sarah stood rigid in Dorothy's attempted embrace, before pulling away and moving to the nearest table. She faced Casey Mitchell, the young American. 'Can I sit here?'

'S… sure,' he stammered, pushing his glasses into floppy, dark hair.

'I thought I wanted to be alone,' Sarah began, speaking to no one in particular. 'But it turns out I'm not as comfortable with silence as I thought I was,' she added numbly.

Dorothy touched her shoulder, causing the young girl to instantly recoil. 'As I said, you shouldn't be alone right now.'

Sarah turned to Hugo. 'How did my father die?' she breathed.

Hugo fought the urge to turn his head from her because he knew how she would interpret it. And she would be correct. There was no getting around the fact her father's death was brutal. 'We can't be sure. The local police will be here soon and they will be better placed to explain what happened.'

Sarah glared at him. 'You're lying. You and Dr. Chapeau examined my father.' She turned to Wolfgang. 'And so did you. What are you keeping from me?'

Wolfgang Huber took what appeared to be a deep breath. 'Child, your father is dead. That is all you need to know. The rest should not trouble you,' he answered finally. 'It serves no purpose and as we have seen here,' he glared at Maurice, before continuing, 'if allowed, it gnaws at you like cancer.'

'I want it to trouble me,' Sarah hissed. 'So, tell me the truth, and tell me right now.'

'Your father was also stabbed,' Wolfgang responded, flashing Hugo a message. *She doesn't need to know all the details, does she?*

Hugo nodded. He did not disagree. The manner of Tony Wilkinson's death was something that needed to be explored, but this was not the time. He stole a look at Edith Lancaster, still knitting, and he had to wonder how her missing needles had ended up being used as murder weapons. Was it as simple as they were just at hand when the murderer was about to strike, or was it premeditated?

There was something about the entire picture he was not seeing, and while it would ordinarily trouble him, he found at that moment it was something he would rather leave to the local police to investigate. He wanted to return to his nice home. He wanted to feel safe again and, more than anything, he wanted his loved ones to be safe. As it was, the village of *Chemin des Pèlerins*, was a powder keg likely to erupt at any time.

'Is this because of the affair?' Sarah asked.

'The affair?' Hugo responded, his voice rising sharply.

She nodded, staring at him from beneath her dark, lank fringe. It was a look he recognised because it was one he had used himself for most of his life. Hiding beneath a veil of hair, hoping no one would look too closely at him.

Wolfgang coughed, his eyes widening in surprise. 'You knew about it?'

Sarah smiled. 'There have never been any secrets in my family,' she responded bitterly. 'We're terribly British, you know. We just chose not to speak of them. My mother used to say we were like swans. All beautiful, regal and calm on the surface, but underneath, paddling like our life depends on it.' She turned to Maurice Rousseau. 'Yes, I knew about the affair, but there's something about it you don't know,' she added triumphantly as if she had a burning secret she could no longer keep. 'Your wife isn't dead. She never has been. It was all an elaborate scam. You killed my father for the wrong reason, you stupid old fool. He didn't kill your wife. He stole her from you.'

Sarah

'My earliest memory is of the war being waged between my parents,' Sarah began. 'But it wasn't a war of fighting or screaming. It was a war of silence. It was a war of hatred, all neatly covered up by the damn stiff British upper lip.'

'I don't know when I first became aware of my father's affairs and what had happened between my parents before their wedding,' she continued. 'But I remember it not coming as much of a surprise. My mother was always ill. My grandparents called it her "sickliness" but I imagine psychiatrists would have probably described her as manic-depressive, or bipolar, or something like that. They've been trying to diagnose me ever since I was a kid but they've never come up with an answer that sticks. When I was six, mum disappeared from my life for almost a year. I later found out it was because she'd tried to kill herself, and not for the first time as my father so casually explained to me like it was her fault or something and nothing but a terrible inconvenience to him.'

'I was about ten when she finally started talking to me. Properly talking to me, I mean. I think it was a comfort for her to have someone to talk to who wasn't a paid professional with very little genuine interest in what she had to say. She was an only child, and her parents were aristocracy, so really she was raised by a nanny, and certainly not by them. Anyway, as the years went on, she started telling me about how she met my father. He was the son of a business acquaintance of my grandfather's, and though I never really understood the reasoning, it seems my grandfather owed a favour to dad's father, so a deal was cut, and my mother was the prize, it seems.'

Sarah took a deep breath, reaching across the table and pouring a glass of water. 'The pilgrimage was my grandfather's idea as well. He was a devout Catholic and wanted to make sure his daughter was, too. He had ties to the Church, you see. I can't imagine my father was keen on it, but he wasn't stupid either. He knew it was a price he had to pay for marrying a multimillionaire's daughter. Anyway, they came here and as my mother later described it, my father didn't even bother to hide the fact he was shagging some local tramp. In fact, I think he took great pride in showing her he was the one in charge of her now, and that it was no longer her father who pulled her strings. Put up and shut up, were his words.'

'After they returned to London, my mother went to her father and begged for the wedding to be called off, and apparently, he laughed at her. He told her marriages were built on such situations. Of course, her husband would have affairs. It was part of life and part of their class, and he told her she should grow up and accept her reality. So she did, and they were married and it was on their wedding night that my mother first tried to kill herself because my father didn't spend his wedding night with her, he spent it in the penthouse apartment overlooking Tower Bridge he had just bought for his mistress.' She stopped and turned her head. 'And who do you imagine that was?'

Maurice Rousseau's face crinkled with confusion, his eyes darting from side to side. 'I don't understand what you're saying. Olive died a long time ago.' He spoke the words without the confidence on display earlier. He eyed the young woman as if she terrified him.

Sarah Wilkinson shook her head. 'That's not what happened. And I'm sorry for you. I'm sorry that you got caught up in this whole mess. I actually really am, believe it or not. But I happen to know for certain Olive has been living in the swanky penthouse apartment my father bought for her when they left here together forty years ago.'

'Is this really true?' Hugo interrupted. It sounded fanciful to him.

Sarah nodded.

'I don't believe you,' Maurice spat.

Sarah shrugged. 'I don't know what you expect me to do about that, but what I can do is I can give you her address. When the damn phones finally start working again, why don't you call her up?' She laughed angrily. 'That should be a pretty interesting conversation, I would imagine.'

Maurice stared blankly at the telephone on the counter, his eyes narrowing as if he was looking at something horrible, something that might hurt him.

'How did she manage to leave the village?' Hugo asked.

'I don't know,' Sarah responded.

Hugo leaned forward. There was something about her tone which had caused the hairs on the back of his arm to stand on end. He was certain she had just lied, and he could not understand why. What possible reason could Sarah Lancaster have for lying about how Olive Rousseau had managed to leave *Chemin des Pèlerins*? He could not imagine any scenario and therefore he assumed his assumption had to be incorrect.

Maurice looked at Xavier. 'I don't believe it.'

'Nor do I,' Xavier agreed.

Hugo moved his eyes between the other people in the room. Dorothy Chapeau, Elke Humer and Edith Lancaster were all looking at each other in a way which suggested to him the three women were exchanged in a conspiracy of their own. He exhaled. Whatever the truth, it did not alter the fact two men had died, and it was most likely a direct result of whatever had transpired decades early.

'There's something else I don't understand,' Hugo addressed Sarah. 'Why are you and your father even here on the pilgrimage now?'

'What do you mean?' she countered, biting her fingernails anxiously.

He shrugged. 'Only that you have spoken clearly about your feelings for your father. Why would you accompany him now if it was all so painful for you?'

'My mother has been planning on doing the pilgrimage again for longer than I have been born,' Sarah stated. 'But it was never the right time. She was either in hospital or just incapable of leaving her house, usually because of the drugs my father and grandfather kept her dosed up on. Or I was in hospital. There was always a reason to put it off.'

'Anyway, after my mother died, I told my father we had to do the Camino for her,' Sarah continued. 'I'd seen the emails from the original pilgrims, and it seemed the perfect way to honour my mother.'

She laughed haughtily. 'I have to say it also amused me. Making my father return to the scene of the "crime" - it seemed poetic almost, you might say.' She looked at Maurice. 'I wanted to see if he would have the shame to look you in the eye all the time knowing he'd ruined your life as well as mine and my mother's.'

'And he was happy to come back?' Wolfgang asked, clearly confused.

Sarah laughed again. 'Not even close. But I told him it was my mother's dying wish, and that he owed it to the both of us to make this journey.' She smiled. 'He was still reluctant and then I reminded him that in her will, my mother had made me her proxy in all business dealings. He needed my signature for every deal he made, every cheque he wrote. She may have had little choice in how she lived her life, but in the end, she found a way to control him and that was through me. It didn't take him long to see sense.'

'If it's true about Olive,' Dorothy began cautiously, stealing a worried look at Maurice, whose head was lowered, slowly shaking in apparent disbelief, 'then I have to wonder: if she's still alive, did she know he was coming back?'

Sarah shrugged. 'I have no idea what that bitch knows or doesn't know. The only thing I know about her is my father spent every weekend, every summer, and every Christmas with her, not with me and my mother. I've hated Olive for most of my life.'

Edith Lancaster dropped her knitting. 'Did you ever meet her, child? Can you even be sure it's her?'

Sarah shook her head. 'I never met her, but I used to go into London and look up at her in her ivory tower, tossing copper-coloured hair over her shoulders just because she thought that was what men wanted.'

Maurice gasped. 'Copper-coloured hair,' he repeated slowly.

Sarah laughed. 'It's still the same shitty colour, but at her age, I doubt it's natural.'

Maurice's nostrils flared. 'I don't believe you,' he stated again. 'I don't believe you! I don't believe you! I don't believe you!' he repeated, his voice rising sharply each time.

'What proof do you have, child?' Wolfgang demanded.

Sarah shrugged again. 'I don't need to give you proof. Go to

London, I'll give you her address and you can tell her yourself her sugar daddy is dead, and that you killed him.'

'I didn't kill your father!' Maurice roared.

'The hell you did!' Sarah retorted. 'And once the shock wore off, I realised I owe you a debt of gratitude. I'm finally free of my entire crappy family and rich enough to do what the hell I want with the rest of my life.'

She stood. 'I'm going to my room now and I'll stay there until the police arrive,' she stared at Maurice. 'I want you to know the only reason I told you about Olive was that I realised when I was upstairs the favour you did me deserved a favour in return. You'll die in jail, old man, but at least you'll finally know what happened to your tramp of a wife. She walked out of this village and she never looked back, and I doubt she even thought of you once. I wanted you to know the truth because I want the whole world to know what sort of bitch she was and what kind of bastard my father was. And in the end, it seems as if you were the only one who had the guts to do something about it.'

Everyone in the room watched her leave, but no one spoke.

Casey Mitchell jumped to his feet. 'I'm going too,' he said breathlessly, pushing his glasses up his nose. 'I can't be around you people any longer. You're freaks.'

'Help will be here soon,' Elke Huber cried to no one in particular. 'And we can all leave and put this behind us, finally.'

Hugo stared at the doorway again, sending a silent prayer. *Please hurry, Ben.*

Ben, Viviane & Jean

'My name is Captain Jean Allons. I work between all the villages in this area. It is a job which mostly gives me little trouble. Usually, the worst I have to contend with is a tourist who has partaken in too much wine,' he added with a cheerful chuckle.

He tipped his head towards the bar. 'The bar owner told me to get over to Millieure as quickly as possible,' he stopped, tired eyes twinkling with amusement. Allons was a small man, with a round face framed with long, thin hair. His lips were thin, lined with a pencil moustache. 'Because they said two kids had shown up claiming there has been a double murder in *Chemin des Pèlerins*.'

He paused again. 'I couldn't believe it, not for a second. There's been no kind of trouble like that around here for as long as I've been a police officer.'

Ben felt his patience deserting him. The journey from *Chemin des Pèlerins* had been long and arduous, hampered by the rain and sodden paths, but once they arrived in Millieure they had been informed by the bar owner that it would be at least several hours before the police would arrive. As he waited, each minute felt like an eternity dragging ahead of him, one he thought would never end. It had also given his imagination plenty of time to create scenarios about what was happening back in the village, images which he could barely stand.

'It's true,' Ben blurted bluntly. 'Two people are dead and there's no doubt they were murdered. I don't really understand what happened, but as far as I can tell a man called Maurice Rousseau has some kind of cockamamie idea about something that may or may not have happened to his wife decades ago and he's somehow or other orchestrated bringing together people he thinks are involved to...' he trailed off, 'well, to Dieu knows what. But this is serious. This is really serious.'

The police captain and the bar manager exchanged a long look. The bar manager raised a concerned eyebrow.

'Tell me more,' Allons prodded.

'I don't know what more I can say,' Ben suggested. 'Other than it's all a bit of a mess. The bridge to the village has been destroyed. We only got in and out by climbing down the trees and swimming across, but that's not an ideal solution for everyone in the village. Some of them are elderly and because the conditions are terrible, it will not be easy. And the fact is, there is a murderer on the loose and we have no idea what they're going to do next. That means the people stranded there are in very serious danger.'

The police officer tapped his chin. 'It's not an ideal solution,' he said after a minute of contemplation, 'but I can have the pompiers here in an hour or so. They have extendable ladders which should be able to bridge the gap between the banks, allowing at least some of us into the village.'

'We need to get people out!' Ben cried.

Allons nodded. 'Obviously, but that will take time. If we secure it enough, we may be able to evacuate the people there.' His lips twisted as he considered. 'But more importantly, at this point, we just need to get in and secure the scene and take control of the situation. Only then will everyone be safe.' He gestured to the bar owner. 'Bring me the phone. We need the pompiers here urgently.'

Ben took a deep breath. 'Please tell them to hurry, I beg you. We have no idea what's going on there.'

Hugo, Irene & Dorothy

Hugo knocked on the door to Irene's room, Dorothy close behind him. Irene opened the door and gestured for them to enter, quickly closing the door behind them. Hugo ruffled Bruno's hair. The five-year-old beamed at him, and Hugo was pleased to see he was in good humour, happily playing a game on his iPad.

'What's going on down there?' Irene asked quietly, ensuring Bruno's headphones were in place.

Hugo quickly explained what had happened in the Café. As he did, Dorothy sank into a chair in front of the window, her head staring through the net curtains.

Irene waited until he had finished. 'Well, what do you make of it all?' she asked with a frown.

Hugo shrugged. 'It's practically impossible to say.' He turned to the window. 'Dorothy, I have to ask: Do you think it's possible Olive Rousseau left the village to begin a new life in London?'

It took her a long time to answer. 'I only really knew her for a second, truth be told. And while I think we all had an idea what was going on, I find it hard to reconcile that the young woman I met could be so cruel as to let her husband believe she had died when in fact she had just chosen to run away.'

'Perhaps she didn't know?' Irene reasoned. 'She could have just decided to leave her husband and didn't think about her actions.'

'Then why not tell him? Why not leave him a letter?' Dorothy responded, before shaking her head with determination. 'No, I can imagine a young girl being impetuous, running away from her parents, a life she didn't want...' she trailed off, laughing sadly. 'Hell, I did the same thing myself. I left Scotland without giving it a second thought, leaving behind everyone and everything I knew and loved for a man and a country I knew nothing about, and I did

275

it without a moment's hesitation or thought, probably because I was young and impatient. And I never regretted it for a second.' Her face clouded. 'Perhaps Olive felt the same way.'

Irene shook her head. 'Mama, I don't believe you would have allowed people to think you were dead just so you could run off to a new life.'

'There is another possibility,' Hugo suggested. 'There has been a suggestion that the Rousseau's marriage was not a happy one, possibly even a violent one. We've seen this sort of thing before. Olive Rousseau wanted to escape, and she didn't want an abusive man coming after her.'

'Oh, this is awful!' Dorothy wailed. 'To think of her living a life so far away all this time, while Maurice was here... well, here imagining whatever he has been imagining.' She looked at Hugo. 'You think he killed Alain and Tony because of their involvement?'

'I'm not sure what to think,' Hugo reasoned.

Irene dashed across the room and rubbed her mother's shoulder. 'As far as I can see, there's very little reason to think someone else might be involved. The stabbing in the back is a good example. If Maurice Rousseau discovered his best friend had information about his missing, or dead wife, then it might just have pushed him over the edge, and far enough to murder the man who took her from him.'

Hugo nodded. 'I understand that, mais...'

'But what?' Dorothy demanded.

'I don't know,' Hugo exhaled. 'Only that there was something about Maurice's reaction to it all that struck me as genuine.'

'Hugo, we've looked into the eyes of men and women many times, and believed their lies, have we not?' Irene asked. 'Some people lie very easily, and I'm not sure it's always easy to tell because they are very good at it. That could be all we're seeing here.'

'Je sais.'

Dorothy looked at her watch. 'It's getting late. Perhaps we should make some food again while we wait for help to arrive?'

'I'm not sure that's a good idea, mama,' Irene reasoned.

Dorothy rose to her feet. 'What else do you suggest we do? We have to eat, and we have to pass the time and I know I can't just sit around waiting to be rescued. I haven't been a feminist all this time to wait for a man to rescue me. If someone wants to come to me with a knitting needle, well, they'll soon see the wrath of a Scottish woman wronged!'

Irene moved to her mother. 'I love you, mama, and I agree no man or woman can get one over on you. You taught me well.'

Dorothy laughed. 'I did, didn't I?' She kissed the top of Irene's head. 'Stay with Bruno and I'll call you when the food is ready.' She gestured to Hugo. 'You'll join me?'

Hugo stood. 'Of course.'

Dorothy and Elke moved around the Café, placing plates of food in front of everyone. The mood was tense and there had been very little chit-chat. Hugo watched as people smiled their acknowledgement and began idly playing with the food that had been placed in front of them.

'Thank you very much,' Hugo said in English, looking at a plate of food he had no stomach to eat. He looked around the room. Maurice Rousseau and Xavier Cadieux were at the table next to the exit, their backs to everyone else. Hugo watched as Dorothy finished serving the food. Maurice lifted his head, his lips twisting into words he seemingly could not speak.

Hugo stood, moving across the Café, suddenly feeling very claustrophobic and realising it had been a long time between cigarettes.

He pulled at the door, realising that Xavier's foot was blocking it. 'I'd like to go outside,' Hugo said. 'I'd like some air and I need a cigarette.'

'No one leaves,' Xavier stated. 'We told you that already.'

Hugo kicked his foot away. 'I'm not leaving. I'm going outside for a cigarette, so get out of my way.' He yanked the door open and stepped into the rain. The wind and rain slapped against his face, so he moved quickly, taking shelter under a gazebo.

He quickly lit a cigarette, shuddering as the door to the Café slammed behind him. The smoke escaped his mouth, and he sighed contentedly. As bad a habit as it was, it was a habit he had spent most of his life being unwilling to even attempt to break. He narrowed his eyes and reached into his pocket and extracted his glasses. It took him a moment to realise what he was seeing and then his mouth broke into a wide smile when he realised what was in front of him. Ben was running down the steps from the top of the village two at a time, often slipping and having to steady himself on the handrail.

'Ben,' Hugo exhaled. *'Ben.'*

Les Pèlerins - Onzième nuit

'My name is Captain Jean Allons, and I am taking charge of this... of this *situation* as of now. And I want to reassure you everything is going to be alright.'

Despite the fact they had just met moments earlier, there was something about the demeanour of the small police officer with a kindly round face and thin moustache, which Hugo recognised. He was sure Allons was an experienced and capable officer who was more than capable of dealing with a difficult situation.

'The first thing that is going to happen,' Allons continued, 'is that I have officers who are going to escort you from this Café and take you to the nearby village of Millieure, where we have reserved rooms for you in a hotel there, and where you will be quite safe, I can assure you.'

Edith Lancaster snorted. 'And we're supposed to believe that?' She pointed towards the door behind the counter. 'I think the two men lying in there would disagree.'

Captain Allons pointed to the officers who had accompanied him. They were standing sentry around Maurice Rousseau and Xavier Cadieux. 'Whatever happened here will be understood later, I'm sure, but right now all you need to know is we are going to move you from this village to a place of safety, a place we are in control of. That is all that matters at this moment.'

'And how do you propose getting us across a river with no bridge?' Edith sniped.

Wolfgang Huber chortled. 'You could always use your broomstick, Edith,' he laughed.

Edith dropped her knitting and stared at him. 'I could think of a more appropriate place to stick my broomstick, Wolfgang Huber,' she retorted, 'and I'm not so sure you'd be so flippant then.'

280

Captain Allons raised his hands. 'The pompiers have secured their rescue ladders to either side of the river. It is perfectly safe to cross that way.'

'It really is,' Ben confirmed. 'It's very sturdy.'

'I'm not sure,' Elke Huber stated anxiously.

Dorothy rubbed her hand. 'It will be fine, Elke,' she reassured. 'You heard, Ben, it's perfectly safe, and it's much better than staying here, don't you think?'

'And I'll have your hand, dear,' Wolfgang reassured. 'I won't allow anything to happen to you,' he added sincerely.

'Tres bien,' Allons said. 'Well, if you would like to collect your belongings, then we can leave as soon as possible.' He looked at a trio of officers. 'You guard the door to the kitchen,' he directed one of them, 'and you two stay by the suspects.'

'We're not suspects!' Maurice shouted.

Allons looked at him. 'There'll be time to talk about that later.' He turned to Hugo. 'Captain Duchamp, are you available to go for a walk with me? We have much to discuss.'

Wolfgang clambered to his feet. 'I should come too. I may be retired, but I was a decorated police officer for three decades.'

Allons nodded. 'I understand that, monsieur. However, you were also present during the murders, so until I am satisfied with what happened, I'm afraid I have to treat you all not just as witnesses but potential suspects. I am sorry, but these are the facts.' The small, round police officer raised his hands again, as Wolfgang's face reddened. 'As a former police officer of such a long time, I'm sure you would react in exactly the same way.' He spun around before Wolfgang had a chance to respond. 'Captain Duchamp, shall we?'

Hugo & Jean

Hugo was pleased to see that despite the ominous dark clouds which still hung heavy over the village, the rain had decreased to a light drizzle and the wind was now also barely noticeable. He walked slowly behind Captain Allons, his height dwarfing the small and rotund police officer.

'We'll talk in front of the church,' Allons instructed. 'It seems an appropriate place under the circumstances,' he added with a cheerful wink.

They continued the short walk in silence. When they reached the small, ancient church, Hugo was pleased when Allons reached into his raincoat and extracted a packet of cigarettes. He extended the pack to Hugo, and he took one with a grateful smile.

'I see you have the same terrible habit as I do,' Allons stated, lighting both their cigarettes.

Hugo inhaled cheerfully. 'I used to say I only smoked because it helped me think, but the truth is I just enjoy it and need an excuse to do so.'

Allons nodded knowingly. 'My wife says the smell is so bad she won't even kiss me,' he laughed. 'Not that she was very fond of kissing me in the first place, you understand! I suppose your wife feels the same.'

Hugo's eyes widened as they always did in such circumstances. 'Husband,' he corrected.

Allon's own eyes flashed, but Hugo was sure there was no malice or judgement in them. Allons laughed again. 'How very modern.'

The two men enjoyed the rest of their cigarettes in silence, finishing at the same time and stubbing them out.

'It appears we have quite a situation here,' Allons broke the silence. 'I know what Ben and Viviane told me, but I'd like you to tell me in your own words what you think has happened here.'

'I only came to the village after the events unfolded,' Hugo explained. 'But I'll tell you what I know.' He took a deep breath and relayed the events he had witnessed and experienced since arriving in the village. Captain Allons listened intently, his round head cocked to the side, and a stubby finger toying with his thin moustache.

'So the German cop and the French pathologist played at being investigators?' Allons questioned.

'I know Dr. Chapeau very well. I've worked alongside her for many years now,' Hugo reasoned, 'and I have to say, I trust her implicitly. And because of that, I know she did only what she had to do to preserve the crime scene and the evidence. Valuable information could have been lost otherwise. As for the interviewing of witnesses.' He paused. 'Well, there are legal issues with that, but under the circumstances, with no telephone lines and no way to get out of the village, I would reason that talking to the witnesses, and recording their oral statements while their memories were still fresh, was very important.' He shrugged. 'I don't see what they could have done differently under the circumstances. I would have done the same.'

Allons grimaced. 'You're probably right. The circumstances were not ideal. However, regardless of your personal knowledge of the doctor. She and the German were both present for the murders and therefore have to be suspects. It's that simple, n'est pas?'

'Peut être,' Hugo conceded. 'But for me, because I know her, I feel confident in her ability and innocence, though I understand you don't have to share that. Either way, we have the recordings because of Irene and I'm sure they will prove important in the investigation.'

'And you've listened to them?'

Hugo nodded. 'I have.'

'And have you come to any conclusions?'

Hugo considered his answer. 'I'm not sure,' he answered honestly. 'I listened, and I have made observations since, but I think it's too difficult to say with any certainty. However, the manner of the deaths and the persons who died, do point towards Maurice Rousseau, and by extension Xavier Cadieux, who is Olive's nephew.'

'And what opinion do you have of Maurice?'

Hugo was not sure how to answer. He had found Rousseau's denials plausible, but he also was not sure he was telling the truth. He sighed. 'The fact is, I've spent very little time with him to form a firm opinion. If you're asking me do I believe he committed these crimes, then I would have to answer his surprise seemed genuine to me, mais...'

'Mais?' Allons asked.

'Mais, the facts suggest something else altogether,' Hugo responded. 'I think you need to get him in an interview room and maybe then it will become clearer.'

Allons nodded. 'I know Maurice well,' he began. 'And it's fair to say he can be a troublesome man. He's spent more than a night or two in a police cell.'

'For what reason?' Hugo enquired.

'For many reasons,' Allons replied. 'Mainly that he is, occasionally, an angry man, and that anger manifests itself badly sometimes. I have always held the belief he is angry because he is broken. It has been my experience the two tend to go hand in hand.'

'Then you imagine it could be possible? That he could have reacted in such a way as to murder someone if he felt provoked?'

Allons kicked the ground with his foot. 'I never met Olive,' he began, 'but I know others who did, and there was talk of abuse. I know this because the reports of her disappearance noted they wondered whether he might have been involved. I can't talk too much of that, other than the original reports suggest he was genuinely upset by her, shall we say "death."' He paused. 'As you said, maybe he's just an excellent liar.'

Hugo stuffed his hands in his pockets. 'If he discovered Tony Wilkinson had taken his wife away and been with her this entire time, whilst I don't condone it, his actions aren't entirely difficult to understand.'

Captain Allons tapped his chin contemplatively. 'Let's get him in custody and we'll see, but as it happens, I agree. Maurice is a complicated man, and he's waited a long time for the truth. Whatever we think of him, I think we have to accept the case appears to be an open and shut one.'

'You're probably right,' Hugo conceded. 'So, what happens next? We stay in the hotel in the next village, for how long?'

'A day or two,' Allons replied. 'I expect to charge Maurice quickly and then you all can move on. There has been a tragedy in this village, and it seems to me who know who the guilty parties are.'

'Maurice is adamant he is innocent,' Hugo interrupted.

Allons scoffed. 'Obviously. Don't they all? I have come across very few criminals who hold their hands up to a crime. Most of them have watched enough television to know the importance of,' he stopped, adding with a grimace and air quotes, '"reasonable doubt."'

He sighed. 'In the end, we must accept the likelihood of Maurice Rousseau never admitting his guilt. However, even from my limited understanding of the matter, it seems as if there is no doubt of his guilt, and I'm sure a court will agree.' He smiled at Hugo. 'You will be able to leave soon and hopefully everyone can put this whole terrible business behind them.' He clapped his hands. 'Shall we have one last cigarette while we wait for them to gather their belongings, and then we can leave this village once and for all? I've never liked it, and I can't wait to see the back of it.'

Hugo nodded. 'I understand that feeling,' he replied distantly, staring at the Café. He sucked impatiently on the cigarette, trying desperately to ignore a feeling that was nagging away at him. Something was not right, he was sure, but he could not understand what it might be. And it appeared as far as anyone was concerned, the case was closed and Maurice Rousseau was guilty. They smoked the rest of their cigarettes in silence.

'Shall we?' Allons asked.

Hugo nodded, pulling up the hood of his jacket and dashing back towards the lights of the Café.

Les Pèlerins - Onzième nuit

The group moved slowly up the steep steps leading from the square to the top of the village. The weather had finally taken a turn for the better and the generators which supplied the hastily erected floodlights, flickered on and off, giving them just enough illumination to move forward.

Hugo glanced over his shoulder, noticing Maurice Rousseau and Xavier Cadieux were now in handcuffs, flanked by two police officers, their hands nestling on the rifles on their hips. A forensic team had also arrived and was already taking charge of the crime scene, and Hugo was immensely relieved about it all. Whatever had taken place in *Café Compostelle*, it would all become clear eventually. What mattered now was making sure everyone was safe and away from the volatile situation.

Ben slipped his hand into Hugo's, wrapping fingers scarred from a fire around Hugo's own. As always in such times, Hugo's free hand reached to the scar on his cheek. Both were reminders of times in the past when they had come close to their own demise. Hugo glanced over his shoulder. *Café Compostelle* was now shrouded in police tape and police officers were hurriedly moving in and out of the Café. He spotted Captain Allons and understood the difficult path he was about to tread. Whatever had transpired, it would not be easy to unravel, Hugo was sure of that.

The progress to the top of the steps was slow, the women helping each other up the worn stones. Finally, they made it to the top, stepping into the clearing where the bridge had once been. Hugo was relieved to see the pompiers had erected what appeared to be a sturdy enough makeshift path between the two banks.

'You expect me to cross that?' Edith Lancaster demanded.

'It looks perfectly safe to me,' Dorothy stated. She smiled at a pompier. 'In fact, I'll go first just to show you how safe and easy it is.'

The pompier nodded, took Dorothy's hand and escorted her over the narrow walkway. Dorothy stepped onto the other side and extended her hand. 'Ta-da!' she exclaimed triumphantly.

Edith Lancaster stepped onto the walkway, thrusting away the hand of another pompier. 'I don't need your help, young man,' she snapped. 'I'm perfectly capable of making my own way. I've been doing it for eighty years, you know, and most of them without a man telling me how to do it.'

Ben snuggled closer to Hugo. 'Merci Dieu, we're getting out of here and this is all finally over. We'll be home soon and can put this all behind us.'

Hugo glanced over his shoulder at the village below them. 'J'espère,' he whispered.

SEMAINE TROIS / WEEK THREE

CHEMIN DES PÈLERINS / PAMPLONA / MONTGENOUX

Hugo stepped out of the hotel in the centre of Millieure and lit a cigarette. He lifted his head, relieved to see the sun shining down on him. The warmth on his face was a welcome relief after feeling nothing but rain. After leaving the village two days earlier, everyone had been sequestered in the hotel and were now restless and eager to move on.

'Got one of them for me?'

Hugo turned around, instantly recognising the soft voice of the diminutive flic he had only met a few days earlier but had warmed to. 'Bien sûr, Captain Allons.'

Allons took a cigarette from him. 'Merci, and it's Jean.' He tipped his head towards the hotel. 'How are things?'

Hugo shrugged. 'Fine, I suppose. Everyone seems to be well enough. It's been reassuring to have police officers around for them, but I think they're mostly keen just to get on with what they came here for in the first place.'

Allons nodded. 'I finally may be able to help with that.'

Hugo raised an eyebrow. 'You have news?' he asked keenly.

'I do,' Allons replied. 'This morning, we charged Maurice Rousseau with the murders of Alain Bonnet and Tony Wilkinson.'

Hugo gave him a surprised look. 'He confessed?' he asked, wondering why he did not feel more relieved.

'Non, but the Procurer thinks we have enough to prosecute.'

'He does?' Hugo demanded, his voice rising sharply. He bit his lip. 'Désolé, I know it's not my place.'

Allons chortled. 'I understand your reticence. As I said the other day, I've known Maurice for a long time and while he has a temper, I found, still find, this whole sorry business a surprise. But he has no explanations for it and still maintains he didn't know about the affair. However, we found two pieces of evidence which contradict his assertions.'

'You do?'

'Oui,' Allons replied. 'Firstly, forensics found evidence of his presence in the storeroom.'

Hugo scratched his head. 'That's hardly surprising, surely?' he retorted. 'I expect he spent a great deal of time in the Café, and it stands to reason he may have helped out from time to time, which would perfectly explain his presence.'

Allons nodded. 'I can't say I disagree. However, the evidence is highly suggestive. As you no doubt recall, Monsieur Rousseau has rather distinctive shoulder-length dark hair. Well, one of those hairs was discovered amongst the blood congealed around Alain Bonet's wound. The forensics team believe it fell during the struggle which resulted in the death.'

'I see,' Hugo mused. 'Still, it could have been transferred a number of ways, non?'

Allons shrugged. 'That no doubt will be for a defence avocat to claim, but the procurer is satisfied enough with it to proceed. I can't profess to understand forensic evidence, but the report is clear in its conclusion. The examiner states the hair wasn't *under* the blood, it was *amongst* it. Which they suggest is quite a different scenario.'

Hugo frowned. The evidence, while certainly suggestive, was not conclusive as far as he could tell. The position of the hair was interesting, but he was still not sure it would be enough to convict. 'You said there were two pieces of evidence?' he continued.

'That is what you might call a smoking gun,' Allons smacked his lips with satisfaction. 'When we searched Maurice's belongings, we found a photograph of his wife.'

'Hardly surprising,' Hugo reasoned.

Allons continued to smile. 'A photograph of his wife is normal, oui. A photograph of his middle-aged wife against the backdrop of the Tower of London is something altogether different.'

'Ah,' Hugo responded. 'That does rather change things.' He was surprised at himself because he had thought Maurice Rousseau's reaction to news of his wife's infidelity was entirely genuine. But now it appeared he had known all along. Had that been the plan all the time - to wait for Tony Wilkinson to return to the village and murder him?

'I sense your reticence, and I understand it,' Allons continued, 'mais, the case is really quite simple.'

'You're probably right,' Hugo conceded. 'I suppose my biggest problem is this: if Maurice Rousseau knew about the affair and that his wife was alive and well and living a new life in London, then why not just go and see her himself? I know he said he didn't want to leave the village, but I'm sure he would have made the exception if he'd known the actual truth. It makes no sense. If murder was his plan, then why not just go to London to do it?'

'Peut être the location is the issue,' Allons reasoned. 'Maurice waited for Tony to return to the scene of the crime, so to speak, to exact his revenge.'

Hugo ran his hands through his hair, floppy blond hair falling over his face. He pushed it away and lit another cigarette as a thought occurred to him. 'There's another alternative,' he suggested. 'Tony Wilkinson could have just given him the photograph this week.'

'It's possible, I suppose,' Allons said with obvious reluctance, 'but it would seem a rather cruel thing to do.'

Hugo shrugged. 'People can often do terrible things when it comes to love. I'm sure you've seen as much of that as I have in our profession. We can't ask Tony Wilkinson and as you said, Maurice Rousseau isn't talking, so until he does, we may never know the actual truth.'

Allons snorted. 'I think matters might become clearer when the trial approaches and Maurice's defence avocat convinces him of the likelihood of being found guilty. Maybe then, when they try to secure a plea bargain, we might get more information and answers to our questions.'

Hugo dragged on the cigarette and exhaled. 'What happens next?'

'As I said, the procurer is happy to proceed,' Allons replied. 'So, there is nothing left to do other than wait for a trial date. All of which means you can all go about your normal lives again. I have taken everyone's statements and there's a chance they may be called back to give evidence, but the procurer seems sure most of it can be done via video link, especially for those out of the country.'

'And what about Olive Rousseau?' Hugo asked. 'Have you confirmed she is still alive and living in London?'

Allons face clouded, and Hugo could see he was not satisfied. 'I sent a copy of the photograph to the London Metropolitan Police, but so far they have been unable to locate her,' Allons answered. 'However, they have confirmed a woman matching her description has been living in an apartment owned by Tony Wilkinson. Her neighbours describe her as a "beautiful French woman" and confirmed it was her in the photograph.'

'And so did Maurice?' Hugo continued. 'He confirmed it was Olive?'

Allons nodded. 'All he said was, "she's still so beautiful." He would say no more, other than he was adamant he did not know where the photograph came from.'

'I worked for the Metropolitan Police for over ten years,' Hugo stated. 'I could make some calls and try to pull some strings. I imagine when this goes to trial, it will be important to either confirm or deny that she is dead or alive.'

'I'd appreciate that, Hugo. It could make all the difference,' Allons smiled. 'The chances are, she's just on holiday herself. With her lover away, she could be on a beach somewhere,' he chortled. 'I mean, it's not as if she could have come along here, is it?'

'You're right. I'll call my ex-colleagues and see if they can help,' Hugo said. 'Did the autopsies of Alain Bonnet and Tony Wilkinson reveal anything?'

'Non, I'm afraid not,' Allons stated glumly. 'They were pretty much as your Dr. Chapeau described. Alain died as a result of blunt force trauma to the cranium. The knife wound was entirely post-mortem. As for our English Romeo, his death was attributable to the two rather large knitting needles being plunged into his brain. Death would have been more or less instantaneous. The only odd thing is that his blood showed extremely high levels of warfarin.'

'Warfarin?'

Allons nodded again. 'Apparently, it's a blood thinner used to prevent blood clots,' he explained. 'Not so unusual in itself, but there was rather more in his system than would be expected. I'm not sure what that means,' he continued, 'other than the pathologist seems to think he may have been ingesting too much, but whether that was by choice, or someone was giving it to him, we can't say.'

Hugo raised an eyebrow. 'Interesting all the same, non?'

Allons shrugged, pushing a finger across his squidgy cheek. 'I'm not sure it is. Maurice Rousseau murdered the man. The pathologist says that even though there were high doses of warfarin, it wasn't enough to kill him.' He moved his head. 'Non, I'm afraid, it's pretty much an open and shut case.'

Hugo moved. 'And what about the young man, Xavier Cadieux?'

'As slippery as Maurice, I'm afraid, if not more so,' Allons replied. 'And as cocky as hell, it was all I could do to not smack the smug smirk off his face, mais...' he trailed off wearily. 'There isn't actually any direct evidence he was involved, however, after many heated debates with the procurer, he has agreed to charge Cadieux with false imprisonment. The procurer's not convinced it will go anywhere, so I suppose we'll see, but I wanted to at least attempt to wipe that damn cocky grin off his face.'

He glanced anxiously at his watch. 'Speaking of the procurer, I have a meeting with him in half an hour. I wonder, could I impose on you to relay the facts to the group and tell them they are free to leave but we will be in touch with them all at a later date?'

Hugo nodded. 'No problem. I'm sure they'll all be very pleased.' He shook Captain Allons hand. 'It's been a pleasure meeting you, Jean.'

'And you Hugo,' Allons replied. 'Hopefully next time it will be under better circumstances. Until then, au revoir.'

Dorothy Chapeau exhaled. 'Oh, thank goodness,' she gushed at Hugo after he had finished relaying his discussion with Captain Allons.

'Yes, indeed,' Irene agreed. 'We can all get out of here finally and go home.'

Dorothy turned her head abruptly to her daughter. 'What are you talking about? We've barely begun the pilgrimage.'

Irene's eyes widened. 'Well, it's just that I assumed after everything that happened...'

Wolfgang Huber interrupted. 'We've been discussing it, and because we've come all of this way, it seems foolish not to at least attempt to complete the journey.'

'And besides, Captain Duchamp just told us the madman is safely in police custody, didn't he?' Edith Lancaster demanded.

'He is,' Hugo confirmed. He looked around the room. 'Is everyone going to continue with the pilgrimage?'

'Well, I certainly am,' Edith confirmed brusquely.

'I have to,' Sam Mitchell added, ruffling his son's head. Casey Mitchell pulled away, fixing his father with an angry glare. Sam's face crinkled, obviously sad by the reaction. 'I have a book to write,' Sam continued, 'and I already spent the advance,' he added with a tight smile.

'What about you, Sarah?' Elke Huber. 'You'll be wanting to go home and deal with... deal with...'

Sarah shook her head. 'No, I'm going to continue the walk as well.'

'You are?' Elke asked, clearly surprised.

'It was what my mother wanted,' Sarah replied. 'I want to do it for her.'

Elke nodded. 'I understand, and for Tony, of course.'

Sarah rounded on her. 'He didn't even want to do this in the first place, so no, I won't be doing it for him. He ruined my life, my mother's life and Maurice Rousseau's life.' She smiled tightly. 'As far as I'm concerned, he got exactly what he deserved.'

Edith Lancaster sharply sucked in a breath. 'You shouldn't talk that way, child.'

Sarah bit her fingernails. 'You want me to lie?' she retorted. 'Isn't that, like, against God, or something?'

'God always knows the truth, young lady,' Edith snapped. 'He is more interested in our behaviour than you can imagine. It is what we must discuss with Him on our day of reckoning.'

Dorothy cleared her throat, looking at Hugo and Ben. 'I expect you'll be going back to Montgenoux with Irene and Bruno?'

Ben nodded. 'Oui. I'm in the middle of building a hotel…'

'I can't believe you're going ahead with this, Mama,' Irene interrupted, ignoring everyone else. 'Especially after everything that's happened.'

'It's all over,' Dorothy said forcefully. 'You heard Hugo. Maurice is in custody, so there's no reason to not continue as far as I can tell. I mean, that was the intention to begin with, wasn't it? Nothing has really changed.'

'You don't even have a guide anymore,' Irene said, her tone soft but forceful as if she was attempting to stop the situation from escalating.

In the corner of the room, Viviane Auclair raised her hand. 'I'm a guide. I'm not the most experienced but I can do it, I'm sure. And besides, there's not much work for me at the moment. So, if you'd like, I could go along with you.'

'Oh, would you, dear?' Dorothy replied. 'That would be wonderful.'

'What about the bus that was supposed to follow you in case you need a rest along the way?' Irene continued.

'I could bring the bus,' Viviane suggested. 'I guess it's just sitting in *Chemin des Pèlerins*. It's not like Maurice Rousseau is going to need it again, is it?'

Dorothy clapped her hands. 'There you go. Everything's sorted. We'll leave first thing tomorrow.'

Hugo, Ben & Irene

'I can't leave,' Irene declared abruptly to Hugo and Ben.

The three of them were seated outside in a bar next to the hotel. The rest of the group had retired to their rooms to prepare for restarting the pilgrimage the following day.

'What do you mean?' Ben asked.

'I thought I could leave mama,' Irene explained before her face contorted with confusion. 'Well, actually, I was only really half invested in that idea,' she added with a shy smile. 'I had thought it possible before, and I was coming off as a Jewish grandmother, even though I'm not Jewish. Mais now, after everything that's happened, I just don't know. I don't feel comfortable leaving her.'

Ben reached over and hugged her. 'It's fine to worry, but I think everything is okay now. But if you need to stay, you should, or else you're just going to work yourself up back in Montgenoux. What about Bruno? I thought you were keen to take him home?'

Irene slowly sipped from her glass of wine. 'I did, but I just can't leave Mama, not yet, at least. Can you take him home with you? It would mean the world to me, and it would be a weight off my mind.'

Ben rubbed her hand. 'Bien sûr, we can. Do what you need to do. You know Bruno will be fine with us. In fact, we'll have a hell of a time making trouble when Maman is away,' he added with a wicked laugh.

Until then Hugo had been quiet, silently nursing the beer in front of him, sucking absently on a cigarette. He lifted his head sharply. 'How long is the next section of the walk?' he asked abruptly.

Irene reached into her handbag and extracted a notepad. She flipped through it. 'We're about halfway to the next checkpoint, which is at a place called Pamplona. According to my estimation, we're about twenty kilometres away from it.'

Hugo nodded, his face clouded by the smoke.

'What's going on in there?' Ben asked, tapping Hugo's head.

'I think we should walk with them to Pamplona,' Hugo blurted, surprising himself. He was not sure why, but instinctively he knew whatever had happened in *Chemin des Pèlerins* was not yet finished. There was a missing piece to the puzzle.

Ben spluttered, the curls on his forehead bouncing. 'What on earth for? Have you suddenly found religion?'

Irene leaned forward and took Hugo's cigarette from him, taking a quick drag. 'Non, he hasn't. It's something else altogether. I recognise that look. You think something is wrong, don't you?'

Hugo took the cigarette from her and took his own drag, something he would never have thought to do a few years earlier when his life was staid and solitary. 'I don't know what I think,' he answered honestly. 'But I think another day with these people wouldn't be such a bad idea, that's all. Even if it's just to alleviate a concern I'm not sure is real.'

Ben nodded, smiling warmly at him. 'Then we'll walk.'

'Then we'll walk,' Hugo agreed, hoping he would not come to regret his decision.

The line of pilgrims ambled along the side of the road. For the first day since they had begun, the sun was beaming down on them and there was not a cloud in the sky. Hugo and Ben were at the back of the line, their hands entwined walking in silence.

'Do you believe in all of this?' Ben asked finally.

'The pilgrimage to Camino?' Hugo asked.

Ben nodded, gesturing in front of them. 'They all seem to be taking it so very seriously, and I'm just wondering if I'm missing out on something.'

Hugo considered his response. 'I don't think I believe in God, not a physical one at least, but I understand the power of belief in all its forms, good and bad, judgmental and non-judgmental. I suppose the walk is a way of showing that belief and hope.'

'A crazy way, if you ask me,' Ben laughed.

'Peut être,' Hugo agreed, 'but a lot of good can come from it, I'm sure. I would imagine a lot of people do it for a myriad of reasons, to make decisions about their future, their life, par example. Or just to get away from normal life and see if it makes a difference. A long walk with little else to do but listen to your own thoughts can be quite illuminating, or infuriating,' he added with a laugh.

Ben raised himself up and kissed Hugo on the cheek. 'Je t'aime, oh wise one!'

They continued on in silence for a while. Hugo's attention drawn to the slow-moving line in front of them. Sarah Wilkinson was walking alongside Casey Mitchell, though they did not appear to be engaged in any sort of conversation. He supposed it made sense, particularly since they were the closest in age. As for the rest of the pilgrims, they seemed to have recommenced the walk with a renewed vigour. Even Edith Lancaster, the eldest of the group, was striding ahead, her walking cane stabbing against the ground like a weapon.

Irene and Bruno stepped back. Ben swung Bruno upwards, throwing the giggling youth onto his shoulders.

'Everyone seems to be happy to be on the road again,' Irene stated. 'It's like the whole nightmare never happened.'

'Except it did,' Hugo corrected.

'Did Captain Allons happen to mention the autopsies?' Irene asked.

Hugo relayed the information Allons had passed on. Irene listened intently. 'It's pretty much as I thought,' she stated. 'Though the warfarin addition is interesting.'

'Is it?' Hugo questioned. 'Apparently, it wasn't enough to kill him.'

'Warfarin, like anything else in high enough quantities, can be fatal,' Irene replied.

'You think it's possible someone was poisoning him?' Ben interjected. 'From what you told me about his daughter, Sarah, it seems as if there was no love lost between them.'

'It's true,' Hugo conceded. 'Though I have to agree with Captain Allons. Someone clearly murdered him another way and he could have just taken too much of his own regular medication.'

Irene nodded. 'It's possible.' She sighed. 'Oh well, I suppose everyone is right. This really is over.' She studied Hugo's impassive face. 'And yet, you don't believe it is, do you?'

'I'm not saying that,' Hugo replied. 'Because the truth is, I don't know what to believe. All I know is that I believed Maurice Rousseau when he said he didn't know about the affair and I suppose that keeps niggling at me.'

'But what about the photograph?' Ben asked. 'Even if he didn't know, it makes sense that if Tony Wilkinson gave him the photograph, then it likely pushed him over the edge. And then imagine him finding out his best friend and confidant knew about it all the time.' He shrugged. 'I'm no flic, but I can see how that kind of info could be the final straw for someone already on the edge.'

'I have to say I agree,' Irene added. They lapsed into silence again. 'Are you going to go back to Montgenoux once we get to Pamplona?' she asked after a few minutes had passed.

Hugo did not answer immediately, there was still too much noise in his head and it was bothering him. 'I think so. I'm not sure what else we can do here,' he said with more reluctance than he knew he should have.

Ben clasped his hands together. 'Merci Dieu, or whoever,' he said, looking up, 'because I don't think my little old feet could do the whole walk.'

Irene laughed. 'You should take a leaf out of Edith Lancaster's book. She's more than twice all of our ages and I honestly think she could complete this pilgrimage without breaking a sweat.'

Ben blew a raspberry at her. 'Have you made your mind up? Shall we take Bruno home with us, or will you be coming back?'

Irene studied her mother in front of them. Dorothy Chapeau was engaged in a light-hearted chat with Elke and Wolfgang Huber, laughing happily. Irene sighed. 'I haven't seen my mother so happy for a long time. I think I'd like to stay with her a while longer. Not for the entire way. I think she'd have a better experience without my keeping a beady eye on her all the time.' Her face tightened. 'But after losing Papa, I'd like to spend as much time with her as I can.'

At the front of the procession, Viviane Auclair stopped and raised her hands. 'There's a village about one kilometre away, seems a perfect time to stop for lunch, non?'

Edith Lancaster tutted loudly. 'If we must. Saint Jacques de Compostelle has been waiting a long time for us. I'm sure he won't mind waiting a little longer,' she said, her voice laced with sarcasm as she pushed past the young tour guide.

'I spoke to your former colleague in London,' Etienne began. 'Gemma sends her love, by the way, and told me to remind you, you promised to visit London again soon,' he added.

Hugo stared at his feet. Gemma Anderson was one of the first people he met during his time working in London. He had left France with nothing, ready to embark upon a new life and Gemma had been one of the first people he had met. A tough-talking Londoner with strong opinions which had landed her in trouble with more than one of her former superiors. For some reason, Hugo had taken to her, and she to him, and together they had formed a team of detectives affectionately nicknamed "The Met Outsiders Club."

The team had proven to be very successful and despite his depressing personal life, Hugo had found himself with friends for what seemed like the first time in a very long time. He had allowed himself to take a chance, and it had almost worked. However, a doomed love affair had changed the course of Hugo's life once again, forcing him back into his reclusive shell. After several years of distance, Hugo had come to the realisation he would always be grateful to Gemma for being the first person who had made him feel practically normal.

'I'll call her,' Hugo replied to Etienne. 'Going back to London has never been high on my list of priorities, but I should make the effort.' He took a deep breath. 'Anyway, what did she find?'

'Not a lot, I'm afraid,' Etienne answered glumly. 'Other than what you already knew. It appears as if a woman matching Olive Rousseau's description has been living in London for a long time. Although she doesn't appear to be officially registered anywhere. She also doesn't seem to have paid taxes or have a passport, or anything like that. The apartment is owned by Tony Wilkinson. Gemma spoke to the neighbours and although they mention him being a regular visitor, they don't believe he actually lived there, but the French woman most certainly did, they say. The neighbours also report not seeing her for at least a week or two.'

'Hmm,' Hugo murmured. 'That's interesting, non?'

Etienne whistled. 'Not necessarily. If she was Tony Wilkinson's mistress, she might have just chosen to go on holiday herself because he was going away.'

'That's what I thought too, but I'd be happier if we at least knew where she was,' Hugo stated. 'You said there was no official trace of her?'

'That's right,' Etienne replied. 'I checked. Olive Rousseau was officially declared dead thirty-four years ago in France, five years after her disappearance. If this mystery woman is indeed Olive, I imagine she assumed another identity, because there is no passport held in that name. The Wilkinson family are very rich, so it's not too much of a stretch to assume they could have facilitated a new identity and a new passport for her.'

'It's certainly possible,' Hugo agreed wearily.

'What is it about all of this that's bugging you?'

Hugo sighed. 'I wish I knew, truly I do, because believe me, I want nothing more than just to put it all behind me and come back to Montgenoux.'

'Then what can I do to help facilitate that?'

'I hate to waste your time on this,' Hugo replied. 'You have more than enough work of your own to do.'

Etienne laughed. 'Not that I'm saying you attract trouble, but with you out of town, the crime rate seems to have gone to zero.'

It was Hugo's turn to laugh. 'Oui, I suppose I am the common denominator. D'accord,' he said decisively. 'I know you've looked into these people already, but could you try again?'

'Bien sûr,' Etienne replied. 'But what am I looking for?'

Hugo snorted. 'Well, if I knew that...' he trailed off. 'The only thing I know for sure is that if anyone is capable of finding a needle in a haystack, it's you.'

'Sweet talker!' Etienne gently mocked. 'Okay, I'll see what I can do. How long do I have?'

Hugo turned his attention to his fellow travellers, all enjoying their lunch in a picturesque village. 'Well, we'll be in the next village by nightfall. I had planned on leaving tomorrow, alors...'

'You don't ask much of me, do you?' Etienne demanded cheerfully, clearly relishing the challenge. 'Is Irene coming with you?' he asked hopefully.

Hugo felt his heart sink. 'I'm not sure,' he intoned. 'I think she needs to spend some time with her mother, so we may bring Bruno back with us, but I'm sure she won't be far behind,' he added, ensuring his tone was light and hopeful.

Etienne cleared his throat and. 'I'll see what I can do. In the meantime, try to have a bit of downtime, d'accord?'

Hugo smiled. 'Right now, I'm going to have a beer, a cigarette and a plate of frites, and do a little bit of people-watching. Speak to you soon, Etienne, and merci.'

Hugo watched as the pilgrims ate their lunch. He was again surprised at how light the mood was, particularly after everything that had taken place in the preceding days. He supposed it had a lot to do with the young tour guide, Viviane Auclair, who had somehow managed to bring her natural exuberance to the group and invigorated them with a new sense of purpose. As far as Hugo could tell, there had been hardly any discussion of the murders, even from Sarah Wilkinson, who seemed to be bonding well with the young American Sam Mitchell.

Ben moved across the bar, placing a beer in front of Hugo. 'How's the people watching going?' he asked warmly.

Hugo sipped the beer, his shoulders dropping. 'I think we should just go home,' he announced glumly. 'I'm seeing darkness in the shadows again and I'm not sure why, and frankly it's getting on my nerves now.'

Ben touched Hugo's cheek. 'You think something is off? I get that. And as far as I'm concerned, that's all I need to know. Something is off, if you think it is.' He reached over and kissed his husband. 'So, talk to me. I know you, Hugo Duchamp, and I can think of only one reason why you might be reluctant to tell me something, and that's because you think it might upset me. So quit worrying about upsetting me.'

Hugo took a deep breath, again surprised by how well Ben knew him. 'There are so many things that seem off about this whole thing, but there's one thing in particular at the moment which is troubling me and until I clear that from my mind, I won't be able to move on.' He glanced around, ensuring no one was listening to them. 'When I was talking with Dorothy, she commented about the way Tony Wilkinson died and she mentioned the knitting needles. And I have to wonder, how did she know that?'

Ben frowned and scratched his head, pushing the curls away. 'What are you talking about? Obviously Irene told her.' He gave Hugo an incredulous look. 'You can't possibly be suggesting Dorothy Chapeau had something to do with it,' he snapped, lowering his voice to ensure no one else could hear their conversation.

'I don't know what I think,' Hugo reasoned. 'And it's highly possible Irene mentioned it to her mother, mais…' he trailed off because he knew he did not need to finish the sentence.

'Irene would never talk about a case,' Ben said finally. 'Not even to her mother.' He shook his head. 'But that's not to say Dorothy didn't find Irene's notes or listen to the recordings.' He took a deep breath. 'I can't begin to imagine what you're getting at.'

'I'm not getting at anything necessarily,' Hugo replied. 'And as I said, I'm probably reading too much into everything. You're probably right. Dorothy probably overheard, or read something…'

'What's the alternative?' Ben asked, wide-eyed. 'I can't for a second imagine Dorothy would do something so heinous. Mais…' he stopped abruptly, 'then how did she know?' he asked, confused.

'There's a possibility she could have seen Tony after he was dead,' Hugo suggested. 'It was easy for anyone to get into the storeroom. Curiosity could have just gotten the better of her.'

'Then why didn't she mention it?' Ben countered.

Hugo shrugged. 'There could be any number of reasons. She might not think it important and that I hadn't noticed her saying it. She could also be embarrassed and doesn't want us to think of her as being nosy.'

Ben mused. 'We could just ask her?'

Hugo shook his head. 'It's not my investigation and besides, I don't think it's something we want to get involved in, particularly because I don't think Irene would appreciate it.'

'Then what do we do?' Ben asked, seizing Hugo's hand. 'Just

go back to Montgenoux and pretend as if nothing happened? Are you able to do that?'

Hugo did not answer immediately. 'I'm not sure what choice I have. Two crimes were committed, and someone is in custody. The fact he doesn't admit to it is neither here nor there at the end of the day. Most criminals don't admit their crimes. And I suppose my own reticence is based purely on the fact I don't tend to trust a word most people say because I'm used to being lied to.'

Ben wrapped his arm around Hugo. 'We'll go home tomorrow when we reach Pamplona,' he said simply, 'but until then, do what you do best.'

'And what's that?' Hugo asked.

Ben pushed him forward. 'Walk on your own for a while. Go and listen. Go and talk. And maybe then you'll find answers to whatever it is that's bothering you. Let's hope it's nothing, but if it isn't, you'll know what to do about it, because you always do.'

Hugo looked ahead at the people in front of them. He nodded. 'Let's hope you're right.'

Dorothy & Wolfgang

'Do you think you'll make it to Compostelle?' Dorothy asked curiously.

Wolfgang Huber patted his expansive stomach. 'I can't imagine why you would ask that. After all, I'm fitter than the rest of you old folks, aren't I?'

Dorothy threw back her head and laughed. 'Don't be cheeky, Wolfgang Huber.' She looked glumly at the road ahead. 'The truth is, we've barely begun and we've spent most of the time with our feet up, not on the ground. No, it's going to be hard, whether we're old or not,' she added with a tight smile.

He lightly touched her arm. 'But you will make it because you have Willum sending you the strength you need. We'll get each other to the end. You'll see if we don't.' He pointed to Edith. 'And if need be, we can borrow Edith's broomstick!' he said to lighten the mood.

Dorothy laughed again. She glanced over her shoulder, noticing Hugo a few steps behind them, flashing him a smile before turning back to Wolfgang. 'It's strange,' she continued, 'Elke was always keen on doing the Camino again, but each time, there was always a reason why she couldn't.' She paused. 'Those reasons were usually to do with you.'

Wolfgang snorted. 'I was a police detective in West Germany. My time was not my own. No matter what I wanted personally, I didn't have the time to… to…' he stopped, 'to do something that would consume me,' he added, his voice lowering. 'And I always believed there were some things best left behind.'

Dorothy nodded, her face clouding. 'I understand. Once Willum and I were married and we had Irene, our lives were taken over by, well, just taken over by life, everyday life in all its forms. And yet… and yet we always knew we would have found a way to

312

come back if everyone else was. For some reason, we felt an affinity with those we'd travelled with in the first place. We knew if they came back, we HAD to come back. After all, we had shared so much,' she added, her tone whimsical. 'And after everything that has happened recently, I have to say, I'm not proud of my part in it.'

Wolfgang's eyes darted around them anxiously. 'This isn't the time, nor the place, to discuss this.'

Dorothy laughed, extending her arms around her. 'On the contrary, Wolfgang, I think this is *exactly* the place to discuss it. We all did a terrible thing back then,' she began, before shaking her head. 'I don't remember it being a terrible thing back then, but looking back now, here and now, I can see we all became involved in something we shouldn't have, and I think in one way or another, we've been running from it ever since, and not to mention what it did to Maurice and his family.'

Wolfgang rolled his eyes. 'You and Elke are the same. Stupid women living in a world of nothing but pure imagination. You imagined you did something wonderful back then, but you did nothing of the sort.'

'What are you talking about?' Dorothy snapped. 'We did the only thing we could.'

He shook his head angrily. 'No, you didn't. You answered the siren call of another female. A female who bleated about how unhappy she was, about how cruel her husband was, so you did the only thing you could. You reacted as women and created a situation that was nothing short of a disaster. Stupid, foolish females.'

Dorothy glared at him. 'You really are the most monstrous sexist man, Wolfgang Huber. You were back then, and it only appears you have become worse with time. I can't imagine why Elke has put up with you all of this time.'

Wolfgang shrugged nonchalantly. 'I am a man of my time,' he conceded. 'But one thing you should be in no doubt of is that while

I am not perfect, I have always done the best for my Elke.'

Dorothy turned her head. At that moment, Elke was smiling, happily chatting with the young American Casey Mitchell. 'Elke was always good at making the best out of things,' Dorothy mouthed.

Wolfgang nodded. 'I would like to have given her more, but there were some things I could just not give her. Like a child, for example. If I regret anything, I regret that.' He ran a finger across his wide face. 'In the end, it was down to me, according to the doctors, but I don't think she blamed me. She could have left me for a man who could have given her more and what her heart ached for, a baby, but instead she chose to stay with a dinosaur like me.' He frowned. 'In my darkest hours, I used to like to imagine it was because she thought me a catch, but I suppose it's much more likely that she is a saint and a woman who doesn't believe in divorce. Either way, I try to count my blessings, and I know you may find this hard to believe, but Elke is the love of my life.'

Dorothy laughed. 'Careful, Wolfgang, or you'll have me believing you actually have a beating heart under there,' she said, tapping his chest.

The two of them walked in silence for several minutes.

Wolfgang finally broke the silence. 'Olive had no right to do what she did,' he stated. 'And more importantly, she had no right to ask for help. She put us all in a very awkward position.'

Dorothy nodded. 'Then why did you help?'

He snorted. 'Because I was trying to impress Elke,' he explained. 'I could not care less about the sordidness that was going on. Whatever monstrosity took place four decades ago, it was nothing to do with me. In fact, I spoke to you all and told you my concerns. But of course, you all ignored me.'

'That's not true,' Dorothy interjected. 'We all agreed that night in the Café we would help Tony and Olive.'

Wolfgang stared at her. 'I know. I was there and just because

I'm a man, it doesn't mean I don't understand what was going on. But I WAS the only one who understood what was wrong about it, and none of you wanted to hear that at the time, did you?'

Dorothy gave him a curious look. 'We have very different recollections it appears, Wolfgang, don't we?'

'I'm not sure what you mean,' he retorted.

Dorothy moved forward, waving to her fellow pilgrims before she spoke again. 'You're right about one thing,' she spoke softly, 'we all realised the error of our ways and we told Tony and Olive as such, and yet she left the village anyway. It wasn't down to us, but it was down to you.'

'I have no idea what you're talking about,' he snapped.

'Yes, you do,' Dorothy retorted. 'The day of that terrible storm, Elke and I went to Tony and Olive and told her we wanted no part of it. We told Olive we felt bad for her, but we wouldn't be part of such a terrible scheme. Whatever Maurice had done, we didn't believe he deserved what they were planning.'

Wolfgang shrugged. 'I know all of this. I was there. I never bought the whole "he'll never give me a divorce" stance Olive took. She could have walked out of the village anytime she wanted…'

'You're delusional, Wolfgang,' Dorothy interrupted. 'Back then, women's rights weren't a patch on what they are now, and even now they're not so great as far as I'm concerned. Olive grew up in this village and I imagine she thought she would die in it. She didn't even have her own bank account or any money of her own. Until Tony arrived her only choice was to stay with a man who loved her in his own way, but wasn't very kind to her.' She stopped, shaking her head slowly. 'I can't say I agreed with Olive's choices, but I also can't say I didn't understand her. It wasn't much different in Scotland. I got lucky, she wanted the same. So she took a chance to get away. We can disagree with it as much as we like, but we have to accept her reasoning as being sound enough.'

Wolfgang raised an eyebrow. 'And yet you decided not to help her in the end,' he stated. 'You can't have been that worried about her so-called female rights.'

'I told you,' she responded. 'We realised it would be wrong. But luckily, you didn't.'

He clenched his fists in front of him. 'I don't know why you keep saying that. I had nothing to do with her escaping the village. I wouldn't have done that, not even to impress Elke.'

Dorothy gave him a curious look. 'Well, that's odd. I saw Olive that night and I apologised again. She hugged me and said it was fine, she'd found someone else to help her.'

'And you assumed it was me?' Wolfgang demanded.

'Well, yes, I did,' Dorothy conceded. 'I saw you talking to her outside the Café shortly before she disappeared.'

He shrugged. 'You may well have, but I'm sure I was just telling her I wouldn't help her escape. I thought it was cruel. I remember saying that to her. *If you do this, you'll be as cruel to him as he has been to you.* That's what I said to her. She looked at me with the face of a defiant child. *This might be my only chance to get out of here,* she said, *so if you won't help me, they will.* I walked away from her. I couldn't be bothered to argue any longer.'

Dorothy cocked her head. 'She said - *so if you won't help me, they will?*'

Wolfgang nodded. 'Yes. I'm sure she did. Does it matter?'

'I don't know,' she replied, staring off into the distance. 'Only that if you didn't help her and Elke and I didn't help her. Then who did?'

'I could not care less,' Wolfgang replied. 'And I don't wish to talk about this anymore,' he said, breaking away and moving further into the group.

'You knew my parents well?' Sam Mitchell asked.

Edith Lancaster did not answer him, instead continuing to focus on the road ahead of her.

Sam Mitchell followed her, struggling to keep up with the octogenarian English woman. 'They spoke of you often,' he blustered.

Edith did not look back, nor slow down as she spoke. 'I can't imagine for a second that either Anne or Frank were happy to have a child who became,' she paused, her face crinkling, 'a *football* player,' she added as if she was uttering a curse word.

Sam laughed. 'You're probably right. Mom wanted me to have a nice, safe job like a doctor, or a dentist or something like that. And pop wanted me to follow him into the family drywall business. I suspect it was a huge disappointment to them both that not only didn't I have the brains to do anything clever, but also the only thing I could do well with my hands was to throw a ball. But until I was injured, I threw a ball pretty well.'

'You were a dreadful child,' Edith stated matter-of-factly. 'Precocious and clearly bored and a dreadful waste of all of your time here. You were always complaining, throwing stones in front of you as if you were hoping one of us was going to trip over just for your amusement.'

'I probably was a bit of a brat,' Sam confirmed with a mischievous smile. 'My parents made me leave my girlfriend behind because they caught us having sex, so you can imagine how happy I was to be dragged to rural France and Spain for no real reason. I hated them and I hated my entire time here.' He gave her a wry smile. 'Though I am sorry for throwing stones at people!'

'Well, if I'd tripped over one of them, you'd have been eating them for your supper, that's all I can tell you!' Edith snorted, hiding a smile. She fixed him with a curious look. 'If it was such an ordeal the first time around, what are you doing back here?'

'It's all about the book,' he responded. 'My last few haven't sold well, and my publisher was threatening to bail on me, which would have meant returning the advance I already spent a long time ago. Anyway, one day Casey came to me with an idea.'

'This was your son's idea?' Edith asked in amazement.

Sam nodded. 'He knew his grandparents were desperate to do the walk again, but they never had the opportunity, or the time, or to be honest, the money. I guess Casey overheard me talking to my agent and realised I was in trouble, so he suggested I pitch the book about fulfilling my parents' ambition and doing the walk for them.' He smiled sadly. 'I had to admit, it was a pretty good idea, and though I never really got on with my folks, it seemed like a good enough way to honour them.'

Edith nodded curtly. 'I suppose it's an honourable enough idea.' She paused, pursing her lips. 'Tell me, what do you make of what has transpired here since we arrived?'

Sam shrugged. 'I can't begin to imagine. It's pretty shocking.'

She raised an eyebrow. 'Although a rather interesting twist for your book, no?'

Sam met her gaze, his cheeks reddening.

'So, the thought has occurred to you,' Edith mused. 'Then tell me, how does it end? If you thought about it, you must also have some ideas.'

Sam nodded to Hugo, who was walking near them, quietly smoking a cigarette.

'I don't know,' Sam continued. 'Mom and dad talked about Olive's death, or rather her "apparent" death.'

Edith gave him a curious look. 'And what, pray tell, did they have to say about that?'

Sam's eyes flashed wide. 'Well, not a lot really.' He stopped as if considering something. 'I guess they were sad. My dad was pretty straight-laced. I can't imagine he approved of the affair, but mom could always wrap him around her little finger.' He laughed sadly. 'She could pretty much do that to anyone she met. So when Olive came to her with her sob story, of course she wanted to help, and she got pop to help too.'

'Help in what way, exactly?' Edith demanded.

Sam stepped ahead of her, scampering along the path.

Edith threw her carpetbag over her shoulder and stabbed her cane into the grass, trying desperately to keep up with him. 'Answer my question, young man?' she called after him.

Sam stopped abruptly, causing her to crash into him. 'I'm fifty-five years old. I haven't been called a young man for a very long time, nor have I been told off by an old matron for even longer.'

'Less of the old,' she growled.

He laughed. 'How old are you? Like a hundred?'

Edith raised her cane. 'Do you want to see how hard an old matron can hit with one of these? Because I can assure you, I can pack a punch.'

Sam's eyes flicked over her. 'You know, it's quite incredible. Forty years ago, you practically looked the same.'

Despite herself, Edith Lancaster laughed. 'Nice attempt to distract me, but I'm still waiting for a response to my question. How did your parents help Olive Rousseau?'

He shrugged. 'I don't know.'

'I don't think I believe you,' Edith retorted, fixing him with a withering look.

Sam laughed sardonically. 'I don't know what to tell you. My parents never actually confided in me and I can't say I was particularly interested.' He paused. 'The only thing I can tell you is that when we got home, the only time my folks talked about what happened in France was behind closed doors and in whispers. And before you ask, I didn't ask because I didn't care. You were right about one thing, I was fifteen years old and I could not care less about what happened to old folks I didn't even know.'

Edith stared at him. 'I don't think I believe you,' she stated again.

He shrugged again. 'Same here. I don't believe there's a single thing that went on forty years ago and last week that you don't know about, for that matter.'

Edith Lancaster's thin lips pulled into a tight smile, but she said nothing, instead striding away from him.

Elke & Casey

Elke Huber watched as Dorothy Chapeau stepped away with Irene, Bruno skipping between them. Her face clouded as if she was lost in thought.

'You got kids?'

Elke jumped, startled by Casey Mitchell, the young American who was watching her.

'I'm sorry, I didn't mean to frighten you,' Casey said, pushing his glasses up his nose.

She smiled warmly at him. 'Do you know something, young man? You have a kind face.'

Casey blushed.

'And to answer your question, no, I was never blessed with children of my own.'

He snorted. 'Blessed? I doubt my father would ever describe me as a blessing.'

Elke looked ahead. At that moment, Sam Mitchell was engaged in what appeared to be a heated debate with Edith Lancaster and it caused her to smile because it appeared as if Edith was winning. 'Oh, I'm sure that's not true,' she whispered.

Casey pointed at his father. 'Yeah right. Look at him, he's the all-American hero. Blond hair, square jaw, athletic.' He ran his hand through his own black, greasy hair. 'And then there's me. Scrawny with spots and zero ability in anything other than playing video games.' He snorted. 'Yeah, he's super proud of me,' he added sarcastically.

'And your mother?' Dorothy asked before biting her lip. 'Sorry, it's none of my business.'

Casey shrugged. 'It doesn't matter. Mom hated my father. She said she was terrified of him, but that didn't stop her from leaving me with him when she went off to start a new life with a doctor in California. Yeah. It's pretty obvious how highly she thought of me, too.'

Elke cleared her throat and glanced around as if she was having trouble deciding how to respond. 'Anyway, it's good that you came with your father to walk the Camino,' she said finally. 'It must mean a lot to him.'

'He's here because he's broke and he can't afford to pay back his publisher,' Casey snapped. 'He figured it would make a good story. Not just the walk, but weaving in his parents' story, the mysterious death of Olive Rousseau,' he laughed, 'and now that we know different, I imagine my father is seeing a Hollywood screenplay in his future.'

Elke continued staring ahead, her face tightening as if she was unsure what to say. 'Well, still it's good that you came along with him,' she said finally.

He laughed. 'He didn't really give me a choice, because he rented out our house for the summer. And besides, I've never been out of the state before, let alone the country, so I figured, why not? It's not like I have a lot of friends to hang out with.'

Elke touched his arm, and he recoiled instantly, a look of concern passing over her face. 'Who knows, young man? The walk to Camino might just be the best thing that ever happened to you. It has the ability to do that. Trust me, I know.'

Casey gave her a doubtful look.

She smiled. 'When I did this the first time, I came as a young woman who did not know what she wanted to do with her life, and I went back to Germany and realised that whatever I needed, whatever my life was supposed to be, I had to trust and imagine it would be what it was always meant to be.'

'And has it been?' he asked. 'Did you get the life you wanted?'

Elke nodded. 'I got the life I deserved. It is all any of us should expect.'

Hugo continued walking on his own. The sun was warm on the back of his neck and despite the smell of rain in the air; it appeared as if the worst of the storm had passed them and they were walking into something better.

He inhaled the cigarette, slowly blowing smoke above him. He had been on his own for only a short time, but it had been enough. Although he knew eavesdropping was probably not the nicest of pastimes, he also understood that, as a police officer, it was sometimes necessary. But what had he discovered? He was not sure if he had overheard anything which might be helpful, but he was also acutely aware that often amid an investigation, even the smallest details could prove invaluable.

'How's it going?'

Hugo looked over his shoulder. Viviane Auclair, the young tour guide had appeared by his side. She was dressed in baggy clothes, a beanie cap pulled over her head. Despite the clothes, she was a thin woman, with anxious dark eyes.

'Everything's fine,' Hugo replied.

'Your husband said you're probably going home tomorrow,' she said. 'We can't tempt you to stay?'

Hugo smiled. 'Even if I didn't have to get back to work, I'm not sure this is for me,' he said gesturing all around them.

'Then you're not "looking" for anything?' she asked.

Hugo considered his response. 'I'm not sure I am, although I'm also not sure how to answer a question like that. I suppose as a police officer, I am always looking for things, but as a man, non, not so much. Not anymore, at least.'

'Have you ever lost anyone?'

Hugo regarded her with curiosity. They hardly knew one another and he was not used to sharing his private life unless it was really necessary. 'Well, I imagine we all have. Oui, I've lost people. Some I have cared more about than others, but if you're suggesting the walk to Camino might provide me with something I have lost, or reconnect me with them, then I am fairly sure it's just not true.' He held up his hands. 'Mais, s'il vous plaît don't think I am being disrespectful when I say that. Whatever my own beliefs, I don't ever wish to infringe on someone else's, so long as they are not illegal or illogical. Alors, oui, I will return to Montgenoux when we reach Pamplona.'

'And you have the answers you are happy with?'

Hugo shrugged. 'Again, I'm not sure how to answer that. This investigation is not mine, therefore it is not my responsibility to understand what happened.'

Viviane nodded. 'Is Xavier going to jail?' she asked as if she was hopeful he would not.

'It's possible,' Hugo conceded. 'I'm not privy to the investigation, but there is a possibility they will convict him of some crime.' He appraised the young guide. 'You were close?'

She turned her face away from him. 'Yeah and no. You've seen him, he's gorgeous, but he's also cool, always kind of distant. I guess we know why now, mais… I'd hate to think of him ending up in jail because of his family and something that happened a long time before he was even born.'

'For what it's worth,' Hugo replied, 'as far as I know, it's not clear what his involvement was, or how he took part. He prevented people from leaving, oui, I'm not sure how that act would translate into a court of law because they were in a terrible storm and there was no actual safe way to leave the village anyway. He may be convicted, but unless the police find more evidence, I can't imagine a court sentencing him to a prison term.'

Viviane gave him a grateful smile. 'I hope so. I'm glad it's over, at least.'

Hugo looked at the pilgrims in front of them. 'How long

until we arrive in Pamplona?'

Viviane looked at her watch. 'In about an hour, just in time for supper. I've reserved a hotel, so we can rest up and you can be on your way tomorrow.'

Hugo nodded, inhaling on the remains of his cigarette, staring into the distance.

After several hours the pilgrims finally arrived in Pamplona, a larger village than the others they had passed through, and it was filled with people enjoying the abrupt respite from the rain. The day had been long, but the bad weather had not returned, and as the summer day moved into evening, the group had moved into the village and taken refuge in a hostel with a large, secluded veranda lined with honeysuckle trees.

'It's beautiful here, isn't it?' Ben said, appearing by Hugo's side and snuggling him.

Hugo nodded slowly, his face pensive.

'What's wrong?' Ben asked with a frown.

Hugo shrugged. He had spent the proceeding hours ruminating and listening and instead of allaying his concerns, he was more confused than ever. 'I know it's not my case, so I shouldn't get involved,' he began cautiously, 'but I have to admit I am still troubled, and I just can't shake the feeling I'm missing something. And if I'm missing something, then there's a chance Captain Allons and the investigating team will be as well. I'm not criticising them, they were presented with what appears to be an open and shut case and I would likely have reacted the same way under similar circumstances.'

Ben rubbed Hugo's shoulder. 'Can't you go to Captain Allons with your concerns?'

Hugo shook his head. 'I would if I had anything tangible to go on, but I'm not at all sure it isn't my overactive imagination playing tricks on me.'

Ben touched Hugo's face. 'I know you and I believe in you, so if you think something is off, then I'm sure there is,' he said. 'Did you hear anything on the walk that might help?'

Hugo's cheeks flushed with embarrassment. He was not

proud of eavesdropping, no matter the reason for it, especially when he was not even sure it had been worthwhile. 'I'm not sure, other than it seems as if there were a lot more people involved in Olive Rousseau's disappearance than we originally imagined. Quite what the relevance of that is, I can't say, or what, if anything, I should even do about it.'

Ben considered for a while. 'It seems to me there's only one thing you can do. The thing you do best, and it's probably all you can do to understand whether any of it is relevant. And that's sitting everyone down and talking to them,' he suggested. 'Maybe then you can try to figure out what's important or not.'

'I really shouldn't because it's not my case,' Hugo responded.

Ben smiled. 'Well, that hasn't strictly stopped you in the past. But seriously, as you said, Captain Allons isn't looking at this case any further, so the question you have to ask yourself is very simple: are you happy just to let it go if there is even the smallest of chances your concerns might be legitimate?'

Hugo watched his husband and reached over, pushing his hand through the curls that bounded on Ben's forehead. 'You're right. However, before I do anything, I'd like to speak to Etienne again. He has a knack for helping me figure out what it is I'm missing.'

'Bon. Make your call and we can finish this and get home,' Ben said, clapping his hands. 'I've had my fill of walking. I think I just need to sit around the pool and try to put this all behind us.'

Hugo nodded. 'Me too. Why don't you see if you can round everyone up and tell them I'd like to talk to them in a couple of hours after they've eaten?' He pointed to the enclosed veranda. Its seclusion was perfect for a private conversation. He was not looking forward to it, particularly because he had no clear idea or plan as to what he was going to say, but he was certain of one thing. The whole truth had not yet been revealed.

'I know you're going to expect me to have performed miracles,' Etienne began wearily, his voice soft down the telephone line, 'but I'm afraid in this instance I must disappoint you.'

'You found nothing?' Hugo asked in clear disbelief. '*Rien?*'

'Not nothing, but more questions than answers,' Etienne replied. 'Gemma executed a warrant and searched the alleged home of Olive Rousseau,' he added. 'They found no trace of her having been there recently, but the forensic team found evidence of some kind of struggle. They used luminol in the kitchen area and found there had once been a lot of blood there. It had been cleaned with bleach, so it's difficult to say how old it was, but the volume and condition of the blood suggest it hadn't been a great deal of time.'

Hugo pursed his lips. 'That's interesting.'

'Peut être,' Etienne conceded. 'Although I can't imagine how helpful it will be to you.'

Hugo laughed sadly. 'At this point, I can't say I disagree with you. Anything else?'

Etienne cleared his throat. 'I've been looking for connections between the members of the group, as you asked, and other than letters and cards, I don't think they have had much interaction over the years.' He paused. 'The only potential link between them, and this is tenuous, do you remember I told you about Sarah Wilkinson being in and out of clinics?'

Hugo nodded, vaguely recalling the discussion. 'Oui. Wasn't there a suggestion of drugs or possibly anorexia?'

'That's correct,' Etienne confirmed. 'Well, when I was going through the newspaper reports again concerning the Wilkinson family, I saw something which rang a bell,' he explained. 'It took me a while to figure out what it was. Sarah was in a clinic called "The Priory" five years ago. I don't know for what reason exactly, but it was shortly after her mother's death, so that might provide an explanation. Anyway, "The Priory" is a pretty unusual name, which is why I suppose I remembered it. I'd been flicking through one of Sam Mitchell's books, searching for anything that might help, and in it he talks about visiting his son in London where he was staying at...'

'The Priory,' Hugo concluded in surprise. 'Hardly the subject to discuss in a book. I can't imagine Casey would have been thrilled about having his life exposed in such a way.'

'I agree,' Etienne replied. 'I don't know if Sam Mitchell was seizing headlines for his book or something, but he talks a lot about his son's battles with substance abuse and being thrown out of one school after another. I also read the blurb his publishers have released about the book he's writing about this particular trip, and it's not just about following in his dead parent's footsteps, it's also billed as, and I quote, "the journey of a father and son walking side-by-side in an attempt to confront the past and face the future," end quotes.'

Hugo scratched his chin. There was something about the blurb which troubled him. 'It seems an odd description, or is that just me?'

'Je ne sais pas,' Etienne conceded. 'It could just be some ad agency's way of drumming up interest in the book. Anyway, I checked the dates and they match. Unless I'm very much mistaken, Sam Mitchell was in "The Priory" around the same time as Sarah Wilkinson.'

Hugo lit a cigarette, allowing himself time to consider the information Etienne had just given him. 'Well, it's interesting, I suppose,' he said, 'but it still could be just a strange coincidence. I've seen no sign they know each other, and I imagine in clinics like those, it's possible they may not have met even if they were there at the same time.' He stopped abruptly, his forehead creasing.

'Are you okay, H?'

'Oui, oui,' Hugo blurted. A thought had popped into his head, but it had left as quickly, and he found he could not retrieve it. Whatever it was, he suspected it was something important.

'Are you sure?' Etienne pushed.

'Oui,' Hugo repeated. The thought returned and at first he imagined it was foolish of him to think of it, and yet there was something about it which made sense.

'Is this about Sarah and Casey?'

'It's all connected, I think,' Hugo replied. There were too many thoughts running through his head, and he was not sure what to do with them all. Finally, he made a decision. 'I need you to check three things for me. Can you do that?'

'Bien sûr,' Etienne confirmed.

Hugo told him what he needed.

'D'accord,' Etienne replied. 'How urgent is this?'

Hugo took a drag on the cigarette. 'Two people were murdered this week, but I have a feeling they weren't the first. And if I'm right, the wrong person is currently sitting in jail. And therefore my concern is, this might not be over.'

Etienne gave an anxious chuckle. 'No pressure there, then. Leave it with me and I'll get back to you as soon as I can.'

Hugo turned around and looked to the hotel where he could see the pilgrims were all making their way onto the veranda. He stubbed out his cigarette and immediately lit another.

'Why did you ask for us to be here, Hugo?' Dorothy Chapeau asked. The tone of her voice was light, but Hugo could sense she was concerned.

Wolfgang Huber gave Ben a frosty look. 'As far as I can tell, it wasn't a request. It was an order.'

Ben raised an eyebrow, an innocent look appearing on his face.

Hugo suppressed a smile. 'I assure you, it wasn't meant that way. We're leaving tomorrow and I just wanted to talk to you all before I go.'

Edith Lancaster frowned. 'About what?' she demanded. 'Maurice Rousseau is behind bars where he belongs and this whole sorry affair is over, or have I completely lost my marbles?'

Wolfgang chortled. 'Well, that's debatable, but to answer your question, yes, the man responsible for these heinous crimes is currently locked up, no doubt where he will remain for a very long time to come.'

Hugo took a deep breath. 'I'm afraid I'm not sure that's true.'

Irene pulled herself up in her chair, running her hand through her smooth red hair, green eyes wide and alert. 'What do you mean, Hugo?'

Hugo stepped in front of the group. It was the same path he had walked many times before. The places and faces were always different, but the scenario and truth were not. It was always about confronting truths which someone had taken great pains to hide or erase. No matter the number of times he had experienced such situations, it had never gotten easier, and he had never become entirely comfortable with it. More often than not, he found himself dealing with men and women who were infinitely better liars than he was.

'I realise I came late into this situation,' Hugo began. 'And that these events were triggered by prior events which took place decades ago, but I believe from the second I arrived here, I was aware something was wrong, I just couldn't put my finger on it.'

'What are you talking about?' Wolfgang interrupted. 'Maurice Rousseau is clearly the culprit. Must we keep going over and over this whole damn thing? Maurice had more motive than anyone to kill Tony Wilkinson, and if he imagined his oldest friend had betrayed him, well then it's not too difficult to extrapolate that in the imbalance of his mind, he did something very wrong.'

'I don't disagree,' Hugo replied. 'However, from the beginning, my instinct told me that for all this time, Maurice Rousseau believed his wife Olive was dead.'

Wolfgang threw his hands in the hair. 'My point exactly!' he shouted. 'That's why he reacted the way he did.'

Hugo shook his head. 'That's not what I meant. I believe his reaction was genuine AFTER the murders. Not just about his wife, but also about the deaths of Alain Bonnet and Tony Wilkinson, and the manner of them.'

'And what do you base that on, exactly?' Edith Lancaster asked haughtily. 'Your vast experience? You're practically a baby. You know nothing about life.'

Hugo covered his smile with his hand. 'I appreciate the compliment,' he said lightly, 'but I have been a police officer for over twenty years. Many of them spent dealing with violent criminals who committed terrible crimes. And I'm afraid to say, I think I have become accustomed to it, and because I have become accustomed to it, I tend to be able to spot something others might not.' He paused. 'I'm not always right, but either way, I believe it to be my obligation to at least consider all sides of the puzzle.'

'And what conclusions have you arrived at concerning this puzzle?' Wolfgang demanded, sarcasm biting through his tone.

Hugo ignored the German's combative stance. 'I believe, to

understand what happened this week, we need to understand what happened in the past and the circumstances in which Olive Rousseau left the village in the first place, and there is only one way I can see to do that.' He turned, addressing the group. 'And it is simple. Each and every one of you needs to stop lying and finally start telling the truth.'

The outdoor veranda descended into silence. In the distance, Hugo could hear indistinct chatter, the lightness of which made him sad because it reminded him of the path he had chosen in life. The path of walking in darkness. He did not often regret it because he was aware he had done a lot of good, but there were occasions when he wished he could sometimes enjoy being carefree.

Irene finally broke the silence. 'What are you suggesting, Hugo?' she asked softly, glancing at her mother from the corner of her eye. Dorothy Chapeau's head was lowered.

'I think we can agree on the first fact,' Hugo began. He turned to face Sarah Wilkinson. 'I am sorry if this hurts you, Miss Wilkinson, but we must address the fact that shortly after he arrived in the village of *Chemin des Pèlerins*, your father began an affair with Olive Rousseau. A young woman, by all accounts, in an unhappy marriage not of her own choosing. I can't profess to know all the details of what went on…'

Sarah lifted her head slowly, dank hair falling over her face. She pushed it away with her hand and Hugo noticed her fingernails were so bitten back they were bleeding. 'She was a whore. That's all you need to know about Olive,' she spat.

Hugo stared at her. 'Did you know she had faked her death to be with your father?'

'Not really, not at first at least,' Sarah answered. 'All I knew was the two of them never even bothered to keep their affair a secret,' she added, dark eyes widened with anger. 'In fact, I'd go so far as to say my father went to great pains to rub my mother's face in it because he knew she could do sod all about it.'

'In what way?' Hugo asked.

Sarah poured a glass of water and slowly sipped it. 'You could say my mother was the one who held all the cards. The money was hers. The high society name and contacts were all down to her and her family. My father was nothing without her and he knew it. But he also knew my grandfather would never allow a divorce and therefore he could do what the hell he pleased. And that French bitch lived the life of a queen in an apartment paid for by my mother.'

Hugo took in a sharp breath, recoiling when he noticed she had chosen the word *lived* not *lives*. It had been on his mind for some time. Where was Olive Rousseau now?

Sarah moved her head slowly, turning and facing everyone sitting on the veranda. 'And you all helped her. You're as guilty as the both of them.'

It was Dorothy Chapeau who broke the silence. 'I understand why you might be angry, Sarah,' she began cautiously. 'All I can tell you is that Olive Rousseau was a fine young woman who had all her choices taken away from her. Married off to a man she didn't care about like she was some cattle at a market. The very first time I met her, I knew her secret. She was scared.'

Dorothy stopped and shook her head, 'I don't mean scared in the sense she was worried about violence from Maurice, although, as far as I could tell, that was a very real possibility, no, her fear was based on something entirely different. The realisation of a life ahead of her of which she had no control.'

'And that's why you agreed to help her leave?' Hugo asked.

Dorothy glanced slyly at Elke before answering. 'The conversation was difficult because basically we were all helpless to do anything about it. It wasn't our place, and the fact was she was not prepared to stand up and do something about it herself. She was terrified of Maurice, and she was terrified of her family.' She exhaled wearily. 'You have to remember this was a lifetime ago. Times were different. Divorces were rare, and non-existent in villages such as these. They wouldn't have let her go easily.'

'I understand that,' Hugo reasoned, 'but to go to such

335

extremes as to fake her own death. Who came up with the idea?'

Dorothy stole a look at Wolfgang. 'It was you?' Hugo demanded.

Wolfgang snorted. 'No, it most certainly was not. I told them it was a foolish thing to do, and I forbade Elke from getting involved.'

'That's not how I remember it,' Edith Lancaster interrupted.

Wolfgang's head jerked in her direction, eyes narrowing angrily. 'Then you remember incorrectly, foolish old woman,' he hissed through gritted teeth.

Elke Huber slammed her hand on the table with such force a glass fell over. She quickly picked it up, wiping the spillage with a napkin. She looked at her husband. 'It's all going to come out now, Wolfgang. It has to, and does it really matter anymore?'

He glared at her, pressing fingers against his bald head as if he had a headache. 'Of course its matters!' he roared.

Elke faced Hugo. 'Tony Wilkinson paid my husband to help Olive escape.'

'Elke!' Wolfgang roared, his voice echoing angrily around the enclosed space.

Edith placed her knitting in front of her on the table. 'Except he backed out and kept the money. That's the truth, isn't it, Wolfgang?'

Elke turned to her husband. 'Wolfgang?'

'Oh, it's true all right,' Edith scoffed. 'I know because I heard the deal being made.'

'That's because you spend your time hiding around corners, eavesdropping because you have no damn life of your own,' Wolfgang stated, his tone harsh.

Edith picked up the knitting again, moving bony shoulders into a nonchalant shrug.

'You've lied to me all these years?' Elke whispered.

Wolfgang shook his head. 'We never spoke of it, so no, I

didn't lie.'

'What were you supposed to do for the money and why didn't you go ahead with it?' Hugo asked.

The German sighed, pushing his plump body into the chair. 'Tony came to me one night after everyone had gone to bed. We all knew about the affair. Everyone except Maurice, it seems. Tony told me he and Olive were in love and that she was going to come to London with him, only the problem was Maurice would never allow it. So they had to come up with another way.'

'And that was to fake her death?' Hugo asked, shaking his head. 'I understand Maurice not wanting to let her go, but I still can't fathom them going to such extremes.'

'I said much the same thing,' Wolfgang agreed. He shrugged. 'But they were in love, or worse, in lust with one another, and we all know how dangerous that can be.' He smiled sadly at his wife. 'I may be old, but I can still remember the first flush of young love and the crazy things it can make you do.'

He turned back to Hugo. 'Of course, they wouldn't listen to me. And then Tony made me an offer. More money than I had ever seen. More than a year's salary, in fact. A lot of money now, but back then it was a fortune. I took the money, of course, I did, I wasn't a fool..'

'And what were you supposed to do?' Hugo pushed.

'All I was supposed to do was drive Olive to Saint-Jean-Pied-de-Port, where Tony had arranged for someone to pick her up and take her via boat to London. I was then supposed to come back to the village and say I'd seen Olive fall to her death in the storm.'

'But you changed your mind?' Hugo asked.

Wolfgang nodded. 'A few hours before, I saw Maurice in the Café and how much he was in love with Olive. I'm not saying he was perfect, but let's face it, none of us is. I suppose you might say my conscience got the better of me and I just didn't have the heart to go through with it.'

Elke's face creased, a dawning realisation crossing her face. 'You had the money. I know you did. I suppose I always have. You used it for the deposit for our house. You made up some excuse about inheriting it from a long last aunt, but I knew it wasn't true.' She lowered her head. 'But I didn't care, not really.'

He smiled wryly as if he was pleased with himself. He turned back to Hugo. 'Yes, I kept the money. Tony wasn't happy about my refusing to help and wanted it back, but I refused and reminded him he could do nothing about it, not unless he wanted me to come clean, and if he did that, then his dirty little plan would fall to pieces.'

Hugo was about to ask another question when he was distracted by a beep from his cell phone. He pulled it from his pocket and flicked on his glasses, reading the screen:

Hugo, it's Etienne. Can you call me? It's urgent.

Hugo rose to his feet. 'Please excuse me, I'll be back in a moment.'

'Are you sure?' Hugo asked, his voice cracking at the shock of what Etienne had just told him.

'Oui. I'm afraid there's little doubt. Gemma executed a search warrant a few hours ago,' Etienne replied.

Hugo sunk against a wall, cradling the cell phone against his ear as he looked at the group gathered on the veranda. 'But we can't be sure it's her,' he mumbled. 'And as far as I'm aware, there are no dental records on file.'

'That's true. According to Gemma, though, they found enough evidence in the apartment to be fairly certain it was indeed Olive Rousseau,' Etienne added. 'They found bills in her name as well. She's been living under the name Olive Wilkinson, it seems.'

Hugo exhaled and lit a cigarette. 'How did she die?'

'They haven't done the autopsy yet,' Etienne replied. 'Although it appears from the initial examination, she was stabbed to death, but there's something else which is interesting. Her face was badly slashed, most probably post-mortem. Whoever murdered her really went to town.'

Hugo took a long drag, the smoke soothing him. All he could hope was that Olive's death had been as quick and as painless as possible. 'And where did they find her body?'

'A cleaner at Tony Wilkinson's mansion found blood in the pool area so went investigating,' Etienne explained, 'and found what appeared to be a shallow grave behind the pool house. She called the police.'

Hugo scratched his chin. 'I thought there was blood in Olive's apartment?' he questioned.

'There was, and a lot, but it's not clear if it was the primary scene. Forensics say it's going to take some time to figure it all out. I'm sorry I don't have a clearer picture for you.'

Hugo smiled. 'You don't need to apologise, Etienne. I'm just grateful for your help. What about the other matters I asked you to look into?'

'Oui, although I'm not sure how much help it's going to be,' he replied before quickly explaining what else he had discovered.

Hugo mulled it over.

'See, not a lot of help, is it?'

The fact was, Hugo was unsure whether or not it made a difference, but all the same, it suggested a very troubling scenario to him. 'I'm not sure,' he answered honestly. 'However, it lends itself to a somewhat fanciful possibility.'

Etienne gave a loud laugh. 'That pretty much sums up our lives these last few years of working together, don't you think? Is there anything else I can do?'

'Non, merci,' Hugo replied. 'Except tell everyone I'm coming home tomorrow.'

'Then you know what happened?'

Hugo turned back to the veranda. 'I'm about to find out for certain. Au revoir, Etienne.'

'Merci, for your patience,' Hugo said as he walked back onto the veranda.

'Is everything okay?' Ben asked.

Hugo nodded towards his husband. 'It will be,' he mouthed.

Irene searched Hugo's face. 'Has something happened?'

'We'll come to that in a moment,' he responded before turning his attention to the others. 'First, I'd like to go back to forty years ago. We know that someone was talking to Olive Rousseau next to the bridge, most likely a man. We also now know Tony Wilkinson paid Wolfgang Huber to help Olive make her escape, but that Wolfgang backed out. So, the question is: who did help her? And who was the man, or possibly woman, who was with her by the bridge?'

Irene frowned. 'Couldn't it have been Tony himself?'

Dorothy shook her head. 'That night, your father and I had dinner with Tony and Jane,' she answered. 'As far as I can remember, neither of them left the Café. The storm was terrible.'

'If the storm was so bad, why did Olive decide to leave that night?' Ben asked.

'It was part of the plan,' Wolfgang answered. 'Tony said people wouldn't look too closely at her supposed accident.'

'And we were planning on leaving the next day,' Dorothy added. 'I suppose they ran out of time and, as Wolfgang said, the storm was a perfect cover.'

Hugo nodded, pacing in front of them. He inhaled the scent of the honeysuckle and for a moment it made him feel better because he knew what was coming next, and it made him feel sick. Several people had died because of one illicit love affair forty years in the past.

'Then who helped Olive escape?' Hugo asked the group of

pilgrims. Nobody responded.

'Perhaps Alain,' Dorothy suggested. 'After all, it would also explain why Maurice murdered him.'

Elke Huber shook her head. 'They were best friends and I just can't see Alain doing something so cruel to his friend and then having to face him every day afterwards for decades.'

'For what it's worth, I don't believe it was Alain either,' Hugo responded. 'However, I believe Olive had help.' He turned to Sam Mitchell. 'Was it you or your parents who helped Olive escape?'

The American writer lifted his head slowly. He sipped the glass of wine in front of him. 'Do you know I walked in on them fucking? Tony and Olive? My mother was outraged and went to my father, demanding he do something about it. So he did. He went to Tony and just as he had with Wolfgang, the obnoxious Brit threw money at my father. Only my father, being dirt poor from Hicksville USA, couldn't resist.'

Hugo nodded. 'And what did he do?'

Sam pushed his hand through his short blond hair. He pointed to Wolfgang. 'Just like he said. Pop took Olive to Saint-Jean-Pied-de-Port and dropped her off. A lot of money for not a lot of effort.'

'I don't recall your father having said he'd seen her slip into the river,' Dorothy interrupted.

Sam shook his head. 'He didn't. Mom wouldn't let him,' he gave a sarcastic laugh. 'I guess they were happy to take the money, but not to lie to the authorities. In the end, it didn't matter because no one really bothered to look too closely at it,' he stated. 'I mean, everyone bought the story, didn't they?'

Hugo stepped closer to him. 'Did your parents keep in touch with the Wilkinson's? I know everyone in the group of original pilgrims kept in touch in one way or another, but I just wonder if your parents paid particular attention to them?'

Sam nodded. 'Mom said she wanted to make sure Olive was

okay. I think it was also a way to ease the guilt she felt. We even went over to London three or four times over the years. All paid for by Tony, of course. He even arranged for Casey to go to college in London. He paid for that too.'

Hugo took a deep breath as the pieces started to come together. 'And did you see Olive during those visits?'

'Not me,' Sam answered. 'But mom and pop went to see her. They didn't talk about it. All mom said was that she was happy and I think finally they came to accept they hadn't done such a bad thing in helping her escape.' He stopped. 'I don't get what this has to do with anything. This was all a long time ago. I had nothing to do with Tony or Alain's death, I can assure you.'

'I know,' Hugo replied. 'But your son did.' He turned to Casey Mitchell. 'Isn't that right?'

Casey Mitchell's face pulled into a tight smile. He pushed his glasses up his nose, challenging Hugo with his eyes.

'What are you talking about?' Sam Mitchell yelled. 'My son had nothing to do with any of this. How could he? He didn't even know any of these people. What on earth motive could he possibly have?' he spat.

Hugo noticed that Casey Mitchell was now looking at Sarah Wilkinson and he saw the message passing between them and he understood it. They were in love.

'When did you two first meet?' Hugo asked. 'Was it at college? Or rehab perhaps?'

'That's none of your business,' Sam clapped back.

'Did Tony pay for Casey to come to rehab in London?' Hugo asked.

Sam took an extremely long breath. 'The waiting list in our state was ridiculous. It would have been years before Casey got the help he needed, and we couldn't afford to go private. And then I remembered; we knew someone who could help. Someone rich and someone very likely to want to make sure they kept us happy, so I called Tony and asked him to help.'

'You blackmailed him?'

Sam shrugged. 'I didn't need to. Tony knew I could throw a spanner into his nice, perfect little world. It's not like he'd committed much of a crime sneaking Olive out of France. No, he was more worried about the grenade being thrown into his nice, cosy set-up. Jane had been turning a blind eye to it all that time, but if the scandal was made public, the chances were she wouldn't. Rich folks don't like scandal. Anyway, he said he understood because he was having trouble with his daughter and he knew a very good rehab centre and he could get Casey in the same place.'

Casey reached across and grabbed Sarah's hand, gently squeezing it. 'I met Sarah on my first day at the clinic and it was like

- WOH! Something had punched me in the gut and I knew nothing would ever be the same again. My life changed forever at that moment.'

Sarah smiled lovingly at him. 'Mine too,' she whispered.

'And it was like our family connection only strengthened it,' Casey continued. 'We got talking, and it soon became clear what her father had done and what my grandparents had done to help.' His face clouded. 'They destroyed Sarah's life.'

Hugo leaned forward. 'I don't understand.'

Sarah took over. 'As I said earlier, my mother knew all about the French whore and my father lorded it over her because he knew there was nothing she could do about it. My mother tried to kill herself on her wedding night because my father chose to be with his whore instead of her. They patched mum up, but it never really made any difference. She never got any better. And the worst part was my father didn't care at all. He never cared about her, so long as she kept signing the cheques.'

'And yet she kept signing them?' Hugo asked.

Sarah nodded. 'She was always zonked out on one drug or another, practically willing herself to die because she couldn't take the embarrassment of her life and what dad did to her. And then in the end, he got bored waiting for her to kill herself because he wanted all of her damn money without having to go to her and ask for it every time.'

Hugo raised an eyebrow. 'You're saying your father killed your mother?'

'Not himself,' Sarah hissed, spitting into the air. 'Dad wasn't the sort of man to get his own hands dirty, but he certainly knew people who would for the right price.'

'Are you sure?' Hugo pressed.

Sarah nodded. 'Afterwards, I heard him talking on the telephone. It was pretty clear he was paying off the man who ran my mother off the road. The bastard,' she hissed clenching her fists. 'I hated him and all I could think of was making him pay for ruining our lives. But before I could do anything, he had me shipped off to a clinic again.'

She stopped and reached over, kissing Casey on the cheek. 'But in the end, he did me a favour. He sent me a knight in shining armour. Casey walked into the room and it was like somebody was finally listening to me for the first time in my life.'

Hugo considered for a moment. 'Did you know each other before?'

'No,' she replied. 'But dad told me who Casey was and that I should look out for him. I admit I was curious. My father wasn't the sort of person interested in doing favours for anyone unless it was in his own best interests. But once Casey and I got talking, it didn't take me long to figure out the story.'

'You knew what your grandparents had done?' Hugo asked Casey.

'Yeah. I'd overheard them talking about it once with dad,' he answered. 'And I told Sarah about it and she went crazy. At first, I didn't understand why, but then she explained what they had done and how it had affected her. Her father and my grandparents destroyed Sarah and her mum's life and they didn't even care. All they cared about was money and they pretended like they were these God-fearing people!' He snorted. 'Fucking hypocrites.'

Hugo began pacing in front of them. 'Sarah, your mother died in 2017 and two years later you met Casey and then,' he paused, 'one year later Casey, your grandparents Anne and Frank died, also in a car accident. No one was ever caught for crashing into them. We've checked.'

Sam Mitchell scratched his head. 'You can't possibly be suggesting my son had anything to do with that. It's ludicrous.'

'No, it isn't,' Casey interjected. 'You've always treated me like I was a fool and that I wasn't good enough for you, the great American football hero. Your parents always preached about God when all the time they'd done something so heinous, just for a few pieces of silver. And you never cared, none of you, because you kept taking money from the bastard.' He laughed. 'So yeah, I ran them off the road. You should have seen Gramps' face when he realised it was me coming for them. It was priceless!'

Sam clenched his fists together, gawping at his son as if he wanted to punch him, instead he punched his own chest, his eyes wide as tears fell from them. 'What have you done?' he wailed. 'What the hell have you done?'

Casey smiled at his father. 'We've righted some wrongs, dad, that's all.'

Hugo glanced around, noticing the anxieties etched on everyone's faces. But he also knew at this stage it was important to keep Casey and Sarah talking before they were given legal advice. He turned to Sarah. 'Why was it important for you to come back here to walk the Camino?'

She shrugged. 'I wanted to see where it all began. When the invitation came, my father threw it straight in the bin. He had no intention of doing it. With my mother out of the picture, I imagined he was planning on moving his French bitch home wrecker into my mother's house, into her bed. And I wasn't going to have that. When I pulled the invitation out of the bin, it became clear to me what I needed to do. I was planning on telling Olive's husband the truth right in front of my father and seeing his reaction. I wanted to see the realisation dawning on my father that his perfect new life wasn't going to be quite as he imagined.'

Hugo took a deep breath and decided to be blunt in the hope it gave them the answers they needed. 'Why did you murder Olive Rousseau?'

Behind him, Dorothy gasped. 'Olive's dead? But I thought…'

Hugo held up his hands. 'I'm afraid it's true. But it seems she only died recently, in the last few weeks, in fact. Which begs the question - why? Why now?' He faced Sarah again. 'You've already said you'd known about Olive for a long time. So what changed?'

'Because she wanted to stop my father from coming here,' Sarah explained. 'And I couldn't let her do that. She came by the house. Can you believe that?' she asked with incredulity. 'Like she owned the fucking place. My father was out, but she said she would wait and that she had to see him to talk him out of walking the Camino. She said in that annoying accent of hers. *Oh, maybe I'll wait for him by the pool.* I was so mad and told her she had no right to be there or to tell us what to do. And then she looked at me straight in the face and without blinking said, *I have every right. I am the only woman your father has ever loved.* I swear I didn't know what I was doing until she was lying on the ground in a pool of blood. But for the first time in a long time, I actually felt alive, and it was pretty ironic that it took her finally dying for it to happen.'

'Did your father know?' Hugo asked.

'No,' she replied. 'I called Casey, and he told me what to do. So, I went into her apartment, spread some blood around and then cleaned it up. I figured if someone came looking for her, it would be better if they assumed she had died there, not in my father's house. Then I went into her computer and emailed my father and made it sound as if it came from her. I just typed some nonsense about how she didn't want to see him before he went because she was upset about him choosing me over her. And that was that. Bitch dead. Another one down,' she said finally with a snide smile.

Hugo frowned. 'You must have known your father would discover what happened once you got back to London?' He paused, his jaw tightening. 'Unless you knew all the time he would not be returning to London. Was it the plan all the time?'

Sarah nodded, clutching Casey's hand tightly. 'After what happened to Olive, I knew my father couldn't go back to London, but I also knew I couldn't afford to have people looking too closely at me, or where I'd buried Olive. So we came up with a better plan. Kill my father and blame the betrayed husband. We figured everyone would buy it and once we were home, no one would look for Olive. We could just send another email saying she'd taken off again now her secret was out.'

'What about Alain Bonnet?' Hugo pursed his lips. 'What did he have to do with any of this? Why did he have to die?'

'It wasn't part of the plan,' Casey answered. 'Sarah and I snuck off into the storeroom. It was the only place we could think of to be alone without anyone spotting us. Anyway, we were talking, and he suddenly appeared and it was clear from his face he'd overheard us. It was just a gut reaction, I swear it was, but I socked him on the chin and he spun around and fell against the wall. There was so much blood and we didn't know what to do.'

'And that's when you stabbed him in the back after he was already dead,' Hugo took over. 'Not just to confuse the issue, but also to point the investigation in a different direction. Why pin just one murder on Maurice Rousseau when you could have him blamed for two?'

'You've got to admit it was quite clever,' Sarah reasoned. 'Even if you'd figured out the knife wound came after he was already dead, I didn't think it would matter too much. No one would believe Maurice and that was the only important thing.'

'And then came your father's murder,' Hugo continued. 'Tell me, why did you choose to murder him that way? Stabbed in the eyes with knitting needles.'

In the veranda's corner, Edith Lancaster dropped her knitting. 'So, that's where my other needles went!' she exclaimed.

Sarah laughed. 'Yeah, sorry about that, old lady. I just saw it lying on the table and the idea came to me. I admit I'd thought of a million different ways to kill my father, each more painful than the last, but I'd never really decided until that moment.'

'Were you poisoning him, as well?' Hugo asked.

She raised an eyebrow. 'Ah, so you know about that,' she smiled. 'I've been trying to up his warfarin dose, but it was taking too long.' She turned to Edith, smiling at the old lady. 'And then seeing your knitting gave me a new idea. After the knife in the back looked symbolic, I thought if my father's death looked symbolic too, it would be a distraction and keep the police guessing. But more importantly, I didn't want him to look at me ever again. He was a cruel man with cruel eyes.'

'It appears Olive Rousseau was murdered in a similar way.' Hugo stared at her. 'Was it on purpose?'

'She was a vain woman,' Sarah stated calmly. 'Always with a face full of makeup. Like my father, I couldn't stand for her to look at me and,' she stopped, laughing manically, 'I thought it was kinda cool that she'd go to hell looking a mess because I knew she would hate it and so would he.'

The pilgrims around the veranda murmured aloud in dismay.

Sam Mitchell turned to his son. 'Casey, I don't want you to say another word until I get you a lawyer.'

Casey shook his head. 'What for? The police can't prove a damn thing.'

Sam threw his hands in the air. 'You've just confessed in front of all of these people, you idiot!'

'So what?' Sarah interrupted. 'It's your word against ours, and once we have lawyers, we can throw a lot of confusion in the air, probably enough for reasonable doubt.' She stabbed her finger in the air, pointing to the other pilgrims. 'You were all involved in one way or another.' She stopped and smiled at Wolfgang. 'And you've just admitted blackmailing my father. Seems to me you've got as much motive as I do.'

She shrugged nonchalantly. 'Either way, it doesn't matter. Thanks to our parents, everyone already thinks Casey and I are nuts, so even if we are convicted, the chances are we'll never do a day of jail time. And who's to say my father didn't kill Olive himself? You've got to admit folks, we've been pretty smart. I even pulled a hair from Maurice and made sure it was in Alain's blood, not just around it, but in it, so that if it did go to court, they'd never really be able to prove it wasn't there to begin with.'

'And then I snuck into his house and hid a photo of Olive,' Casey added with a grin. 'Let's see him explain how he had a recent photograph of his long-dead wife.'

'The fact is,' Sarah continued. 'Maurice Rousseau is going to stand trial and there's enough evidence to send him down. Even with all of you saying otherwise, it doesn't really matter, because I'll just say you were all involved and are only protecting yourselves and your reputations. And if all that fails, I'll just have my shrink speak up for me. At worst, I'll do another stint in a nice clinic and be out before you know it, the sole heir to a great big fucking fortune.' She reached over and kissed Casey on the cheek. 'And as for my Casey, you'll never be able to prove he did anything, either. We've been smarter than all of you.'

Ben whispered to Hugo. 'Is that right? Can they get away with it?'

Hugo kept staring at Sarah and Casey who were now embracing. Between them, they had murdered at least five people and it appeared to him they showed no remorse. Despite his experience, he knew how difficult convictions were under the best of circumstances and therefore he could not predict how a court might deal with Sarah Lancaster and Casey Mitchell. He took a deep breath. 'Not if I have anything to say about it. I'll telephone Captain Allons,' he said decisively.

The sun felt soothing on Hugo's face, and for the first time in days it seemed as if the tension was beginning to leave him. As he moved his leg, he felt reassured by the bag next to his feet. The taxi was on its way and within a few hours, they would be back in Montgenoux.

'Is it really all over?' Elke Huber asked from the chair opposite him.

'I believe so,' Hugo answered. Captain Allons had arrived late the previous night and arrested Sarah Wilkinson and Casey Mitchell and taken them away for questioning. A shellshocked Sam Mitchell had followed them, mumbling apologies to the rest of the group.

'When did you first start to suspect them, Hugo?' Dorothy Chapeau asked.

Hugo suppressed a smile. 'Actually, at one point, I suspected you.'

Dorothy's eyes widened in horror. 'Me?' she gasped, her voice rising sharply.

'You couldn't possibly have suspected my mother,' Irene said, shaking her head in disbelief.

'Not seriously,' Hugo conceded. 'But I had to wonder how you knew about the manner of Tony Wilkinson's death.'

Dorothy frowned. 'What do you mean? Didn't everyone know?'

'Not me,' Edith Lancaster sniffed. 'Filthy thieves stealing my knitting. There's an orphan in Rwanda who's going to go cold this winter,' she added bitterly.

'I didn't know either,' Elke added. 'And I'm glad. How macabre!'

'The truth is we never actually mentioned the real cause of death,' Hugo continued, 'and there were always people around, so I

353

thought it would be difficult to explore the walk-in freezer without being seen.'

Dorothy took a sharp breath. 'I heard Sam and Casey talking about it, that's all. Casey said he'd heard you and Irene talking about it. I didn't mention it because, well, I didn't think anyone needed to know the horrific details about how poor Tony died.' She stopped, lowering her head. 'I am sorry if you thought I was misleading you. It was not my intention, and for what it's worth, I didn't really think Olive had left the village, not after we'd refused to help her.'

'We were embarrassed about what we'd almost done,' Elke continued. 'And we didn't want Maurice to know we had been willing to help Olive leave him. We believed she was dead, so what was the point in diminishing his memory of her?'

Dorothy covered her mouth with her hand. 'If I had told you, it might have stopped this all happening.'

Hugo shook his head. 'I don't think it would have mattered. Alain Bonnet was murdered because he was in the wrong place at the wrong time and the plan to murder Tony Wilkinson was already decided before he'd even arrived in France. I don't think there's anything we could have done to prevent this.'

He stopped, noticing the troubled expression on Dorothy's face. 'And for what it's worth, and to answer your question, I'd already started to suspect them by then, and it was actually thanks to you. I overheard a conversation between you and Casey where he informed you that this trip was the first time he had left America.'

'That's right, he did,' Dorothy confirmed.

'But then when I had my forensic expert do some investigating for me, he informed me that not only had Casey Mitchell spent some time in the U.K. it was also likely he was at a clinic at the same time as Sarah. It seemed feasible they knew other, a fact confirmed by Sam Mitchell earlier. So, they knew each other.

It meant little necessarily, but then why pretend otherwise?'

'And additionally,' Hugo continued. 'They were also the only two people without an alibi at the time of Alain Bonnet's murder. I didn't give that a lot of thought at first, because I couldn't imagine a reason why they would murder a man they'd never met. But adding it to everything else, it began to build up a picture I couldn't ignore. I listened to the recordings Irene made, and I didn't think too much of it, but Casey Mitchell made a point of talking about not being able to go to the bathroom at the time of Alain's death. And in hindsight, I think it might have been because he and Sarah were the only people without corroborated alibis, so perhaps it was a way of giving each other one. Sarah was in the bathroom and Casey was waiting. It certainly worked because we didn't look too closely at it. After all, as far as we knew, they were perfect strangers.'

He smiled at Dorothy. 'But thanks to you, I realised it was not necessarily true.'

'And thank God for that,' Elke exclaimed.

Wolfgang Huber gave Hugo a curious look. 'Credit where credit is due. You're not such a bad cop, after all.'

'Wolfgang!' Elke cried.

Hugo laughed. 'It's okay. I can take this as a compliment.' He stopped, noticing a taxi pulling up. 'Ah, I think our ride is here.'

Ben stood, moving across the veranda towards Irene. 'You've changed your mind again, haven't you?'

Irene nodded. 'I need to stay a while longer. I'd like for us to be with Mama for as long as we can.'

Ben smiled. 'Well, call me, and this time I mean it. Don't make me drag my ass back out here, I don't think I can cope with the stress,' he added with a chuckle.

'You could always join us on the pilgrimage,' Edith Lancaster interjected. 'I'm sure God would like the chance to get to know you both better.'

'I'm not sure about that,' Hugo replied, emerald green eyes twinkling. 'But more importantly, I don't think my legs could take it.'

The elderly English woman rose to her feet, hurrying back towards the hotel. 'You young people can't take the pace. Goodbye!' she called over her shoulder, waving her cane in the air.

Hugo turned to face the rest of the group of pilgrims. 'Well, we have to go, but I just wanted to say it's been a pleasure getting to know you all, and I wish you a safe journey.'

'I second that,' Ben added. 'But no more helping unhappy housewives disappear, okay?'

Irene laughed. 'Oh, I'll make sure of that, don't worry! I can promise you this: the rest of this pilgrimage will proceed without incident, or there'll be hell to pay.'

Above them, thunder growled across distant storm clouds.

Dorothy Chapeau tutted. 'You had to tempt fate, didn't you?' she laughed, linking arms with her daughter and resting her head on her shoulder.

HUGO DUCHAMP WILL
RETURN IN A NEW
INVESTIGATION:

Hotel Beaupain

Made in the USA
Columbia, SC
11 March 2023

1133d813-5cf9-4266-9365-ccdd629058f4R01